BLACK ZODIAC

Zizi Cole

BLACK ZODIAC

By Zizi Cole

ISBN-13: 978-1-7347151-0-1

Introduction

Ghosts are everywhere. Every day you may interact with them, or are near them, without ever knowing. Some ghosts leave an impression that you can feel as you walk through the room. A chill, goosebumps, a bad feeling. It could also be a warmth, like a hug, if they were someone that you loved.

There are also the types of ghosts that are commonly known as poltergeists. They move things and cause mayhem wherever they go. Not necessarily dangerous, but annoying. Then, there are ghosts that are dangerous. They have the power to end lives, but they also can culminate power.

Twelve ghosts are linked to the Black Zodiac. The Black Zodiac is the dark side of the zodiac signs. The black zodiac signs are: Tyrant, Fallen Demon, Basilisk, Serpent, War Maiden, Maelstrom, Ravenous, Poisoned Dart, Tempest, Leviathan, Beast, and Sword. Each of the ghosts represents a sign of the black zodiac.

There is a story behind every ghost. These are their stories . . .

Black Zodiac Ghost 1
Golden Boy

Chapter 1

Bourbon, MO 1882

I smirked as I heard Mother berating Charles yet again. It amused me I could do things that he was constantly blamed for. It was incredibly easy to get away with anything. All I had to do was look at mother, tear up a bit, and tell her Charles was the one who did it. Then I would beg for him not to get into trouble because he was my brother, and I didn't want to see him in trouble again. She would kiss me on the top of the head and send me to my room so I could play.

Even in my room, I could still hear her yelling at Charles. Poor Charles. He would just listen and apologize for anything that happened, knowing he was innocent of the infractions he was accused of doing. He would then be lashed for the behavior. Mother had a very heavy hand when she was angered.

I rarely saw her wrath firsthand, but seeing what Charles went through made me to want to keep it away from me. Then again, Mother wouldn't do anything like that to me. I was her baby. She didn't believe I could do anything wrong. I had seen her fire maids because they tried to tell her I was the one actually guilty of something instead of Charles.

I was lying on my stomach playing with my toy soldiers as I listened to the unfolding scene downstairs.

"You little bastard! How dare you break my best china tea pot? Do you realize how much gold it will cost to replace it?" Mother's voice was shrill, making my ears hurt from one floor away.

"I apologize, Mother." Charles's voice was calm. I could barely hear it from my position on the floor.

"You do not truly care that you are wasting your father's fortune. You think that it is already yours, don't you?"

"Of course not, Mother. I will work to replace the teapot. I will speak to Father about working for him to make up the difference."

The sound of her hand connecting to his face echoed through the house.

"You do not deserve the family fortune. It should be given to William instead. He is your father's legitimate child. You are just a bastard from his first marriage. I know that your father only married your mother then because she was with child. He pitied your mother and doesn't even know if you are his actual child. He wanted to make an honest woman out of your mother because he felt sorry for her."

I giggled at the end of her rant. I knew that she hated the fact that she was Father's second wife instead of his only wife. I also was aware that it hurt Charles to know that Mother despised his being even more. He tried to be a good son, but he would never be good enough for Mother. He wasn't me.

The silence was a signal that she was done with him and dismissed him for the evening. I waited patiently for him to come up and tell me what happened. I heard his footsteps on the stairs, and the bedroom door opened.

I looked up as Charles walked into the room and closed the door behind him. He sank down onto the floor and wrapped his arms around his legs. His forehead was resting on his knees, his dark hair hiding his face.

"Are you alright, Brother?" I asked, hoping concern was heavy in my voice.

He nodded but didn't speak.

"I'm sorry Mother is like that. She must be off her pills again. I will speak to Father for you about it. I will tell him how unfair Mother is treating you. She shouldn't speak to the Wellington heir in such a manner."

"Thanks, Brother, but it will just make things worse if you do," his voice was muffled by his legs. "I don't want her to get mad at you as well. We both know Father won't do anything about it."

He had a point. Father tended to ignore issues in the house. He let Mother deal with it. He always said the house was the wife's domain and responsibility. I shrugged.

When he didn't say anything, I turned my attention back to my soldiers. While I was playing, I wondered what I could do next that would completely get under Mother's skin. It was funny when she had a fit.

We sat there in our own worlds quietly for a while, then I noticed that Charles was speaking softly. I strained to hear what he said, but it wasn't making any sense. Looking up, I saw that he was staring straight ahead, like he was looking at someone but nothing was there.

It gave me the ammo needed to set Mother off. I acted like I wasn't paying attention to him while he kept talking softly. When we were called down to dinner I stood up, leaving my toys where they laid. As I headed out of the room, I heard Charles sigh as he began picking up my stuff. I knew that he would clean up after me. He always did.

When we were all seated around the table, Father led in the prayers over our meal, and we began to eat in silence. Biding my time, I watched the expressions on everyone's faces while they ate. Father looked like he had been hitting the bottle rather heavily. Mother's face was pinched. Her brown hair was pulled back in a tight bun that had to hurt her head. Her cheeks were slightly red, telling me that she wasn't happy.

"Pass the potatoes," Father slurred.

She set the potatoes in front of him with a resounding thud. "You need to pray for forgiveness before you end up in hell."

"What are you mouthing about, Ingrid?" Father gently set his fork on the table.

Things were about to get interesting. Father already looked annoyed, now his expression was pinched. Red was beginning to rise in his face. It looked like Mother and Father were going to be in a fight. I would have bet on Mother winning. Father was larger but she was brutal and had deadly aim.

"With the gambling and drinking, you are going to go to hell. You come to church on Sundays and have the congregation convinced you are the ideal deacon. That isn't even mentioning your demonic child. If anyone knew what he did, they would burn him or drown him as a witch."

"Enough!" Father roared as he surged to his feet. "I will not allow you to accuse Charles of witchcraft. We all know he is not demonic or a witch. I forbid you to utter those words again. Ingrid, I will show you how a true deacon deals with a disobedient wife if you do not stop with the nonsense."

"It isn't nonsense. I am the one with a clear head, I know what is happening in this house. He has scared little William with his wi— behavior."

I took my cue to pout and carefully nod my head. My eyes shifted toward Charles, who was sitting at a separate table. His head was down and he was pushing his food around with his fork. He wasn't allowed to sit at the table with us. Mother had declared that after he spilled a glass of water on the tablecloth one time.

"He was talking to himself again," I said softly. I made my voice quiver like I was afraid.

"See Charles? Your bastard child is speaking to the demons!" Mother crossed her arms satisfied that she won that argument.

Unexpectedly, Father's hand shot out and slapped Mother hard enough that her head jerked backward, and she almost toppled out of her chair.

"I said you will stop accusing him of devil work. My son is not a devil or a witch. He is a little boy who lost his mother at a young age. He is not a bastard. Everything will go to him when I die, so you best keep that in mind." He stormed out of the room, slamming the door behind him. The pictures on the walls rattled from the force of the door.

Mother stood up, walking out of the room without a word, heading into the kitchen. I figured she was going to go in there and stew while she calmed down. Or if she was angry enough, she was going to be plotting something especially vile.

I finished eating and went upstairs to get ready for bed without bugging Mother. Charles wasn't going to get up from his seat until Mother excused him, so I had no idea when he would be able to go to bed. He wasn't allowed to leave the table without Mother's permission. He did once and for punishment, he was lashed with a leather strap.

I readied myself for bed then settled in when I heard footsteps coming to the room. I looked at the door expectantly, smile on my face. The door opened, and Mother appeared in the doorway. She smiled as she walked in and shut the door.

"Are you all ready for bed, darling?" she asked softly. There was tenderness in her voice.

I nodded. "Yes, ma'am."

"You are such a good boy." She sat on the edge of the bed and tucked the blanket around my legs. "You deserve to be the heir, not Charles. The household would do good with you in charge of it. You are so smart and kind."

"Thank you, Mother," I began to relax as she continued to tuck me in.

"I have a plan for to get exactly what you deserve." She kissed me on the forehead, then blew out the candle beside my bed.

When she left the room, I heard the door close with a click. I listened for the sounds of any commotion going on in the house. It didn't take long to hear the muffled sounds of voices along with the sharp crack of the belt to skin. I wasn't sure what happened, but I knew that Charles was in trouble yet again.

As I closed my eyes and began to fall asleep, I wondered if Mother found the surprise that I had left for her. I knew she would think that

Charles did it. Maybe that was why he was being punished again. I fell asleep with a smile on my face.

Chapter 2

I hid in the cabinet, listening to Father and Charles work on something in the study. If I moved just right, I could see them sitting at the desk through the crack between the doors of the sideboard. Father had been spending more time with Charles as he got closer to his twelfth birthday. He was getting closer to becoming a man and taking over Father's empire.

"This is important, so pay attention, Charles," Father ordered as he pointed to something on the desk.

"Aye, Father." Charles leaned in to look at what Father was showing him.

A wave of jealousy washed through me. Father rarely paid any attention to me. Mostly it was just to shoo me out of the way or send me to play. I was nothing in his eyes while he spent time with Charles and admired Charles. The roaring was so loud in my head that I couldn't hear what they were saying any longer. I didn't want to hear anyway. I wanted Charles to disappear so I could have Father's attention.

My life would have been perfect without Charles. I wished he had never been born, or had died as an infant. I knew that Mother felt the same; I heard her speaking with Aunt Regina about it before. When they noticed me, they changed the topic rather quickly.

"Do you understand, Son?" Father asked. I could feel the resentment growing more and more.

"I think so, Father." Charles looked up at our father. "I will do my best to be fair in all things. Especially with Mother and William."

"You are a good lad and will grow up to be a fine man." He tousled Charles's hair.

"Father. Why does Mother hate me so?"

Father hesitated, causing me to perk up. I couldn't wait to hear his answer to this. "Son, Ingrid has some issues of her own she has to work out. She doesn't hate you. She just doesn't understand you. I think she partly resents the fact you are like your mother in many ways."

"How am I like my mother?" Charles asked, with a frown on his face. "I don't even know what she looked like. I have no memory of her."

"You wouldn't, Son. Your mother, Charlotte, was a delicate, sweet woman. You have a lot of her features and personality. Sometimes when you speak, or get a particular look on your face, I see her. You also seem to have some of her other gifts as well."

"Like what?"

Father's face closed up and demeanor changed. "That is a conversation for another time, Charles."

They walked out of the room, but I stayed in the cabinet for a while longer. I needed to think about what was said. I knew Mother wasn't jealous of Charles. Mother believed that I, the legitimate child, should inherit everything.

Another thought raced across my mind. I wondered what gifts Charles's mother had that Father refused to speak about. It would be interesting to find out. Maybe I should go through Father's stuff again to see if I could find anything.

**

The following weeks had been intense, the anger escalating between Mother and Father. Once night for dinner, she made potato soup. It was creamy, with chunks of ham and potatoes in it. She placed Father's bowl in front of him, smiling sweetly.

"Here you go, husband-dearest. I made it just how you like it. Now eat up." Mother smiled and handed Charles his bowl, carefully, offering him a chunk of bread to go with it. Charles thanked her quietly, then began to eat without making any other noises.

Mother winked at me as she sat down at the table and began to eat her dinner. There was a calmness in the room that was unnerving. Mother was acting like nothing had been bothering her. I hadn't seen her this calm in a long time.

Before dinner was over, Father was acting differently. He swayed slightly in his chair. Gripping his stomach, he attempted to leave the table. Father staggered and fell back into the chair. Mother rushed to his side and helped him stand.

"Let's get you to bed. I hope you aren't getting the sweating sickness." Mother wiped at the sweat that was beading on his forehead.

After they disappeared toward the staircase, I looked at Charles, who had also been watching the scene before us.

"Do you think Father will be alright?"

I watched as Charles slowly nodded his head. "Yes. Father is strong and can beat any illness that comes his way. Now, please excuse me. Let Mother know that I am also ill."

He dashed from his table. It didn't sound like he made it to his room before vomiting commenced.

I decided to finish eating then searched for the goodies that I knew Mother had made during the day. She always made a lot of sweets before the holidays that were coming up. When I found them, I ate my fill and went up to bed. I spent the rest of the evening listening to Charles vomit and cry for a mother who never came to comfort him.

A week had passed. Father remained ill, but Charles was feeling better. He took over the majority of the chores to keep Mother from having a fit. He also kept a low profile as not to rile her. She seemed on edge since the night Father had fallen ill.

Mother refused visitors and told the doctor that she wouldn't leave his side. The doctor wasn't sure what caused the ailment but suggested that we take a vacation. Mother refused to let Father out of his sick bed, so we stayed at home and the doctor was there almost around the clock.

Father slowly regained his strength and was well enough that he was able to get up and move around on his own. The doctor told Mother that since Father was feeling better, he didn't plan on sticking around much longer. He had other patients to attend.

"Thank you for all your help. Charles will be fine under my watch. You go ahead and attend your other patients. If we need anything, we will have you fetched. Thank you again, Dr. Marino."

I watched from the hallway as Mother and Doctor Marino shook hands, and she walked him to the door. Once the door was closed, she turned back and winked at me as she headed in the direction of her and Father's bedroom.

That night we had a roast for dinner with mashed potatoes and gravy and a side of fresh green beans. We ate in silence, Charles especially silent. He was hunkered down in his chair, eyes down, attempting to be invisible. Now that Father was better, Mother would surely start in on Charles again.

Father had insisted that Charles be seated with the rest of the family from now on. He wasn't to be treated like an outsider and was old enough now not to make messes. Mother agreed reluctantly but kept him as far from her as she could manage.

Halfway through dinner, Father set his silverware down and looked at Mother. "It is delicious, Ingrid. However, I am not feeling the best and think I should lie down."

He stood up and staggered a bit as he made his way to his bedroom. He made it to the doorway before Mother replied. "Good night, darling. Hope you feel better in the morning."

After dinner, Mother sent us to bed immediately. "I'll do the chores this evening. You two go wash up and go to bed. Charles, that includes you."

Charles and I glanced at each other. Mother never let Charles out of chores. Silently, we got up and went to our rooms. After the house settled into a sleepy quiet, I got out of bed and slipped into Charles's room.

"Are you awake?" I whispered.

"Yes."

I padded over to his bed and crawled in next to him. "I'm worried about Father."

"Me too."

"Charles?"

"Can I sleep with you?"

"Mhmm."

"Charles?"

"What William?"

"What do you want to do when you grow up?"

There was a long silence then he spoke. "Be normal."

"Do you want to take over Father's business?"

"No. You can have it. When I'm old enough, I'm leaving."

"Where are you going?"

"Somewhere no one has ever heard of me."

Charles resituated and I could tell he had his back facing me.

"Charles?"

"Go to sleep, William. We don't want to anger Mother."

"I'm glad you're my brother," I whispered as I cuddled into the quilts. It was true. Even when I was mean, Charles would let me come sleep with him. The house was scary at night when I was alone. Sometimes I felt like I was being watched.

The sun was just beginning to peek over the horizon when Mother's screams woke us. Shooting out of bed, we raced downstairs to

Mother and Father's room. I shoved the door open with Charles on my heels.

Mother was sprawled over Father. He wasn't moving. She continued screaming, her hands fisted in the pillow on both sides of his head.

"Nooooooooo!" she cried. "Wake up you bastard! Don't you widow me with two kids to raise. Charles, fetch the doctor at once."

Charles ran off to do as she bid. Once the physician arrived, he declared what we dreaded the most.

"Ingrid, I am so sorry to have to tell you this. It looks as if the illness got him. He has gone to a better place." He pulled the quilt over Father as he spoke.

Tears pooled in my eyes and rolled down my face. I heard Charles sniffle behind me. I just stared at the quilt that had been my father. Out of the corner of my eye, I saw the doctor draping a black cloth over the mirror on the vanity. I turned my head to watch and saw as he opened the window as well.

"What are you doing?" I asked Dr. Marino.

He smiled at me with a sad smile. "I am covering the mirrors and opening windows, so your father doesn't get trapped inside the house. It helps him move on to a better place."

Looking at Charles for confirmation of this story, Charles just shrugged. He didn't know the truth either. I watched as his attention turned away from me to a spot in the corner. He stared at it so intently that I looked to see what was there. Nothing. My brother was doing the weird thing again.

I couldn't decide if I hoped Mother caught him or not. If she did, he would be punished. It scared me when he did that. I never knew what was going on. He almost seemed like he was somewhere else. Within a few heartbeats, Charles turned looked at me then looked away quickly.

I decided that it would be best if Mother didn't know about that incident. She was still speaking with the doctor in hushed tones.

"I will have him removed from the house shortly," Dr. Marino explained.

"Thank you. I will prepare the boys for the coming days and funeral." She walked him to the door. Once the door was shut, she turned and faced us. "Children get dressed in your Sunday best. It is going to be a long few days with a lot of company. Once the excitement dies down, we will go over how things will be done from now on."

It sounded ominous and even made me a little nervous. The look she gave Charles as she turned and walked away sent chills down my spine. I felt bad for him but at the same time, I couldn't wait to see what happened next.

Chapter 3

The funeral came and went in a whirlwind of activity. Charles and I pretty much just stayed out of the way during all the excitement. Mother was tense, and I worried that she would have fits if anything happened.

Charles was more nervous than I. He had more reason to. It was obvious Mother didn't love him like she did me, but when we were under the spotlight, she acted like a loving tender mother. Her affection seemed scarier to Charles than her complete lack of interest or her dislike.

We were sitting on the couch in the sitting room as the guests milled about when Aunt Gertie approached us. She pinched my cheeks making them hurt. I jerked away from her, rubbing the sore spots carefully.

"Don't touch me," I commanded.

"You need to be taught manners, young man." She smoothed her dress then hair as she spoke.

"You need to be taught manners," I mocked. I didn't want her near me. "You touch me again, and I will scream. Then when everyone comes in here, I'll tell Mother you hit me, and she will kill you."

Aunt Gertie stormed off, huffing about disrespectful children and needing to be seen and not heard. I grinned at Charles who just stared back at me. I was sure he couldn't believe I did that. He had to find it a little funny.

There was commotion in the kitchen where voices were raised. I shrugged at Charles. It was probably Aunt Gertie. Suddenly an old lady rushed up and grabbed Charles by the arms. She pulled him up to her and whispered in harsh tones. I couldn't hear what she said, but he was visibly shaken. Once he was released, he shook his head and sat back down. His skin was pale, and I was positive he was going to throw up.

The scary looking old lady disappeared as fast as she had appeared. I looked around the room but didn't see her. I had no idea which way she had gone. Looking back at Charles, I noticed that he was still sitting there staring straight ahead. His reaction had me startled. I expected him to just shake off whatever that crazy lady had said. The rest of the evening, we sat in silence watching the scenes around us.

***

Things were different around the house since Father passed. Mother was unusually friendly to Charles. She continued to let him sit with us at the table and hadn't punished him since before the funeral. It was awkward, and Charles did his best to stay on Mother's good side.

The bank and Father's lawyer had come and gone a lot, explaining how things would work now that Charles was in charge of the estate. He was still too young to take over so Mother was supposed to oversee everything until Charles reached the age of 13 years. She would be in control for another year before everything was handed over to Charles.

Mother had to keep the lawyer informed of anything she did and Charles had to be present during the meetings with the lawyer. There were times that Charles had to meet with just the lawyer without Mother's presence. When they met by themselves, Mother would watch the study door like a cat waiting for a mouse.

Charles never mentioned what went on in those meetings to anyone. He would just come out and return to whatever chore he had left when he was pulled in there. It was almost as if the meetings never occurred.

One afternoon, Charles was in a particularly long meeting with the lawyer, Mr. Faye. He showed up and pulled Charles into the office in a semblance of urgency. Mother kept watching the door, waiting for it to open, but it didn't. I sat outside the door in the hall, trying to hear something, but they were speaking so low that I couldn't hear anything. I knew Mother would want to know anything that was said if I could hear it.

The sun quickly set and darkness set in. Mother had fixed dinner and it was just the two of us that ate at the table. She frowned down the hallway the entire time we were seated at the table.

"Mother, I couldn't hear anything," I told her, disappointment swelling in me.

"It's alright, William. You did the best you could. They will let me know what is going on if they feel it necessary." Even though she said it was okay, her tone and body said that it was a problem. Her eyes narrowed at the door and she mumbled under her breath, "Six more months. I have to do something before then."

I was confused by what she was talking about but decided not to say anything. She had the look on her face that meant things could get scary. A thrill run through me. I was always a little excited when I saw Mother being mean. It gave me ideas.

When Charles emerged from the study, he was stopped by Mr. Faye for a moment. After a couple of nods and indecipherable whispers, they parted directions. Mr. Faye showed himself out while Charles joined us at the table.

He slipped into his chair and didn't say a word. Just bowed his head, prayed silently, and began eating. The silence that followed him into the room was deafening. I glanced at Mother and saw she was studying him with a glint in her eye.

"What did Mr. Faye have to say, Charles?" she asked through gritted teeth.

He looked up at her and gave a half shrug. "He was explaining the accounting books to me and how to keep track of household expenses."

"I have been doing that since I married your father. I will continue to do so until you fully take over the household."

"Okay, Mother," Charles knew better than to argue with Mother about anything. He slowly began eating again.

After dinner, Charles cleared the dishes for Mother, then went into the kitchen to wash them. She didn't tell him to, he just did it. I figured it was to try to keep her calm and happy so she didn't beat him again.

On my way to the stairs, I heard him talking to someone in the kitchen. I stopped and peeked in, hoping he didn't notice me.

"No, I didn't tell her anything that Mr. Faye said." He was staring off into the corner of the room, holding a plate that was dripping soap. "Mr. Faye told me that it was important not to tell anyone what we discussed in our meetings. He said that Father wouldn't want Mother, or anyone one else, knowing."

He paused for a moment as if listening to someone else. "Yes, I know she isn't my mother. That's what I have been raised to call her though. Father always told me to call her that so it wouldn't hurt her feelings."

Another long pause. "Yes, I know she hurts me. Father said it was because she was scared of me and jealous that I was from his first marriage, and William wouldn't be the heir to Father's estate. But honestly, I don't want the estate, so I don't care if William has it."

He rinsed the plate and carefully dried it with a towel before starting to wash the next. "William isn't all bad. He is just a child taught that he is entitled to everything. Yes, he gets me into trouble, but he cares about me. He is the only one that does now that Father is gone. I don't think he does what he does intentionally. William was just raised to be a brat."

The last thing he said made my stomach churn and anger flood through me. I wasn't going to let Charles speak like that about me, even to himself. I raced quietly into the sitting room where Mother was working on needle point.

Breathlessly, I told her what I heard. "Mother, Charles is doing it again. He is speaking to himself aloud like he is speaking to someone that isn't there. He said you aren't his real mother and that I am an entitled brat."

She carefully set her needlepoint down and smiled at me. "Thank you, William. Now go ahead and get ready for bed, I'll be up to tuck you in shortly."

She grabbed the leather strap that hung on the wall as she walked out of the room. I headed up the stairs and stopped at the top to listen to what went on down below. I could hear Mother as soon as she entered the kitchen.

"Who are you speaking with, Charles?"

"No one, Mother," he answered quickly.

"Yes, you are speaking with no one. I am going to teach you that speaking to no one is unacceptable. I will get the devil out of you if it kills me. Remove your shirt, turn around, and get on your knees."

"Please, Mother. Don't. I'm sorry. I won't speak to myself or no one anymore. I will just sit quietly. I don't have to talk at all. Please don't."

"I will not repeat myself. Do as I say!"

There were several heartbeats of silence then the sound of the strap hitting his back. He didn't cry out, but I knew he had to be in pain. I listened as Mother let out her frustration on Charles's back. A part of me felt bad that he was being beaten like that, but at the same time I was glad. That would teach him to call me a brat.

Chapter 4

Charles became more closed off and didn't speak to anyone after that. He kept to himself, did his chores, and spent the rest of his time alone in his room. Silent. The silence was more unsettling than him speaking to thin air. It was eerie.

I was sitting in the kitchen with Mother, watching her prepare different desserts. She always liked baking. She smiled at me and handed me the spoon from the cookie dough, so I could lick it off.

"We are going to make a banana cake just for Charles." Her voice was cheerful.

"Why for Charles?" I felt a frown form on my face.

She looked at me sharply. "Because his birthday is coming up. I want him to know that we love him. He has been working hard around the house and deserves a little treat. I want you to stay away from the cake. Do you understand, William?"

I huffed. I loved Mother's banana cake. It was one of my favorite desserts. She knew that I loved it, so I wasn't sure why she was making it for him and not allowing me to have any. It wasn't fair. I never got in trouble and always did what I was asked. I also wasn't a freak that talked to nothing. I deserved the cake.

Under Mother's stern stare, I lowered my head and nodded. "I understand." My voice was low, barely a whisper.

It didn't take her long to whip the cake up. She was a professional at baking cakes. Once it was done and out of the oven, she placed it on a cake stand and frosted it with buttercream frosting. She then set it in the middle of the counter and walked out of the room.

I continued to stare at the cake. It beckoned me toward it. The smell of the fresh baked bananas teased my senses and lured me closer. Before I knew it, I was sitting on the counter next to the cake staring at it. I couldn't help myself. I had to taste it.

My hand shook as I reached for the cake to stick my fingers in the frosting. I didn't want to upset Mother, but at the same time, I wanted and needed that sweet goodness. With one swift motion, I coated my finger in the frosting and popped it into my mouth.

Mmm. The sugar and cream coated my mouth and slid down my throat as I swallowed. It was the best feeling in the world. I closed my eyes to savor it, then decided I had to have more. Throwing caution to the wind, I grabbed a handful of cake and shoveled it into my mouth. Before I had that swallowed, I was already reaching for more.

Before I realized what I had done, I had eaten the whole cake and my stomach hurt. I had eaten way too much, and I would regret it later. Mother was going to be upset with me for eating Charles's cake.

Climbing down from the counter, the first wave of pain hit me. I dropped to the ground, curling up into a ball. The pain was unbearable and overcame all my senses. I had never felt anything like it in my life. I began to vomit and it went everywhere.

Screaming with what breath I could catch, I tried to get Mother's attention. "Mothe- Mothe- MOMMY!"

Even though it sounded like I was screaming, I wasn't truly sure if any sound came out of my mouth. Forcing my eyes open, I looked up to see Charles kneeling beside me. His face was pinched, his eyes wide. He looked almost as scared as I felt.

"William, are you okay?" His voice sounded like it was in the cavern we played in when we were far apart.

Tears were rolling down his face as he pulled me onto his lap. It felt like I was being stabbed with a knife and set on fire as the pain intensified and overcame everything. I could no longer see, it hurt so bad. Suddenly, the pain and everything stopped and darkness washed over me. It was a relief to be away from the pain and torment I had suffered.

When I could see again, I stood in the kitchen next to Charles. I looked down and frowned. How did I get on my feet? Then I noticed that Charles was holding something. Upon closer inspection, I realized that he was holding my body.

"What?" I asked. It was the only thing I could think of.

Charles's head shot up and he looked at me. "William?"

"Charles, what is going on?"

"I don't know how to tell you this, but you're dead."

Not sure what to say, I just stood there staring at him. I didn't have much of a chance to process what was said because a whirl of commotion happened.

Mother walked into the room, took in the scene and began to scream. She jerked my body away from Charles.

"What in the hell did you do to him?" she yelled as she held my body close.

Charles began shaking his head no. "I didn't do anything to him, Mother. I found him like this. I'm sorry. I don't know what happened."

"You little bastard! You killed him!"

"I didn't . . ."

"That cake was meant for you! Not him. He wasn't allowed to have it, so why did you feed it to him?"

Charles's eyes got wider if it were possible. "What do you mean?"

"You were supposed to be the one dead, not my precious William."

31

She put my body down and charged Charles, hitting him with her hands fisted up. Reaching for something on the counter, she grabbed a wooden spoon and continued to hit him with it.

Charles tried covering his head and scurried away from the abuse.

"Get back here, you bastard! You were supposed to die like your mother did. You were never supposed to live. I don't know how you survived as a babe, but you won't live much longer. Everything will be mine then."

Charles was cornered by the kitchen door that led the backyard. He huddled into a ball in the corner as the blows kept coming. Every hit made a resounding thud. I watched, mesmerized by the violence. I had never seen it up close before. Mother usually sent me away before she punished Charles.

A quivering hand felt around behind him, his fingers wrapping around the handle of the ax Father kept in the house for firewood.

Charles swung and struck Mother on the arm. She staggered back, and Charles got to his feet advancing. He continued swinging the ax. Blood splattered everywhere. Once he was finally spent, he dropped the ax and looked around the room.

"Charles," I said stunned.

He made eye contact with me. "I'm sorry, William."

He walked out of the room and up the stairs. He came back down with a statue. Placing it beside Mother's body, he leaned over her and chanted something so quietly I couldn't hear. A light flashed around Mother then the statue. It was gone as suddenly as it appeared.

"Charles? What did you just do?"

Standing he walked over to the china hutch and opened it. Placing the statue in it, he shut it and locked it, pulled the key from the lock, and pocketed it. When he finally turned, he looked at me with tears in his eyes. "I've freed us both from a demon. Now you can live here until you are content and ready to move on to be with Father. And I- Well, I can finally get away. I love you, William."

I watched as he walked out the front door to his new future. I looked around the house, realizing it was truly alone with not only my body, but my mother's as well. It was an odd feeling, but at the same time I didn't feel anything at all. I didn't know what to make of it. I decided that I would just see what I could find to do.

Chapter 5

I'm not sure how much time had passed. They eventually came in and removed our bodies. Police spoke about how Charles had either been kidnapped, or he was killed along with Mother and me. They didn't exert too much energy into finding the killer though. There were whispers about how horrible Mother had been and that there was suspicion around Father's death. They had thought that she killed my father. She may have, but it didn't matter anymore.

The house stood completely barren for what seemed like eons. I was alone. Then a family had moved in. They didn't last long. The little girl saw me and was scared. They moved shortly after that.

I had learned how to move objects and hurt people. I found it quite exhilarating. There had been a few accidents along the way, but I didn't mind. They were part of the learning process.

The door opened, and I heard a voice I didn't think I would ever hear again.

"Come on in, Mr. Bane."

"Call me Cyrus," a smooth voice responded.

"I've had possession of this house for years and can't seem to keep tenants in it. That's why I decided to put it on the market. Under the full disclosure laws, I need to let you know that there were three deaths in this house in 1882. The stories are a woman killed her husband and son by poisoning and then was hacked to death by an intruder."

"Quite fascinating, Mr. Bucco."

"Please, call me Bastian. Mr. Bucco was my father."

I was shocked when I saw the face of the man speaking. He looked eerily like Father, but younger. I shook my head. I had to be seeing things. There was no way.

"How did you end up in possession of such a wonderful piece of history?" the man named Cyrus asked as he looked around the house in awe.

"It has been passed down in my family from my great-great-great, I believe, grandfather, Charles. His request was that it stay in the family, but it has become a burden to me."

This was Charles's grandson? I believed it as much as he looked like Father. He looked over Cyrus's shoulder and made direct eye contact with me. He could see me. He had the same affliction as Charles.

"I will write you a check for the full amount today," Cyrus told him, pulling out his checkbook.

"Mr- I mean Cyrus. About the other deal. This is the location that you needed. The one with high activity. I can bring you everything you need for it."

His eyebrows raised in interest. I watched the interaction carefully. I felt like there was something odd here.

"How can you be sure?" Cyrus tapped the pen to his lips.

"This is the home of the first ghost, Golden Boy. The one that could do no wrong in his mother's eyes and died because he was greedy and only thought of himself. This house is located in the middle of the third, and most important, gateway. With the Black Zodiac, you will be able to open the gateway and become the most powerful person on Earth. I know that is what you dream of.

"How do you propose that you bring me the other 11 ghosts for the zodiac?"

"I know where to find them. I know what I'm looking for. I will be able to bring them all to you and put them here. You just have to do what you do best and let me do what I do best."

"What do you want out of this?"

"Pay me for the ghosts as I deliver them. I also want you to fund the travels it will take to get all of them here. With my help, you will have all your dreams come true, and I will get to see the world and travel."

"Deal." Cyrus held his hand out and Bastian shook it.

After Cyrus wrote out the check and handed it to Bastian, he walked out of the room to look around the house some more.

Bastian turned his attention to me. "Hello. William, is it?"

I nodded. "Why are you selling my house?"

"I know you heard what I had to say. It simply had to go. It's been holding my family down for years. A presence and burden that I no longer want to own. You will get to play with others. You won't be alone anymore. I hope you can respect that."

"You are kin to Charles?"

The name stopped Bastian cold. He continued to stare at me for several long heartbeats. Finally, he nodded once.

"You look like my father." I turned and walked away. I had no more interest in that mortal or his past. I found out what I wanted. He was my blood, and he betrayed us by selling the house.

I glanced back once to see him standing in front of the china hutch. His eyes were focused on something in there, but I wasn't going to ask what. There was nothing in there worth looking at.

I was excited about one thing that had been mentioned. I was finally going to get playmates.

Black Zodiac Ghost 2
BUTCHER

Chapter 6

Chicago, 1929

I placed my cards face up on the table, grinning from ear to ear. I had won yet another hand at poker. I was on a winning streak, and if I kept it up, I'd have enough money to pay back Mr. Capone. I still owed him a hefty sum, and he was getting antsy for his money.

Another hand was dealt, and I stared at my cards smiling. I had a flush. This was a sure bet I would win the next hand. After that, I would cash out and take my money straight to Capone to pay him off. Then, I would be able to get back to business as normal.

"I'm all in," I said while pushing my chips into the middle of the table.

"Yous sure you wanta do that?" Tony asked from the other side of the table. He had one eyebrow raised. The look in his eyes made the hair on the back of my neck stand up.

"Yes. If I wasn't, then I wouldn't bet it."

"I raise ya," Tony said tossing chips into the pile.

Glancing over to the dealer, I smiled. "Give me more. Double it."

"Okay, Jimmy," Frankie said as he handed me the chips.

I slid them to the middle of the table and the others, except for Tony, folded. I laid down my hand to show my straight flush. Reaching across, I began to gather the chips in victory.

"Hold on there a minute," Tony placed his cards down to show all four aces. With one giant hand, he scooped the chips to him.

Defeat washed through me. I lost everything. Again. Mr. Capone was going to be furious when I couldn't pay him the money I owed. I sat there unsure of my next move. I knew I had to get out of there before they realized I couldn't afford to pay what I lost.

Standing up, I gave the group an innocent smile. "I must be goin'. Nice playin' with you gents. Frankie, I will get the money when the bank opens in the morning, and I will bring it on over to you."

As casually as possible, I hurried to the door. I wanted to get away from them before they called my bluff. I was going to have to fall back on my ol' reliable to get the funds I needed to pay them back. Frankie was part of Mr. Capone's group, so technically I owed Mr. Capone more money now that I lost that hand.

When I entered my shop, I paced the back room, trying to decide how I wanted to make my next move. Borrowing more from Mr. Capone was a bad idea, so I had to come up with something new. I didn't want him to realize that I was completely broke and in over my head.

Suddenly, an idea hit me. I could get the money out of the savings account that my wife's family set up for us. I would pay some on it and buy some time to get the rest of the money together. With the decision made, I quietly made my way upstairs to the apartment that I shared with my wife and daughter. Slipping into the bed beside my wife, I pulled her close and smiled as I drifted off to sleep.

The next morning, I was down in the shop, chopping up a hog when the bell above the front door jingled. Looking up, I saw Frankie enter the shop. I groaned inwardly, being I hadn't heard from the bookie at the track yet.

Frankie moved slowly, yet purposefully around the shop looking at the different meats I had in the cases. I wiped my bloody hands on my apron and headed toward the counter, hoping that he just wanted to purchase some meat.

He stepped up to the glass and began to tap his fingers on it as he looked down at the ground beef underneath his hand.

My heart pounded in my ears and knocked against my chest hard enough I was certain that Frankie could hear it.

"Yous got my money?" he asked quietly. His voice was barely above a whisper, but the menace and violence were loud and clear.

"Not yet, Frankie. I ain't been to the bank yet, but I will get there soon. I just gots to finish chopping up

"I'll be back in an hour. You best have that money for me." He turned and slammed the door as he left.

Relief washed through me as the door clicked shut. I had just bought myself some more time. I waited several heartbeats to be sure he was truly gone before I walked over and locked the door. I flipped the sign to closed and slipped out the back. I had to see a man about a horse.

***

I had narrowly won enough to keep Frankie at bay. It would only be a matter of time before they came back for more money. I hoped I'd be able to make enough to keep the wolves from the door. I wondered if I could win more at the track after I closed the shop for the evening.

The bell over the door rang, causing me to jump and nick myself with the knife I was using to clean the carcass in front of me. I cursed and glanced up to see who had entered. My daughter, Abigail, stood there a smile on her face.

"Hi, Daddy." She skipped over to the counter and leaned on it.

"Princess, you scared me." Her smile was contagious, and I couldn't help but smile back at her. She had grown into a beautiful young woman. "How was school?"

"It was fine. Do you need any help today?"

"Nah. Go on up and do your homework. Let your mother know that I'll be closing up and heading out for a bit. I'll be home later."

She nodded and trotted to the stairs. That girl had so much energy, and she was always happy. I tried to remember if there were ever a time that I felt like that. I couldn't think of any. Once I was alone with my thoughts, the smile faded. Fear washed over me again. I was going to have to do something quick.

Closing the shop, I slipped out the back door and headed back to the track. I was determined that I had to win. I had a feeling that I was about to get lucky. The tides were going to turn in my favor for once.

I watched with a growing, sickening anticipation as the horse I had bet all my money on lost the lead. I feared that I had been wrong. I prayed to a deity that I didn't believe in that the horse would get another wind and win the race, but I didn't believe it would.

After losing everything that I had plus some that I didn't, I went home in defeat. I was going to have to face the music and Frankie. Mr. Capone wasn't going to like the fact that I didn't have his money and no way to get it.

When Mr. Capone wanted money out of you and you didn't have it, he would take it from you in the most painful of ways. I would have nightmares of what was going to happen when he realized that I had couldn't pay.

Chapter 7

I was jumpy for days after losing the money. Every time the bell above the shop door jingled, my heart would race, and I could feel my anxiety rising. It was making my job more difficult than it had ever been. I cut myself more than I had since I was a rookie, still wet behind the ears.

Looking up, I didn't see anyone in the shop, but I knew the door had opened. I turned back to the carcass in front of me. Slamming my cleaver down into the joint of the leg, a satisfied feeling washed over me as the blade connected to the wood.

It gave me an idea. Maybe I could fight my way out of the mess with Mr. Capone and Frankie. I deflated when I remembered that they had something I wouldn't. Tommy guns. I couldn't outlast automatic guns like that. I'd be dead in seconds.

I was so lost in thought that I didn't see the boy standing there watching me. I jumped out of my skin when I heard him speak to me.

"Excuse me, sir."

Once my heart settled back down in my chest, I studied the boy in front of me. He didn't appear to be much older than Abigail. His eyes, however, were something I hadn't even seen in most grown men. They were haunted. He appeared to have seen more in his few years than what he should have.

"Yes?" I walked around the table to the counter where I could assist him better. Leaning on the counter, I watched as he stared down at the meats in the display case.

"I'd like to purchase some of the roast beef." He spoke softly, almost like he was afraid of his own voice.

"How much can I get ya?"

"Half pound."

I pulled out some of the meat, placing it on the scale. As I weighed it, I told him how much it was going to cost him. Grabbing some paper, I wrapped it as I watched him fumbling around in his pockets. He pulled out wads of cash.

Envy washed over me. I decided that he came from money, and he was running an errand for his mother. No child had that kind of money. It wasn't fair that he should have that kind of money on him. Some of it from the flash I had gotten of the cash, he had enough to keep the sharks at bay for a bit.

I sighed as I exchanged the meat for the money. I wished that I could come up with a way to get the kid to give me the money that he had. I needed it more than he did. I told him to have a good day and watched as he walked out.

The rest of the day was a blur of nerves. I had so much on my mind, I lost track of time. It was like there were gaps in my memory where I didn't remember anything. It was strange.

Right before I closed up for the night, the bells above the door jingled. It was the young man again. I was surprised that I would see him so soon after buying a half pound of roast beef. He approached the counter. The look on his face was awkward.

"Can I help yas?" I asked, slightly irritated. I didn't have time for some kid to be bugging the piss out of me. I needed to close up and go hide upstairs before Frankie came back, or I needed to come up with some money to hold him off.

"Yes, sir. I was wondering. If umm, maybe you would hire me to help out around here." He shifted his weight from one foot to the other before he continued to speak. "See, it's something I've been interested in for a while, and I want to learn the trade. I've heard you are the best butcher in Chicago."

"I don't have time to be trainin' anyone at the moment. I also don't have the moneys to be paying an apprentice."

"You don't have to pay me. I am willing to work with you for scraps of the meat and maybe a pallet on the floor to sleep."

Suspicion arose in me. It didn't make any sense. He had the money for roast beef, why would he want to sleep on my floor.

"Why? You don't look like yous live on the streets. You had enough money to get some of my best roast beef. What aren't you telling me?"

He sighed, shoulders drooping. "I was running an errand for the old lady down the street. She asked if I could pick up the roast for her since she couldn't get around as good as she used to. I have a little money, but who is going to rent to a teenager. Look at me. I look like I'm twelve."

"How old are you?" The wheels were beginning to turn in my head.

"Almost sixteen."

"Where are your parents?"

A shrug was his only answer.

"What's your name?"

"Chuck."

"Just Chuck?"

"For now."

I nodded. The kid had spunk. He made valid points, though. He didn't look old enough to be on his own, and no one would trust a kid to live in a rental. Plus, he didn't look like he would be able to pay his way in the world.

"Here's the deal, kid. I'll let you sleep in the shop, but you will have to do some work for me. I have a bunk in the back that I use sometimes. I'll let you sleep there."

"What do you want me to do?" His eyes narrowed suspiciously at me.

"I need some money and you's gonna help me get it."

"How?"

"We can discuss that in the morning. Now help me get locked up."

He did as I said, and we cleaned up the shop faster than I could do it on my own. Maybe having help wouldn't be such a horrible thing. Also, if he could help me earn some extra money, I could get out from under Mr. Capone and maybe get on easy street.

Chapter 8

Chuck turned out to be more help than I could have imagined. He had a certain skill that involved lightening other people's pockets. Within a couple days of him staying at the shop, we were able to scrounge up enough money to buy me some time. I knew it wasn't going to be much, but it would give me time to come up with my next plan.

He was also extremely eager to learn the ways of butchering. I had never seen anyone as enthused about it before. He would jump right in and start hacking away at the hog or whatever animal that I was butchering at the time. He relished in putting the meat in the grinder, a job that would tend to make other people's stomachs churn.

"Jimmy, do you need me to cut the heart out?" He looked at me with a glint in his eye.

"Go ahead. We gots to get rid of it anyway." I leaned my hip against the table while I watched him work. His hands were steady and concentration strong. "Here's an idea. I need to go out for a bit. You can finish butchering this here hog and clean up for me tonight. I'll be back later."

"Yes, sir."

His eyes didn't once stray from the task at hand. I had a moment of pride overcome me. He seemed to take what I had told him seriously and put it to use.

I took off my plastic apron and hung it up. This was the first time in years that I had felt comfortable leaving the shop in someone else's hands. He may have been young, but he was capable. That I could tell from watching the intensity at which he worked.

On my way out the door, I couldn't help thinking that he would make a great butcher one of these days. Maybe one day he could come into the business with me. I chuckled at the musings. He wouldn't be around that long. No one wanted to stick around here that long. He was young and eager.

Thoughts of Chuck escaped my mind once I entered the bar. The actual bar was in the center of the room, in the shape of a circle so patrons could come from all side. The stage was against the north wall, gold pole in the middle. There was a scantily dressed woman on stage swaying to the music.

Bars like this one weren't common and very rarely spoken about. It was one of those places that you just knew where there. I watched as she pulled her top off. Her tits swayed and bounced with every move she made. Had to admit, it was an enticing show. With enough money, a patron could taste the goods of the dancer of his choice. I rarely had the monies for that kind of entertainment.

Sex wasn't what I was here for anyway. I was going to try my hand at this game. It wasn't one of Mr. Capone's games, so I wasn't as well known. I had only played in Mr. Moran's games a couple of times but won both of those games.

After watching those voluptuous tits bounce around, I turned and headed to the back of the bar. There was a door that led into the kitchen. Going through that door, I was met by a man dressed in a pinstripe suit, the noticeable bulge of a gun under his arm. He had a fedora on his head, tipped to one side, partially covering his right eye.

"Are yous lost?" he asked. His accent wasn't local, it sounded like he was from The Big Apple.

"No. I'm here for the game, see," I answered. I felt the need to sound tough when in a fight he would win since he had a gun. It would only take one bullet to blow me to smithereens.

"Yous got the entrance fee?"

I handed him the wad of cash. I had taken just enough out of the till to cover the fee and buy in. He stepped aside after counting it to let me though the door. Seven men sat around the table, cards in hand, cigars hanging from their mouths.

After a quick assessment of the room, my heart skipped a beat to see Frankie as one of those seven. He smiled at me as his eyes met mine. It sent a chill down my spine. Part of me wanted to back out knowing he was there, but I couldn't let him think I was yellow bellied. If I left now, he would become suspicious that I didn't have the funds to finish paying off his boss, and he would break something of value to me.

I sat down at the table, ironically across from Frankie, being it was the only open seat. I was dealt in one and a couple of words were spoken that had nothing to do with the game. It was a quiet game. No bullshitting, no shooting the shit. They were all concentrating on their cards and whatever they were thinking about.

After winning the first three hands, I began to feel confident and cocky. Maybe the intensity of this game was what I needed to make money. The game wore on, and I continued to win. As I hit two grand, a voice in my head told me to stop, but the louder voice in my head said that I only needed one more huge win to be able to pay off all my debts and get my business back in the black.

The round continued, one by one players began to fold. As I raised the stakes yet again, I glanced at Frankie. He smiled, matching my bet and raising it. I felt sweat pop out across my forehead. Goosebumps broke out across my flesh. I wasn't sure what had me worried. I knew that I held three aces in my hand in a full house with two jacks. Frankie had shit hands all night so there was no way that he had anything that could beat me.

I made a dramatic gesture as I laid my cards down to show my win. "Full house, gents."

Reaching forward, I brought my arms around the chips to slide them to me. The clearing of a throat stopped me mid-movement.

"Not so fast, ace." Frankie gently set his cards down as if they would break. "I believe a Royal Straight Flush beats your Full House."

My mouth fell open. I wasn't sure how he did that. There had been no way he could beat me. No one was ever that lucky. I was having trouble comprehending what the reality of losing this hand meant.

"Please take yous hands off my winnins."

I sank back into my chair completely defeated.

Frankie stood and smiled at me. "I'm going to collect my winnings, so pony up boys. Jimmy, I'm assumin' I need to come to the shop to pick it up from you. I'll be there in the morning."

He collected his winnings and left whistling a tune I couldn't quite reckonize, but one I would never forget.

Chapter 9

I entered the shop through the back door. I was going to by-pass the back room completely until I heard Chuck speaking softly. I stopped to listen to what he was saying. I wondered who he had in the room with him.

"Yes, I still have enough that I can leave when I need to. The skills I've learned from Jimmy will be invaluable. He has been a lot of help. I know when I move on, I will be able to use it to my advantage."

He sounded like he was talking on a telephone, but there wasn't one in the back. I couldn't hear anyone else and there wasn't any movement in the room, so I was assuming that Chuck was on the bunk settled down for the night. There was a long stretch of silence, so I thought that he was talkin' to himself, but then he spoke again.

"I have around three thousand. Yes, I keep it hidden. I don't think anyone will be able to find it. Jimmy doesn't know about it. I don't fully trust him yet. He is nice, but I know he has a penchant for gambling. His daughter has confirmed that for me as well. I want to help him, but I can't. He has to learn to help himself. I learned that years ago when I was living with Ingrid. No one can help you but you."

I frowned. What in the hell was going on? Chuck was starting to act like a freak. He was talking to himself and answering nothing. I was beginning to worry that he was sick in the head and needed help. I would have to look into what kind of help would be useful for him.

I was also intrigued by the fact he had stated that he had three thousand. I could only assume that he meant dollars. That would help me out greatly. I would have to find the loot he was speakin' about. I turned to walk away when I heard his voice once more.

"I will, good night. I love you, Mother."

Curiosity got the best of me, and I opened the door just a crack so I could peek in. The room was still and quiet. Chuck didn't make a sound when I opened it, so I figured his eyes were closed. When I didn't see anything but Chuck, I shut the door and headed up to bed.

The next few days were relatively quiet. Frankie hadn't been by, telling me that he knew that I didn't have the funds to pay him. I was spared a little time to come up with something. It was a relief, but at the same time, my nerves were fried.

I found myself wandering the city while trying to clear my head after going to the bank. I hadn't realized how much time had passed since I left. Running my hands through my hair, I took a deep breath and released it. It was time to head back to the shop.

When I walked in, the first thing I noticed was how quiet it was in the shop. After a cursory glance around, I didn't see Chuck, so I began to look for him. It was unusual for him not to be in the front of the store or cleaning something. The boy was good at cleaning and maintaining the place.

As I walked around the counter to check the back, I thought I heard a female laugh. The door to the back room where is bunk was located was closed. I smiled as I stood at the door. He had found himself a gal to bed. I needed to give the boy some privacy.

Halfway back to the counter, I heard something that made me freeze in place. My blood began to boil. Turning back, I raced to the door and threw it open.

My little Abigail was lying on the bed with Chuck covering her body with his. There were in different states of undress. Her button up dress was unbuttoned to her navel, her camisole askew. Chuck was shirtless, trousers unbuttoned.

"What in the fuck is going on?" The rage I was feeling was beginning to boil over. My voice was louder than I had intended, but I couldn't control it.

I had trusted Chuck. Brought him into my shop, under my wing and he took advantage of my daughter. My daughter who wasn't even out of high school yet. He had turned my daughter into a whore.

Abigail covered her chest with her arms, eyes wide with surprise. She had gasped as she pushed him away.

"Daddy—" she started.

"Don't say a word." I spat out through clenched teeth.

"Jimmy, this isn't what it looks like," Chuck said as he buttoned up his shirt.

"It looks like you ruined my daughter. That's what it looks like." I looked at Abigail. "Get up to your room. I'll deal with you later."

She scrambled away without a word. I would have to calm myself before I could even think about what to do with her.

Once alone with Chuck, my temper snapped, and I attacked. My fists flew at his face. I wanted to kill him with my bare hands. Every logical thought escaped me as I pummeled the kid. There was a satisfying crunch of his nose breaking from the impact of my fist. It made me feel a little better.

Chuck didn't fight back, he curled his arms over his head, protecting it, and let me beat on him until I was exhausted. Once I was done, I stood up so I was towering over him. My knuckles were cracked and bleeding. Bruises already starting to form.

I studied the damage I had done to him. His eye was swollen and blackening. There was blood running down his face from his nose and a crack in the corner of his lip. He wiped the blood off his face with the back of his hand.

"I want you out of here now. If you aren't gone in five minutes, I will chop you into pieces with my butcher's knife. You will know what it is like to be one of the hogs we carve." I walked out of the room, then turned back and grabbed him by the neck. "On second thought, I'll escort you out."

I dragged him out by the neck and tossed him into the street.

"I need to get my things." Chuck's voice was even and steady, which was surprising after what I did to him.

"Too bad. I needed my daughter to stay pure."

"Jimmy, you don't want to do this. Just let me get my stuff."

"Get the fuck out of here, Chuck. I never want to see your face again."

The door shut behind me with a resounding click. After locking up, I slowly made my way up the stairs. I would go through and get rid of Chuck's things in the morning. I still had to deal with Abigail.

Chapter 10

I secured the back room, ridding it of everything that belonged to Chuck. I didn't want any traces of him or his betrayal in my shop. It hurt that he would take advantage of my generosity in that manner. While going through the back room, I found cash banded together. From the quick count, there was at least a grand there.

It would help get Frankie off my back when he showed up for payment. I knew that he would eventually. He always did. This way, I was ready for him. There was a small flicker of remorse over the fact that I was essentially stealing from Chuck. Then I remembered the scene I had walked in on. Him on top of my daughter. He got what he deserved.

Frankie showed up a few days after I kicked Chuck out. When I passed him the wad of cash, he smiled and stuffed it in his inside coat pocket. He whistled on the way out the door. My shoulders relaxed for the first time in a while. I knew that I would be sleeping like a baby.

I tried to stay away from the games, but I couldn't seem to. It was like a magnet. The harder I tried to stay away, the more I was lured back. I found myself in the game night after night, losing hand after hand. Before I knew it, I was up to my eyeballs in debt with Mr. Capone. Again.

The problem remained: I had no money to pay him. The shop wasn't getting enough customers to keep it afloat either. I was beginning to stress over the issue. I wouldn't be able to hide it from my wife much longer. When she found out that I spent all the savings plus the money her family had given us, well her, she was going to be angry. Hell, angry wasn't the correct term for it.

***

When Frankie showed up at the shop this time, my heart raced and sweat beaded my forehead. It was time to face the music. I would have to tell him I didn't have any money to pay. I wondered what he was going to cut off me as payment.

"Frankie, I was just gonna call yas." I attempted a smile even though my insides were quivering like jelly.

"I'm sure you were. You gots Mr. Capone's money, Jimmy?" He leaned on the glass of the counter. His eyes were blank. If I didn't know better, I'd believe he was dead.

"That's why I was gonna call you. I need more time." A nervous sweat rolled down my back between my shoulder blades.

"The boss wants you to see what happens when he doesn't get his money. Come with me." He turned and walked away without looking to see if I was following. Not that I was brave enough to not follow.

We climbed into the car and drove through the city. I felt pins and needles shooting through my body as my anxiety skyrocketed out of control. My heart pounded against my chest and blood thundered in my ears.

The car rolled to a stop. Frankie turned to me. "Yous are gonna do as I say. If you don't, I'll shoot you wheres you stand. Go inside, keep your head down."

My mouth dried out and I didn't think I was capable of speaking. I nodded in agreement as we got out of the car. We headed toward the building, head down as instructed. The building was a garage. We went to the door in the alley. It was abandoned and our clipped footsteps echoed.

When we entered the garage, I took in the scene. There were men lined up facing the wall. Two men stood behind them, tommy guns in hand. They were dressed up as coppers, and they had their guns trained on the row of men's backs.

Frankie approached the men and picked up the gun that was on the floor at their feet. He motioned me over with a jerk of his head. Obediently, I moved across the room, so I was standing next to him.

"Do you recognize these men, Jimmy?"

I swallowed back the fear and studied the men in front of us. A few of them did look familiar. It took a few moments for me to realize that they were the men that we had played in the poker game a while back. The game that I hadn't expected to see Frankie, yet he was there. These were Moran's guys.

One of the men turned his head, looking back at Frankie. Desperation and hope flashed across his face. "Frankie. So glad you're here. Tell these coppers that we ain't done nothing wrong."

"I wish I could, Louie. Bugsy pissed of Mr. Capone, and you know what happens when Mr. Capone is pissed. Things tend to get ugly."

"Frankie—"

"Listen, I'm just following orders. Yous knew what could happen when Mr. Capone was crossed." He turned his attention back to me. "Jimmy, this is a lesson to yas. Get Mr. Capone's money or suffer a fate like this."

Gunfire lit up the room. The sound of the guns' rapid firing echoed deafeningly off the walls. I swore I heard someone laugh, but I couldn't tell with all the screams bouncing around the room. The scene was frightening. I had never seen anything like this in my life.

I felt my control of my bladder slip a little, but I managed to regain control before I completely pissed myself. When the gunfire and screams died down, I stared at the carnage in front of me. Blood poured out of the bodies like miniature streams, pooling underneath them. The walls were filled with bullet holes. I had a feeling the sight would haunt me for a long time.

Mr. Capone got his point across. I was in deep shit and terrified of what would happen to me. I needed to come up with an escape plan.

When he dropped me back off at the shop, I sat in the storage room until the shaking began to subside. I closed my eyes and took several deep breaths just to get myself back under control. When my eyes shut, images of the dead mean flashed back in my mind. I could swear I had seen brains leaking out of one of them.

My stomach revolted at the thought. Grabbing a bucket, I vomited until I was just dry heaving. I wiped my mouth with the back of my hand. The nausea was still very real, but my stomach was now empty.

My mind spun with possibilities and ideas. The only thing I was certain of was that I didn't want to die. I would do anything to keep that from happening.

Chapter 11

The idea hit me like a steam train. I knew Mr. Capone had a fancy for younger women, so I needed to have a word with him directly. I walked into his office trying to conceal the shaking, but there was a slight tremble to my hands

"Jimmy, what is it that you couldn't relay the message through Frankie?" He turned in his chair, so he was facing me. "You got my money?"

"No, that's what I wanted to talk about." I tried swallowing around the giant lump in my throat. His eyebrow raised, and I hurriedly continued, trying not to lose my nerve. "I have a proposal for you. I gots to be honest Mr. Capone, I ain't got the money, but I do have a daughter that is of age."

He frowned. "What are you trying to say, Jimmy?"

I shuffled my feet, feeling like a schoolboy in front of the class without an answer. I hadn't realized he was going to make me say it out loud. "I know yous have a refined taste when it comes to the lasses. My girl is at the ripe age and still innocent. She would be suited for your tastes."

"You're telling me that you are going to give me your daughter to fuck and have as a plaything to wipe out our debts?" He picked up a pen and twirled it between his fingers. "I gotta say, this is the most interesting proposition that I've had when it comes to having debts paid back. Do you have a picture of the dame?"

I pulled the photograph out of my wallet and handed it to him. This was the most awkward moment I had ever been in. It felt like I was selling my daughter, and essentially, I was. I had to shake the thought. She wasn't any use to me now that she had let Chuck touch her. I wouldn't be able to marry her off to a wealthy man like I'd originally planned. I hoped that she would make an impression on Mr. Capone, so I would get something out of the girl.

He set the picture down on his desk and looked up at me. There was a glint in his eyes that made me uncomfortable. He tapped the pen on the desk, eyes never leaving me. I wanted to squirm under the intensity of his gaze.

"I can't lie. I'm intrigued. I want to meet the doll. We will have it set up, and if I like her, we will discuss terms." He dropped the pen on the desk and turned, dismissing me. "I'll have my new errand boy come with the time to bring the doll up."

I nodded my ascent then left the room quietly. The further I walked from the room, the more my stomach churned at the thought of what I was doing. I was selling my daughter to save my skin. I knew it was wrong, but at the same time, I didn't give a fuck. I had to pay this man off.

I hadn't been back at the shop for long when the front door opened. I walked out to greet the customer. As soon as my eyes landed on him, I stopped dead in my tracks. I couldn't believe the little bastard had the nerve to come back here.

Grabbing the butcher knife, I had every intention of showing him that I meant business. The only thought running through my head was that I was going to chop him to bits. I lifted it up as I approached him.

"You don't want to do that, Jimmy." Chuck took a step backward.

"You don't know me very well if you think that I don't want to do this."

The door opened again, stopping my forward motion. Frankie stood there, just behind Chuck. His eyes narrowed as he glared at me.

"What's going on here?" Frankie asked.

"I'm getting rid of a problem," I took another step forward.

"Don't touch the boy. He is Mr. Capone's newest errand boy. Back off, Jimmy." Frankie's words penetrated my head, and I stepped backward, lowering the knife.

If he was the errand boy for Mr. Capone, then there was nothing I could do about it. I had to let him live. I cursed under my breath. This was putting me in a precarious situation. I wanted the bastard dead, but if I touched him, I would die.

"You are supposed to bring Abigail to Mr. Capone tomorrow at nine pm. She is supposed to dress in her best outfit." Chuck glared at me as he gave me the instructions.

When he turned to leave, I spoke up. "I wouldn't have to use her like this if you hadn't ruined her for any other man. Now let's just hope that she can become Capone's whore and get some use out of her."

He looked at me over his shoulder. "You're making a big mistake, Jimmy."

***

"Alright Abigail. You need to listen closely. We are going to go see a very important person. I need you to be on your best behavior. You are a lady, and you need to act like it." I stared at her, watching her expression.

She nodded and smoothed down the front of the dress she was wearing. I had lied to her mother and told her that we were going on a father-daughter date for ice cream. She didn't need to know what was going on. If Capone agreed, then I would come up with something to tell her.

I knocked on the door and glanced at Abigail, making sure she was presentable. Chuck answered the door, allowing us to enter before returning to Mr. Capone's side. Frankie stood behind the big man, looking intimidating.

I was starting to second guess myself, but there was nothing I could do about it now. We stood in front of his desk, waiting. I wasn't sure what the next move should be, so I just stood there like a statue, feeling like an idiot.

"I'm Abigail," Abigail held out her hand to Mr. Capone, seemingly unaware of the precarious situation she was in.

Mr. Capone stood, walked around the desk and took Abigail's hand. Instead of shaking it like she had intended, he turned it, so the back was up and bent at the waist slowly to kiss her hand.

I watched as Abigail's cheeks began to flush with color. She wasn't used to the attentions of a man. She openly stared at the man before her.

"I'm Alfred. You may call me Al."

"Alright, Al. You can call me Abby."

"Do you know why you are here, Abigail?" He ignored her request for the use of her nickname.

She swallowed and shook her head no. The room became increasingly tense with each tick of the clock. Mr. Capone continued to stare at her while she stared back. There was a slight tremor running through her body while she stood there.

I had to admire the girl. She had balls. I didn't know if I could stare down the mob boss like that myself. If I was honest, I knew I couldn't. I would have pissed myself or dropped eye contact long ago.

Finally, the boss walked away and seated himself on the edge of his desk. Lifting a hand, he made a simple gesture that had Chuck moving forward. Capone looked at over at the boy. "Give me your impression of the situation. You have impressed me thus far."

"I think Mr. Demelo is a sick bastard for pimping out his only daughter to pay his debts. The poor girl is sweet. She wouldn't willingly agree to that kind of arrangement. What kind of father would do that to their child?" He looked at me with a glint in his eye. "If it were me, I wouldn't be able to make the bargain. You've given the butcher plenty of chances to pay the debts."

Chuck headed back to his position, touching Abigail's hand and giving it a squeeze before walking away. The atmosphere in the room seemed to intensify yet again, making me anxious.

The evening took a sudden turn. Capone spoke without looking away from me. "Chuck, take Abigail into the other room. We need to talk, and a lady doesn't need to be involved in it."

Chuck led Abigail out the door. Pulling it closed behind them, the door clicked shut with a finality that scared the shit out of me. I didn't know why, but I was suddenly very afraid to be alone with Mr. Capone and Frankie.

Chapter 12

I debated on whether I stood a chance trying to make a run for it or not. The problem was, I wasn't much of a runner and they had guns. Glancing over my shoulder, I noticed there were two more goons in the room that hadn't been there before. They were standing in front of the door, so there was no way out.

"Jimmy, we have a problem." Mr. Capone stood and straightened his suit. "You see, I agree with Chuck about what you had planned for your daughter. The problem with that is, I can't accept the offer being that it feels wrong to me."

"Mr. Capone—" I started but was silenced by a look.

"Don't interrupt me." He walked around his desk and opened a drawer while he spoke. "You admitted to not having my money, now you have nothing to bargain with. I know how the shop is doing and there is nothing to squeeze from there."

He produced a cigar cutter and box of cigars. Pulling a cigar out of the box, he clipped it, then lit it. He took a deep drag off it, releasing the smoke into the air.

"What am I going to do with you? I need that money back. It belongs to me, and I want it. I am not a patient man. You know what happens when my patience runs out."

"Mr. Capone just give me some more time; I'll get the money. I'll do whatever I need to do to pay you back."

"Jimmy, Jimmy, Jimmy. I have told you not to interrupt me." He waved a hand.

Before I knew what was happening, two sets of burly hands had my arms and were forcing me down into a chair. Frankie approached and tied my hands down then my legs so I couldn't get off the chair. Once he was certain I was secure, he went back to the desk and picked up the cigar cutter.

When he came back over to the chair, he slipped my pinkie in the cutter and forced it closed with a resounding snap. The pain was immediate and severe. I couldn't help but cry out.

"Don't interrupt the boss again," Frankie said, letting the tip of my finger drop to the ground.

"I'm done, Jimmy. Done with you." Mr. Capone walked to the door then stopped and turned back. I hoped that he changed his mind. "Your daughter is done in this as well. She will be returned home with your wife. I hope she makes better decisions than you did. Frankie don't do it here. Too messy."

There was a click of the door shutting behind Mr. Capone. I suppressed a shiver and tears burned the back of my eyes. I had never been so scared in my entire life.

Frankie stepped up in front of me. I didn't see the blow coming; suddenly there was a ringing in my ears, and everything went dark.

***

Opening my eyes, I stared at a ceiling that looked familiar. There was a terrible pounding in my head. I turned it slowly in attempt to take in my surroundings. Shock hit me like a ton of bricks when I realized where I was. I was at the shop.

Trying to sit up, I couldn't move. There was a tightness across my arms and chest. I looked down to see ropes tied tightly around me. There was no getting away. Frankie and a couple other men that I had only seen a couple times stood there. It was dark except for the light above me. I was lying on the carving table where I butchered my meats. Frankie was wearing my plastic apron.

"Let me go," I said, struggling against the rope.

Frankie clicked this tongue on his teeth, tsking at me. "I can't do that, Jimmy. Mr. Capone wants his money, and since you ain't got it, we are taking it out in flesh."

"My wife will hear you down here. She will call the coppers," I tried to reason with him. Maybe I could convince him that it was a bad idea to kill me here, and I'd have a chance to escape.

He laughed then. It was a loud rumbling kind of laughter. The laughter that you only hear when you are with the insane or demented. It stopped as quickly as it started. He leaned over me and spoke softly. "No one is going to hear you. Chuck told your wife that you ran off with some broad after trying to pimp out your daughter. Mr. Capone, being the generous man that he is, provided them with tickets and the funds to go back to her family and start over. Your family is gone."

He grabbed a cigar, lighting it in the same manner Capone had done earlier. After blowing out his first puff of smoke, he smiled at me. "You can die knowing that your family was spared and that they won't suffer from your crimes. Now, if you believe in the Lord, it may be the time to start praying."

He didn't waste time after that. Picking up a butcher knife, he swung it downward, chopping off my fingertips. After the first bout of agony, one of the goons put a burlap sack over my head.

I screamed and pleaded for my life, but the pleas fell on deaf ears. The pain intensified with every slice that he made. I wasn't sure how long I screamed, but my throat became hoarse, and I couldn't make any more sounds.

He took the cigar and burned my skin with it. The smell of burned flesh along with the pain was nauseating. As I began to black out, I knew that I wouldn't be waking up again. Giving up to the darkness, I welcomed the feeling of nothingness and floated away from the pain.

Chapter 13

Next thing I knew, I was standing next to the table, watching Frankie work on the bloody mass on top of it. It took several long heartbeats for me to realize that I was staring at my own body. It didn't look like me. It didn't even look human anymore.

"He's dead, Frankie," a voice from the back of the room said quietly. Even though his voice was barely a whisper, it sounded like he was shouting.

"Time to get to work boys. We have our orders." Frankie dropped the knife and picked up a handsaw from beside the body.

I watched with disgust as he began to saw my body into pieces starting at the feet. As parts fell on the floor, one of the goons picked them up and dropped them into a trash bag. They stopped when there was nothing but the torso left.

Anger washed over me, making me lunge at Frankie. Nothing happened. I just fell through him. I couldn't touch them. They took everything from me. Now I was helpless but to watch the scene unfold in front of me.

Frankie wrapped the torso up in plastic, then secured it with adhesive tape. Without a word, they packed the body pieces out of the shop. The goons came back in and began cleaning up the blood.

"What is Frankie doing with them remains?" one asked as they were scrubbing the table.

"Don't ask questions, Mikey. That's what gets you killed," the other one answered.

They didn't speak anymore as they cleaned up the mess. Once the majority of the blood was cleaned up, the one called Mikey walked out and returned with cans of gasoline. They splashed it around, making sure to soak as much as possible with it.

The other one lit a book of matches, dropping it on the pile of bloody rags that had been left from cleaning up. There was a whoosh as flames caught the gasoline.

They stayed long enough to make sure that the fire was going to catch, then left. I was left inside, watching everything I worked for go up in smoke and flames.

After the shop was burned to the ground, I was lost. I wandered the streets, in and out of buildings. The longer I was lost, the angrier I became. It wasn't fair. I just tried to do what was best for everyone and it came back and bit me in the ass.

I lost everything because of one little boy. I lost everything because of lies. I started plotting my vengeance. I would get even with them, starting with Frankie.

It was more difficult to locate people as a spirit than it was when you were alive. I was lost and confused by my surroundings. It felt like I was easily turned around and couldn't get a sense of direction. It was also more difficult to see where I was going with the burlap sack over my face. I could see though it, but it made visibility shitty.

I finally found my way to Frankie. I walked into the back of a club to see that I had interrupted a poker game. It was only fitting that I would find him in one of them. With a glance around the table, I saw that the two goons that helped kill me were there also. Sitting in a corner in the room, reading a book, was Chuck. I was going to enjoy this.

I focused all of my energy on the anger. It wasn't hard. I just had to unleash it. Cards and chips flew across the space. There were gasps and curses around the room. It was a mix of shock and surprise. I grabbed at a lit cigar and shoved the cherry side into Frankie's right eye.

The smell of burned hair and flesh filled the room. Guns were drawn, swinging around wildly, since no one knew where to aim and what was happening.

As chaos ensued, Chuck put his book down and stood up. I approached him, looking down at him.

"You're mine," I whispered.

"You're making a mistake," Chuck whispered back.

I lunged but was stopped by an invisible force. I couldn't move closer to him no matter how hard I tried. A growl slipped out of from between my lips. If I couldn't get him, I'd finish my original mission—Frankie.

I turned my attention back to the big man. He had blood and intraocular fluid running down his face. The cigar was still protruding from his eye. I couldn't suppress the smile. It felt good to see the damage on him.

I grabbed a knife that one of the men had sat on the table and attacked. I stabbed Frankie in the throat. I stepped back when blood sprayed from the wound. The room fell silent as Frankie stood there and died, choking on his own blood.

***

I found my way back to the butcher shop; however, it was no longer a butcher shop. It had been torn down and rebuilt to be a massage parlor. I couldn't believe they ruined it. I stayed close to the shop. It was where I was most comfortable. I did, however, mess with the masseuses. I liked to kill their clients while they were out of the room.

There was talk of a psychic coming in and looking around. I scoffed because no one had seen me. I was invisible. There was no such thing as ghosts like little kids were told at bedtime, so they weren't scared of the boogieman under the bed.

When the psychic showed up, I frowned at him. He looked familiar, but I couldn't quite place it. It was confusing. I had memories flashing through my mind, but it couldn't be. It had been close to ninety years. My memories must be fuzzy.

"Thank you for coming, Mr. Bucco. I heard you are the best." The owner of the parlor shook hands with the man in question.

"Not a problem, Mrs. Hyde. I heard about your predicament and planned on visiting anyway. Losing clients like that gives you a bad name. I will see what's going on and take care of it for you."

She showed him around, I couldn't help but follow. There was something about the man that drew me to him. I couldn't put my finger on it, though.

She left us alone, and he turned looking right at me. "Come on, big guy. I'll take you somewhere that you will be free to be you."

"You see me?" I had a hard time comprehending that idea.

"Yes. Come on."

"No. I'm staying here."

He shook his head. "I'm sorry, Jimmy, but I can't let you."

How did he know my name? I didn't have a chance to ask because next thing I knew, I was being pulled by a force I couldn't fight and all went dark.

I'm not sure how much time passed before I was released from the darkness. I found myself in a room. It was a dank room, but somewhat comforting. The room was decorated in dark colors and something called to me there.

"Welcome to your new home, Butcher. I'm your new keeper, Cyrus Bane." The man smiled at me after introducing himself. "You will be allowed to roam the house. Any guests enter at their own risk and you can do whatever you please. There are rooms you aren't allowed in, but that's not a problem, you can't get in there."

With that, he walked out of the room and left me alone in what I was assuming was my new room. I felt an energy buzz through me, making me want to kill everything in sight. I didn't know why, but I knew that great things were waiting for me in this house.

Chapter 14

Unionville, Missouri, 1982

The teacher droned on and on. I couldn't help but watch the clock, wishing that last ten minutes would pass, and I would be free for rest of the day. Okay, I had to go to cheer practice, but that wasn't a big deal. Cheerleading was my passion.

Cheerleading and Andrew. Andrew was the perfect man. Well, almost. He had his insecurities, but they were cute. It made him more attractive to me. I liked to push his buttons to see how far I could drive him before he couldn't take anymore. I always pulled back just before he completely lost his mind.

My eyes settled on the girl sitting in the front row. She had her long blonde hair pulled back in a tight bun. She was dressed like it was still the seventies. Why didn't anyone tell Ashley that bellbottoms were out? I supposed I would have to do so myself.

When the bell rang, I got up and made my way to her desk to block her in before she could escape. I leaned against the desk and smiled down at her.

Ashley's eyes widened, pupils dilating. I was certain she was intimidated by me and I loved it. The idea I was feared sent a rush of adrenaline through my body.

"Hello, Ashley." I said her name slowly.

"H-h-hi Susan," she stuttered and her hands trembled slightly as she gathered her books. "I need to get to my next class. Mrs. Sutton hates it when you're late."

"Mrs. Sutton will get over it." I flipped my hair out of my eyes while I spoke. "I just need to give you a little advice."

She swallowed audibly. "What's that?"

"Bell bottoms were last decade. If I were you, I'd kill myself before I wore something like that to school again."

"My mom gave them to me."

I laughed. "I don't care if the Pope gave them to you. They are ugly and make you look fatter than normal. You need to get rid of them. Your mom obviously has bad taste also."

She stared at me blinking rapidly.

I straightened and began to walk away. "Don't wear them again."

As I passed through the hallway, boys and girls alike got out of my way. I loved being the biggest bitch in the school. Those who didn't fear me, worshipped me. No one dared to cross me. Teachers even kept their distance. The women anyway.

The men looked at me with desire. There was a twinkle in their eyes that told me they were picturing me with my knees touching my ears. A couple were even brave enough to brush against me when they walked by. I enjoyed the power over them.

I walked into my next class and took a seat next to Andrew. Smiling, I leaned over the arm of it and grabbed his shirt. Pulling him closer to me, my mouth pressed against his in a firm kiss. I wondered if I could get him to cut class with me and fuck in the janitor's closet.

My thoughts were interrupted by someone clearing their throat. I turned my head, breaking the kiss so I could see who it was. The principal stood there, arms crossed.

"If I can have your attention, please. Mrs. Taylor will be out the rest of the year. In her place, we have a new, long-term substitute, Mr. Welsh," Mr. Shaw explained.

My eyes drifted to the young man standing next to him. He was a handsome young man. If I had to guess, he was fresh out of college. He had a smile on his face, but his eyes were dark and mysterious. I would enjoy finding out his secrets.

I glanced over to see Andrew glaring at the new teacher. He looked between me and the teacher, expression dark. An idea flashed through my mind. I did my best to suppress the evil smile that was forming at the corner of my mouth. I was going to enjoy this immensely.

Mr. Shaw left the room, leaving the new teacher alone. He walked to the front of the room. He studied us, his eyes landing on me. "Hello, boys and girls. I'm Mr. Welsh and I am happy to be here. I am going to go over my rules and expectations of the class."

He turned and began writing on the board. The chalk squeaked and tapped against it as he wrote out his rules. When he turned back, he rolled the chalk between his fingers.

"I only have a few rules, and I expect them to be followed. We are to treat each other with respect. It's okay to have differing views, but it's not okay to criticize or degrade. There will be participation."

As he continued to drone on, I lost interest in what he was talking about. I didn't care about rules or expectations. I just wanted to get out of there and have fun.

"Are you going to actually teach or just bitch at us over your new rules? This is a classroom of seniors. We know how to sit in a classroom and listen to you talk. Now teach or shut up." I grabbed a nail file from my purse and began to file a snag I noticed on my pinkie nail.

The room fell silent, and I could feel all eyes on me. I knew I had made an impression on the new teacher. He was going to have to learn the rules around here as well.

"Excuse me?" His eyebrows shot up, then furrowed.

"You are boring us. We don't need the lecture. Just teach. Like my mother says, 'shit or get off the pot.' "

"I think you need to go to the office."

"You think?" I laughed. It was a sarcastic laugh.

"I'm not kidding. Get out of my classroom. Go see Mr. Shaw. I will be in there to discuss the rules and maybe have a conference with your parents."

I stood up, slipping my purse on my shoulder. "Oh, yes my father, Superintendent John Hatcher, will know."

Stopping at the doorway, I looked over my shoulder, meeting eyes with Andrew. I blew him a kiss and winked as I exited.

***

I reclined as much as I could in the uncomfortable chair in front of Mr. Shaw's desk. I had my fingers laced together resting on my stomach.

Mr. Shaw completely ignored me as I pretended to sleep. This wasn't the first time I had been sent here and wasn't going to be the last.

When the door opened, rolled my head back so I could see who was walking in. It was both Mr. Welsh and my father. I bit my cheek to keep from smiling. If I knew daddy, he would put Mr. Welsh in his place, and I'd be back to class in no time at all.

"Is there a reason that I was pulled from my busy schedule to come down here?" his gruff voice was directed over my head at the principal.

"John, thank you for coming." Mr. Shaw stood and leaned out to shake daddy's hand.

Mr. Welsh stepped up then. "I'm sorry to bother you, sir, but Susan was out of line in class. Her language and attitude were inappropriate for a classroom. Her tone was disrespectful."

My father looked down at me. "What do you have to say for yourself?"

"If he was actually teaching and not beating his chest like a caveman, I wouldn't have said anything." I stuck my bottom lip out in a pout.

A dark eyebrow rose seconds before he looked away from me. "It sounds as if someone needs to explain what the hell is going on in this school."

There was a recap of what went down in the classroom as I sat there listening, pretending I gave a damn to what was happening. It really didn't matter to me since I wouldn't be in trouble either way, but I needed to keep up appearances.

When Mr. Welsh finished talking, there was a debate on the appropriate course of action. I rolled my eyes when the word detention came up. Like hell I was going to stay for detention. I had better shit to do.

As I was opening my mouth to say as much, daddy spoke up. "Gentlemen, it seems to me like we have a case of teenage angst and dominance struggle of the classroom. Detention isn't necessary with the charity work and cheerleading practice. I will make sure she will learn her lesson about respect. Thank you."

I assumed the meeting was over, so I grabbed my purse and stood up. I made it halfway to the door before Mr. Shaw stopped me. "Susan, do you think you need to say something to Mr. Welsh?"

I turned my head and glanced at him over my shoulder. "I suppose I do. I apologize for making you look weak in front of the rest of the class. It won't happen again."

With that, I flipped my hair and walked out the door.

Chapter 15

"Be aggressive! Be, be aggressive! Go Midgets!" The chant echoed through the gymnasium. I smiled and did a cartwheel. The crowd cheered and screamed.

Once the student body was in a frenzy of excitement, the football players ran in. They were wearing their jerseys with jeans. Faces were painted to show spirit and determination. Just because we were the midgets, didn't mean that it would keep the team down. They were fighters.

I loved being on the floor with the football team during pep assemblies. It was a rush to have all eyes on me while I showed off my skills. It was during these assemblies that I knew all the girls were jealous of me. They wanted to be able to do what I could do. They wanted to be me. It was a glorious feeling.

When the pep assembly ended, I watched as the kids filed out of the gymnasium. The football players were jacking around, being boys as the crowd emptied out. When it was just us and the football players, I walked over to Andrew and kissed him.

The boys hooted and hollered. There were a couple that made comments about getting lucky or laid or something. I tried to tune them out. I liked the attention; however, I didn't encourage the moronic behavior. At least I didn't encourage it in a way that they were aware of it.

Breaking the kiss, I stepped away from Andrew. "You are going to kick ass tonight. Then when you are done beating the Tigers, we are going to celebrate."

I turned and walked away. I could feel their eyes on my ass as I walked.

***

The team won the game by a landslide. It was almost as if the tigers hadn't even tried. The way we wiped the floor with them was embarrassing. I couldn't believe how lousy they had played. Since we won, the team threw a giant party. There would have been a party anyway, but the team was excited about it.

I weaved through the crowd, looking for Andrew. He had gotten there way before I had. He had to help set up the kegs, so we had agreed to meet there. I had taken a little longer getting ready because I wanted to look my best. I had a feeling that things were going to interesting. If not, then I would make it interesting.

When I couldn't find Andrew, I decided to just mingle in the crowds. He would find me when he was ready. I sat on a couch, crossing one leg over the other. I waited, knowing someone would bring me a drink if I waited long enough, then I wouldn't have to go get it myself. I never got my own drinks.

"Here, I saw you sitting here, and thought you looked thirsty." A cup was handed to me.

"Thanks, Brian." I smiled at the football player.

He sat down next to me, slinging his arm across my shoulders. I didn't mind the attention, so I smiled at him as I took a sip of the frothy beer. I wasn't a fan of beer, but I would drink it if it was given to me. Most of these parties didn't have anything besides beer. Occasionally, there would be mixed drinks but not often. High schoolers had troubles getting their hands on the hard liquor.

"Where's Andrew hiding tonight?" he asked as he leaned closer to me.

I gave a half shrug. "He'll find me when he's ready."

"Andrew is stupid." He leaned over so he was speaking softly in my ear. "If you were my woman, I'd never leave you alone. I wouldn't want another man to come and sweep you off your feet from under my nose."

I smiled. This was exactly what I was looking forward to. "Oh? Well, maybe you should teach Andrew that lesson."

I slid a finger down the side of his face. In response, he reached over and slid his fingers around my ear in an erotic gesture. I had a shiver run down my back as my nipples hardened.

"Let's dance," I whispered.

Standing, I pulled him to his feet. I led him to the middle of the dance floor and began to dance around him. It only took him a couple seconds to join in on the dancing. It made me think that he was trying to weigh his options on whether or not it was a good idea.

He slipped his arms around me, pulling me closer to him. I smiled as I took the half step necessary to be pressed up against his body. I could tell that he was excited and aroused to be pressed against me. He spun me as he reached around sliding his hand up the back of my miniskirt to grab my bare ass.

Just then, hands went around Brian's neck, jerking him away from me. He was tossed against the wall. The impact was hard enough that pictures fell. Andrew had a grip on him tight enough to cut off oxygen.

Brian's face turned red and was changing to a purplish color. Andrew then threw a punch, hitting Brian in the middle of the face. Blood squirted everywhere. Andrew threw three more punches before Brian decided to fight back. They began rolling around on the floor throwing punches back and forth.

A few of the other players broke them up. One held Brian while two held onto Andrew. Andrew was struggling like a caged, rabid animal.

Brian was being held more for support than to keep him from jumping back into the fight.

"You ever touch my girl again, I will kill you where you stand!" Andrew shouted from across the room. He attempted to charge, but they pulled him back.

I stepped up to Andrew, deciding it was time to be placating. I had pushed him as far as I felt was safe. I gently placed my hands on his face, looking deep into his eyes.

"Andrew, don't worry about Brian. He's harmless. We were just dancing, waiting for you to come back from where you were." I gave him my most sincere look. "Come on, lets just go."

He jerked his arms free from the other guys' holds. He wrapped an arm around my shoulders, leading me out of the party. We climbed into his truck, and he sped off.

We drove for miles through the country and on gravel roads. I wasn't sure where he planned on taking us, but I couldn't wait to see the destination.

Finally, we turned down a lane that was more path than road. We took another sharp curve as he hit the brakes and came to a stop.

His headlights shone on the fence and the tombstones beyond. The name of our location was on the archway entering cemetery: Dickson Cemetery.

He got out without a word. I hopped out my side and walked around the truck cautiously. Being this far out, you never knew when there would be a snake in the grass.

Climbing into the truck bed, I settled down beside him. I leaned against his side, and he put his arm around my waist.

"I don't know why you do this to me, Susan. You know it makes me crazy seeing you even talking to other dudes." His confession was soft, but his tone had an underlying twinge of danger.

"I don't mean to." The lie slipped off my tongue smoothly. "It's like they see me as a toy to play with. I don't understand why your friends do that."

"Really, Susan? I've seen you flirt and lead them on. That skirt you're wearing is so short that your ass cheeks hang out of it."

"Are you saying you don't like the skirt?" I stuck my bottom lip out in a pout.

"That's not what I said." He leaned forward and kissed me, nipping hard on my lip. "I don't want anyone else near you. You're mine."

A smile tugged on my lips. "Then show me."

He pulled me down, so I was lying down in the truck bed. He took off his jacket and shirt, wading them up so they were a makeshift pillow for me.

He began kissing me and working his way to the junction of my legs. As he worked me into a frenzy, he tried his best to make me his.

Chapter 16

I sat in Mr. Welsh's classroom, listening to him drone on. His voice was relaxing and had a nice rumble to it. I wasn't sure of what he was talking about, but I couldn't care less.

His class had actually been better than what I imagined after the first day, and I tried to be overly helpful. At first, he seemed leery, but he started to warm up to my helpfulness.

My being so considerate in this class was doing weird things to Andrew. He didn't joke and bullshit with his friends as much. He would sit and watch me as I moved around the room or did anything to assist Mr. Welsh.

If I spoke up in class, he would say something or glare at me. I found it titillating to say the least. The passion seemed to consume him.

I wasn't sure how many times he'd pulled me to the janitor's closet for a quickie or blow job. I wondered if I could push it so he'd fuck me during one of the games. That would be amazing. Either in the locker room or hallway.

I glanced over at him to see him staring at me. I blew him a kiss and winked. He only partially smiled back. I bit my lip and turned my attention back to the teacher.

As the bell rang, Mr. Welsh addressed me. "Ms. Hatcher, can you hang out for a moment. I need to speak with you before you go to your next class."

"Sure, Mr. Welsh." I smiled, but my stomach did a flip. I couldn't imagine what he wanted to speak about.

Andrew was the last to leave the room. He stared at me as he walked out the door. It was an intense stare with a fire that I wasn't accustomed to.

The door shut with a resounding thud. I knew he would be waiting outside the room for me to exit.

"What can I do for you, Mr. Welsh?" I smiled and crossed my legs.

He walked over, looking down at me. "I would like to thank you for the improvement of your attitude. It is a pleasure having you be as helpful in the class."

I raised an eyebrow. "That's the whole reason you are keeping me after class? To thank me?"

"No. I want to ask you how well you know Andrew Pipes?"

"Better than most," I shrugged. I was confused what Andrew had to do with anything. "Why?"

"I'd be careful with him. You are a bright, beautiful young lady and I would hate to see anything bad happen to you. You have a great future ahead of you."

I couldn't help but laugh. "You are concerned about me? About my safety? That's crazy. Andrew wouldn't hurt a fly."

"Are you sure about that? I've seen the boy play football."

The memory of his fight with Brian flashed through my head. Standing, I smoothed my skirt. "Positive. May I go now?"

He nodded as I walked out of the room. Sure enough, Andrew was leaning against the wall with his hands in his pockets. He pushed off the wall, grabbing my arm and leading us into the janitor's closet.

I couldn't help but smile when the door shut behind us. I didn't think we really had time for anything, but I'd give him a quick hand job before getting back to class. Staring at him, I decided that I didn't care if I were late for class. It wasn't that big of a deal.

"What the fuck was that?" he asked, teeth grinding together.

I felt completely lost. "What?"

"What did that bastard want to talk to you about?"

"Uh, he just thanked me for being polite."

"That's it? Why would he keep you after class for that?"

"I don't know, Andrew. Maybe because I was the one that was sent to the office on his first day because I mouthed off. I almost got detention over that. If I would have gotten detention, I would have been kicked off the squad."

"They wouldn't have kicked you off the squad, Susan. I know better than that. I'm not stupid. Your father would have never let them do it. That's ridiculous. Be nice, be polite, do whatever. Don't push my buttons on this. I don't trust this guy."

If I wasn't so unnerved, it would have been funny that neither man trusted the other. I wanted to laugh, but the situation was too serious.

I opened my mouth to say something, and his mouth pressed against mine. I wrapped my arms around his neck and held on for the ride. He rode me hard and on the verge of painful. I wanted to scream out in pain, not pleasure, at first.

When he was spent, he let go of me so I could put my legs on the floor. My legs were shaky, and I was sore from the middle of my back down. It felt like my back was bruised. I wouldn't be surprised if it was, with as hard as he had slammed me against the shelves.

After walking out of the closet, I headed toward my next class, not sure how much time was left in it but decided that I wasn't going to.

I turned and headed the other direction. I was going to cut class for the rest of the day and spend it in Oskaloosa. I could do some shopping and have lunch. That sounded like a great idea. I wondered if I could get my best friend to go with me. I decided not to ask her, since it would involve going into a classroom, and I wanted out of there.

***

"Is he really that jealous over Mr. Welsh?" Veronica asked while painting her long nails.

"Seems to be. He doesn't like Mr. Welsh even talking to me. It makes him crazy." I sprayed more AquaNet into my hair.

"What are you going to do about it?" She popped a bubble with the gum she was chewing. "Jealousy is really hot on guys. Especially guys like Andrew. I wish Jonathan was more jealous."

She was right. It was hot. I didn't know exactly what to do about it though since it unnerved me a little. I remembered the crazed look in Andrew's eyes. They seemed more than jealous.

"Don't know but can't let it go to waste."

We both laughed over my last comment. When it died down, the room was silent. Apparently, we were both lost in our thoughts.

"Did you see Ashley's attempt to be stylish today? A pleated skirt." Veronica cackled over the memory.

Glad of the subject change, I chimed in. "Yeah. The girl is a real loser. She can't get out of the seventies. Too bad she won't just end it."

"Maybe we could help her out." The suggestion was quiet, but the implication was loud and clear.

It had been a while since I pushed another girl to the brink of her sanity, and it sounded like fun.

"What do you have in mind?"

We began to plan what we could do to remind Ashley she was nothing but a pawn in my school. She needed to either get with the times or be gone. I had already told her that she needed to catch up with fashion. She needed another reminder.

The next day at school, Veronica and I set out to find Ashley as soon as we got there. She was sitting in the library, nose in a book.

She looked up as we approached her, one from each side to keep her from trying to take off.

She was wearing worn out bell bottoms and a Grateful Dead t-shirt. She looked up at us with what appeared to be defiance in her eyes.

"What did I tell you the other day?" I asked quietly. I didn't want to get the librarian's attention turned to me.

"I don't know why you think it's okay to pick on me," Ashley murmured.

Leaning down, I spoke in her face. "Because you are so stupid and ugly, you don't deserve to live. If I could murder you and get away with it, I would in a heartbeat."

"That's because you're an insecure bitch."

Veronica slapped her then, reminding us of her presence. "How dare you talk to Susan that way, scum."

I silenced Veronica with a wave of hand. "Don't worry about her. When I'm done with her, she won't be able to show her face at school again."

Without another glance at Ashley, I turned, walking out of the library with the mindset that I needed to take care of business. On my way through the halls to class, I stopped anyone I could telling, them a different story about Ashley.

Before the end of second period, rumors were running rampant. Everything from Ashley having headlice to AIDS was going around school. My favorite was that she got crabs from the skaters that she was fucking.

During lunch, I watched with glee as whispers, stares, and insults were flung at her. She tried to sit in her usual spot near the back way, but she wasn't being left alone. Ten minutes before lunch came to an end, she left the building.

I smiled as I chatted happily to Veronica about the cheer team. This was a reminder to not only Ashley, but the entire student body, that I was in charge and no one messed with me.

Chapter 17

Mr. Welsh was explaining his theory on a Shakespeare piece while I doodled in my notebook, pretending to take notes. I glanced up occasionally to check the clock and sneak a peek at Andrew.

Andrew wasn't listening to the teacher at all. Simply sitting there staring at me or he would turn to talk to Jonathan. I smiled and blew a kiss at him before looking back down to write down more ideas for my prom dress.

The door opened, causing me to look up to see who was coming in. Mr. Shaw. He walked, over speaking softly to Mr. Welsh before standing in front of the class. He simply stood there waiting for the whispers and movement to die down.

"I have an announcement to make that I felt was better to say in person than over the intercom. We had a student, Ashley Stevenson, commit suicide last night. She was found hanging in her closet by her little brother. From what I was told, her wrists were also cut." He paused taking in everyone's reactions.

"I have been informed that some vicious rumors had been spread about the poor girl. I am going to assume that they didn't start here. If anyone needs to talk, the counselor is available the rest of the week. School will be closed on Friday for her services."

After he left the room, there was complete silence. I chanced a glance around to see half the class looking down at their desks. I was sure shame and guilt were washing over them. I felt none of it. I wasn't surprised by this.

I had grown up with Ashley and knew she had suicidal tendencies. She was a habitual cutter. She had also threatened to kill herself for attention in the past. In my opinion, there was no need for guilt when she just followed through with her threats.

The rest of the day was almost funeral-like it was so quiet. I let the posers mourn the loss of someone they didn't care about. I was almost amused by how two-faced people were. The irony of people crying over the death of someone they cared so little about wasn't lost on me.

At cheer practice, the coach made an announcement that practice was going to be canceled the rest of the week due to Ashley's death. My temper flared then. I shot to my feet.

"Coach Dixon, that's stupid." The words didn't come out the way I planned, but the sentiment was still there.

She spun around and glared at me. "Excuse me?"

"Why cancel practice because someone not on the team died? I mean come on. No one liked her here, and her death doesn't affect our cheering. We have games coming up and competition. We need the practice." I crossed my arms, glaring right back at the coach.

We stared each other down, Coach Dixon looking away first. I knew I had won and cheer practice was going to continue.

She spoke to the squad. "Susan is correct about needing to practice. I am going to leave it up to you, as a team, to decide if you want to have practice or take the rest of the week off. Ashley's death is hard on everyone, so this shouldn't be taken lightly."

I turned and faced the other girls. "If you want to practice raise your hand."

I raised my hand, watching the others expectantly. One by one, they began to raise their hands, eyes not leaving me. I knew that I had them eating from the palm of my hand, and they would do anything that I wanted them to. Practice was going to resume as usual.

Once practice was over, Veronica and I walked home. It was a daily routine after practice, since the town was so small. We had a population of a couple thousand, mostly elderly and teenagers. The teenagers wouldn't stick around in the town but would come back as they got older. My mother called Unionville a retirement town.

We were walking down Garfield street toward my house on the end of Putnam. It was a twenty-minute walk, but the weather was nice, so it was a nice stroll. We crossed tenth street and made our way up the hill to the house, Veronica stopped, touching my arm.

"Is Ashley's death our fault?" Her voice was soft and guilt ridden.

"No." I grabbed both of her hands, squeezing reassuringly. "We both grew up with her. This wasn't the first time she attempted. Just the first time she succeeded. This was her choice; she chose her path."

"I feel responsible."

"Don't feel responsible. You aren't. I'm not. None of us are."

She nodded, but I had a feeling that she didn't believe me. It would take time for her to get over it, but eventually she should. She always did after we did something that we weren't supposed to do. Veronica was a good lackey. She was the one that always did as she was told and followed along with the ideas.

"Everything will be alright. I promise." I kissed her cheek, and we began walking again. To lighten the mood I asked, "So is Jonathan taking you to the prom?"

She gave me a small smile that made me feel better. I knew she would be fine before too long. "Yeah, he already asked me, and we are coordinating our outfits. He's wearing black with a powder blue vest to go with my blue dress."

"Sounds rad. I'm planning my dress now. We are having it made in Kirksville at the Bridal Shoppe. I am so excited."

"We are going to have to go shopping for accessories soon."

"Totally."

We walked into the house, dropping our bags on chair beside the door. I lived in a modest two-bedroom house with my parents. There were two doors off the living room to the right. One led to dad's office. The other led to my bedroom.

To the left, there was an archway that led into the kitchen. Off the kitchen was the master bedroom, bathroom, and a mudroom.

We went into the kitchen, Veronica plopping down in a chair while I got into the refrigerator and grabbed two bottles of water. I set one down in front of her and took a seat across from her. We sat and discussed prom dresses, limos, flowers, and other necessities for the most important dance of our high school career.

When my mother came in, she smiled at us and began her evening routine of fixing dinner and cleaning up. She didn't usually say anything to us when we were doing our thing. The good thing about Mother was she gave me my space. She wasn't like the other mothers that hovered over their kids and monitored everything that went on.

"Veronica, are you staying for dinner?" she asked while adding something to a pan.

"If that's alright with you, Mrs. Hatcher," she answered politely.

"You are always welcome over here."

Dinner was just being served when my father came in. He walked over and kissed my mother on the cheek then headed toward his bedroom. As his routine, he would change out of his suit to some jeans and a shirt. Then he would come back in and join us for dinner before going to his office to do paperwork or watch a football game or something like that.

We were all seated at the table, food dished up when my father spoke. "Did you hear about that girl?"

"What girl?" Mother asked.

"Ashley Stevenson. She killed herself last night." I answered for him.

"Oh my! How horrible." She took a sip of her water. "I'll have to call Glenda in the morning, see how she's holding up and if she needs anything."

"Weren't you girls and Ashley close at one time?" My father looked directly at me.

"That was a long time ago, Daddy. We grew up and went our separate ways. Can we please change the subject now?"

The rest of dinner we only talked small talk. School, sports, cheer, the usual. After dinner, Veronica left to go home, and I retired to my bedroom. Once in my room, I changed into my sleep clothes: a body-hugging tank top and daisy duke pajama pants.

I settled into bed, turning off the light. There was a light shining in through the window in the bedroom. The light was from a light post that was over the shed in the back. I must have dozed off for a bit because the next thing I knew, I woke up to a shadow looming over me.

I gasped, with the intention of screaming, but a huge hand covered my mouth. The shadow slipped into bed with me, kissing me on the neck. I recognized the smell of the man next to me and relaxed immediately. Andrew.

"How did you get in?" I asked in a breathless whisper.

"Through the sliding glass doors in the living room. Don't worry, your parents have been in bed for probably an hour now."

I should have been concerned with the fact that Andrew watched my house and knew when my parents were in bed, but I couldn't gather a coherent thought at the moment. All I could think about was the passion and how I was feeling. I wanted him to be closer to me so we were joined. I wished that we could stay like that forever, but I knew that it would have to come to an end eventually.

He slipped out of the house before the alarm clocks went off so he wouldn't be detected after promising to see me at school the next morning. I barely heard him leave the room.

Chapter 18

Prom was fast approaching, and school year was winding down to an end. I couldn't believe how fast it was going. Almost everyone had forgotten about the death of Ashley, except to honor her, the yearbook was dedicated to her memory.

Mr. Welsh was starting to eye me in a "more of a woman than student" sort of way. He maintained eye contact with me through a lot of classes, which infuriated Andrew to no end. I found it intriguing.

At the end of class two days before prom, I decided to stay and "get help with homework". I wanted to test the waters to see if I was right about the way he looked at me.

"Mr. Welsh, can you explain to me what Fitzgerald was discussing in Gatsby?" I leaned forward at my desk to be certain he could see down my top. "I know there was a hidden message behind it, just not sure what it is."

He leaned against his desk watching me. His eyes were dark and intense, making my stomach do little flips. The left side of his mouth pulled into a half-smile. "Fitzgerald was a fascinating man. He wrote Gatsby from the heart. The story is about longing and long-lasting love."

He pushed away from his desk and walked my direction. While he slowly came closer, he continued to speak. "He wanted to show passion and how it can transcend time."

I tilted my head back to look up at him. The look on his face made my mouth to dry out. I swallowed hard. "I don't get all of that from his writing. He confuses me."

"Re-read it, and then tell me what you think. The greatest works takes several times of being read for you to understand what the author was trying to say."

I nodded, then stood with the intention of leaving the room to head to my next class. When I stepped from my desk, I accidentally bumped against him. Mr. Welsh reached out putting his arm around my waist in an effort to keep me from losing my balance.

"Thank you," I whispered. I stepped on my tiptoes, gently pressing my lips against his.

His lips were firm yet soft at the same time. He pulled me a little closer and deepened the kiss. I wrapped my arms around his shoulders. As I was melting into the kiss, he ended it abruptly and stepped back.

"I apologize. I can't do this. I shouldn't have done that." He broke all physical contact with me, taking refugee behind his desk.

I stood there half stunned. The kiss had been amazing. I had never been kissed with so much expertise and tenderness before. I touched my lips with my fingertips. They tingled slightly. I assumed it was from the kiss. There was one thing I did know. I wanted more.

I mentally shook myself, trying to bring myself back into the now. I smiled as my arm dropped back down to my side. "Mr. Welsh, you don't have to apologize. I should be the one to apologize."

"Let's just forget that it happened. Okay, Susan?"

I nodded and I gathered my things to head to my next class. I knew that I wasn't going to forget it. I wanted more. I just had to work on a plan.

In the hallway, Andrew waited for me. He was standing by the door, staring at the wall. He pushed off the wall and walked with me to the next class. Andrew was unusually quiet and distant. I didn't think much of it though; my mind was on the kiss.

We went our separate ways without a goodbye kiss. That was unusual as well, but it didn't hit me until in the middle of lunch while I was sitting with the other girls from the squad. I brushed it off, figuring we were both distracted.

"So, the limo will be picking us up at Veronica's around six. That way, we have time to go to dinner in Centerville before the dance," I explained.

"Sounds good," Veronica said, everyone else nodding their heads in agreement. The bell rang, and we all stood up, going our separate ways.

***

The final bell rang, causing chaos and a flurry of movement as students and teachers alike hustled around, trying to get their stuff together to leave for the weekend. Prom was the next night and there was a lot of getting ready to do. Girls had hair and nails to do while guys needed to have haircuts, shaves, and tux preparations.

I walked down the hallway toward the one classroom where I knew the teacher wasn't in a hurry. Mr. Welsh sat at his desk, grading a paper. He didn't look up when I entered. I wasn't sure he heard me come into the room.

I stopped about a foot from his desk. "Mr. Welsh?"

He looked up, focusing on me. "Susan. Why are you still here? I figured you would be out of here by now with prom coming up. You should be heading to the salon like the other girls."

"Wow, that's totally judgmental of you, Mr. Welsh." I cocked an eyebrow at him. "It sounds like jealousy to me. Are you jealous?"

He chortled. "Maybe I am. I didn't get to go to my prom. I was sick."

"That's sad. I bet your date was upset."

"I was going solo. I didn't have a date."

"You didn't have a date for your own prom? That is so sad. I am having a hard time believing this."

"Why is that, Ms. Hatcher?"

"I mean look at you. You're handsome. You had to be even more handsome in high school."

"You are going to make it me blush."

I leaned over the desk to him. "I can make you blush if that's what you want."

He groaned and leaned back. "I told you we can't do this."

"I know what you said, but I fully disagree with you on this. We can. No one has to know. It'll be our little secret."

I walked around the desk and knelt in front of him. Slowly, I unfastened his belt and unbuttoned the button of his slacks. I unzipped them, slowly releasing him from his pants. I crawled around so I was hidden by his desk. I grabbed the sides of his chair and rolled him, so he was concealed. If anyone came in, they would see him just sitting at his desk.

My mouth went over him, and I could hear him moan as his body tensed up. My tongue swirled around him, and he made noises that indicated that he was purely enjoying it. I closed my eyes and let the sensations and feeling of him in my mouth overcome me.

I heard the door open and Mr. Welsh jumped, straightening in his chair as much he could.

"Mr. Welsh? Have you seen Susan?" Andrew's voice vibrated through the room.

My heart began pounding in my chest as anxiety and adrenaline raced through my body. I paused for a moment to see what his answer was going to be.

"No, she probably went with Veronica and the other cheerleaders to get ready for the uh—" he stuttered slightly when my mouth went over him again, "The big dance."

"I just saw Veronica, and she hasn't seen her. They are meeting up later this evening. She usually meets me at my truck, and I drive her home."

"She's somewhere around here then or she walked. I haven't seen her. If I do, I will let her know you are looking for her."

"Thanks," Andrew said a few seconds before I heard his footsteps and the door slam shut.

"That was close," Mr. Welsh murmured.

Since he had the ability to speak coherently, I decided I wasn't doing my best, so I began to work him along with sucking and licking. It didn't take long after that for him to lose complete control. He began to tense and shake, seconds before he exploded into my mouth. He shuddered out a breath, indicating that he was spent.

I crawled out from under the desk while he fastened his pants. Grabbing up my backpack and books that I had set down, I walked to the door. Turning, I looked back at him. He looked wild and exhausted. Turning back to the door I walked out. I had to get to Veronica's so we could make our appointments for hair and nails.

Chapter 19

I walked into the dance on Andrew's arm. The day had flown by, and I was worried that I wasn't going to be ready on time, but I managed to be. I smiled largely as we walked across the dance floor. The night was going to be magical.

There were balloons and streamers everywhere and the gymnasium floor was covered in a protective covering to keep the floor from being scuffed by the heels and other shoes. Once on the left side of the room, we sat at the table that had the reserved sign on it. I had made sure our table was saved so no one would sit there except us.

We all sat at the table, laughing and making jokes. My favorite slow song came on, and I jumped up, grabbing Andrew by the arm.

"Andrew, let's dance! I love this song."

We went out onto the dance floor. I wrapped my arms around his neck and pressed up against him. We gently swayed back and forth. Staring up into his eyes, I couldn't believe how much I actually loved him. I couldn't stop smiling.

Andrew wasn't smiling, but he didn't look upset. He just looked like he was deep in thought. His hands gently rubbed my lower back as he pulled me closer. When the song ended, I didn't want to stop dancing. I wanted to stay like that forever.

After we were seated back at our table, Jonathan waved his hand and a waitress brought drinks to the table. I was surprised that there were waitresses. It wasn't something that had been discussed at the meetings about prom.

I looked up when the doors opened to see Mr. Welsh enter the gym. He was wearing a tux and had a rose in his lapel. He was stunningly handsome. He looked like he was made to wear the tux. I wanted to go over and touch him but knew that would be a bad idea with Andrew looking over my shoulder as well.

I excused myself to go to the snack table. I wanted an excuse to get away for a moment. It didn't hurt that Mr. Welsh was at the snack table pouring some punch into a glass. I stood next to him, reaching across him to grab a napkin and plate.

"You clean up nicely," I said, putting vegetables on the plate. I didn't really want them but it gave me an excuse to talk to him.

"Thank you. You do, too. Very beautiful. You and Andrew make a nice-looking couple." He sipped from the glass and made a weird face.

I giggled. "You know that the punch is probably spiked."

"Definitely spiked. Too much rum."

I turned from him and slid my hand across his shoulder. He was as firm as I imagined. I felt his arm tremble under my fingertips. I loved that I could cause him to react in such manner. It was empowering. I loved having power over men.

Joining the others back at the table, Veronica and Alyssa were giggling and whispering softly. They turned their attention to me.

"Oh my god, Mr. Welsh is hot. I wouldn't mind touching him. Did he look as good up-close?" Alyssa asked.

"Oh yeah. He looks amazing and smells great," I answered back quickly. I didn't want Andrew to become upset.

Before anything else could be said, Mr. Shaw stood at the microphone on the stage. "Can I have your attention, please?"

The music stopped and chatter died down. Turning in my chair, I looked at him standing on the stage. I knew what was coming next.

"I would like to introduce Danielle, the Senior class president to announce this year's prom king and queen."

There was a short burst of applause then it died down when she stepped to the microphone. "Thank you all for coming and making this the best prom that Putnam County High School has had in years. Now, here is the moment you have all been waiting for. This year's prom king and queen are . . ." she trailed off while opening the envelope. There was rustling and ripping of the paper. "Andrew Pipes and Susan Hatcher."

There was applause and hooting around the gym as we stood up and walked to the stage together. Once on the stage, we were crowned by staff members, I was crowned by Mr. Welsh, Andrew crowned by Ms. Sutherland.

It was a proud moment as I stood next to Andrew, wearing our crowns. It proved we were the best couple in the school. All eyes were on us. It was amazing to be worshipped and looked up to.

The music started back up; Andrew led me down to the dance floor. While we were pressed close together, he whispered in my ear. "Let's cut out. I have a surprise for you."

It sounded like fun. I couldn't wait to see what he had in store for me. I loved surprises. I kissed him lightly on the lips. "Let's go."

We slipped out of the gymnasium and made our way down the street toward his house. When we got there, we headed over to the truck and he helped me in.

Once we were both inside, I looked at him and smiled. "Where are we going?"

"You'll see."

He pulled out of the drive and drove back down the street toward the school. We turned into the parking lot of the football stadium. When we parked, I shifted so I could look at him.

"The football field? Why are we here?"

"Come on."

He hopped out and headed to the back of the truck. He pulled out a large duffle bag and opened the door to help me out. We walked down to the field. He set the bag down by the fifty-yard line.

Unzipping the bag, he pulled out a blanket and spread it out on the Astroturf. He also produced a couple of glasses and bottle of wine. He set everything down and helped me down to the blanket. Joining me, he opened the wine and poured us both a glass.

"Now what's the surprise?" I asked, feeling impatience wash through me.

"You'll see." He clinked our glasses together then took a sip of his.

We drank the wine in silence, then he set the glasses to the side. I smiled as my focus went in and out. He would become blurry then come into focus. I blinked a couple of times. I wasn't sure what was going on, I was feeling weird, suddenly.

"Andrew, I don't feel so well."

He leaned over me, pushing me so I was lying down completely. I tried to sit up, but the spinning increased by tenfold. I shook my head trying to clear it, but the movement made it worse.

Andrew flipped me over onto my stomach, pulling my arms behind me. I heard the sound of duct tape. Panic washed through me, not sure what was happening. I felt the duct tape wrap around my wrists, binding them together. Once that was done, he flipped me back over and straddled my waist.

"The surprise is that I know you are a slut," he whispered in my ear.

"What?" My brain felt like it was full of cotton balls.

"I know you've been fucking the teacher. It's all over the school. I've seen how you look at him and know you better than that. You will fuck anything that looks at you twice."

"No."

"Don't lie to me!" he screamed in my face. Spittle sprayed me.

Jerking his tie off his neck, he wrapped it around my neck and began to pull. I struggled as my air supply was cut off. I tried to move my arms, but they weren't going anywhere. I was helpless while he held me down and strangled me.

"I told you that you were mine. Now you are going to learn what happens when you don't listen. I warned you that you were making me crazy, but did you stop? No. You didn't. You kept fucking around. I thought I could ignore it, but obviously I can't. Now, no one else will touch you again."

Everything went dark as I listened to his crazed rambling. Maybe he was right, and I did this to myself. I shouldn't have messed with his head. I should have just been a good girlfriend. I wasn't sure how, but that's what I should have done.

I felt my soul separate from my body as my heart stopped beating. So, this was what it was like to be dead. I watched, completely detached as he stood up from my lifeless body and went to his truck. Andrew pulled a shovel out of the back and began to dig a hole at the edge of the fifty-yard line.

Once the hole was big enough, he gently laid my body into it after wrapping me in the blanket. He uncovered my face and kissed me lightly on my lips.

"Now you will always be here, supporting the team like you love to do. I love you, Susan." He covered my face back up and began to scoop dirt back into the hole, getting rid of all traces that I had been there.

Chapter 20

I was still in shock that I was dead. I had been killed on my own prom night. The night that I was made Queen. It was supposed to be the most magical night of my life but turned into the biggest nightmare. I wandered around the field and stadium, not sure what to do next. I sat on the bench where the team waited to be put into the game and stared lost into the field.

After time had passed, I started to mess with the equipment, causing it to malfunction. I also caused injuries to the football players on both teams. I did the best that I could to help the Midgets win or stay ahead in the games.

Years passed, students came and went. There had been talk about my disappearance, but it was almost like no one was too concerned about it. Andrew had also disappeared after the prom. There were whispers that we ran off together. I wasn't sure where he went but hoped one day, he got his.

I started to haunt the school as well. It was amusing to mess with the teachers and students. Mr. Shaw retired and so did most of the staff from when I went to school. Trends and clothing changed as the years passed on.

I was standing on the sideline, watching the homecoming game, and debating on what I wanted to do next. We were down by two, and I wanted to see the Midgets win, especially homecoming. It was raining and wind was blowing.

The cheerleaders were huddled together on the sideline, not cheering. I was annoyed they weren't cheering. When I was a cheerleader, we cheered no matter the weather. It was the job of the squad to keep the team motivated and pepped.

I stood next to the captain, debating on what I could do to make her do her job. I shoved her with all of my might, and she stumbled into the other girls.

"What the hell?" she shouted at the girl next to her. She shoved her and a fight ensued. It had to be broken up by the cheer coach and the football coach.

"That's enough, ladies!" The cheer coach glared down at the two girls. "You are supposed to be cheering, not fighting. Now get out there and cheer."

The squad grumbled as they moved away from the bench to spread out so they could cheer. As they cheered, they went into a pyramid, I grabbed the flyer's ankle and yanked her off the top of the pyramid. She fell and landed on her neck. There was a loud crack as her neck snapped.

The game was called due to the accident, and she was rushed to the emergency room. The bleacher and stadium cleared out, and I was alone yet again.

I walked aimlessly around the field, debating on what to do next. My life needed purpose. I was tired of being alone on the field all the time.

"You know, that was mean." A voice said from a distance.

I turned to see a man standing on the bleachers, rain pelting him. He was wearing a dark coat and hat. He looked very mysterious.

"You don't know what mean is." I didn't think he was speaking to me. No one had talked to me since I died, but I was bored so I answered.

He laughed, which surprised me. "Oh, Susan you have no idea what I have seen."

He knew my name? I couldn't believe it. I stared at this man trying to determine if I knew him.

"Who are you?" I frowned at him.

"Call me an old friend." He came down off the bleachers and walked closer to me. "I want to help you."

"Help me how? I'm dead."

"I want to take you to a new home. Somewhere where you will be with others. You won't be alone all the time. Somewhere you can kill and hone your skills."

"Why would you do that for me?"

One shoulder lifted in a shrug. "Because I like you. I always have."

"Who are you?" I felt like a broken record.

"You will find out soon enough." He smiled. "You ready?"

I hesitated. It sounded too good to be true, especially after being alone as long as I had. Was there really a place that I wouldn't be alone and could kill?

"I may even be able to help you get even with a certain man that put you in this position."

"You know Andrew?" Interest and intrigue peaked in me. The thought of getting even with Andrew was too tempting.

"Perhaps I have located him and could get him to the new house for a visit. Would you like that?"

"Let's do it."

***

Next thing I knew, I was in an elegant room. There were pom poms and a picture on the dresser. Walking over, I saw that the picture was a prom picture of Andrew and me. I was shocked that someone had it. How did they get that picture?

Two men walked into the room. One younger, the other older and graying at the temples. The younger man spoke softly to the other, then addressed me.

"Susan, this is Cyrus Bane. He is the owner of the house. We wanted to personally come in and make you feel at home, but also lie down some ground rules." He smiled. I thought it was familiar, but I couldn't place it. "You aren't to attempt to kill Cyrus or myself. Anyone else roaming the house is free game. The rooms you aren't allowed in you won't be able to enter. The other ghosts aren't exactly the friendliest, so you may not want to speak with them."

"What other ghosts?" It seemed the most logical question.

"Right now, there are two. The Golden Boy and Butcher. The Butcher is especially surly, and the Golden Boy prefers to stick in the shadows."

"What about the promise of Andrew?" Then I raised an eyebrow. "What's your name?"

"I'm Bastian Bucco. I will get Andrew here for you as promised. It may take some time, but it will happen."

I nodded and the men left me alone to my devices.

It hadn't been that long when Bastian came into the room with a giant smile on his face. "Susan, you would be happy to know that Andrew and his wife are going to be staying the night in this very room this evening."

Wife? Andrew was married. I couldn't believe it. He killed me then moved on with his life like nothing happened. I was mortified and beyond angry. I couldn't wait to get even with them. I simply nodded at Bastian, and he left me alone with my thoughts.

Memories of my death flashed through my head, infuriating me even more. When the door opened again, I watched Andrew and his wife come in. Shock and anger washed through me when I recognized the face of the woman that he was married to. Veronica.

"Mr. and Mrs. Pipes, this will be your room for the evening. I hope you enjoy you stay." A lady set bags down and backed out of the room slowly.

Once the door was closed, Veronica roamed around the room, studying the décor. She stopped at the photo and picked it up, eyes wide.

"Andrew, look at this." She handed him the framed picture.

He looked at it, his face clouding up. "Where in the hell would they have gotten this? Why put it in our room? We are going to check out. There is no reason to taunt us like this."

"Maybe they got it at a garage sale or an estate sale." Veronica set the picture back on the dresser.

They settled in for the night as I watched from the corner of the room. I wanted to kill them both, but I wanted to do it slowly.

Once they were asleep, I stood over them and whispered. "Andrew. Andrew. Wake up."

His eyes opened, and he stared at me. His eyes widened as they focused.

"I'm back. You are going to get what you deserve."

I reached into his chest, grabbing his heart and squeezing it. I didn't know that it would work until I did it. The more he struggled, the harder I squeezed. I watched as the lights began to fade in his eyes.

"Why?" he whispered.

"Why?" I laughed. "You killed me and buried me on the football field. Now I find out you married my best friend. You are both traitors."

I yanked with enough force that his heart exploded out of his chest. There was a loud pop and snap as it came out. The light drained from his eyes as his mouth opened and closed in shock.

I took the heart and shoved it in Veronica's mouth as she snored, completely unaware of the devastation that was going on next to her. Her eyes popped open as she choked and gurgled on Andrew's blood.

The deaths were quick but gave me a sense of belonging that I hadn't had since before I died. I was going to like it at this house.

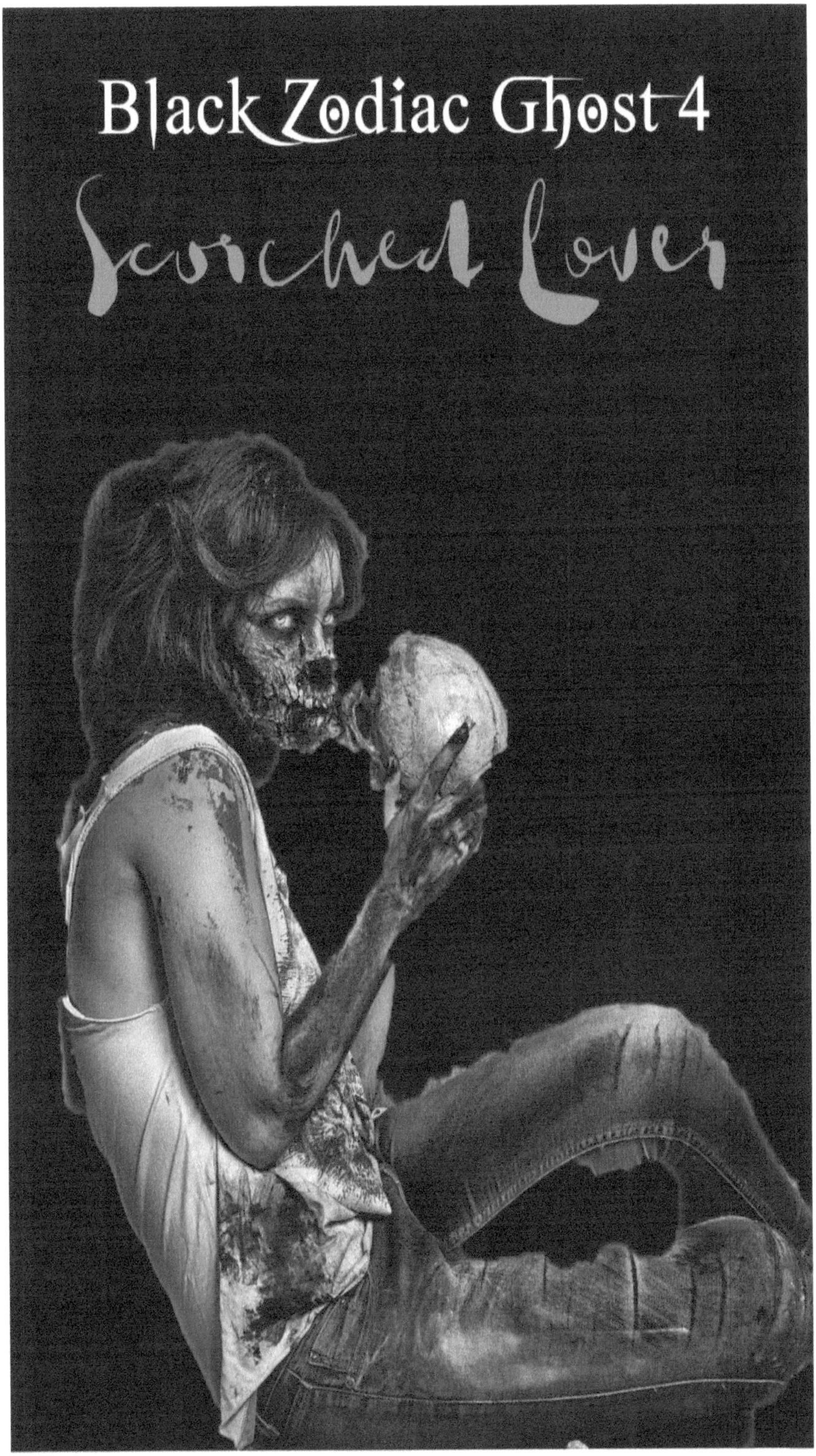

Black Zodiac Ghost 4
Scorched Lover

Chapter 21

1976 Fort Worth, TX

I stood outside the church looking up at it in awe. It was different than I pictured. It looked more like a giant house instead of a church. There were people milling about tending to the garden and other things I could only describe as chores.

I looked over at my sister. We had heard about the church while at work, and it was intriguing. We had asked to hear more, and they told us all about the Children of the Great Divine. They said it was a community that had the same beliefs and worked together so they were in complete harmony.

I had been skeptical at first, but Adrianne insisted it would be fine to check out. She claimed she just wanted to see what it was like, and we didn't have to commit to anything. We had agreed that if we both weren't certain about it, we wouldn't join.

We had grown up in an extremely strict Catholic family. I had rebelled against them and moved out as a teenager; Adrianne followed shortly after. Now we both felt lost and were looking for a place to belong.

A handsome young man came to the door, walked down the stairs to greet us. His smile was huge, making me feel like he was genuinely happy to see us.

"You must be Jean and Adrianne. I heard so much about you from Samuel and Isabel. My name is Peter, and I'll be showing you around today. First I have to ask: are you devoted to the Lord?" Peter continued to smile while waiting for our answer.

I hesitated. I wouldn't have claimed to be devoted. I didn't truly believe in God. Looking over at Adrianne, I decided to go with honesty. "No. I am not devoted."

Adrianne shook her head no. "I want to be devoted, though."

"That's perfect. We are going to take a tour of the church, then you can talk to our leader, David." Peter motioned us forward and we followed.

My stomach flipped as we stepped across the threshold, but I ignored it. It had to be just nerves. I had never been in a church quite like this. It reminded me of a home. It smelled like a home. The smell of fresh baked bread wafted through the building. There was a sense of homeliness that I hadn't felt in years.

When we walked into the sanctuary, we stopped. There was a group of women on their knees praying near the front of the room. Instead of benches, there were folding chairs lined up in rows filling the expanse of the room. There was a scent in the air that was floral, most likely incense.

He led us from the sanctuary toward a room he called the family room. There was a man sitting in a giant chair, reading a newspaper. He set the paper down when we walked in and stood. He was around six feet tall with dark, neatly-styled hair.

"Reverend David, these are the Marlow sisters that Samuel and Isabel told us about. They decided to come tour our little family." Peter smiled and stepped to the side.

Reverend David walked up so he was standing directly in front of me. My breath hitched as I looked up at him. His eyes sparkled as they met mine. I was almost certain he felt the instant connection as well.

When he spoke, his voice was deep and smooth. The tones almost hypnotic. "Ladies, it is a pleasure to finally meet you."

He held his hand out to shake ours. Adrianne shook his hand first but didn't speak. I had the feeling she was a little star struck as well.

Finding my voice, I spoke up. "I'm Jean, this is Adrianne. It is a pleasure to meet you, Reverend David."

"Please, call me David. The pleasure is all mine." He motioned to the chairs. "Let's have a seat and chat."

We all took a seat, and Peter left the room. This had to be a conversation for just the three of us. It made me a little nervous, but I did my best to keep still and calm on the outside. A few minutes later, Peter returned with four glasses of lemonade.

My nerves settled, and I tried not to laugh at the silliness of my nerves. There was no secret meeting or underlying reason for the privacy, just getting refreshments. Peter handed me a glass. I took it gratefully and took a sip. The liquid was really sour, yet sweet at the same time.

"So, tell me. What are you looking for here?" He stroked his chin and leaned forward.

"A new church." I wasn't sure what answer he was looking for.

He laughed a deep rolling laugh. "Y'all aren't here for just a new church. Let me put it this way. Do you believe that you are going to be allowed through the gates of Heaven?"

I shook my head no. "I haven't been right with God most of my life. Our family is Catholic, but I walked away from the church. I couldn't stand being under my parents' thumbs any longer."

He reached forward and grabbed my hand, squeezing it gently. "I'm sorry you didn't feel like you belonged with your family. Have you considered they may be your blood family, but not your spiritual family?"

I glanced at Adrianne, she shrugged. It was an interesting concept. I hadn't considered there was a difference between my family by blood and my spiritual family. Maybe he was right. I frowned as I thought about it.

"Here's is how I see it. You have multiple families. Your physical family: mother, father, siblings. Then you have your spiritual family. The family that completes you. That you can depend on in a spiritual and emotional level. The ones that are beside you on your journey to Heaven. It is the family that you truly belong to. That is what the Children of the Great Divine is about."

"Sounds great, but what's the catch?" Adrianne finally spoke.

"The catch..." David scratched his chin. "That's easy. The catch is you find your family, your place of belonging. You get your key to the Pearly Gates. You get all that you desire."

"You are convincing, David." I smiled hoping to take the sting out of the words. "I'm not entirely convinced that this place is right for us."

"I was hoping you would say that. I want to invite you to spend the evening here so you can see what it is like here. You are welcome to join in the festivities."

I turned my head toward Adrianne. "What do you think? Should we?"

She shrugged. "We did say that we were going to be open so why not?"

"Groovy."

David stood up. "Follow me and we will head out to the back patio. That's where everything will begin."

He winked at me as he passed. We followed him down the hallway to the back of the house. We walked out on the patio where there were several people were beginning to gather. It was going to be an interesting evening.

Chapter 22

I woke up the next morning and blinked rapidly, trying to adjust to the light that was shining into my window. I looked at the clock, seeing that it was still early, and I didn't have to get up just yet. Pulling the blanket up to shield my eyes, I sighed as my mind drifted back to the party at the church.

It hadn't been what I expected. There was laughter, music, drinks, dancing. It was almost a normal party, but there was no nudity or inappropriate misconduct. No one pawing at me or trying to get down my pants. The food was delicious, and the people were pleasant.

It was the wee hours of the morning before we left to come back to our studio apartment. It wasn't much, but it had been ours for years. I stumbled into my bed as my sister had stumbled into hers. We had giggled and talked about the church until we passed out.

Sighing, I rolled on my side. I had felt comfortable and part of the group at the Children of the Great Divine. It had been well, great. I loved every minute. I felt special. I hadn't felt like that in a long time. It wasn't just the church members that made me feel so good. It was David. He had paid extra attention to me and barely left my side.

David had even walked us to the apartment building, claiming that it wasn't proper for two women to walk home unescorted. He walked us to our door and waited for us to enter the apartment and lock the door before he had left. I watched through the peephole as he stood there, then turned and left.

Sitting up, I knew reminiscing wasn't going to get me anywhere. I needed to get ready and make my way to the diner that I waitressed at. I hated the job, but it paid the bills. Slowly, I climbed out of bed and made my way to the bathroom to shower and get ready for my day.

Once ready, I slipped out of the apartment and went to the diner. I was scheduled for a long shift and the customers were generally rude. I entered the back of the diner and donned my apron. I was ready for a shit day.

Rolling my neck, I tried to relieve some of the stress building there before I added more stress to it. I stuffed my order pad in my pocket. The pencil I slid into my hair so I could keep track of it. I walked out into the dining area and started taking orders with a smile on my face. They tended to tip something if I was smiling.

"Howdy, welcome to Granny's Diner. What can I get ya?" I poised my pencil over my pad and waited. I hadn't looked up yet to see whom I was speaking to.

"Well, howdy. I'll take a burger and fries with a glass of Coke. I also wanted to see you again."

My head shot up and eyes met with the one man that had captured my interest last night and couldn't get my mind off of. Reverend David. The smile was genuine that crossed my face this time. "Now why would you do that?"

He shrugged. "I'm not sure, but your pretty brown eyes are stuck in my head. Have you thought anymore about coming to my church?"

"A little, but we still aren't sure."

"Don't worry, I am inviting you and Adrianne to come with me personally to church. I have a special place for my guests."

"Sounds like a good time. Do you want us to meet you at the church?"

"No. What kind of southern gentleman would I be if I didn't escort you? I will pick you ladies up at your apartment, and I'll drive you to the church."

"I'll be right back. I gotta put your order in." I turned and walked away. My cheeks were red from the encounter and heart was racing.

After his food was ready, I brought it back out and set it down in front of him. He thanked me. I walked away with a spring in my step. I felt like I was floating. I was looking forward to going to church with Reverend David.

***

6 months later . . .

We had lived at the church for a while, then David had Adrianne and I moved to the main compound. It was much larger than the church, with a lot more people staying there. I had found out that the church was mainly for recruiters and new members. The others stayed at the compound and were given jobs to do.

My main job was gardening so I could spend the day outside in the dirt. It helped ground me and was better than working with people who were rude and grabby.

When I wasn't gardening, I studied the bible, cleaned, or spent time with David. My favorite was time spent with him. It wasn't often that I got alone time with him, and I cherished those precious moments.

I was kneeling in the garden humming one of the hymns that we sang in church while pulling weeds. A shadow loomed over me, blocking the sun that beat down on my back just seconds before. Looking up, I saw the shadow was made by David as he stood there watching me.

"Come, let's talk," he said as he held his hand out for my dirty one. I hesitated for several heartbeats before I dusted my hands off and allowed him to help me to my feet.

We walked down the path that curved to the left and led down to a small pond. There was a bench halfway, nestled under a tree. He led me to the bench, helping me sit down. He sat behind me, keeping my hand in his.

"What did you wish to talk about, David?" I felt self-conscious with him holding my hand after I had been in the sun and dirt. I was hot, sweaty, and caked in mud. I worried what he thought about me.

He shifted slightly so our legs were touching, thigh to thigh. "I'm not sure how to tell you what is going on in my head."

"Just say it, I guess. Did...did I do something wrong? Are you kicking me out of the church?" Anxiety washed over me as I thought of the different things that he could be trying to tell me. I was certain that he wanted to send me away.

He smiled at me. "Calm down, Jean. This conversation isn't bad. It's just that I haven't thought of anything except you since we met. I was wondering if you would be willing to be my lady?"

"You want to date me?"

"Of course. You are gorgeous, sweet, kind, and devoted. I have watched you blossom over the past several months. Children of the Divine suits you. You were made to be part of it, part of me."

"Okay. I will be your lady."

He leaned over, kissing me on the cheek. "Groovy."

Chapter 23

Being the girlfriend to the leader of the church definitely had its advantages. I was required to do less work and no recruiting. I sat behind him at the pulpit.

Watching the congregation worship and look up to David was an amazing thing. They also acted like they admired me as well for just being there. They watched with a longing visible on most faces. Some of the other women were envious of me, and I secretly reveled in it.

I hadn't come up with any negatives while dating him. David was absolutely perfect in every way. He even insisted on abstaining until marriage. He told me fornication outside of marriage was a sin and he didn't want to taint my soul with such a blemish.

I wasn't sure if we would get married, but I loved the fact that he thought that much about me and my soul. No one had ever cared about my spiritual well-being and soul before. It was an exhilarating feeling. I knew the signs of falling in love, and I was head over heels with him. Just thinking about David made my heart race and butterflies flitter in my stomach.

I listened to David speak to the followers about devotion. I was completely devoted to the church now. I had even closed my bank accounts and added my funds to the community funds of the church. Those funds were used to better our living condition and provide for those things that we couldn't supply ourselves within the community.

After services, I stood at David's side and greeted the parishioners while they came by to thank David for the wonderful service. Service always took place in town, that way we could hopefully get more followers coming in to find us. At least the Sunday service was done in town. We had other services throughout the week at the compound. Those who weren't staying at the compound would spend an hour an evening before going to bed in silence as they worshipped God.

Once the church was clear, I walked about straightening things up and doing the maintenance necessary to keep our church clean. I felt responsible for helping keep things running smoothly. It was important to me that the church was kept in pristine condition.

"Jean?" David said my name in a question.

I turned my head, looking at him after I straightened the brochures on the table by the door. "Yes, David?"

"Come."

I walked to where he stood on the dais by the podium. He had a habit of lingering there until it was time to leave to head home to the compound. When I was even with him, I looked up and smiled. "Do you need something?"

"Yes, I do." He grabbed my hands, squeezing them gently. "I want you to be my wife."

My mouth opened and closed a few times before I was able to speak. I was surprised that it would come out of nowhere like this. "Yes! I would love to. I can't wait to start planning it."

He frowned. "There is no need to go through the hassle of planning a big fancy wedding. They are too expensive, and we need to conserve our funds. We will have our wedding at the compound in front of the family. That is the most important thing, the family being there, is it not?"

I deflated at his slight reprimand, but he had a point. We didn't need a big wedding. Our love and being with our family were all we needed. I tried to recover the smile that had been on my face previously. I worried that I wasn't able to completely hide the disappointment though. "You're right, David, as always. Family and love are all we need. When do you want to get married?"

"Tonight, when we return to the compound." His smile widened. "In fact, I already have everyone setting up for it. We will have the ceremony then a huge feast to celebrate. Everyone will be there, from all the compounds. Then you and I will be together as husband and wife for the rest of our lives and beyond."

"Wow, I don't know what to say."

"You don't have to say anything. Just be by my side forever."

"Forever."

***

Marriage was all that I had ever imagined and more. I loved waking up beside David every morning and going to sleep next to him every evening. Doing things for him made my heart and soul happy. I didn't think I could ever be happier.

"Adrianne, how are you enjoying living here?" I sipped my water during our lunch period.

She half shrugged. "It's not what I imagined. I thought it would be more harmony, less work. All I get to do is work and pray. My hands are so sore that they are beginning to bleed."

"What do they have you assigned doing?"

"Lately, pulling weeds from around the compound and garden. Before that they had me digging out post holes for the new fence that is being put in. I wouldn't be surprised if they make me build the fence." She picked up her sandwich and took a small bite of it. She then dropped it back down on the tray in front of her. "Hell, I don't have an appetite anymore. I'm too tired to be hungry."

"I'll talk to David and see what I can do to get you some light duty work for a while. I'm sure he will listen to me."

"Thanks, I appreciate it, Sissy."

"You're quite welcome. I'll speak with him as soon as I get back to our rooms."

After we ate, I went back to my rooms so I could see if David was there. I wanted to get my sister something more light duty as soon as possible. When I walked in, he was sitting at his desk with a notebook in front of him. I stepped a couple steps closer so I could see over his shoulder. The notebook wasn't just a notebook, it was an accounting ledger. In the ledger, there was a list of names with amounts beside them.

Before I announced my presence, I stepped back so I could no longer see what he was doing. I had a feeling it wasn't something that he would want me to see. "David?"

Shutting the notebook, he turned and looked at me with a smile on his face. "Yes, my dear?"

"I have a favor to ask of you."

His eyebrow raised in curiosity. "What is that?"

"Do you think you could have Adrianne's job changed? She has been assigned labor that is too physical for her. She is in constant pain from the sores and blisters on her hands. I'm worried about her overall health."

"We don't make special exceptions for anyone."

I knelt in front of him, taking his hands in mine. "I know, but I'm asking just this one time. Please, give her something light duty. I will do anything you want, if you please do this for me."

Reaching out, he brushed his fingers though my hair. "You want this for her this badly? That you will get on your knees and beg for me to help her?"

"Yes."

He leaned forward and kissed me lightly on the lips. "Then it is done."

Chapter 24

I woke up with a start. I couldn't remember all of my dream, but I did know that it consisted of going through different rooms in a hotel. A sense of urgency was in the air and I ran from floor to floor looking for the right room. When I found the right room, it wasn't what I expected. There were elevator doors inside and the staff constantly walked through the room. The staff was faceless, Ω though. I couldn't recall what any of them looked like. I didn't know the meaning behind that dream. It was strange.

I climbed out of the bed and made my bleary-eyed way to the bathroom. After washing my face and getting rid of the last remnants of sleep from them, I studied my reflection. The past year had been fairly difficult adjusting to the rules and schedule of the church. David would have evenings where he kept us in the compound sanctuary while he would preach on the word that he had just received from God. Those nights were difficult, especially since he expected us to stay alert, active, and involved in the sermon all night long.

I was sitting off to the side, where I always sat at the compound sermons, watching David as he preached. He was animated and had so much energy, it made me slightly envious. He was always animated when giving his sermons, even when they lasted all night long. He was in his element when preaching the Good Lord's word.

I glanced at my watch, realizing we had been here for hours now. I could feel the exhaustion creeping up my shoulders, but I was determined not to show it. I had to stay strong for everyone else. In the back of the room, I saw a young man, probably early twenties, dozing off. His face was red from the sun, shirt dirty. I hoped the man next to him would nudge him awake. It wouldn't be pretty if David caught him sleeping.

I had a knot building in my stomach knowing that it wasn't going to end well. David tended to catch those who fell asleep. He would even catch the ones who just closed their eyes for a moment and become upset that all eyes weren't on him at all times. To ignore David when he was sharing God's word was blasphemy.

He did the worst thing he could possibly do besides fall asleep. He snored. The room fell silent, heads looking around until everyone was focused on the sleeping man. My stomach flipped as anxiety raced through me. I could hear my heart pounding in my ears. I knew what was going to happen, or had a good idea, at least. Hopefully David took mercy on him.

David walked away from the podium and headed down the aisle. When he approached the young man, he stared down, towering over him. He didn't say a word, just stared at the man. The guys next to him shifted out of their seats so they were out of the line of fire. David rose a hand and two big men that I hadn't seen before approach. They stood on each side of David; fists clenched.

David kicked him on the foot, startling him awake. His head shot up. Eyes darting around obviously disoriented before settling on David. They just stared at each other for several heartbeats.

"What's your name?" David asked softly. There was an undertone of something in his voice.

"Phillip," he answered. His voice was raspy. If it were possible, his red face reddened some more.

"How dare you sleep during our service! Are you dedicated to our Lord? Are you fully committed- heart, soul, and body?"

"Yes, sir."

"Then you need a reminder and recommitment."

With a slight nod from David, the two men helped Phillip up and led him from the room. The sound of the door closing echoed through the sanctuary. The stillness made me uneasy. David turned and made his way back up to the podium.

"Alright, I am going to call this a night. Sorry for the interruption, but we will have to finish the sermon later on. Have a good night and get some sleep. I will see you in the morning."

He turned and walked out of the sanctuary without waiting for the followers to file out. That was unusual for him. He always waited for everyone to leave before he did. I stood and watched everyone leaving, slowly and exhausted. I wanted to do something for them. To show our appreciation for all they do.

When the last parishioner was gone, I stood there a moment watching the door that David had gone through. It was a door I had only seen him go through once before, and I wasn't allowed to go back there. It was David's private space. He told me that the only ones allowed back there were the ones that needed recommitment of their faith, but it was mostly where he kept the books and other necessities.

I wanted to go in there and see what was happening, but fear washed through me, keeping me from breaking the rules and seeing what was happening. I didn't know what was involved with the recommitment phase. A part of me didn't want to know what it consisted of, yet at the same time, I was extremely curious.

Fear and caution got the best of me, and I went back to my room to go to bed. I wasn't sure when David joined me, but when I woke up in the morning, he was lying next me. I didn't know what I was looking for, but I studied him closely. Maybe I was trying to see remnants of the night before, but I saw nothing. Maybe I was reading too much into it, but I didn't like that there was an area that I wasn't allowed into in the compound. I was basically the Queen of the Community; I should be allowed everywhere.

Climbing out of bed, I got ready for the day. I needed to think.

Chapter 25

I was sitting out in the garden when I saw a young man standing at the edge of the property. He looked like he was lost and lonely. Standing, I slowly approached him. I hoped not to frighten him away as I got closer. Every step I took toward him made his eyes widen just a little.

"It's okay. I'm not going to hurt you," I said softly. "Do you need help?"

It felt like I was coaching and placating a wounded animal. He watched me warily until I stood a few feet away from him.

"Do you need help?" I repeated.

He shook his head no.

My heart went out to this young man. He didn't look any older than seventeen and was so skinny. He looked like he hasn't had a good meal in a while. I was determined to change that.

"Please come with me. Get something to eat and a chance to clean up. Once you've eaten, you can leave. It'll be left up to you." I held my hand out to him. He studied me for several moments before he took my hand.

I led him to the compound. Instead of going through the main doors, we went in through the doors that led to the kitchen. I don't know why, but I felt it would be best if a few people as possible saw him.

He took a seat at the countertop while I pulled out some leftover casserole that we had the night before. It wasn't much, but it would fill him up. As I warmed it, I cut a hunk of bread off the loaf. I handed him his plate with a fork.

"Eat," I smiled gently.

After the first tentative bite, he shoveled the food in his mouth, hardly giving himself time to chew. He almost looked like he was swallowing it whole.

When his plate was clean, he set down the fork gently and looked me directly in the eyes. "Thank you. I should be going."

"Wait." I put my hand atop of his. "Where is your family?"

He shrugged haphazardly. "Don't have one."

"Everyone has a family. What happened?"

"I just don't have one. Some people are born into situations that require that they don't have family. Just because someone gives birth to you or raises you, doesn't make them family. I've never had a family."

I gently squeezed his hand. "I'm so sorry that you went through that. I can help you now. You can stay here and be part of our family. We are a diverse group and would welcome you with open arms."

He shook his head no. "I don't think that's a good idea. I should just go. Thank you."

"I insist. Please let me show you are around and meet everyone. You will see they are great people and you'll love it here." I smiled and hoped he would say yes.

He glanced at the door, then back at me. With a sigh, he slowly nodded his head. "Fine. Just know that it isn't going to sway me to stay."

Smiling, I stood up and held my hand out to his. "Once you see everything, you will love it. I promise you this. We can be a big happy family. Now may I have your name?"

His eyes were serious when he answered. "Sebastian."

After showing him around, he reacted almost like I expected. He agreed to stay for a couple days, just to see if it was somewhere he could call home. I showed him to the rooms for the young boys and introduced him to his new roommate. When I left the room, they seemed to be getting along really well.

Climbing into bed, I was surprised that David was already there. It was fairly early for him. It was the perfect time to tell him about Sebastian and how he may be joining the church. I knew David would be proud of me.

I looked over at him. He was curled on his side. I couldn't tell if his eyes were closed, but his breathing was even and smooth.

Reaching over, I gently placed my hand on his shoulder. "David?"

His head turned my direction, look in his eyes intense. "Yes?"

"We may have a new member. I found him out by the garden and showed him around. He agreed to stay for a few days, sees if he likes our compound."

"What's his name?"

"Sebastian."

"That's good, sweetheart. We also have some new recruits coming tomorrow also. It's a family. They are going to be there for the morning service, then Peter will show them around. If we snag them, we will have quite a bit of funds coming into our compound. They are a wealthy family."

Leaning over, I kissed him lightly on the lips. "They will join us. How could they not?"

***

Things had gone according to plan, and the Church began to rapidly grow. That was when things had started to go downhill for me. David had become distant and distracted. It felt like my world was starting to crumble and did the best I could to keep it from falling apart completely. I decided that I wasn't going to let things end and would do my best to save my marriage.

I planned an elaborate dinner for just the two of us. The day of the dinner, I approached him as he was doing some of the accounting work for the church.

"David, I have dinner planned out for just the two of us. It will be served at seven p.m. Do you think you will be on time for it? It means the world to me."

He looked up from the ledger with a smile on his face. "Of course, anything for you, darling."

With that, I left the room with a smile spread across my face. I knew that the night would be wonderful. It was the beginning of a fresh start. I couldn't wait for him to see what I had planned. It would make David so happy. I was making his favorite dish.

The entire day felt like I was walking on air. I was so happy. I simply knew that it would make everything good. David would see my devotion to him and our love. I couldn't wait to find Sebastian to tell him that our plan was going to work.

Sebastian had told me that he would help me with the planning. He wanted to see me happy. We had grown close over the time that we had spent together. It wasn't a typical relationship between a man and woman. We were more like brother and sister, yet closer. The bond between us was strong and sometimes he felt like he was much older than he actually was.

He was stirring something when I entered the kitchen. I walked over, leaning on the counter and studied him. He had gained a little weight since he came to us. He looked happier as well. The shadows were no longer lingering under his eyes.

"Did he go for it?" He asked without looking up at me.

"Yes. He sounded genuinely happy about it." I smiled. "What are you making?"

"Texas sheet cake. It has always been one of my favorites. I think David will love it, and I know you will."

"Sounds amazing."

I couldn't wait for the evening and to fix my marriage.

Chapter 26

Tears filled my eyes as I stared at the clock on the wall. He was late. He hadn't come back for dinner now everything was cold. I sat at the little kitchenette, napkin in my lap as I continued to blink and watch that damned clock. He hadn't come. He promised he would be there. My heart was slowly breaking. It was excruciating.

It was well after midnight when I finally stood. My legs were asleep and tingling. Pins and needles shot through them as I slowly backed away from the table and walked toward the bedroom. Pulling my shirt over my head, I tossed it into the corner of the room.

I stalked around the room, preparing for bed. With every step I took, the angrier I became. By time I was in my pajamas and make-up was washed off, I was boiling angry. I could feel the anger balled up in the pit of my stomach. I couldn't believe that he lied.

Determined to face him and ask why he didn't show up; I took off toward the sanctuary. Since he wasn't in our room, he had to be in one of the offices there. When I pushed the sanctuary doors open, I stopped for a moment. It was completely empty. The rows of chairs that had been here were gone. I frowned and looked around. Everything else was in place, just not the chairs.

It didn't make sense. Where could the chairs have gone? My eyes drifted to the back of the room where the door to the recommitment area. I slowly walked toward it, the hair standing up on the back of my neck. I didn't know why it made me so nervous, but the anger washed away in one swoop of nerves, replaced by fear.

My hand trembled as I reached out for the doorknob. Fingers wrapping around the cool metal, I took a deep breath to steady myself. I didn't know what I was going to find when I opened the door, but I was about to find out.

Slowly turning the knob, I pushed the door and it opened silently. The room that it opened into was large. It reminded me of a sitting room for a doctor's office. On the left side of the room, there was another door. It was closed as well.

As I made my way to that door, every fiber of my being told me that I needed to go the other way. There was something on the other side of the door that I didn't want to see. Pulling the door open, I stared into the darkness. There was a staircase leading down into the inky black. Hesitantly, I took my first step onto the stairs.

I almost turned around when I heard voices. I couldn't make out what they were saying or who they belonged to, but there were a lot of them. Curiosity overcame my fear as I followed the sound of the voices. I had to know what was going on.

When I reached the bottom of the stairs, I looked around trying to make out what room I was in. I tried to get my bearings. It was dark, but a light was coming from the end of a long hallway. I walked cautiously down the hallway.

The voice in my head was back. It was telling me that I needed to turn around. I needed to head back to my room and forget about being stood up by David. I needed to pretend that nothing was wrong. I should just turn a blind eye and be the devoted wife that I vowed to be. The voice whispered warnings in my head saying that I would regret it if I kept digging.

I shook my head. It was too late to turn back. I would forever hate myself if I didn't go find out what was going on. I was still angry and hurt that he had stood me up and I wanted, no deserved, answers. As I walked,

I thought about all the late nights and awkward moments over the past year that we had been married. There had been secrets, and I was tired of them. It was time that I was let fully into his life, or maybe we needed to rethink our marriage.

At the end of the hallway, there was another closed door. The light that I had seen was coming from the crack at the bottom of the door. Standing at the door, I hesitated. The voice in my head now screamed to turn back. It said it wasn't too late to go back, it would only be too late if I went through that doorway.

There was the sound of something hitting something else and a muffled sound that made me open the door and walk inside. The sight before me stunned, shocked, and repulsed me. It was so horrific that I couldn't process what I was staring at.

The chairs were set up in a circle in the middle of the room. The congregation was there, sitting calmly in the circle. They were facing the center of the circle where a pile of bloody clothing was heaped. It didn't make sense. Why would they sit there staring at clothes? Why were the clothes bloody?

The longer I stared at the heap, the more I started to make out more shapes that seemed recognizable. Something moved in it causing me to gasp. It was a finger. That heap wasn't just a pile of clothing, it was a human. My brain quickly processed the rest of the scene before.

A tingle went rushing up my neck onto the base of my head. If it was possible, my hair tingled as well. I had goosebumps raise on my arms. My eyes raised upward, coming into direct contact with David's dark gaze. I couldn't blink or look away from the look in his eyes.

"Jean," his voice was full of disapproval. "What on Earth are you doing down here? You aren't supposed to be here."

"David, what is this?" My voice was weak and wavered, giving away that I was afraid.

He sighed deeply before he walked around the circle of chairs to stand directly in front of me. "Darling, you weren't supposed to see this yet. You aren't ready. But now, I guess you will have to adjust, like it or not."

I crossed my arms over my chest and took a small step back from him. I wasn't sure why, but the gleam in his eye and the tone of his voice scared me. The fear consumed me quickly like a fire in the dry forest. "What?"

"This is the recommitment room. We come down here when the followers are having troubles with believing and being true to us." He stepped closer, fingers curling around my arms. "Everything that happens down here is God's word, His plan. He demands that we follow these rules and expects those rules to be obeyed."

My gaze tore away from his and went over his shoulder to the bloodied person on the floor.

"Who is that?" Even as I asked the question, there was a knot in my stomach that told me I already had the answer to that one.

"Sebastian." My eyes flew back to his as he spoke. "He has broken the commandments and needed recommitment. He needed to be reminded of his place here."

"How?"

"That isn't your concern. Just know that he will be better when we are done with the recommitment process. He won't make that mistake again." He smiled at me. The smile made my insides freeze in terror. "Now that you are here, you can dole out the final lashes for his punishment. That way he remembers his place and yours in this society."

"Mine? What do I have to do with it? What lashes?"

"No questions," David's voice boomed across the room.

He released one arm but kept his grip on the other and pulled me into the circle. He picked up a leather razor strap, placing it in the hand of my free arm. I stared down at the strap in my hand, not sure what to do with it. Peeling my eyes from it, I looked up to David questioningly.

"Use it. Give him another twenty lashes, and he will be able to go back to his room. Then we can go to bed. It's late. I know you are tired. Just do this and everyone can go."

At the word everyone, I looked around the circle. Faces were blank, most facing where Sebastian was lying. The looks were expressionless. It reminded me of a trance.

David kept encouraging me to use the strap on Sebastian as I stared. I couldn't help but stare at the helpless pile. My heart ached for Sebastian and the torment that he went through and was going through.

I looked back down at the strap. I couldn't do it. I couldn't inflict more pain on him. He needed nurturing, not pain. The strap fell from my fingers as I collapsed to the ground in heap of tears.

Chapter 27

I sat up, confused. I was now in my bed. Alone. I looked at the clock, surprised that it was morning. The previous night was a fog. I wasn't sure what was real and what I had dreamed. Climbing out of bed, I made my way to Sebastian's room to check on him.

The memories of the dream I had made my stomach churn. It was so bloody, and Sebastian had been in bad shape. I opened his bedroom door, slipping in silently. I didn't want to wake anyone. I moved silently through the bedroom until I was next to his bed.

He was covered from head to toe in his blanket. I could barely make out this shape under the blanket. I sat on the edge of the bed and placed my hand on his shoulder, gently shaking it to wake him. As his shoulder moved, he cried out in pain.

I froze for several heartbeats before I pulled the blankets down, exposing his shoulders and back. They were black and blue. He had cuts all over his back. As I stared at the wounds, I realized that I didn't dream all that up. It had really happened.

"Oh my God! Bastian, are you okay?" My voice came out as a high, airy whisper. Panic was lacing my voice and my hands began to tremble.

"Uh." He carefully turned and opened one eye balefully at me.

"Are you okay?" I repeated, more insistently.

"No. You aren't either."

"What do you mean?"

"I mean that this place isn't what it seems. You aren't safe here. We need to get out of here. David is a liar, a charlatan."

"What are you talking about? David isn't a fake."

He reached out, grabbing my hand. Squeezing it, he looked me dead in the eye. "I came to find you because I heard about the Wilson girl—"

"What about her?" My stomach began to hurt as nausea rose up.

"There is a rumor that he married her the other day. He is married to both of you. He has been messing around with both the Wilson girls, but chose the older one to marry. He did this because he didn't want you to know."

"No." I shook my head slowly back and forth.

"Yes. I'm worried about what he will do now that you know. You could be hurt."

"You just rest. David wouldn't hurt me. Trust me. I know him better than that. He loves me."

I wasn't sure who I was trying to convince. Sebastian or myself. Carefully, I covered him back up and kissed him on the forehead. While I was waiting for him to fall back asleep, I considered my options. I could do as he suggested and pretend I didn't know anything, or I could face David and find out what was truly going on.

I knew I had to find out the truth. I wasn't the type of woman to sit in the background and let secrets overshadow our lives.

As soon as I was sure Sebastian was back to sleep, I got up and headed toward my room so I could gather my thoughts before I confronted the man in question. Halfway to the room, I changed my mind and veered to the left toward the office where I knew David would be with the accountant and property manager.

Opening the door, I was shocked to find David in the room, but he wasn't alone, and he wasn't with the accountant or the property manager. He was leaning against the desk, pants open. There was a girl, who I thought was older of the Wilson girls. She was on her knees in front of him, mouth suctioned around his penis.

His eyes opened and looked directly into mine as his breathing picked up and one hand went to the girl's head. He bunched her hair into his hand, pushing her head closer to him while she gagged. This continued until he began to shudder. His eyes didn't stray from mine as he orgasmed into her mouth. When he finished, he pushed her away, then grabbed a tissue from the desk, cleaning and drying himself off.

"What is going on here?" I managed to sputter out. My throat was dry and had constricted from watching my husband cheat on me.

"Darling, I would like you to meet the newest member of our family. This is Darla. She is now your sister, my wife."

"Excuse me?"

"I was going to find a more delicate way to tell you, but after your debacle last night, I knew that you were bound to find out sooner."

"Why?" I couldn't seem to gather a coherent thought that made it possible to speak a full sentence.

"You were slacking as a wife. You couldn't be obedient as much as I need, so I thought I would get you some help. This way you can focus on your other tasks and I can have all my needs met when I demand it."

"Why?" It seemed like the most reasonable thing that I could utter.

He sighed. The sigh sounded exasperated. It made me feel like he was explaining himself to an idiot. He stared at me for a full thirty seconds before he answered. "Because it's what I want. What God demands of me. He thinks I need to have more than one wife to do everything that is needed to be done. You will be okay with this. It is happening, and you are going to have to accept it."

I shook my head slowly back and forth in a no motion. It was something that I couldn't accept. I had been raised and believed in one man, one woman in a marriage. That didn't include adding other women into the mix.

I didn't see him rear back and was taken completely off-guard when the blow landed on my face. I stumbled backward into the wall, hand going over the stinging on my cheek. I stared at him; eyes wide as he approached me. His hand came to my neck, wrapping around my throat and squeezing until the air started to cut off.

"You are going to learn the ways of being my wife. You seem to need a recommitment to our marriage and the Church."

I was seeing dark spots when he finally released me. I dropped to the ground, gasping for the precious air that I had been denied. My throat and lungs burned with the deep inhalations that I was taking while attempting to catch my breath.

His hand in my hair scared me. David began to pull on it, causing me to cry out. My hands went up to his hand and grabbed on, trying to free myself of his grip. He wasn't letting go. I opened my eyes after I realized that I had squeezed them shut from the pain.

He was taking me to the door on the far end of the room. The door that led downstairs. I knew I didn't want to be downstairs. I was going to have to fight for my life.

I struggled with all the effort and strength that I had. I felt the urgency to escape before we made it to that door. If I went into that hell, I knew I wouldn't come out alive. My nails raked against his skin. When his grip didn't loosen, I shifted and sank my teeth into his leg. I bit as hard as I could until I heard a pop and tasted copper.

He screamed tossing me to the ground. "Fucking bitch! I will kill you!"

I scrambled to my feet and raced to the door. My hand was on the knob seconds before I felt the crash. Pain exploded in my head as the floor rose up to meet me as everything went black.

Chapter 28

The light was blinding as I opened my eyes. Nausea washed over me. My hands automatically came up, covering my eyes to protect them from the light. As I dug my palms into my eyes, I tried to remember what happened. All I could remember was going to find David, after that it was a blank.

After what seemed like an eternity, I sat up and looked around. My eyes felt like they were being stabbed, but the room slowly started to come into focus. I didn't recognize it. I was sitting on the floor in the middle of the room. The walls were gray, and it appeared to be a basement of some sort. Beside me on the floor was a drain that had some copper stains around the rim. The room smelled strongly of bleach. That's when it me. I was in the recommitment room.

"It's about time you woke up. I was worried that Darla may have severely injured you. She hit you pretty hard with that Mother Mary statue." David was leaning against the door. His arms were crossed against his chest.

He reminded me of a caged tiger I saw at a zoo once. Dangerous. Deadly. I didn't know how I didn't see it before, but he didn't look like the kind, loving man that I had married anymore. All I could see was pure evil. It amazed me how different a person he was.

"David, let me go." It sounded weak and stupid even to my ears, but I had to try.

He inhaled and exhaled slowly in a big, disappointed sounding sigh. I had never known the sound of air could sound disappointed, but there you have it. "Jean, you know I can't do that. You are my wife in the eyes of God. We both spoke the words "til death do us part'. I meant every word of my vows. I thought you did, too."

"I did mean them, David. You are the one that broke our commitment when you started fucking Darla. That goes against all of what we promised each other."

His head turned as he clicked his tongue. "Actually, our vows said nothing about being with you solely. It said that you would honor and obey me, but there was nothing about being married to only you."

"That what a marriage is. A promise to stay just the two of us forever."

"No. It's a promise to love one another." He pushed away from the wall. "I'm not going to argue the semantics of marriage with you. There is one part of the vows that you have deliberately broken. To honor and obey. Now as much as it pains me to do this, I am going to have to teach you to keep your word."

Suddenly, he had the razor strap in his hand. I hadn't seen him grab it or where it came from. It had appeared like magic. The first blow hit my back with enough force that it threw me forward. I faceplanted on the ground and felt the crunch of my nose breaking.

Struggling to sit up, I slipped but managed to get back in the sitting position. There was a coppery taste in my mouth that had to be from the blood running down my face. I had never tasted blood before, but it was something I couldn't deny. I knew that was a taste that I would remember for the rest of my life.

The second blow was from his fist. It landed on my jaw, knocking me backward. My head smacked the floor, and I saw stars. The strength of the impact made my already spinning head worse. My stomach revolted. I barely had time to get on my side before I vomited all over the place.

The blows kept coming in different ways, but each attack as vicious as the last. I knew that I was going to die while I was lying in that room. David's hand was going to be the one to end my life. I could hear myself begging for him to stop even though I didn't intend on giving him the satisfaction of my tears.

"Please." I coughed, expelling blood from my lungs. "Stop. David. I love you. Please. No more. You're going to kill me. I'm dying."

There was one more kick to the ribs before he stopped and crouched down, so his face was close to mine. "You aren't going to die, wife. You will live, and you will remember this. This is a reminder that you are mine, and you do as I say. Do you understand me?"

I nodded once. There wasn't much else I could do. I felt defeated.

He stood back up but continued to look down at me. "Good. There is a mattress in the corner for you to get some sleep. You are going to stay down here for a few days while the bruises on your face heal. I'll take care of you."

I watched as he walked to the door. He stopped as he had opened and turned back toward me. "Oh, and in case you think anyone will come looking for you, I am going to spread word that you mother is ill and you went to take care of her for a few days."

He walked out and left me alone in the room that I now dubbed the room of horrors. I curled up into a ball and cried. The pain was so intense that it even hurt to cry. I didn't have one spot on my body that wasn't broken or injured.

I wished I was back home. I should have never joined this church. I couldn't understand how I thought it was the loving, caring environment that I belonged in. My mind reeled about it while I listened to the demons of the room come to life.

***

I wasn't sure how long I had been in the room. It could have been days, hours, or minutes. It was impossible to tell. I just knew that I felt like a prisoner. The thought stopped me. I didn't just feel like a prisoner; I was a prisoner.

I was so sore, I couldn't move. I didn't know about anatomy or injuries, but I was certain that my nose and possibly a rib or two were broken. It hurt to breathe. I couldn't breathe through my nose. My sides and chest hurt. Moving was painful and slow.

I was seated on the mattress, huddled in the corner furthest from the door. I had spent an insane amount of time trying to find a way out with no avail. All I managed to do was make the pain unbearable. Tears rolled down my cheeks as I sat there, hopelessness washing over me.

The only human contact I had gotten was when David brought food down. He didn't stay and he didn't speak. He just set the tray down and left. I figured he couldn't be gone very long or people would ask where he was wondering off to.

I leaned my head against the wall, looking at the ceiling. Despair and pain overwhelmed me. I felt as if I were suffocating on it. I wasn't sure if I had my head back to try to get air or to stare at something different.

I closed my eyes as depression crept up me while I tried my best to fight it off. I couldn't let the darkness overcome me. I needed to stay strong so I could escape. Getting out of the prison was my only priority.

A strange smell caught my attention. I opened my eyes, squinting at the ceiling as I tried to identify the smell. It reminded me of a bonfire or a campfire. It wasn't quite a campfire smell. There was an underlying stench of chemical in it. Something had to be burning.

The longer I sat there, the warmer I became. My anxiety began to ratchet up as the hair stood up on the back of my neck. Something was wrong. The smell was getting stronger. I felt like it was starting to catch in my throat.

The sounds in the building changed. I had been listening to mice scurry in the walls, but now it was different. There was a crackling sound that made me even more nervous. I didn't think that it was possible that I had become more nervous, but it happened.

There was a crack and a loud thump from above that made me jump. Pain shot through me causing nausea to rise. I cried out from the pain, having to breathe slowly through it.

The burning smell intensified as the pain subsided. I stood and walked to the door, placing the back of my hand on the doorknob. It was so hot that it burned my hand. I jumped back from the door, all thoughts of the pain in my body long forgotten.

Smoke began to slip into the room from the crack under the door. Before I realized what I had done, I was pressed against the opposite wall watching flames eat the wooden door. It was the only thing that was barring the fire from me.

The flames came into the room with a whoosh and ate up everything in sight. It only took seconds for it to reach me. The heat made my skin boil and sizzle. I could hear the popping and cracking of the flames licking my skin. Blisters were emerging and bursting as soon as they were full size. I screamed as I was burned alive.

My last memory was thinking that it was too hot to even cry.

Chapter 29

I wasn't sure how long I had my eyes closed, but when I opened them again, things were different. The room was completely changed. I stood up and realized that the mattress I had been sleeping on was gone. I looked around, hoping the cobwebs would clear from my mind.

I remembered flames but they couldn't have happened. I was still alive. Looking down at my arm, it didn't look any different than normal. It must have been a nightmare. I couldn't have survived a fire without a mark.

My focus shifted back to the room. It had carpeting that wasn't there before. I couldn't have slept through that. The room looked like a living room, but weird. There was a black square on the wall that looked like it was a screen, but I didn't know how it was possible to have it hanging like it was.

I turned and headed to the door. It was open, and I walked through it out to the hallway. Stopping dead in my track, confusion washed over me. It was changed. The hallway was gone. I was standing at the base of a staircase that led up.

What happened to the hallway? How could it have changed? What was going on? Questions raced through my mind. I didn't see how this was possible. I tried to figure it out, but there was no clear explanation. I slowly started up the stairs to the main floor. The door there was open as well. I slipped through quietly into a kitchen.

This was supposed to be David's office, not a kitchen. I frowned as I stared at the island in middle of the room. It should not have been there. None of this was right. I couldn't figure out what happened or what was going on.

The longer I stared at that island, the angrier I became. There was a whoosh and flames shot from the stove. I jumped back, startled. The flames grew, and I raced from the room. There was an alarm that started to go off. A woman ran past me without a second glance. There was a shout with cursing. Clanging followed and a hissing sound. The alarm died down; the woman came back out carrying a fire extinguisher.

"Excuse me?" I asked as I followed her. She didn't acknowledge me or even hesitate as she went into a living room and set it down on the floor beside a couch. She sat down and I stood in front of her, arms crossed. "I said excuse me. Why aren't you listening to me?"

Music started playing and she pulled a small thing out of her pocket. "Hello? John, the weirdest thing happened. The stove caught fire while it was turned off. . . Yeah. . . Everything is fine, I was able to put the flames out. No, I don't know why it did that. There was nothing around the stove. Yeah, I'll call an electrician. Love you too. Bye."

I almost believed she had been talking to someone on that contraption. She set it down, stretched on the couch, then closed her eyes. I walked away with anger simmering in the pit of my stomach. She completely ignored me, and I wasn't sure what was going on. She acted like I wasn't even there. Nothing made sense.

***

I had found through exploring that the compound had become some kind of housing units. I wasn't sure what happened to the compound, but it was gone. I still didn't know what had happened to me, however. It was as if I were taken from what I knew and placed in something unfamiliar. It made me so mad that I felt as if my head were going to explode.

There was a knock, and the woman answered the door. I couldn't see who was at the door, but the voice rang a bell. I just couldn't place it though.

"Good evenin', ma'am. We received a call about a pest problem in the condo next door, so I was wondering if I could come in and look around." The voice was pleasant and professional sounding.

"I don't know," the woman hesitated. "I haven't heard anything about pests."

"Ma'am, you can call the building manager if it would make you feel better. Mr. Andrew Davidson called this afternoon. I will be more than happy to wait out here until you can confirm."

"Well, if Andrew called, then it is surely okay. Come on in."

The young man that entered to room sparked a memory from me. I still couldn't quite place him, but I felt like I knew him. It was making me crazy. I followed them around as they roamed the house, checking in nooks and crannies for whatever these pests were.

When they ended back in the living room, he turned and looked my direction. "There are signs of the vermin in the house. I want to treat it for you. I will go get my equipment. Is there anywhere you can go for about two hours?"

"Um, yeah. I can go to my sister's. Will the house be ready for me to come back in two hours? I'll have to have dinner made before my husband comes home."

"Of course. We caught it before it became an infestation, so it won't take long to treat."

After going over details, she left quickly so that he could get back to work. After she was gone, he set his stuff down on the floor and took a seat in the recliner on the other side of the room.

"Jean, are you alright?" he asked, shocking me. I couldn't believe that he was addressing me. No one had addressed me since I woke up.

I looked around the room. "Me?"

"Yes. You're Jean, correct?" His voice was soft and calming.

"I am."

"I heard about what happened to you. Do you remember what happened?"

I shook my head no. "I remember nothing."

"Would you like to know what happened?"

There was something in his voice that made me stare at him. Something like regret was in his voice. I nodded.

"You were locked in the recommitment room. There was a fire, and the compound was destroyed. No one knew you were there until the fire fighters found your remains. Your friend Sebastian was devastated when he found out what happened to you. After you were identified, he disappeared."

"What happened to David?"

"He fell off the grid. No one heard what happened to him. That is until your friend Sebastian located him. He is currently staying in a mansion in the state of Missouri. I can take you there if you would like. That way you can get your revenge."

The idea of revenge made me giddy. It was something I wanted more than anything. David had ruined me and my life. I wanted to return the favor. Yet, he wasn't the only one I wanted to get even with. I owed Darla as well.

"And Darla?" Anticipating his answer put me on edge.

"She is there, also."

An energy shot through me. "Let's go."

Chapter 30

I walked into the room that the man had told me David was staying in. There were two people lying in the bed, facing away from each other. I approached the bed. Once I was standing over the man, I stared down at him.

It was David. He looked the same, but he was much older. His hair was graying and wrinkles were around his eyes. I hadn't realized how long it had been since I apparently died. As I stared at him, I felt the anger growing within me. I wanted him to know how I suffered.

He stirred, eyes opening in slits. The moment he saw me, his eyes widened, and he sat straight up in the bed.

"What the fuck?" his voice was a harsh whisper.

"Yes, darling. What the fuck? You let me burn to death!"

"Jean?"

I glared at him as he gaped at me.

I blinked, and the next thing I knew, I was leaning over him. My hands stretched out, wrapping around his neck. As I squeezed, I felt my hands warming up. He struggled as he screamed and tried to escape. I could feel the skin under my hands cooking.

"What in the world?" Darla's voice, heavy with sleep, came out of the darkness beside us.

My eyes turned toward her and just stared, causing her to freeze in place. Knowing she wouldn't move; I focused my attention back to David. Leaning forward, I pressed my lips to his. As we kissed, I felt his lips heat up as well. I blew my breath into his mouth. Smoke moved out of my lungs and went into his.

He coughed and choked. I leaned back and watched with glee as he struggled to breathe. I knew that he was burning from the inside out. I looked over at Darla and there was an explosion, then she burst into flames. I smiled as I watched them burn.

The man that brought me to the house was standing next to me, fire extinguisher in hand. Once the screams stopped, he put the fire out.

Turning, he looked at me. "Feel better?"

I nodded. "Yes."

I looked town to see my skin was now blackened and covered in blisters. It felt more natural than the perfect skin I had when I had first woken up.

"This is your home now. You may do as you wish as long as you don't cross Bane. I want you to be comfortable here."

I simply nodded. There wasn't anything else that needed to be said. He was right. I was home, and I planned on staying, having fun. Living my afterlife. I just hoped they had plenty of fire extinguishers around.

Black Zodiac Ghost 5

MANGLED CAPTAIN

Chapter 31

Omaha, Nebraska 1965

The fans in the bleachers cheered as I swung the bat. The ball connected with it, vibrating up my arms. I watched for a moment as it sailed through the air. Tossing the bat behind me, I ran toward first base. Glancing toward where the ball had gone, I saw I had plenty of time for me to go for the next base.

I loved the attention my skill at playing ball gained. The gals loved that I was the captain of the team and MVP. My parents showed off my pictures and strutted around telling everyone I was going to be a pro. The coach had scouts come watch me play. There was talk that a recruiter was going to come from the St. Louis Cardinals to pick me up.

As much fun as baseball was, it wasn't where my true passion lied. I was going to do what I loved as soon as the game was over. Don't get me wrong, I loved baseball as well, but not as much. It was just something that I was good at. My foot touched home plate and everyone cheered. Another homerun. It was almost too easy.

After the game, the team celebrated at the ice cream shop. I sat in the booth with my arm slung across Melinda's shoulder. She was my current girlfriend, but it wouldn't last long. They never did. I had too many girls chasing after me for me to stick with just one.

"Overton, that was a great game," Daniels said as he jumped up and sat on back of the booth.

"Yeah it was, we wiped the floor with them." I chuckled and kissed Melinda on the side of the head.

"You comin' to the party tonight?"

"Nope. Got other plans."

He leaned forward and dipped a fry in the milkshake sitting on the table. After popping it in his mouth, he responded. "Again? You are taking too many risks."

"Only pussies say that, Daniels. There is no fun without risk."

"You're crazy."

I leaned forward and lowered my voice. "That may be, but I'm the one that gets all the girls."

"What was that?" Melinda asked, voice careful.

"Nothing babe."

I leaned back and sipped my soda. It would be better with a little vodka in it.

***

The engine revved as I pressed the pedal down. I loved the sound of a roaring engine. The vibration raced through me, causing my heart to race. Adrenaline surged through my body as I looked over at the other car. The guy was from Omaha South, our rival school. He looked my way and flipped me off.

I smiled. He was nervous, and I could tell. He was going against me for the first time. The loser didn't stand a chance. By the end of the night, I was going to own his car. I loved the look of despair on my opponents' faces after they lost. It was almost as great as winning. Well, not quite.

Melinda waved the flag for the race to start. I let off the brake and listened to the tires squeal as I peeled out and shot forward. Looking over my shoulder I saw the other guy gaining on me. Smiling, I let up on the gas to give him the glimmer of hope that he would be able to be beat me.

When he was even with me, I hit the gas again, and my car lurched forward. I shot passed the finish mark, hitting my brakes. My car did a full three-sixty before stopping and facing the opposite direction. Another win in the bag. If things kept going as they were, I was going to have a fleet of cars to race.

"You are a bastard, you know that?" he grumbled as he handed me the title to his car. "My dad is going to kill me."

Shrugging, I slipped the title into my back pocket. "I guess you shouldn't have bet it. Not my problem."

I walked away without another word. I didn't need to waste my time on another loser with a sob story. He needed to be better and smarter, yet he wasn't. Maybe one day he would learn. Either that, or I would get another car out of him down the road. If I knew the type, he would bet me again trying to gain back some of his pride.

Draping my arm across Melinda's shoulders, I kissed her below the ear. "Let's get out of here. I want to celebrate my winnings with my favorite girl."

Corbin stopped us before we made it to my car. "Y'all aren't coming to the party tonight?"

I cocked an eyebrow at him. "Did you say party? Where at?"

"Jeff's place. The 'rents are out of town for the weekend. He got a keg."

"Hell yeah. We will definitely be there."

A deep sigh escaped from Melinda. Her shoulders had also tensed up as I had been talking to Corbin. I looked at her. Her head was turned away from me.

"What's wrong, Mel?" I didn't really care, but she didn't need to know that.

"Do we really have to go to Jeff's? I mean my parents are gone for the night, too, and I hoped you would spend the night at my place."

"What we will do is go to the back of the car for a quick somethin', go to Jeff's party, then I'll stay with you afterward, and we can take our time. Trust me baby, I can go all night."

She smiled, and I leaned forward to kiss her.

"Okay, let's go." She tugged on my shirt.

I glanced back at Corbin. "See you in a bit."

Chapter 32

There was bass coming from the house as we pulled up to it. I put the car in park and studied the house for a minute before getting out of the car. There were people all over the yard and the smell of booze and weed wafted through the air. I had a feeling the party would be a blast.

I got out of the car and slid across the hood. When my feet hit the ground, I pulled the door open for Melinda. She still had the mark I left on her neck, and if you got close enough, you could still smell me on her. That was intentional as I wanted everyone to remember that she was mine for the moment.

After slamming the door behind her, we walked up to the open door. I stepped across the threshold without knocking. Being polite wasn't part of the protocol for the parties. The house was filled with a heavy layer of smoke.

When we entered the living room, there was a bong being passed around a circle of people. I took Melinda's elbow and entered the circle. We settled onto the couch between a couple of the football players. Lane handed me the bong. I took a hit and held it is as long as I could. I exhaled and coughed a bit as I handed it to Melinda. She followed my lead and hit it as well.

I wasn't sure when cups of beer were handed to us, but next thing I knew I was chugging it. After slamming my cup down on the table, a new one was handed to me. After several more beers, I got up and headed upstairs to use the pisser. I knew the downstairs one was probably occupied. I planned on using the bathroom off the master bedroom. It wasn't the first party here.

Walking out of the bathroom, I finished zipping up my jeans. I stopped dead in my tracks when I saw the woman sitting on the bed. She was wearing a tank top that left nothing to the imagination. It was black and so tight that I could see the shape of her nipples through it.

"Hey Royce." Her voice was sultry. I could picture her underneath me, moaning my name as I lost myself in her.

"Do I know you?" I didn't recognize her, but I wasn't really looking at her face. Her other assets had my full attention.

"I'm Maggie. We met a while back at a party in Lincoln." She leaned forward and smiled at me. "We had a groovy time."

"I crossed my arms loosely across my chest and cocked and eyebrow. "Are you sure about that? I'm pretty sure I'd remember a groovy gal like you."

"Oh yeah I'm sure. You were with some blonde, but you said she was a dud. We spent the evening in the coat closet."

Standing up, she walked over to me and pressed herself against me. Her lips brushed my ear as she whispered, "I can give you a reminder."

She brought her hand up and slipped her fingers into her tank top. She produced a plastic baggie with brown, dried stuff in it. When she stopped swinging it back and forth in front of my face, I saw that the baggie contained shrooms.

I didn't remember ever taking shrooms, but she seemed certain I had. No matter how much I thought about it, the memories didn't surface. "That's not what I thought you were talking about."

"Oh yeah. We did more than shrooms." Her lips brushed mine. "That comes after."

She opened the baggie and produced a shroom out of the bag. She held the shroom up to my mouth. I did the only thing I could think of was to open my mouth and let her place it on my tongue. I closed my mouth and chewed it slowly, watching as she did the same.

It didn't take long for my vision to begin to blur. The room spun, and she became distorted. Her tits were ten times larger than they had been originally, but her head was the size of a pinhead. I had to suppress the laugh that was threatening to bubble out. She looked hilarious, but I wanted to shove my cock deep inside her. As the drugs took effect, I remembered her from before. She had been a good fuck. There had been a group of us that she gave it to that night.

I watched as her body swayed to the music that was either in our heads or coming from downstairs, I couldn't be sure. My hands reached out on their own accord and ran up and down her sides, grabbing her hips. I stepped closer so she had to look up at me.

As my mouth came down on hers, there was a noise at the doorway of the room. I turned, ready to yell at who interrupted what could have been a great time, but stopped when I saw Melinda standing there. Her eyes were wide, mouth open a little and tears were rolling down her cheeks.

"Fuck." My hands dropped off Maggie's hips and I stepped back. "Melinda, wait."

"Fuck you!" she screamed as she turned and ran from the room.

I debated on whether or not I should chase after her. I didn't really want to, but there was an obligation there thinking I should. I glanced back at Maggie, who pulled her shirt off while this was going on and climbed onto the bed. As she pulled her pants down and off, all thoughts of Melinda vanished.

I climbed onto the bed after her and shoved her down. I pressed my body on Maggie and kissed her long and hard. Her legs wrapped around my hips, pulling me tighter onto her. At that moment, I just wanted to get myself freed so I could take care of the needs that were building. I had planned on letting out all the tensions of the evening into Maggie.

Chapter 33

I sat in the back of the classroom, waiting for the bell to ring so I could get out of that damned place. I just wanted to play ball and drive cars. It wasn't too much to ask. The parties over the weekend had ruined any chances that I had of getting back with Melinda, but I honestly didn't give a damn. Like they always said, there was a lot of fish in the sea. That fish had been dead anyway.

My eyes drifted to the front row where she sat. I watched as she crossed her legs one way, then the other. I didn't know what her deal was, but she wasn't my concern. She glanced over her shoulder, eyes meeting mine, then she quickly turned back to the front of the class. I had seen tears in her eyes and they were puffy. The girl looked like hell, which made me glad I was done with her. I couldn't have something looking like that on my arm. I needed someone that looked good next to me.

I needed to find a new piece of ass to waste my time left here with. I was going to be graduating in a couple months and was more than ready to get out of this hellhole they called Nebraska. I was going to go to New York and play with the Yankees. Then I could have all the cars and women I wanted.

My eyes landed on Serena. She sat adjacent from me. Her skirt was shorter than the school policy allowed. I always enjoyed watching her walk down the halls. Maybe she had her eye on me too. I was going to have to find out.

The bell rang, I got up, stopping her before she was able to get out of her seat. "Serena."

"Hey Royce," she smiled up at me.

"You got plans after this?"

She sucked her bottom lip in and chewed on it while she watched me. "Not really."

"Groovy. You should come watch me practice ball, then I'll take you for a burger and soda."

"Okay."

She stood up, I slung my arm across her shoulders and took her books with my free hand. We walked out of the classroom like that and everyone knew that I had just lay claim to my new girl.

***

The car sped down the street, Serena screaming with joy in the passenger seat beside me. She loved riding in the car while I raced, always found it exhilarating and arousing. We turned the corner sharp enough that she slid across the seat and pressed into me. I took one had off the wheel and wrapped an arm around her shoulders.

The finish line came into view. I slammed on the breaks and the tires squealed and car fishtailed across the line. I came to a stop and smiled. This time the bet had been money. I enjoyed money as much as I enjoyed winning cars.

Climbing out, I walked to the opponent's car and leaned into the window. "Better luck next time, chump. Now hand over the green."

A fist shot out the window, hitting me in the eye. I was knocked on my ass. Next thing I knew, the driver of the other car jumped out of the car, wailing on me. I was blindsided by the attack and wasn't sure why he was beating on me.

Corbin and one of his friends ran over, dragging the guy off me. I struggled into a sitting position and watched as the dude struggled to get away from them. Using the back of my hand, I wiped blood off my mouth. Slowly, I got to my feet. My head spun a little, but it wasn't anything that was unbearable.

"What the fuck was that?" I stormed over to him, towering over the driver.

"You fucked my sister. Took her virtue, then dropped her like she was nothing. She is devastated and late. She is going to have to go to a special school because of you," he ranted.

"Who? And what the hell are you talking about?" I was confused, but my stomach dropped.

"Melinda Fessler. She is my sister, dirtbag. She found out that she is going to have a baby, and it's all your fault. My parents have decided to pull her out of school and are enrolling her into the special school starting Monday. You ruined her life."

"If she's having a baby, it sure in hell isn't mine. That chick would put out to anyone that wanted it." I was provoking him and knew it, but I couldn't and wouldn't admit to having impregnated her. That would be the end of my baseball career. I would have to get a job and marry the twit. "Now give me the cash so I can take my girl here to dinner and get on with our lives."

Corbin reached down and pulled the guy's wallet out of his pocket, emptying it of all the cash and handed it to me. I didn't count or even look at it. It didn't matter how much was there, I knew that the bet amount was since he had showed it before the race. The rest I was considering payment for attacking me.

I nodded once at Corbin, then turned and walked to my car without looking back. The first sound of Corbin's fist connecting to the guys flesh was music to my ears. I climbed back into the car, leaned over to Serena and kissed her on the cheek before turning the key. The engine roared to life, and we drove off. Not a word shared between us. Serena had been in the racing world before. She knew the rules and what went on. Nothing needed to be said.

After dinner, Serena insisted we go to a party at Barlow's house. It was supposed to be the last, biggest party of the year. It didn't take much to convince me, since I was down for a good party. According to what Serena said, she had a really good friend that was going to be there and that friend would make sure we had a great time.

When we entered the party, I looked around at the crowd. I didn't recognize many of the people. It looked like more people were from Omaha South than Omaha North. It would be nice partying with a different crowd of people, but at the same time, I was skeptical about who I would be able to trust.

Serena grabbed me by the hand, pulling me through the crowd. She spoke to several people in passing, but didn't stop to carry on a conversation. We wound our way through the room until we came to a group of girls. When we approached them, they turned and stared at us. One stepped forward, and pulled Serena into a huge hug.

"Debbie, this is Royce. Royce, my friend Debbie." She introduced us as she sidled up against my side. "I promised him a good time."

"Heya, Debbie. Nice meeting ya." I held my hand out and shook hands with her.

"Nice meeting you as well. Follow me." She turned and led us from the group to a door. She opened it and took us downstairs to the basement.

The basement was where the real party was taking place. There was more than just drinking and dancing going on. I looked around, curious as I had never been to a party quite like this one. In one corner, there was a couple sitting in a chair, the girl riding the guy. Her skirt was bunched up around her waist, ass bare. In the middle of the room, there was a glass coffee table. White powder, razor blades and rolled up dollar bills were on the table. The powder, I assumed, was cocaine.

Serena walked straight to the table, knelt, cut a line and snorted it up her nose. She smiled at me and held out the dollar bill. "Come on. I told you we would have fun. You need to loosen up. After this, we can go get some beer and dance."

I did as she asked, knelt, and did a line. I blinked as I felt the drug go up my nose and down the back of my throat. "Okay, let's go dance."

She jumped up and grabbed my hand, dragging me back to the stairs. When we made it back upstairs, cups of beer magically appeared in our hands, and we danced while drinking them. Serena had been right. I was having a good time.

We were standing around talking to some of the football players from Omaha South when someone pushed past me, spilling my beer all over the front of my shirt.

"Watch what you're doin', you asshole." I shoved the guy back.

He turned around. "Sorry man, I didn't mean to."

"You're going to think sorry." Anger rushed through me, and I threw a punch at him.

The guy fought back, and next thing I knew we were in an all-out brawl in the middle of Barlow's living room. I knew I got a couple of good hits in before the sirens could be heard from down the street. The sounds of cops broke up the fight like cold water being thrown on my face. I shook my head and ran to the car, Serena directly behind me. We rounded the corner as the flashing lights came into view.

***

Leaning against my car, I waited for my opponent to make an appearance. All I knew was that it was a guy from Omaha South and that he was new to the circuit. I couldn't wait to beat him in the race. Winning was another kind of drug for me.

Serena brushed up to me and held out some pills. "Here, these will help build up the excitement."

I popped them in my mouth and swallowed without a second thought. Taking pills didn't bother me. I was willing to try anything. "Thanks, babe."

A car pulled up beside us and a guy climbed out. I recognized him from the party we had been to. He had a black eye and fat lip that I had given him during the fight. The guy was the one that I had fought because he shoved me.

He walked around the car, eyes never leaving me. When he was directly in front of me, he stopped and held out his hand. "I'm Sebastian."

I crossed my arms and glared at him. I wasn't going to shake hands with the prick. "Royce."

His hand dropped, then he shoved them in his pockets. He rocked back on his heels then nodded once. "Let's do this then."

"We're racing for pink slips." The look on his face made me smile. He didn't like that one bit.

"No. We are racing for money. I have a hundred-fifty to put down on it."

I debated that. He was willing to put up a lot of money on this race. Glancing over his shoulder, I studied his car. It was sleek and new. I wondered what was under the hood that would make him so confident in his car.

"Fine." I held out my hand, and we shook on it.

Getting in the car, I turned the key and started the engine.

Chapter 34

Sebastian's car shot off like a rocket seconds before mine went into motion. We drove like maniacs down around the track, I had my gas pedal all the way to the floor. I watched as the needle on the odometer slowly climbed higher and higher. I shifted gears in hope to pick up some speed and catch up with him.

My car finally met his. I turned my head to look at him. He stared straight ahead and looked like he was out for a Sunday drive. I had to suppress the smile because he wasn't putting any effort into it, and I was going to win.

Suddenly there was a loud pop and my car began to swerve around the road. Serena screamed. I turned my head to look at her, which was my fatal mistake. The impact of the car hitting the pole was strong enough to throw me through the windshield. I slid down the road, the pavement and rocks peeling my skin away in ribbons.

When I came to a stop, I turned my head to see that the whole front end of my car was wrapped around the light pole and Serena was lying on the hood where she had been thrown from the car also. I tried with all my might to get up, but I couldn't move. My arms and legs felt like lead. I could barely breathe. It felt as if there were something in my chest. I managed to half roll to my side and look down. There was a large piece of glass from the windshield protruding from my chest. I rested my head on the ground, determined to give myself a minute to regain my strength so I could get up. My eyes closed and I felt my breath slip away as I lost consciousness.

***

When I came to, everything was different. I was no longer on the ground, and my car was gone. I stood up, looking around. I recognized where I was— the cemetery above the ballfield. The question was, why was I at the cemetery?

I stared down at the ballfield. I was supposed to be down there. A game was going on. Turning, I looked for my car so I could get there and suit up. It was the big game and there had been rumor that the scouts from the Yankees were going to be there. It was the game that was going to determine my career.

My car wasn't to be seen. I started walking toward the road that led down to the school when a tombstone caught my attention. Freezing mid-step, I pivoted and headed back to the stone so I could read it better.

ROYCE MICHAEL OVERTON

B: DECEMBER 12, 1947   D: AUGUST 10, 1965

BELOVED SON

I couldn't believe what I was seeing. Was that really my tombstone? Did I die in that accident? No, it couldn't be me. I was standing right there looking at the stone. If I were dead, I wouldn't be able to see it. I would be gone, but I was standing there looking at it. It was really strange, though. This tombstone had my name and birthday on it. It was also placed next to my grandparents' plots. I thought only family was allowed to be buried on this section of land.

The more I thought about it, the more I dismissed the idea that it was my tombstone. If I had died, the ground would still be mounded up. I wouldn't be around to see it. Maybe this was a joke by the guys to teach me a lesson for taking so many chances when racing.

Without another thought about it, I turned away from the tombstone and made my way down the road to the ballfield. I was going to have to walk the entire way, but it would be worth it. I hoped Coach would put me in the game even though I was late. We weren't supposed to play when we were late, but I was sure he would make an exception for me. They weren't going to bench the best player on the team.

Once at the stadium, I made my way to the locker room. People were scattered everywhere, but no one acknowledged me. Normally, they would say hello or something and gush at me about how wonderful I am. No one even looked my direction. When I was almost to the locker room, I stopped. A nagging feeling was washing over me. Instinct had me changing direction and heading to the memorial hall that led out to the bleachers.

What I saw stopped me in my tracks. It was a picture of me with a nameplate and "In memoriam of" above it. Panic began to set in as the realization of what I was starting to hit me. The light reflected off the glass at an angle so I could see my reflection. What I saw horrified me. The skin on the left side of my face was mostly gone. The meat and parts of my cheekbone were visible. The markings went down the left side of my face and neck. Glass protruded from all over my face. Looking down, there were shards of glass sticking out of my chest as well.

I made my way to the field, determined to talk to Coach. When I made it to the dugout, I frowned. No one looked familiar. The coach that was standing there wasn't someone that I knew. What happened to everyone? Anger washed over me while I considered the possibilities of what was going on. It seemed like everything changed in the blink of an eye.

Grabbing a bat, I began to swing it, letting out the building frustration. I didn't hear the screams of panic and fear at first. I turned toward the coach. He was pressed against wall of the dugout. Swinging the bat, I attacked him. The sound of his skull collapsing under the bat was glorious. I continued to bludgeon him until he was nothing but a bloody heap on the ground at my feet. Turning, I saw that the team had evacuated the dugout and were standing on the field. The look of horror on their faces made me smile. I closed my eyes for a second and when I opened them again, I was on the field in the midst of the team. Swinging the bat, I attacked anyone that was close enough to feel my wrath.

There was an announcement over the loudspeaker. "Can we have everyone please evacuate the stadium in a calm, orderly fashion? Thank you."

The crowd didn't evacuate in a calm, orderly fashion. There was shoving and screaming, chaos everywhere you looked. It was a pandemonium. The elderly were being trampled by youth to escape and avoid the punishment of my bat. I had never seen a place clear as quickly as this did. The fear was empowering. It had a taste. I knew I would need more.

Chapter 35

It hadn't taken me long to learn the ropes of being a ghost. There wasn't much to learn. I knew that my presence alone would scare the shit out of normal people. Some thought they were brave, but I would prove them wrong. Causing the players injuries in the locker room was great fun as well.

Listening to the ghost stories the players came up with was hilarious. A lot of the stories were things that never happened. They didn't know who the ghost was, but they guessed a lot of people. I would listen to them tell the stories before I unleashed my anger and let the bats fly, literally.

"I heard that it's the player, Royce Overton, that is haunting the stadium." The player with the name Lambert on his shirt said as he leaned forward.

"Royce Overton?" The coach said as he walked into the room. "I haven't heard talk of him in years."

"What really happened to him, Coach?" Lambert asked. "I heard he was murdered on the ballfield."

The coach laughed and shook his head. "Nah, Royce died in a car accident. He was racing when a tire blew and he hit a light pole. Killed both him and his girlfriend. She died on impact, but they say he lived a few minutes after the accident. He was buried in the cemetery on the hill. His grave overlooks the ballfield so he can watch the games. Baseball was his passion."

Serena had died with me. I had a fleeting moment where I felt guilty for that, but it quickly passed. I mentally shook myself. It didn't do me any good to feel guilt, or anything, for her death when I had died, too.

"That really sucks balls," Lambert said. He finished tying his cleats and stood up. "Least we can do is make sure to win for him."

I would make sure it was a game that he would never forget.

***

I stood under the lights, blood dripping from my bat. I had killed two players from Omaha South and seriously injured another before the game was cancelled. I heard one of the officials saying they were going to finish off the season going away, there wouldn't be any home games. It had become too dangerous.

Suddenly, I knew I wasn't alone. I heard footsteps behind me. Turning, there was a man with a baseball cap low over his brows so I couldn't see his face. He held a box in his hands. I pulled my eyes away from him to look down at my bat.

"I wouldn't do that if I were you, Royce." His voice was soft, but I heard him clearly. I was surprised that he knew my name.

"You can see me?"

"Yes, I can. Now put down the bat. We are going to go on a trip."

"Fuck you. I'm not going anywhere with you. I'm having too much fun." My grip on the bat tightened.

"We can do this the hard way or the easy way. I prefer the easy way, but the choice is yours."

I didn't answer him. Instead, I swung the bat. He somehow moved so it glided passed him. I swung again, this time hitting him on the shoulder. He hit the ground, the box flying from his hands.

186

"Fine. We will do this the hard way." He got to his feet and grabbed the box. Turning, he ran, making me chase him.

The game of cat and mouse was always amusing. People tended to forget that the mouse rarely won. I ran after him, firm grip on the bat. I wasn't going to drop it. I planned on splattering his brains all over the wall before I was done with him.

He turned and slid into the locker room with me right on his heels. I stepped over the threshold and everything felt different. I felt different. I couldn't explain it, but I felt weaker. It was as if some of my life force was drained from me.

The box was in the middle of the locker room, but the guy was nowhere to be seen. I decided he had to be hiding in the showers, so I headed that direction. To mess with him, I dragged the bat on the ground, every once in a while, bouncing it off the floor. Stepping into the showers, I slowly made my way down the stalls, finding them all empty. Frowning, I walked back toward the main part of the locker room.

The guy stood on the other side of the doorway, out in the hallway. I raced over there, but was knocked backward by an invisible force as soon as my foot hit the threshold. I slid across the floor, stopping next to the box.

I looked over at the box and inside was a crystal. The crystal was glowing faintly. I leaned closer. I heard the guy saying something, but I couldn't understand him or pull my eyes away from the crystal. It started to glow brighter. As I tried to move, I felt a pulling sensation. I tried to get away, but it was too strong. Then everything went dark.

***

I paced the room, anxiety rushing though me. I needed to get out of there. I wasn't sure how long I had been trapped here or how I even got to the room. I hadn't seen or heard anyone since I had been trapped in that damned crystal. I had to have been tapped in that crystal, because I didn't know how the hell I got there. Maybe this was my hell. The silence was torture. Being away from the ballfield was horrible.

The door opened slowly. On the other side there was the man that brought me to the house. He looked familiar, but I couldn't put my finger on it. Maybe I recognized him from the field, but I never saw his face. I glared at him, wanting to put a baseball bat through his skull. As I thought it, a bat materialized in my hand. I took two steps forward before he spoke.

"Hold on there, cowboy. You can't come out of that room until after we talk and come to an agreement."

"Why shouldn't I bash your head in right now?" I felt the rumble of a growl in my voice.

"You try it and you will spend the rest of eternity in that crystal. Or I'll come up with a worse fate for you." He crossed his arms and leaned against the doorjamb. "I'm Bastian. We will call me your liaison. I will be able to speak to Bane on your behalf."

"Who?" I lowered the bat but kept my hand on the grip.

"Cyrus Bane. He's the owner of the house. You are here because he cordially invited you to your paradise."

"What's the agreement?" I didn't care about any of this, I just wanted out.

"You can't kill me or Bane. You will be allowed to roam the house and grounds freely. There are barriers up that will keep you from wandering too far away from the house. If you attempt to kill either of us, you will suffer greatly. You are allowed to kill anyone else that comes into the house. Do we have a deal?"

"Groovy."

"So that's a yes?"

"Yes."

He smiled and stepped away from the door. I stepped over the threshold and smiled to myself. I would eventually get my chance to get even with this Bastian. He imprisoned me, and I would get my revenge.

Black Zodiac Ghost 6
Beauty Queen

Chapter 36

Memphis, TN 2009

Flaws. Blemishes. Imperfections. As I stared in the mirror, I could only see my faults. His words echoed through my head.

If only you were blonde.

Your tits need to be a little perkier.

Your left eye is slightly lower than your right.

Your lips are too thin.

I can't believe how uneven your teeth are.

He was right. I needed to be perfect. I was going to do whatever I could to achieve the level of perfection I desired. Then maybe he would want me again.

Turning from the mirror, I picked up the paper, reading the ad in my head again. Wanted: Administrative Assistant for Cosmetic Surgeon. That was the job that I needed. Maybe I would be able to get deals on procedures if I worked for one.

Smoothing my skirt, I slipped into my red high heels. If my intelligence couldn't get the position, then I'm sure that I could persuade him somehow. Doctor Manning was known for having an eye for pretty young women. I was exactly what he liked.

As I headed out, I had the feeling my life was about to change.

***

Two Years Later...

"Doctor Manning's office, Dana speaking," I answered the phone in a soft voice. Doctor Manning preferred to have a calm, soft atmosphere in the office. He said it helped put the clients and patients at ease. I believed that he just thought it was sexy.

While the voice on the other end of the phone spoke, I stared down at my nails, admiring my new manicure. I loved my nails. They were long and could do some real damage if I wanted them to. I noticed that my fingers were looking a little puffy. I was going to have to look into hand exercises to get the puffiness down.

I hung up the phone after the call ended. Picking up my cellphone, I checked it to see if I had any messages from Brandon. My heart flipped when I saw he had texted me. I pulled up the message and read it quickly.

Can't make it tonight. Something came up.

Something came up alright. Something named Camille. I had been suspecting that something had been going on, and this confirmed it. I could feel the tears building behind my eyes. The heat of humiliation burned my cheeks. I couldn't believe he did this to me again. He promised it would never happen again.

The door that led to the examination rooms opened. One of the nurses poked her head out. "Dana, when you get a chance, the doctor wants to see you in his office."

"Okay, but who is going to man the desk if I'm in there?" I swallowed, forcing the tears back so hopefully she couldn't tell that I had been about to cry.

"I can. Office closes in five for lunch anyway, so go on back. I'll close up for lunch."

I stood, smoothing my skirt before I headed her direction. "Thank you, Janet."

When I entered the office, I shut the door behind me as quietly as possible. Dr. Manning looked up at me and smiled.

"How are you feeling today, Dana?" His voice reminded me of velvet.

"I'm fine. I was a little sore earlier, but it has worn off." My fingers traced my freshly plumped lips. We had decided to try a filler to see how long it would last before I went with full implants. I had wanted the implants, but Dr. Manning wanted to try the other.

He walked up to me, gently turning my face from side to side, examining my mouth. My mouth dried out at the thought of his lips being so close to mine. I wondered what I could get him to do to help make me perfect next. The thought of vaginoplasty crossed my mind. Brandon wouldn't want Camille anymore if I had a perfect vagina.

"I was thinking that maybe we could do vaginoplasty." The words left my mouth before the thought had finished forming.

"Dana, you don't need vaginoplasty. You are sweet and tight as it is."

My bottom lip stuck out in a pout. I bat my eyes quickly, so tears began to well up. "Yes, I do need it. I will show you."

Walking around him, I approached his desk. Turning, I slid up onto it with my legs spread wide, so he had an unobstructed view. He came closer, desire in his eyes. I knew I was about to get my way. His warm hand touched me, sending shivers through my body. I closed my eyes, leaning my head back to look at the ceiling. His hands explored my body. I was aroused and disgusted at the same time.

His hands came to my thighs. He lifted my legs until the were straight up in the air. His mouth came down on me. As his mouth and tongue brought me to the brink, I began to pant. Before I was about to go over the edge, he stopped.

Lifting my head, I watched as he freed himself from his pants. He pulled me from the desk, turning me around so he could enter me from behind. As he pounded himself into me, grunting, I closed my eyes and imagined how I would look once I was perfect.

***

Lighting the candles, I was excited for Brandon to see the newest work I had done. I stopped and stared at myself in the mirror. My newly blonde hair glittered like gold in the candle light. Rushing to my room, I had to put the final touches on my outfit. I slid on my heels and adjusted my breasts. They were still a little sore from the last surgery. Turning, I stared at my ass that I had lifted and shaped. Maybe I would finally be good enough for him.

There was a brisk knock on the door. I took quick steps to reach the door before the third knock. I stood there for a second, trying to get my heart rate under control. Taking a deep breath, I smiled and pulled the door open.

Brandon stood there, shirt wrinkled, days' worth of beard on his face. He hadn't put any effort into his appearance for our dinner date. Granted we were just staying in, but he could have at least put on a fresh shirt and shaved.

He walked passed me with barely a glance in my direction. Closing the door, I reminded myself that he had been working all day on his Harley. He had been working on it for months, restoring it to its former glory.

He went to the refrigerator and looked inside. Reaching in, he pulled a beer out that I kept there for him, popped the top and took a long pull out of it before he turned my direction and acknowledged me.

"Hey babe. Looking good."

My heart fluttered at his compliment. He rarely complimented me anymore, just compared me to Camille. Smiling, I felt my shoulders relax a bit. "Thank you. Have a seat, I made your favorite stew."

His face went serious. "Do you really think you need stew? You look like you've gained a couple pounds."

"I'm still a little puffy from the augmentation and Brazilian lift. I don't think I've gained any weight."

"You wouldn't be puffy around the stomach." He sat and stared at me expectantly.

He is perfect for me. We are soul mates. He doesn't mean it when he says stuff like that. I told myself as I began serving his stew. I set the bowl down on the table in front of him, then grabbed the loaf of fresh baked bread and a bread knife. I sliced a chunk off the loaf and set it on a saucer next to his bowl.

I threw together a quick salad, with no dressing because it was too fatty. I sat down with my lettuce. Watching Brandon stuff his face, part of me wanted to say something to him about his comment on my weight. I knew that I was no where near what was considered obese. I shook my head and picked at my salad.

"Camille doesn't have problems with her weight. She exercises every day," Brandon said without looking up.

"Camille isn't perfect. Why don't you forget about her? We are together now." I dropped my fork, feeling defeated.

"She is a lot more perfect than you will ever be."

The words stung. It was as bad as a slap in the face. I stood up slowly as the anger began to boil in my stomach. "Why can't you just appreciate what you have?"

His eyes flashed as they met mine. "Why would I appreciate a surgery whore that can't even look beautiful with as much surgery and make up that you have?"

My anger possessed me. I slapped him, curving my fingers so that I would scratch him with my manicured nails. Blood welled up in the scratches. I stood frozen after I realized what I had done. The tension in the room was thick enough that I felt like it was trying to strangle me.

Brandon stood and flipped the table in one swift move. He came at me hands balled in fists. I backed away, but my heel caught on the rug causing me to fall backward. Brandon followed me to the ground. He put his weight on me to keep me from moving. His hand went around my throat squeezing hard enough to cut off my oxygen.

"Never touch me like that again," he said through gritted teeth.

I tried to nod agreement, but his hand was so tight on my neck, I couldn't move my head. His mouth crushed down on mine as his grip loosened. I melted into the kiss, wrapping my arms around his neck. He pulled back from the kiss, lifting his torso off of mine.

Grabbing my tank top, he pulled, ripping the front open exposing my breasts. His eyes lit up with hunger and desire. His mouth came down onto my left nipple. His tongue and swirled around it causing me to moan. His other hand covered my other breast, kneading and massaging it while worrying the other with his teeth.

I wrapped my legs around his hips, arching upward to rub myself against him. He groaned, pressing his hips against me. He switched breasts as he reached down to undo his pants. I reached my hands down to help him free himself.

As soon as he was free, he plunged into me hard enough to make me cry out. He slowly pulled out then slammed back into me. He moved faster and hard enough that I could only hang onto him and ride the waves of ecstasy.

After he finished, he stood up, pulling his pants back up. After he fixed himself, he reached a hand out and helped me stand as well. As soon as I was on my feet, his fist shot out, hitting me in the face. I was knocked backward by the impact, falling over the side of the couch. I cradled my eye with both hands staring up at him.

The hurt, shock, and humiliation were almost insurmountable. Tears welled up in my good eye, making Brandon just a blur. He got closer then dug that knife home.

"You will never be as good as Camille in any way shape or form. I'm just passing time with you until she sees the err of her ways and comes crawling back. And believe me baby, she will." He walked out, shutting the door loudly behind him.

Once he was gone, I let the tears fall. The whole Brandon situation told me one thing. I had to try harder to be perfect.

Chapter 37

I sat at the bar sipping the martini that had been bought for me while I waited for Brandon to show up. He was late as usual. I sighed then plucked the olive out of the glass, putting it in my mouth. I would probably sit here and get drunk on drinks that were given to me. I never had to buy a drink while at the bar.

I felt the warmth of a body behind me. Turning my head, I looked up into the intense eyes of a man. His blue eyes looked like the were penetrating all my defenses as they gazed into me. He smiled, making my stomach do a flip. I hadn't had that happen for a long time.

"Can I buy you a drink?" he asked. His voice was soft. It felt like he was speaking directly into my soul.

"Of course. Sex on the beach. Two cherries."

As he ordered my drink, I studied him. He was handsome. If I wasn't with Brandon, I would be all over him like a cheap suit. Thinking of Brandon, I pulled out my phone to check see if he messaged or anything. Nothing.

Anger flared through me. I was being stood up yet again. He would call me tomorrow with some pathetic excuse why he couldn't show up. It was probably Camille again. He was obsessed with the bitch even though he was with me. It seemed like he could never get her out of his mind completely. That was what most of our fights were about.

A glass of orangish pink liquid slid in front of me. I picked it up and took a sip. I loved the taste of Sex on the Beach. It was one drink that I could always over do it on. Looking back at the buyer, I smiled. "Perfect, thank you."

He settled onto the barstool next to me. He shifted so he was facing my direction. "What is a beauty queen like you doing all alone in a joint like this?"

"Thank you so much for the compliment, but I'm waiting for someone."

"If this 'someone' is going to stand someone like you up, they don't deserve you. No lady should be left alone unsupervised. She may get swept off her feet by someone else."

I smiled. There was something about this man that I was drawn to. The way he talked reminded me of the shows that took place back in the olden times.

"How about a dance? That way my night isn't completely wasted, and I get to say I danced with the most beautiful woman I've ever laid eyes on."

What would one dance hurt? Brandon would never know about the blue-eyed stranger. It wasn't like he was actually going to show up anyway. I had been stood up so many times by him, I was beginning to wonder if it was worth staying with him

"One dance would be lovely." I surprised myself with the words that had escaped my lips.

He stood, offering me his hand. Setting my drink down on the bar, I placed my hand in his and joined him on the dance floor. His moves were smooth, he flowed like water. I felt like a klutz dancing with him, but from the look on his face, he didn't seem to mind.

His hand slid around my waist, pulling me closer. We swayed to the music, not keeping with the rhythm of it, but made our own rhythm.

I couldn't pull my eyes away from him. I watched as he moved a little closer. His lips gently touched mine.

Suddenly he was jerked away from me. My eyes widened in surprise. There was Brandon, shoving the man to the ground.

"Who the fuck are you to touch my girl?" he demanded, glaring down at the man on the floor.

"If this is your girl as you say, maybe you shouldn't leave her sitting alone waiting on you. A real man never makes a lady wait for him. He waits for her."

Brandon's fist shot out and connected with the man's jaw. I noticed the bouncers heading our direction, so I placed a hand on his shoulder to get his attention. He jerked out of my grip and flung his hand backward to backhand me across the face. I covered my mouth and could taste blood.

"We are going to have to ask you to leave." The deep voice of the bouncer echoed through the now silent room.

Brandon turned toward him, rage on his face. He opened his mouth when I stepped between them. I made eye contact with Brandon. "It's okay. We're leaving." Lowering my voice so it was barely above a whisper I said, "Let's go home, Brandon."

He took me by the arm and pulled me from the dance floor. His grip kept tightening with each step we took. I glanced over my shoulder at the stranger, who was sitting on the dance floor, hand on jaw. His eyes connected with mine seconds before I was pulled out the door.

I was slammed against his truck. My head hit the side window causing stars to burst in my vision. He jerked on the passenger door, flinging it open, then shoved me into the cab. Slamming the door behind me, he stomped around and got into the driver seat.

He started the engine and put the truck into gear. We drove in silence on the way back to my apartment. I didn't know what to say. I had enjoyed the kiss, but it was just that—a kiss. It wasn't like I was fucking the dude. I sat silently, waiting for the eruption. I knew that he was like a timebomb ticking. I wasn't sure when he would go off, though. I just knew that it was coming.

He slammed the truck in park before he had fully stopped. I opened the door to climb out, but he was around the cab and yanking me down before I could put my foot on the ground. He had one hand around my arm, the other fisted in my hair. He half dragged, half pulled me into the apartment before tossing me on the couch.

"What the fuck were you thinking? You fucking bitch! How dare you cheat on me!" Brandon stalked back and forth across the room.

I attempted to get on my feet, but as soon as I was upright, he shoved me back down onto the couch. "I didn't cheat on you. It was just one dance with a someone I don't know."

"Lies!" he screamed. Spittle sprayed from his mouth at he lost his temper. "You were letting him put his hands all over you. You belong to me!"

I knew the second the eruption occurred. His face turned red as he raged around the room. He picked up a remote and launched it at the television. It went through the screen like the screen had been made from tissue paper. He turned on me, and I knew that it wasn't going to be pleasant.

When his fists started flying at me, I prayed that he wouldn't bruise my face and wouldn't do too much damage.

***

Sitting at my desk, I dabbed a little more concealer under my eye to keep the bruise from showing. Sighing, I stared at myself in the compact. I was beginning to not recognize myself anymore. I was a shell of the person that I used to be. I wasn't sure when I had begun to lose myself, but it was too late now.

The bell above the door jingled. I looked up to see the one and only Camille enter the office. My blood began to boil as I watched her waltz across the room. She was the one person that I could live without ever seeing or knowing. I knew that she didn't have an appointment with Doctor Manning, so I didn't know what she was doing here.

She leaned on the desk, giving me a perfect view of her ample cleavage. I looked up into her eyes. They glittered with something that reminded me of malice.

"I heard about your little tiff with Brandon. He told me all about it when he showed up at my apartment last night. In fact, I helped calm him down from it." The smile she gave me made me want to shove a pencil into her perfect eyeball.

"What are you doing here, Camille?" I put as much disinterest and boredom into my voice that I could. I didn't want her to know how she was affecting me.

"Just wanted to remind you who really is in control here. And if you know what is good for you, you won't piss Brandon off like that again. I would hate to see you having to use more than just make up to cover up the marks." She leaned closer, lowering her voice. "Remember, Brandon is mine."

She straightened and sashayed across the room back to the door. I could see the men in the room follow her with their eyes. She did have a nice ass, but her personality made her ugly. As she stepped out the door, I imagined myself stabbing her over and over until she bled out.

Janet approached the desk and leaned against it glancing down at me. "Who in the hell was that?"

"That," I sighed heavily. "is Camille."

"Wow. She looks like a complete and total cunt."

"She is. I wish she were dead," I said half to myself.

"Be careful what you wish for Dana. Sometimes they come true and not the way you expect."

Chapter 38

"David, my nose needs fixed. It's too big." I stuck my lip out.

"You're beautiful. You don't need any more work, just maintenance," Dr. Manning said as he filled the needle with the Restylane.

"Yes. I do. I need to be perfect. I also think that we should do some shaping on my jaw. It's too square. I want it to come to a gentle point."

I opened my mouth and watched as the needle came closer to my lips. He carefully gripped my lip to hold me still and pushed the needle in. My nipples hardened as the Restylane was injected into my lip. I loved the process of being beautified.

"You are already perfect, Dana." He repeated the process for my top lip.

If I were perfect, then Brandon wouldn't have done what he did. If I were perfect, then I wouldn't be able to pick out flaws as easily as I could. He handed me a mirror. I stared at my reflection, watching as my lips slowly began to swell. I loved to watch the progress of it, the creation of my perfect pouty lips. Dick sucking lips, as Brandon referred to them.

After the procedure was done and David again refused to do another surgery on me, I went back out to the desk. While I was doing paperwork, I looked up to find Janet staring at me.

"What's up, Janet?" I glanced back at my computer. I hoped she didn't stick around too long. Janet was nice but got on my nerves frequently.

"You okay? You look tired."

I looked back up at her, my heart beating faster. "What do you mean?"

"Your eyes are puffy and shadowed." She stuck her hands in the pockets of her scrubs. "It looks like you have been crying or something."

"I'm fine," I answered tersely while I dug in my drawer for a compact.

When my fingers wrapped around it, I flipped it open with my thumb. Looking into it, I could see where the make-up was starting to wear off and the bruise was showing. But she was right, I was seeing fine lines and wrinkles that I had never had before.

"Okay, I just wanted to make sure you are alright. We could talk if you need to."

"No thanks. I'm fine but thank you." I touched up my make up to ensure that the bruise wasn't visible.

The rest of the day went smoothly, but I couldn't get my mind off the wrinkles. I wasn't old enough for wrinkles. After locking the clinic doors, I went into Dr. Manning's office to find him sitting and looking through papers.

"Dr. Manning, I really need you to do something for me."

His eyes met mine with a gleam that made my stomach churn. "What's that, my dear Dana?"

"I need a lower eyelid lift."

He sighed, setting his papers down. Standing, he walked to me, resting his hands on my shoulders. "Dana, you don't need any more work done. This is getting redundant. If you don't let it rest, I may have to replace you. You are beautiful, and I enjoy having you, but there is nothing more I can do for you right now. Let all the incisions heal, think about it. Then if you still need it in three months, I will reconsider."

"I do need it," my voice sounded small, scared. If he wouldn't do the procedure on me, then I was lost. I had to have it done. I needed my eyes fixed. If I had wrinkles, I would never be perfect.

"Go home, rest, have a glass of wine. Take tomorrow and have a spa day, you can use the clinic credit card for it. Come back rejuvenated."

I nodded and left quietly. There was no way I was going to wait months for the surgery that I needed. I was certain that I could talk David into doing it for me. I just had to wait until the time was right. The drive home was quiet. I had the radio off so I could think of ways to convince David into the surgery.

Pulling up to my apartment, I was surprised and delighted to see Brandon's motorcycle sitting in the parking lot. Maybe he was going to apologize for hitting me. I got out of the car, the excitement of seeing him carrying me to the door. I opened it and stepped inside. It didn't look like there was anyone there.

Then I heard a rustling in the bedroom. I followed the sound, thinking he was going to surprise me. When I opened the door, I got a surprise all right. Camille was straddling Brandon, riding him on my bed. Her tits were bouncing as she moved up and down. His hands were on her tits, but his eyes were on me. There was a sadistic smile on his face.

I stood there for a full minute trying to absorb and process the scene before me. Indecision paralyzed me while I watched them fuck on my bed. Suddenly he flipped them, so she was on her back on the bed, their heads toward the foot of the bed, him on top of her. His eyes never left mine as he fucked her. Then he pulled out and came all over her and my bed.

I shook my head and slowly backed away from them. As I reached the living room, I heard him tell her she was perfect. I fled. I raced to my car, climbing in and turning the key. The engine roared to life as I shifted gears and peeled out of there.

I drove aimlessly, trying to get my emotions under control. He brought that skank to my house, my bed. He knew I would find them there, he enjoyed ripping my heart out. I'd show him. I'd show everyone. The longer I drove, the angrier I became.

I found myself parked in front of the clinic staring at the building. I got out of the car and headed inside without thought to what I was doing or going to do once inside. I let myself in and made my way back to the examination rooms.

I turned and went to the supply cabinet. Unlocking it, I took a scalpel out along with a few other tools that I would need. Going back into the examination rooms, I stood at the full-length mirror with an equipment tray beside me. I gently lined up the materials then picked the scalpel back up.

With trembling hands, I brought it to my face to make a small incision next to my eye. I had watched enough videos and Dr. Manning perform enough surgeries, I was confident I could do it. As I began to slice, the pain was immediate.

Fuck! I forgot the numbing agent. I gritted my teeth and continued to work on my eye. There was a loud bang and I jumped. The scalpel jerked, slicing my face, then plunging into my eyeball. I could feel warm liquid gushing down my face onto my hands. I screamed in agony.

The door flew open, a security guard stood there staring at me. I turned toward him, and as I watched him, darkness encroached my vision. I began to lose my balance. As I started to fall, I heard my name called out and everything went black.

Next thing I heard were sirens. I tried to open my eyes, but my left eye was coved with something heavy and my right eye didn't want to cooperate. I moved my head, trying to get myself aware enough to open my eyes.

"Miss Lawson, you need to stay still. We are getting you to the hospital. You are going to be okay." The voice was warm and reassuring. A warm hand rested on my shoulder.

I let the darkness overcome me once again. When I woke up the second time, my left eye wouldn't open, but my right eye did with only a little difficulty. I looked around to see I was in a hospital bed. The beeps and whirrs of machines were like nails on a chalkboard.

A doctor walked in shortly after I had opened my eye. He walked to my side where I didn't have to strain to see him. His smile was sad which caused unease to lump in my stomach. I didn't know what he was going to tell me, but I knew it wasn't good.

"Ms. Lawson, I'm Doctor Geno. I have been overseeing you since you came in earlier this evening. I am sorry, but we couldn't save your eye." He placed his hand on top of mine.

My eye? I took my other hand and carefully lifted it to my face. It was covered in bandages. My eye socket dipped in instead of having the roundness of my eyeball in it.

"My eye. My eye is gone?" I stuttered, overwhelmed with emotion.

"Yes, I'm sorry. We had to stitch up the cuts. I'm not sure how bad the scaring will be. Hopefully it won't be too extensive and over time will become less noticeable. Before you are released from the hospital we will be inserting a prosthetic eye into the socket. We are having one made to match your eye color."

My heart pounded in my chest and the beeping of the machines increased. I was going to be scarred? That was more than I could bear. Not only was I going to be deformed, I was going to be half blind and my eye would be fake. People with fake eyes always looked funny, the eye never moved and was creepy. My heart sank. I didn't say anything else to him while he was there.

A week later, I was released from the hospital. I was on several medications including anti-depressants and pain killers. I didn't feel anything. Being numb was better than hurting. When I got home, I went inside to find no one was there. I was relieved I was finally alone.

Ignoring the texts, calls, and other messages, I let the darkness consume me. I was supposed to have a nurse coming to check on me and help me adjust to living with one eye. I didn't know how they were supposed to help me, but I didn't want to see her, either.

I looked at my phone to see a text from Brandon saying he was going to be over to talk. I really didn't want to see him. Instead of answering him, I decided to draw a bath and soak in the tub while I tried to deal with everything that had happened.

I set up candles around the tub, lighting them to help relax me. The mirror and my reflection taunted me. I hadn't looked at myself since the accident. With shaking hands, I stared at the mirror as I slowly unwrapped the bandages from my head and face.

I was horrified by the creature staring back at me. I looked like Frankenstein's monster. The wound was red and swollen. The stitches were jagged. It hadn't cut straight. The sutures went to my lower eye lid. The eye stared lifelessly ahead. I blinked, my eyelashes sticking on the edge of the wound. My fingers traced the incision. My hand dropped to my side.

I shook my head and walked out of the bathroom. I went into the kitchen, grabbing the chef's knife from my butcher block. I went back into the bathroom, setting the knife on the edge of the tub. I shut the door, locking it. Turning, I watched myself in the full-length mirror as I stripped my clothes off.

I stared at my reflection. My body looked like a shell. An ugly, imperfect shell that needed to be taken care of. I climbed into the tub. The water was on the edge of being too hot, and it burned my skin as I got in. Sighing, I leaned back, closing my eyes.

You will never be good enough. You are ruined for the rest of your life. You are an ugly freak. No one will love you now. Brandon was never going to love you like you wanted him to, the voice in my head taunted. I went through my list of imperfections yet again.

Without thinking about it, I picked up the knife and studied it. Then I lowered it to my left breast. I pressed until I broke and sliced the skin. The pain was fleeting. It was like I was being released. I did it to my right breast. Then my stomach, legs, arms, face, and neck. Then I cut my wrists.

Watching the blood come out of the wounds and mix with the water was mesmerizing. I watched as I felt the strength ebb out of me like my blood. Sticking my index finger into the wound of my left wrist, I let the blood cover my finger. Then I wrote on the wall of the bathroom.

I heard the knocking on the door as everything grew darker. I closed my eyes and let the darkness overcome me as there was a crash in the other room. I had no more concerns.

When I was found moments later, Brandon received my final message. On the wall above my bleeding and rapidly cooling body was the phrase: I'm sorry.

Chapter 39

Next thing I knew, I was watching the scene unfold before me. I was no longer in my body. Brandon pulled me out of the tub, then cradled my cold body in his lap. He held my body close, tears streaming down his face.

"Babe, wake up," he murmured into my wet hair. "Don't leave me, I love you."

Disdain washed over me as the anger burned in my stomach. He wanted to claim that he loved me, yet he had treated me like a piece of shit. He had hit me, cheated on me, stolen from me, and only God knew what else. Now he wanted to act like he loved me? I began to tremble with rage. I wanted to hurt him. To get him away from my body.

The lights flickered. I gripped the knife handle tighter in my hands. I hadn't realized I was still holding it. Raising it, I moved toward him slowly. The idea of the knife going into his heart thrilled me to the core. As I raised the knife above my head, his head came up. He gently placed my body on the floor and walked from the room.

That's when I heard it. The sirens. Next thing I knew the bathroom was a frenzy of activity. People rushing in and out. Paramedics were working on my body, trying to get me to breathe again. I just watched the scene before me with disinterest.

The police and coroner showed up within minutes of the paramedics. I heard them pronounce me dead, then pictures of the scene were taken. I blinked as the flash blinded me momentarily. I was shocked to realize that it didn't affect me like it used to.

My body was loaded onto a stretcher and taken away. I followed it as far as the living room. I noticed Brandon sitting on the couch speaking to a police officer. He brushed tears from his eyes, and he nodded his head.

"Yeah, I was worried about her when she didn't answer her phone. She always answers. So, I came over. When I got here, I couldn't get the door open. She had it locked, but I used my key, but she had it chained too. I had to kick it in. That's when I found her." His breath hitched as spoke.

"How was the body positioned when you got here?" The police officer asked.

"She was in the tub. Her left hand was hanging over the edge of the tub with blood dripping from her finger tips. Her eyes were closed. I, fuck, I can't do this. I'm sorry. Seeing her was so surreal. So hard."

"I understand, but I have a few more questions I need you to answer." Brandon looked up at the police officer. "Tell me about the room. Did you see what caused the wounds? How about any messages from her?"

He shook his head. "I didn't notice a weapon or anything. I don't know what she used to make those cuts. The words 'I'm sorry' were written on the wall."

"What does that mean, do you know?"

"Man, I'm not sure."

"Okay. That is all I have for now. Do you have someone to drive you home? You aren't in any condition to drive after this shock." The officer stood.

Brandon stood as well. "Yeah, Camille is on her way over."

My eyes narrowed at the mention of Camille. I still didn't want that bitch in my apartment, whether I was there or not. There was no way over my dead body that she was going to step foot in this place. Within minutes, I heard her talking to someone outside. I watched as she walked up to the door. When she stepped over the threshold, the anger flooded me again.

Running to the door, I shoved my out as hard as I could, causing her to stumble backward. Brandon raced out to her while I glared at the pair. I watched them walk away, his arm around her shoulders. The anger burned deep in my soul. I decided then that I would see her as flawed as I had been, but first, I needed to get into Brandon's head.

***

Brandon was drinking himself into a stupor. I watched idly as he would wake up in the morning and immediately begin drinking. I felt a slight twinge of satisfaction that he was so fucked up from my death that he turned to the alcohol. He had a drinking problem before we met but had stopped. My death made him pick back up the bottle.

He settled into the couch, bottle in hand, staring aimlessly at the wall. I was behind him. Leaning down I whispered into his ear. "Brandon."

He shot straight up, looking around the room wildly. I couldn't suppress the grin that grew on my face. I knew that he could hear me. This was going to be fun.

I tormented him throughout the day. Finally, he settled down in bed to sleep. I reclined on the bed next to him. He tossed and turned. I watched, feeling nothing. He had caused me many nights of tossing and turning.

I began to whisper in his ear. I was reminding him of what a shitty person he had been to me and how much he enjoyed our time together. I ran my hands down his body, hating the fact that I couldn't actually touch him anymore. His body reacted to my hands moving over him. I watched as he moaned in his sleep.

After bringing him tormenting dreams, erotic memories, and the reminder of my death, I gave him one last message. Walking to his bedroom mirror, I reached out and wrote the words I'm sorry. I wasn't sure if he would see it, but I hoped he would.

213

My thoughts narrowed to my next target. This time, I wasn't going to just play with it. I was going to watch the light leave her eyes. I closed my eyes and smiled. I was going to go after Camille next.

I followed Camille around, watching her every move. I tried to get into her head. I wasn't sure if she knew I was there because she never mentioned me or acknowledged she wasn't alone. However, she wasn't sleeping well, especially since I kept waking her up.

The one thing that made me happy was the fact that Brandon hadn't visited. She hadn't seen him since she dropped him off at his place after finding my body. I couldn't wait until they were in the same room together. I was going to have a lot of fun then.

I stood in the bathroom with her while she showered and the bathroom quickly filled with steam. I rolled my eyes as she began to hum softly to herself. The bitch didn't know how to carry a tune. I smiled when the mirror fogged over. That's when I decided that I would give her a message, so she knew she wasn't alone. I took my finger and pressed it to the mirror. Carefully, I wrote the last message I had given to Brandon as well. I'm sorry.

When she climbed out of the shower, she put a towel to her face to dry it off. I grinned as I watched the towel come down. She was facing the mirror, and I could see the color drain out of it. Her eyes widened, and she looked around wildly.

Focusing my energy, I made the lights flicker right before the bulb burst. She screamed as glass fell from the ceiling. She pulled the door open and rushed into her room. I made sure to stay close behind her. Standing in front of her vanity, she attempted to shake glass out of her hair. I stood behind her left shoulder, watching her face in the mirror.

Camille's eyes met mine. From the widening of her eyes, it was obvious that she could see me. She turned quickly, confusion flashing across her face. Her brows drew together as she searched the room. When she turned back to the mirror she screamed.

On the mirror was a bloody handprint. Blood rolled down the mirror. She backed away from the mirror passing right through me. Her back hit the corner of the room, and she slid down to the floor and began to cry.

I tortured Camille to the point of losing her sanity. I would back off long enough for her to think that she had been just having nightmares, and I would go at her again. She wasn't sleeping. I enjoyed every moment of it. It felt justified.

Then, what I had waited for happened. Brandon showed up. He walked in the apartment, staggering from side to side. From the looks of him, he had been on a bender for a while now. Brandon plopped down on the couch, slouching down. He held his bottle between his knees with two fingers.

"Brandon, I'm so glad you're here. I have had the most horrible week." She stopped short, staring at him. "Oh my God! Are you drunk?"

He shrugged with one shoulder. "What if I am?"

"You promised you would quit drinking."

"Bitch. I do what I want. You don't know what I've been through."

I smirked. They thought they were going through hell now, just wait. I'd show them hell.

"You aren't the only one with problems, dick. My bathroom lightbulb just exploded all over me. Now there is writing on my fucking mirror." She took a deep breath, then continued. "I don't know what is going on, but it has to stop. I can't do this anymore."

He looked over at her. It was a look I had seen many times. Contempt. He stood slowly, then walked toward her until they were toe to toe. "You want to know what is going on? We pushed her to kill herself, now she is haunting us. I told you I should have walked away when we got back together. I don't understand why you didn't want that. Why did we have to flaunt it in her face?"

"She needed to know that she had lost the battle. She wasn't the princess she always thought she was."

His hand went around her neck, then began to squeeze. Her face colored red. I slowly walked closer, fascinated by the scene unfolding before me. I wasn't the only one he hurt apparently.

I stood directly behind him. Pleasure flowed through me as he stopped the oxygen from reaching her lungs.

"Yes, do it. Kill her, baby." My voice was barely above a whisper, but I knew he heard me anyway.

As she turned a mottled red color, he released her and smashed his mouth against hers. She wrapped her arms around his neck as he lifted her. He walked toward the bedroom, holding her against him.

I glared. Anger flushed through me. I followed as they only removed the necessary clothing. When he pushed into her, she moaned causing my vision to go red. I could only think one thing. Kill. I let the anger take over me.

My fingers tightened around the knife that I didn't remember having. Stalking them, I sat on the edge of the bed as the two fucked. Then an idea sprang to mind. I had seen enough horror movies to know that ghosts could possess people. And I would do anything to feel Brandon's cock in me once more.

I directed all of my energy toward her. There was almost a sucking sensation. When I opened my eyes again, I was underneath Brandon. It worked. I had successfully possessed the bitch. I felt powerful. Possessing someone was an amazing experience.

I could feel Brandon pumping into me, or well Camille. As he started to climax, I lighted my upper half and bit his ear. My nails dug into his back as he shuddered. I began to shudder as well. My hands left his back, grabbing the sheets as my release overwhelmed me.

He let his weight press against me in exhaustion. He still twitched inside of me, his breath puffing on my neck. "Baby girl, you are perfect."

The word perfect brought me back to reality. I stared at him. "You told me I would never be perfect."

He raised his head to look into my eyes. Confusion flashed across his face. Rolling off me, he dropped off the side of the bed. When he sprang an instant later, he shook his head. "I've never told you that."

"Yes, you did. I remember it quite clearly. You said I would never be as perfect as Camille."

The color drained from his face. "Dana?"

I smiled. "What are you talking about? I'm Camille. Come back to bed."

I patted the bed beside me. When he didn't move, I glared at him. "Come back to bed, now."

"You said. How did you know–"

While he stared at me, eyes wild, I felt my fingers wrap around the knife again. I picked it up then turned my attention back to him. "Oh, Brandon. We could have been perfect together. But I guess–"

I slit Camille's throat, as deep and hard as I could. The knife hit bone. Her head rolled back and next thing I knew, I was on the bed beside her once again. Blood was spurting everywhere. Brandon stood horrified.

As he gawked, frozen in fear, I stood, knife in hand and walked over to him. It was obvious he didn't understand what happened, and he wasn't expecting what I was about to do next. I stood less than an arm's length away and plunged the knife into his chest.

As his life seeped out of his body, I leaned forward, pressing a kiss to his cheek. "I'm sorry."

Chapter 40

I wasn't sure how much time had passed since I killed Brandon and Camille. I had roamed aimlessly since then. I felt like I had no purpose and wasn't sure what I was supposed to do. I occasionally killed people that were prettier than I had been in life, but it didn't have much thrill to it, until I found myself at Doctor Manning's office. I spent my time there, making equipment malfunction so it scarred or damaged people, so they were no longer perfect.

I would cause the computer to mess up, deleted appointments, added extra appointments. The new administrative assistant was so pretty that jealousy flared up inside me. I would do things to freak her out. One night, it was just her in the office doing some paperwork. She slowly typed out whatever it was she was working on.

There was a pencil sitting on the desk that had been freshly sharpened. I couldn't take my eyes of it. The phone rang, my attention shifting to her when I heard her talk.

"I'm adjusting to the position well, thanks for asking. I don't know when I get to leave, I have to finish the reports and do some filing before I get to go home. Yes, I replaced the woman that died. Yeah. Suicide. Her name was Dana Lawson. No. From my understanding, she had an addiction to cosmetic surgeries. Doctor Manning was going to fire her. The only reason he kept her around was that she put out."

My eyes narrowed at the last statement. I didn't care what else she said, but she wasn't going to speak about me that way. The words I'm sorry appeared over and over on the computer screen, flooding it with the message. The pencil shot up, impaling her in the eye. She screamed, dropped the phone and clutched the pencil.

Suddenly I was behind her. Losing her eyesight in the one eye wasn't enough. I wanted her to suffer for what she had said. She had called me a whore. My grip tightened on the knife I always seemed to have nearby, wanting to plunge it into her heart.

Instead, I slit her wrists. From her perspective, her wrists just split open for reasons unknown and no explanations. I watched as she bled to death sitting in her office chair. What I wasn't aware of was that killing her would be the catalyst of what happened next.

***

After killing the administrative assistant, cameras were installed in the lobby to record all coming and goings of the office. Her death had been deemed as suspicious since there was a pencil embedded in her eye.

People, including police, had been in and out of the office. Her death was unexplainable. She wasn't depressed and never had a history of being suicidal. They had finger printed everything, but nothing out of the ordinary showed up.

I decided that I was going to go after Doctor Manning as well. If it weren't for him refusing the eye surgery, I wouldn't have tried it myself. If I hadn't done it myself, then I wouldn't have become so ugly that I couldn't live. I would have been perfect.

I rearranged his office, making sure that he knew that he wasn't alone. I would lean over his shoulder and try to lick his neck. I would throw things across the room. One time, I managed to cut him with a scalpel. It was the same one that I had mutilated myself with. I wasn't sure how I could tell, I just knew.

It had gotten to the point where the good doctor was too scared to be by himself in the office. Everytime something unexplainable happened, he would check the surveillance cameras. The interesting thing was the cameras didn't work when I was doing stuff. There would be static on the screen.

It was after the scalpel incident that Doctor Manning did something I hadn't expected. He called in a psychic. I couldn't believe it. He had never given them any credence. He claimed psychics were phonies and full of hog wash. I overheard him scheduling the psychic to come in, so I knew it was true.

He showed up after the office closed for the evening. Doctor Manning entered with him. I didn't know what it was about the man, the psychic, but I couldn't take my eyes off him. He wasn't what I would have pictured as a clairvoyant.

He was tall and looked like he lifted weights frequently. His hair was sandy brown and his skin sun-kissed. His blue eyes were alert and observant. It looked like he could see everything. Absolutely mesmerizing.

"Thanks for coming, Mr. Bucco," Doctor Manning said, shaking his hand.

"Not a problem. But please call me Bastian. Mr. Bucco is my father." The man smiled then released his hand. Subtly, his hand went to his side, and he wiped it on his jeans.

That couldn't be the psychic. They didn't look like they just walked out of the gym, or like he could snap the doctor in half like a twig. They were pale, introverted. This guy was definitely not that. He was probably the popular guy when he was in school and the man that all the women wanted to spread their legs for.

There was something about the man that seemed very familiar. I just couldn't place my finger on it. I stared at him while he studied the room. Where had I seen him before? It was going to drive me crazy. I wanted to know why I knew him. I felt a connection there.

"So, tell me what has been going on here. Just facts, not your opinion. I don't want your thoughts clouding mine," Bastian said.

Doctor Manning began to tell him what happened. He believed that things started the night I tried to perform the surgery on myself. That was the first instance he spoke about. I had to swallow a snort. This man was clueless. While he continued, I noticed Bastian kept looking my direction out of the corner of his eye. I was certain he couldn't see me, but I stayed in the shadows just in case.

"Then my administrative assistant died mysteriously at the desk over there. When I found her the next morning, she had a pencil sticking out of her eye, and her wrists were slit open."

One dark eyebrow rose. "Interesting. But I don't think you've had a ghost here for long. The energy doesn't feel like its been here a while. It feels, I don't know how to describe it—fresh I guess. The spirit is angry."

I did snort then. Angry was an understatement. I was pissed. I wanted everyone to suffer like I had. I couldn't stand the thought of them reaching perfection when I never could. Bastian's head turned my direction, and his eyes bore into mine.

I couldn't look away from him. I didn't want to. I stared back, waiting for him to say something or give away my presence. Instead he turned his attention back toward Doctor Manning. They walked through the office together, Manning describing to Bastian the different things that happened in each room as they entered it.

When they reached the office, Bastian stopped, his eyes narrowing. I watched the from the corner of the room as he stared at the desk. His frowned deepened, and I became curious as to what he was thinking. It was the first time I could remember that I actually wanted to know what another being was thinking.

I stepped closer, cocking my head as I watched him. I couldn't read his body language or face. He had a good mask in place. Then he turned suddenly, almost knocking over Doctor Manning in the process. "What has happened in this room?"

Doctor Manning shook his head as he straightened his suit. "Nothing has happened in here."

"You're lying to me. What happened in this room. There is an energy in here that needs explained."

With a shrug Manning looked around the room. "I really can't think of anything that happened in here. It's just my office. The only thing

I can think of is stuff has been rearranged and in disarray. But there haven't been any tragedies in here."

"I see," Bastian crossed his arms, then turned to slowly walk around the room, studying it.

"He's not going to tell you that he would fuck me in here," I whispered. I was sitting on the desk watching the exchange. Bastian whipped around, facing me. Color rose up his face, but only for an instant. He didn't speak, but I knew he could hear me. "He also won't tell you that he traded plastic surgery for sexual favors. I would suck his dick for a lip plumping. It would ruin his reputation and career if that came out."

He walked toward the desk, bringing his hand to rest inches from my thigh. I watched as his eyes held a light I hadn't seen in anyone else's before. He seemed to be lost in time. After a couple moments, he turned his head slightly, eyes connecting with mine.

"David, can I have a moment to myself in here? I want to go through and see what I can pick up on my own. If you will wait outside in the main hallway, I will come get you when I'm done."

Doctor Manning Nodded and slipped out of the room. Once we were alone, I waited. If I could hold my breath, I would.

"Are you Dana?" His voice was so soft it was like velvet rubbing across my skin.

Biting my bottom lip, I nodded once.

"Why are you here? I mean why are you haunting a plastic surgeon."

"It's his fault."

He frowned. "What do you mean?"

"If he would have done the procedure that I asked for, I wouldn't have had to go to the extreme that I did. If, for once, he would have just done it without strings or trying to be in control, I would still be me. I would be perfect. But I'm not. Look at me."

"I am looking at you, Dana. I see a sad, angry, beautiful spirit. You remind me of a beauty queen. There is no reason to hold on to that anger."

My eyebrows shot up. Recognition flashed through me. The man from the bar. I wondered if he remembered me. "Look who's talking. You are the one that was getting angry when you had the vision of him bending me over this very desk so I could get that but lift that I wanted."

"I wasn't angry, I was—" he cut off, taking a deep breath.

"Were what?" I slid off the desk and stepped up to him, so I would have been pressed against him if I was human still.

He shook his head. "It doesn't matter. What does matter is that you are hurting people, and it needs to stop. You need to leave them alone."

I ran my hand down his chest, wishing I could truly feel his body. I had never been so confident during my life. I didn't have anything to lose now. When my hand moved over the zipper of his jeans I heard him release a shaky breath.

Lifting on my tiptoes, I pressed my lips to his ear. "Not until I'm ready. I won't stop. He needs to be punished."

I stepped away and smiled when I saw the bulge in his pants. I had affected him, and he would surely think of me later. I turned and headed toward the door.

"Dana." He stopped me as I made it to the door.

I turned my head and looked at him over my shoulder. "Bastian."

"Let's talk about this."

"Do we have more to say?" I asked, batting my eyelashes.

"You know we do."

I turned back toward him. "I'm listening."

***

It turned out that Bastian was as fascinated with me as I was him. He made several trips to the office to see me, under the guise of helping David get rid of the spirit. He told him that it was a vengeful spirit, and he was trying to help cross me over. I laughed at that. He didn't want to get rid of me. We both knew it.

Things wouldn't be able to continue the way they were though. He was going to have to either confess that he didn't want to get rid of me or let me kill David, either way, I knew that the end of this was coming to pass.

During our visits I had begun to open up to him. I told him some of the darkest secrets I kept in my soul. Things that I hadn't told anyone. I knew if he told anyone, no one would believe him. They would have him committed to a psych ward.

I knew that he was beginning to see things my way, so I figured it was time to persuade him into helping me.

"Bastian, you know David is going to start asking questions soon, right?"

"Yeah, I know. I will tell him I can't help him with his problem." His eyes met mine. "I want to help you with yours though."

I felt the smile tug on my lips. "Okay, this is what we will do."

I outlined the plan I had been coming up with for a while. Bastian agreed to it, and said he would make it happen.

"When this is done, I know somewhere you can go, Dana. Somewhere you can be safe. You can roam freely." Bastian smiled at me.

"We will talk about that later. Now go tell David that you are going to have me expelled from the building."

He left to talk to David and set things up. I couldn't help but feel happy for the first time since I had died. He was helping me get my revenge then maybe I would be free. I would be able to rid the world of the perfect people and people in love.

Later that night, he had the waiting room set up like a scene out of a scary movie. There were candles lit around the room. He also had drawn on the floor with a dark substance. I wasn't sure what kind it was, but I was pretty sure it was blood. I didn't recognize the symbols either. I stood to the side of the room, watching him set it up and explain to David what was going to happen.

"You will stand in the middle of this symbol here. It will lure the ghost out. It wants to hurt you, but you will be protected. Once it is out in the open, I will say the incantation that traps it in this box. Then I will make sure to get it to move on and you can be worry free."

"Thank God. Took you long enough to come up with this," David muttered under his breath.

"Well, I had to make sure it was going to work. This spirit is so angry that it can be unpredictable." He straightened, looking around David at me. "Let's begin."

Bastian began to chant something that sounded like tongues that was supposed to lure me to him. I stood watching, one eyebrow cocked. Then I nodded at him slowly. He pulled the knife from the back of his jeans where he had hidden it earlier.

He plunged it into the doctor's back. He leaned close to David and whispered, "Dana says hello."

Letting go of the knife and body, Bastian picked up the box and began a different chant. Everything changed. There was a tugging and I was pulled toward him and the box he held. He smiled at me.

"You will be free soon. I promise. And you will love where I am taking you."

Like that, I had been betrayed yet again.

Chapter 41

When I was finally released out of the soul box, I was pissed. I looked around the room that I was in, searching for Bastian. I knew that he had been the one that trapped me, and I planned on peeling the skin off his bones. He had no right to trap me in there.

Bastian stood by the door of the room, watching me. The expression on his face was wary. He didn't move, just kept his eyes on me.

"Why?" I demanded.

"You will be happy here. You can roam the house freely and there are others. You won't be alone."

"I don't want to be around others. I want to do as I fucking please."

"Just give it a chance. You will enjoy this place."

I attempted to step toward him, but I was stopped by an invisible force. I tried again, and it was like going against a wall.

"I knew you'd be mad, so I put a barrier up before releasing you. It was for my protection. Don't worry, it will fade in a couple hours. I'll be back in a few days. I want to give you a chance to calm down."

He slipped out of the room, closing the door with a click. I glared at the door, uncertainty filling me. It had been a while since I had felt that way.

The moment the barrier broke, I could tell. There was an audible pop, then the pressure vanished. I began to roam the room as I took in my surroundings.

The room was beautiful. I would have loved it when I was alive. It was decorated in shades of burgundy. The curtains and bedspread were satin. A chandelier hung over the bed with lights dancing from the crystals.

I noticed a door to the left. Upon further inspection, I saw that it was a bathroom. It was just as extravagant as the bedroom. The walls were made from tiny black and white pearl tiles. The bathtub caught my eye. It was the size of a hot tub. It was glorious.

As much as I didn't want to admit it, Bastian was probably right. I would like it here. I went back into the bedroom and settled on the bed while I waited for him to come back to me. I knew he said it would be a couple of days, but time seemed to pass differently now that I was dead. I just sat there, waiting.

I heard noises outside of my room, but I never ventured out to see what it was. I stayed on the bed, waiting. I was getting impatient waiting for Bastian to return. I hadn't expected to actually miss him or want him to come back.

There were heavy footsteps outside my door. It sounded like someone was having hard time walking. Curiosity got the best of me, so I slipped to the door and peeked into the hallway. There was a big man walking like a zombie down the hallway. He had a burlap sack over his head and was covered in blood. He ambled slowly down the hallway like he had to be somewhere.

I couldn't help but watch as it rounded the corner of the hall. Shaking my head, I returned to the bed. I wasn't sure what I was doing here or what this place was, but it was intriguing. I was going to have to ask Bastian when he came back to visit. If he came back.

When the door opened, I sat up and watched to see who was entering my domain. My heart, if I had one still, sped up with the excitement of a visitor. His head popped around the edge of the door, and I couldn't suppress a smile.

He grinned back. "Are you still angry?"

"I'm always angry, but do I still plan on peeling the skin off your body? No. You're safe for the moment."

He let out a breath and walked into the room shutting the door behind him. He reminded me of the eager teenagers I dated back in high school. He fidgeted, staring at me.

Raising an eyebrow, I crossed my arms over my chest. "Are you going to just stand there, staring, or are you going to come sit with me?"

He moved to the other side of the bed and sat down on the edge. He looked like he was ready to spring. I didn't understand where the nervousness was coming from. He wasn't anxious around me at the clinic. He turned so he was facing me but didn't try to sit fully on the bed. He remained at the edge.

"Are you okay?"

"Yeah. I feel guilty for bringing you here. I shouldn't have but—" He cut himself off.

"But what?" I felt a tension go through me. It was an odd sensation since I didn't have a body or nerves anymore. "You are about to piss me off, aren't you?"

"I was paid to bring you here." I watched as his Adam's apple bobbed as he swallowed.

"Excuse me?"

"This house belongs to Cyrus Bane. He, well. Umm. He collects spirits."

"Collects spirits?" I felt my anger rising. I wasn't sure about his meaning, but I knew it wasn't good.

"He has a raison d'être, and he needs thirteen ghosts in order to achieve it. He has been watching for the perfect ones. You fit."

"Why are you telling me this now?"

"I like you, Dana. I can't get you out of my head and thought you deserve the truth. I have thought about you since the first time I met you in that dingy bar."

"You did recognize me! I knew it. Tell me about this house. What the hell was that thing out there?" Since he was opening up, I decided I was going to get the answers I had wondered about.

"This house is the Black Zodiac. It was designed to house the thirteen spirits to open the vortex of power. Cyrus plans on harnessing the power released from the Zodiac." He paused, staring at the wall like he saw something I couldn't. "What you saw is called the Butcher. His name is Jimmy Demelo. He had gambling issues and got in over his head, so to speak."

"I see. What else is here, or is it just me and Jimmy?"

"You are the sixth. There is the Golden Boy, you know about The Butcher, then there is The Cheerleader, Scorched Lover, and The Mangled Captain."

There were six of us. That was interesting as well. He had almost half of the ghosts he needed for this vortex power thing. I frowned. "Everyone has nicknames. What's mine?"

Bastian fidgeted around like he was uncomfortable. I stared at him, waiting for him to tell me. His eyes finally landed on mine and stayed there. I could see the uncertainty and discomfort as he wrestled with revealing it. He swallowed before he spoke. "You are known as The Beauty Queen."

"Why?"

"You were beautiful when you were alive. You still are. You were obsessed with your looks. There is talk that you could get whatever you wanted by a simple look. Men were powerless against your beauty."

I half-shrugged. It suited me fine. The only thing was, I wasn't flawless. That was why I was dead. I couldn't be perfect even though I tried. I still wanted perfection, but I was going to have to find another way to get it.

There was a lot of information to digest, and I would ponder over it when I was alone. I turned toward him so that I was facing him fully. I reached out and ran a hand down the front of his shirt. "I don't want to talk about this anymore. I miss being able to feel skin under my touch. The warmth of another body."

His breathing increased. "I bet you do."

"I just want to be held. I've thought of you as well. You are always on my mind. I don't know how long it has been since we met, but I have thought of you constantly."

"Me too."

"You are different then the others. I can tell. You wouldn't have been like Brandon or Doctor Manning."

"You're right. I am different. I always have been. I've always been a loner. No one wanted to hang out with the weird kid that was abused by his alcoholic parents and could see ghosts."

"Tell me about it."

"I was caught speaking to a ghost my freshman year of high school by Royce Anderson. He beat the ever-living shit out of me for it. After that, I was ostracized for having an 'imaginary friend'. High school was hell. I was beat at home then again at school, so I never had a reprieve."

My heart went out to the boy that Bastian was. He obviously was scarred from his childhood. I couldn't imagine what he had gone through during those times. I wanted to hug him and tell him everything would be okay, even though I knew it wouldn't help fix the past.

"We can get even if you'd like."

Bastian's brows drew together in a frown. "What do you have in mind, Dana?"

"I could kill everyone that tortured you," I shrugged. It wouldn't be hard to do that. In fact, I'd enjoy it.

"Don't worry about it. They are all gone."

"How?"

"My parents are gone. They were killed by carbon monoxide poisoning. Royce," he paused while he snorted out a laugh. "Royce was in an accident. They say he somehow fell out of his moving car and was dragged under it."

The look on his face had me wondering what had actually happened to them, but I wasn't in the mood to press it. If he wanted me to know, he would tell me. I watched his face as he remembered those times. Then he turned his head slowly and made eye contact with me.

"The best part? Royce is here. I brought him here too. He fit the profile of what Cyrus wanted. He is trapped in this house. I have a pendant that keeps him from me, so he can't be anywhere that I am. When I'm in a room, he isn't able to enter it."

"Sounds like you got the revenge that you deserve."

"Yes." He grinned. "I wish I could kiss you."

"Close your eyes," I instructed. As he closed his eyes, I leaned forward and pressed my lips to his. My tongue glided across his and his eyes shot open.

"How did you do that?" he asked. His voice was husky.

"I just did this." I leaned over and pressed my mouth against his again.

When I pulled back, he touched his lips. "My lips are cold and tingling. That's odd."

"Let me show you what else I can do." I pushed at him. He leaned back on the bed.

I straddled his legs above the knees. I ran my hands down his torso to his navel. He shivered. My hands slid underneath his shirt to feel his bare skin.

He reached down, yanking his t-shirt off in one swift motion. He then unbuttoned his jeans, releasing himself. He was stunning.

I sat back, admiring the beauty of him. There were scars all over his upper half, but they didn't take away from the magnificence of him. Leaning forward, I ran my tongue down his body. He inhaled a sharp breath as I gently bit down on his pec.

Using my hand, I stroked him, wishing that I could feel the warmth of his body. He groaned and began to move his hips in time with my hand. As he began to peak, I stopped working him with my hand. I slowly took him into my being. I moved gently at first, then began to speed up. We hit a rhythm where we were moving together as ecstasy built. Looking into his eyes, I could tell he was about to climax, and I let go of what control I had left.

Once spent, Bastian panted while trying to catch his breath. I watched him as he tried to control his heart rate. His eyes met mine. "You are amazing."

"You mean for a ghost?" I cocked an eyebrow.

"No. You are simply amazing."

If my heart was still beating, it would have skipped. It was the first time I could remember someone thought I was amazing.

Chapter 42

I noticed that when Bastian wasn't around, the anger and urge to kill would increase. He tried to come visit daily, but sometimes he was prevented from seeing me. I decided that I was going to search out this Cyrus Bane that Bastian had told me about.

I found Cyrus in the library, pouring over a book. He looked up as soon as I stepped into the room. I wasn't sure how he knew I was there. Most people couldn't see or hear me, and I doubted that Cyrus was an exception to that rule.

"Ahh, here she is. The ever-elusive Beauty Queen, Dana Lawson. I imagined you prettier and less bloody looking. I was told that you were the most beautiful soul that has ever been seen."

I felt my anger spreading through me like a wild fire. The knife reappeared in my hand, and I felt my grip tightening on it.

Cyrus's eye drifted down to my hand. "I wouldn't do that if I were you, tits. In fact, you can't do what you are planning. If you notice, you can't move any closer because of the protection barrier that I had my loyal psychic put up for me. He has done many wonderful things for me."

I glared at him as he spoke to me. He smiled broadly.

"Oh, princess, it isn't all that bad. I can see the appeal that Bastian, and even Brandon, had toward you. You look quite fuckable. Now, I'm sure you have a lot of questions, but fortunately for me, I can't hear you, so I don't have to listen to it. I will answer the one that I know is on your mind. I had special contacts made so I am able to see spirits. I may not be able to hear you, but this helps to know where you are. I also have alarms to notify me when a spirit enters a room that I am inhabiting, and my bedroom is off limits."

It sounded like the bastard had everything figured out. I was surprised that he was that thorough, but dealing with the kind of spirits he did, it was smart. Smart and wealthy was always a dangerous combination. Something sinister or disastrous was bound to happen.

As I turned to leave, he stopped me. "Don't worry, my dear. You will have something to do soon. I promise."

With that, I left to explore the house a little more. It was huge and extravagant. It was no wonder he could house all the ghosts he wanted in it. There was little chance we would be in the same room at the same time. As I wandered aimlessly through the house, taking stock of what was considered my new home, I didn't see any of the other ghosts, but I figured that I would in due time.

I returned to my room to find Bastian sitting on the bed. I hadn't known he was there, but I was elated. I ran to him throwing my arms around his shoulders. When I pulled back, I noticed the look on his face wasn't one of excitement.

"What's wrong, darling?" I asked carefully. If I still had a stomach, it would have dropped.

"Cyrus called. It's time for me to go get number seven."

"Why are you upset by that?" I was confused at his words. It didn't sound like it was a bad thing, but then, I didn't care what happened to the other ghosts. They weren't my concern.

"I have to go to Salem, Massachusetts. The next ghost was a considered a witch during the trials. This one won't be an easy catch. I may be gone for a while."

"Oh." So, he was leaving me. That was why he looked so concerned. "Are you telling me you don't want me anymore?"

"Dana, that isn't what I was saying at all. I am simply saying I won't be around for a while. You are going to have to hold your own while I'm gone. The longer I'm away, the weaker your protection spell will be."

"What protection spell?"

"I placed a spell around you to protect you from the others until you are more experienced as a ghost. You are an infant in the eyes of some of these monsters. They may eat you alive, so to speak."

He reached out to touch my face. I stepped back. "You don't think I can hold my own? Do you fucking know me? I got you to kill for me."

"You didn't convince me to do anything, sweetheart. I knew what I was doing the whole time. Manning deserved what he got."

"Go! I'll show you I can take care of myself. I don't need you around to protect me from the other ghosts."

"Dana, I'm just trying to protect you because—" he cut himself off.

"I don't need or want your excuses, Bastian. You are just as bad as Brandon was. He thought that he could control me as well. I fell for it. I must be stupid. But no more. I can handle things on my own. Now go to Salem and play ghost hunter with Cyrus. Fuck—at least he was straight forward with me."

"I am nothing like that bastard you killed yourself over," Bastian said through gritted teeth. "You truly know nothing of my past or me except what I have shared with you. I have been dealing with the demons for longer than you can imagine. That is my cross to bear. I don't give excuses."

He paced across the room, putting his hand on the door knob. Then he turned back and strode up to me, so we were practically touching. His eyes stared deeply into mine. "When I return, we will speak more about this issue. Trust me, baby, we aren't done here."

He turned on his heel and walked out of the room. The move reminded me of something I had seen on television. It was an old-fashioned move. I stared at the door long after he closed it behind him. I felt the despair wash over me in a wave. I felt like I was drowning in it. My heart was breaking because he left me. I took a deep breath and was determined to pull my shit together.

"He plans on coming back. He said that we were going to talk more," I told myself aloud. I didn't want to break down and show how weak I truly felt.

While he was gone, I was going to show him. I would show all of them that I wasn't just a simple, helpless ghost. I was a badass. I could handle my own. I was able to take care of me. No one would get in my way, especially another ghost, or a man.

I couldn't wait to meet the others to show them what they were up against. I was going to enjoy this.

Chapter 43

The first set of visitors that came to the house after I was brought to it were a married couple. They had apparently been rented the house while Cyrus was gone to keep it occupied and to celebrate their honeymoon. I wasn't sure why Cyrus would do that, but he did.

The agent that was showing the couple around opened my bedroom door. I was reclining on the bed as they entered.

"And this is the room you will be staying in. It's known as The Princess Suite. It's said that Princess Diana stayed in this room during a visit to the United States. It has a jacuzzi bathtub in the bathroom, through that door over there. I think you will enjoy it. Sleep well."

The agent walked out to give the couple privacy. As soon as they thought they were alone, the wife turned to the husband. "I can't believe our luck, Keegan. It's beautiful! Mister Bane is so generous letting us stay here as cheaply as he is. It is a real steal."

"You're right, Angela. We wouldn't have been able to afford this on our own. It still seems too good to be true." Keegan looked around the room as he spoke.

I twirled the knife in my hands while I watched the scene unfold before me. He tossed the woman down on the bed, climbing on top of her. There was rusting and wrestling with clothing until they were naked from the waist down. The woman wrapped her legs around his hips while he plunged himself into her over and over.

Watching them fuck was boring. She was quiet, not making any noise whatsoever, while he grunted and groaned into her neck. The action ended as quickly as it started as well. She immediately got up, walking toward the bathroom.

I followed her into the bathroom, watching her finish stripping her clothing off. She was beautiful. Her breasts were full and perky with high taut nipples. I had never been turned on by a woman before, but she did it. Following on the heels of the arousal came an intense jealousy. Her tits were something my mine never were. Perfect. I could tell that they were natural by looking at them. I knew then, she had to die.

She got into the shower with me close behind. She began to wash off the aftermath of their lovemaking. She turned her back to me to rise off. I stepped up behind her, putting my arms around her. I cupped her breasts in my hands. Her eyes flew open, glancing over her shoulder. Looking confused, she turned back and continued to let the water beat down on her.

I began to squeeze her breasts, feeling the nipples hardening against my hands. I wanted to hear her scream. I pinched one nipple rolling it between my fingertips. Her head rolled back as her breathing picked up. Her hands slid down her body on their own accord. Her fingers disappeared within the junction of her legs.

As her fingers began to work her into a sexual frenzy, I continued to squeeze and massage her breasts. A moan escaped her lips. I smiled. This was what I liked to hear. I ran my hands down her body, covering her hand as she rubbed herself to ecstasy.

She began to climax, her moans getting louder. I grabbed my knife and shoved it into her lower stomach. She screamed as her eyes few open. She had been orgasming as the knife entered her abdomen. I ripped it upward, effectively gutting her. As her intestines spilled out of her body into the bottom on the tub, I whispered into her ear, "I'm sorry."

She looked helplessly toward the bathroom door, her husband hadn't come to her aid. She tumbled and hit her head on the edge of the tub as she landed. The sound of her head hitting was a resounding crack and blood oozed out of the wound. Her eyes stared ahead lifelessly.

I climbed out of the shower, walking into the bedroom. It was the husband's turn. I wanted him to scream as well. Hearing her screams had brought me to the edge of orgasm. I hoped his would finish me off.

I found him asleep lying in the middle of the bed. He was still wearing just a shirt, manhood out for display. He wasn't nearly as impressive as Bastian in the department, but it would work in a pinch. I climbed on to the bed, putting my mouth over him. He moaned as my tongue ran around the head of his penis. I sucked him as he hardened.

"Oh baby, just like that," he mumbled, voice heavy with sleep. "Oh yes, baby. You've never done that before."

I sucked on him until his balls began to tighten. Right before he released, I pulled back. His eyes opened, looking deep into mine. His eyes widened slightly. Before he had time to react, I took the knife and cut his dick and balls off in one stroke.

He screamed as his equipment flew across the room when I tossed it. I took the knife and began to stab him over and over.

"A bit over dramatic don't ya think?" A voice said from behind me.

I turned around to see Bastian leaning against the doorframe. He looked like he had been there a while, but I hadn't heard him come in.

My eyes traveled down to his pants where there was a homemade tent protruding. "You look like you didn't think it was overdramatic in the least."

"I didn't say I didn't like overdramatic, just that that was."

He crossed the room in three long strides. I jumped into his arms, wrapping my arms and legs around him. If it was awkward holding a ghost, he didn't show it. His mouth crashed down onto mine. He kissed me with an intensity I hadn't felt from anyone. He leaned over, placing me on the bed, also lying on top of me while he was at it. My hands slid down his body and fumbled with the zipper of his pants. As I opened it, I pulled him free of the confines of his pants.

His breath came out in pants as he whispered into my ear. "You, my darling, have had enough foreplay."

With that, he drove himself deep inside of me with one powerful thrust. He began to ride me hard and fast. It was extremely arousing to be fucking him next to the body of my last victim. I wrapped my legs around him and held on for the ride of a lifetime.

After we climaxed, he pulled out of me, then shifted so he was lying beside me. A comfortable silence filled the space between us as Bastian worked on catching his breath. He finally turned and looked at me.

"Would you care to tell me why you killed the nice couple?" he asked.

I shrugged one shoulder. "They were dull fucks, and she had perfect tits."

An eyebrow raised. "I need just a little more information, luv."

"She was perfect naturally where I had to be enhanced."

"Darling, you know that you are perfect, always have been. You just couldn't see it. But now I have to dispose of the bodies."

"No, you don't."

"Why not?"

"It's obvious Cyrus wanted to see what I was made of. He had an agent bring them to my room specifically. I figure they will be back in a bit to take care of the clean-up."

I rested my head on his chest, wishing that we could stay like this forever. I knew that he couldn't really feel me, but it was nice to pretend. I listened to his heart beating in his chest and a feeling akin to jealousy washed through me. It wasn't because I was dead, but because he would never truly be with me.

"I am going to have to leave again soon," he whispered.

My head came up. I looked into his eyes. "Why?"

"The collection is almost complete. I know where the next ghosts are going to be, and I want to get them before I miss my opportunity." He paused for a second. "Once its complete, I will be able to finish my plan."

"What plan?"

He placed a kiss on my forehead. "The one where we will be together."

"But how?"

"All will be revealed when the time is right," he promised.

I wasn't sure why, but I had a feeling he was right. He had said all would be revealed, I wondered if I would learn more about him and his past. If we were going to be together, then I would have time to find out. I hoped one day I would have my king by my side and we would be able to terrorize people together.

Black Zodiac Ghost 7

WRETCHED CRONE

Chapter 44

Ozark Mountains, Missouri 1882

"Thou shalt not suffer a witch to live." - Exodus 22:18

The quote ran though my head for hours after the sermon on witchcraft. There had been rumors of witches practicing their craft and worshipping the devil in the woods at night. I knew this to be inaccurate because I lived out there, but I wasn't going to say anything. It was best to stay silent and out of the eye of attention. Those who made a commotion or stood up for others were punished more severely than those being accused of wrongdoing.

The witch hunters were going to be in the area soon. That's how it usually went. The witch trials had ended a long time ago, at least according to the papers. Maybe things died down a long time ago in the original colonies, but in the Ozark Mountains, everything was behind. Where I lived, it was almost as if time stood still. We still had stocks and whipping posts outside the church. They believed discipline needed to be on church grounds so that God could watch over us and ensure that the impureness and evil were taken care of appropriately.

Ever since I was little, I was told that I needed to be careful. Keep my secrets close to my chest, and never let anyone know that I'm special.

I had to live as normally as possible. Go to church. Pray for forgiveness and absolution for my sins and being born. I was told to keep the attention away from me and stay in the shadows. If something slipped out, I would have to run. Go somewhere I had never been before.

My mother told me that I would have to stay pure in order to keep my curse from spreading to my children. The only way to ensure it was never to have offspring. I couldn't get too close to anyone, afraid they would find out about my gifts. So, here I was; an "old maid" as they called me.

I rummaged through my cabinets trying to find a certain pot. I promised that I would make an elixir for my little Allison Agnew. She was sick, and her mother was scared that the little girl was going to die. I couldn't let that happen. The little girl had so much promise and greatness in her. The world would be a darker place if she didn't survive.

Finally, I found the small pot, or cauldron as some people would call it, hidden in the very back of the cabinet inside a large cooking pot. I never had to use it, so it was a convenient place to keep things that I didn't want to normal people to see. I pulled the entire stock pot out of the cabinet and set it down on the counter. Turning, I lit the fire in my wood stove.

Slowly, methodically, I began to put the ingredients in the pot, stirring slowly as I went. It was crucial that I did it in a certain order and mixed them well, or it wouldn't work. I couldn't disappoint Abigail— or Allison. The illness that had been going around was dangerous. Several people in our village had died from it.

There was a knock on the door, interrupting my thoughts. Cautiously, I set the wooden spoon down and crossed the room. Only those who knew I could help came to the back door, but you could never bee too careful. Opening it a crack, I peeked through it to see who it was.

Abigail stood on the other side of the door, wringing her hands. She looked around like she was waiting for someone or something to jump out of the shadows and get her. She was wringing her hands and acting all jittery. If anyone saw her like that, we would both be in trouble for witchcraft. Ushering her in the house, I closed the door firmly behind her.

"What are you doing here, Abigail?" I studied her face. Concern raced through me. "Did something happen to Allison?"

She shook her head quickly back and forth in a no motion. "N-n-no. She is still the same. The doctor was there yesterday and said that she was in God's hands now. If the fever doesn't pass, she won't survive. Isabella, I can't lose my baby!"

I wrapped my arms around her. "Don't worry, Abigail. I won't let you lose your daughter. I will do everything I can to help. I'll bring it to you when it's ready. Give it to her before she goes to sleep, and she should start feeling better in the morning."

"Thank you, Isabella. How can I ever repay you?"

"Please, don't worry about. If you need to repay me, you can do it after Allison is better. Now, come back tonight, and it will be ready."

I led her to the door and hugged her again. As soon as I was alone, I went back to my work. I dumped the previous batch out and stared over from scratch. It had to be perfect. The doctor's words weighed on me. I was her last hope. I couldn't let her die. I wouldn't.

After mixing the elixir, I said a blessing over it. "Watch over the child, Allison. Guide her back to the light of health."

The blessing would have been more beneficial if I had done the blessing over her in person, but this was the best I could do. I couldn't be seen doing a blessing over the child, or I would be killed for certain. I bottled it up and put it in a basket with some baked goods and cheese I had made. It made it look less conspicuous than just the vial.

I put my shawl over my shoulders and grabbed the basket. Walking out the door, I slowly made my way to the Agnew house like the old lady that I was. Coyotes howled in the distance; it was an eerie sound. I had a feeling that there was something dangerous coming this way, possibly the witch hunters.

I knocked on the door softly. I didn't have to knock louder. Abigail would be waiting for me anxiously. Any concerned mother would. The door flew open. Abigail stood there, tears streaming down her face.

"Abigail?"

"She won't wake up." Her voice was soft and tear filled. "I've been trying and can't get her to stir. Please, help!"

I walked in the house, putting the basket down by the door. I grabbed the vial and rushed behind Abigail to the bedroom where little Allison was sleeping. I knelt on the floor beside the bed and placed a hand on her forehead. It was hot. She had beads of sweat along her forehead.

"Abigail, leave us for a few moments." My eyes didn't stray from the small child. I heard the footsteps and the door close with a soft click. Once alone, I gently pressed a kiss to her forehead. "Allison, you need to get better."

Smoothing the blankets, I tucked them in tighter around her. "Let the healing light surround and comfort you. Let it embrace you and send its healing powers into your skin. Drink the liquid of life and rid your body of the fever and ailments that keep you down."

I popped open the vial and opened her mouth. I carefully poured it into her mouth, massaging her neck so that she swallowed involuntarily. Once the vial was empty, I pocketed it and stood up. Going to the living room, I found Abigail pacing back and forth.

"I've done what I can. I'll wait with you to see if she starts feeling better."

We sat in silence as the night slowly passed. The only sound was the grandfather clock ticking the time away. As the sun began to peek over the trees, there was a rustling and coughing from the other room. We rushed in there to find Allison sitting up, blue eyes open. Her gaze landed on her mother.

"Mommy, I don't feel good."

Abigail rushed to the bed and crawled on it with her. She held her trying to comfort the sick child. "I know, dear. Just rest, and you will feel better."

I smiled and backed out of the room. I needed to be gone before Abigail's husband woke up. I didn't like anyone knowing when I helped. Abigail mouthed the words "thank you" to me as I shut the door. I made my way back to my house, glad to help the child survive.

Chapter 45

Word of the death of Mr. Charles Wellington spread through the Ozarks as rapid as a fire catching dry wood. I had known his first wife, Charlotte. She had gifts as well. Hers was vastly different from mine, though. Charlotte's mother had brought her to me when she was a child to help get it under control.

Charlotte could see the spirits of those who had passed. I had learned a lot from her as she had from me. I taught her how to control the urge to speak to those from beyond the veil. I also taught her some basic elixirs and other healing concoctions.

She would come visit me after she married Charles. When she became heavy with child, she told me her fears that the child would have the same gifts. She planned on having me come to the house under the guise of a nanny and teach it what it needed to know so Charles's family was none the wise. She had confessed to Charles of her gifts, and he had still accepted her. He loved her with all of his being.

When Charlotte had the baby, Charles Sebastian Wellington, III, she became ill. I had always felt it was suspicious since she knew how to heal almost any ailment. I had been to visit days before she had passed and held the precious baby. The baby held a great power within him. I worried for his immortal soul. I promised Charlotte I would do whatever necessary to see the child was led down the right path.

Before she passed, she told me of the suspicions she had surrounding her sickness. The memories floated through my head.

"Isabella, I have to tell you something in confidence," her voice was weak. I walked across the room and closed the door. When I returned to her bedside she continued. "I'm not sick, I'm dying. I know I won't get better."

"What are you talking about, Charlotte?" My brows furrowed as I concentrated on the sick woman in front of me.

"I'm not sick. Nothing I can do has helped. We have had Ingrid Sloane here assisting around the house and caring for baby Charles. She has been a wet nurse for him because I don't have any milk. If I did, I would be afraid to feed him. I don't want him to get whatever is ailing me." She struggled to sit up, but I pushed her back gently and leaned over so she could tell me what she really wished to say. "I think I've been murdered. Please keep an eye on baby Charles. He will need guidance."

"I promise."

My heart ached with the memory and the fact that I failed her. I hadn't been able to see Charles since he was a newborn. After Charlotte died, Ingrid made her way into the heart of Charles, and he married her. She banished anyone that had any connection to Charlotte from the house, insisting they weren't needed.

Now was my chance to see little Charles and speak with him. He had to be almost an adult, so hopefully it wasn't too late. I had to at least attempt to make contact. It was important for me to keep my promise, at least to the best of my ability.

Hurrying around the house, I packed some food and other necessities I would need for the trip to Bourbon. If I were to see him, I had to move quickly. I wasn't sure what I was going to say, but I needed to do this.

The trip took several hours, and by time I arrived, I had missed the service. I walked into the house behind a group of women bringing food and condolences. Once inside, I looked around, trying to spot

Charles. I knew he would be there somewhere, greeting guests and taking condolences. It shouldn't be too difficult to pick him out in the crowd, since there weren't many children. It was mostly men and their wives. The wives were gathered around the widow and the men were huddled in a corner, speaking in hushed tones.

Entering the sitting room, I found two boys sitting on the couch. Keeping my distance, I waited for the perfect time to approach them. After studying the two boys, I knew the taller, older one was Charles. He looked so much like Charlotte, my heart ached.

When he turned, the look in his eyes broke my heart. He was a lost soul. His eyes were lonely and sad. I wished I could have done something to take the pain away, but it wasn't possible. I needed to touch him and see what I could get from him before I spoke with him.

He got up and headed into the other room. I followed him, brushing him as I passed him, making my way toward the powder room. The visions I had made me want to cry out. I rushed into the powder room, shut the door, and leaned against it.

Tears gathered in my eyes and a lump formed in my throat. I had failed him. I saw his future, and it was grim. I took a few minutes to compose myself as I thought of what I was going to say to him. I had to say something, had to warn him of a horrible future.

Taking several deep breaths, I opened the door and made my way back to the family room. He was seated back on the couch next the other child. No adults were near, and I could hear voices raised in the kitchen. This would be my only chance.

Rushing to him, I grabbed him by the arms, pulling him off the couch. I held him close to me so he couldn't struggle as I spoke to him quickly and as quietly as possible.

"I have been sent to you by your mother. You are a lost soul and will need assistance soon. You will need assistance soon, and I am willing to help. I'll teach you what you need to know. I live out in the woods, a three-hour walk from here. Come to me, and you will learn what I speak of, I promise. You have been cursed."

I released him and hurried off. I hoped that he would heed my words and come visit before it was too late. I hoped I would be able to help save his soul.

Chapter 46

The days following the funeral, I watched and waited anxiously to see if he would come out before it was too late to see me. I wanted him to visit before the curse took hold of him and clutched his soul. As every day ended and he didn't show up, the more anxious I became. I knew he would come but knew he would have to learn things on his own. No one in their right mind would believe a crazed old lady about a curse, especially a young man of higher standings.

I had finally given up on Charles showing up when I heard a tapping on my back door. It was light, and I thought I was hearing things until it sounded again. Cautiously, I approached the door and opened it so it was only slightly ajar. Peering through the crack, I tried to see what made the noise. I didn't see anything. I went to shut it, thinking I was finally going crazy, when I heard a noise beside the door.

Opening it up further, I looked to the left to see Charles, dirty and covered in blood sitting on the ground by the door. He had his arms wrapped around his knees, forehead resting atop them. I opened the door the rest of the way. Stepping out, I reached out, lift the child, and brought him into the house.

He didn't seem to notice he had been moved. The only movement that he had made when I picked him up was his head coming up. He was lighter than what a boy of his age should be. Gently, I set him down on the couch in the living room and hurried back to the kitchen to shut the door.

Rushing around the house, I drew all the blinds. I couldn't chance anyone seeing the boy, especially in this state. If my vision had been right, he would be in a lot of trouble if he were caught. I needed to know the details. The problem with my visions were they were choppy, and I never received the whole picture. I had a good idea whose blood it was, but I didn't know if he had killed the boy as well.

I pulled the wash basin out of the closet and grabbed the stock pot out of the cabinet. Taking it outside, I filled it up and brought it back in, placing it on the stove to heat up. I didn't have indoor plumbing, it hadn't reached my village yet. Grabbing another pot, I took it out and repeated the process. Once both were on the stove heating up, I pulled out the soap and a washcloth, setting them on the floor next to the basin.

I returned to Charles, kneeling in front of him. The only movement he had made was lifting his head. His eyes followed me, and as I had moved around the room, I could feel them on me. I studying him, seeing the bruises beneath the blood and dirt. His left eye was swollen and black. What had happened to this child?

"Charles," I waited for his eyes to meet mine. When they didn't, I spoke again, hoping to get his attention. "Charles? Charles. I need you to pay attention to me. Can you look at me, please?"

His eyes finally met mine. I expected a vacant stare, but the gaze in his eyes was intense. Maybe he was pulling himself together. I didn't know what happened on the journey here or before he left home, but I knew it wasn't good.

"You need a bath to get the blood off. I'm going to help you get cleaned up. After you bathe, I will see if I can find anything for you to wear and will rid of your bloody clothing. You can't be seen in them again. Can you tell me what happened? Are you well?"

He just blinked a few times but didn't speak. I took that as he wasn't ready to tell me. He would in due time, though. A child, even an older one, would have to vent eventually.

I left him for a moment to go pour the water into the basin. Steam rose from it. I walked to my pantry and grabbed the lavender, tossing a couple sprigs into the water to help soothe him. When I returned to him, I carefully eased the shirt up over his head. There were spoon shaped bruises all over his upper torso.

Those were the freshest wounds. He had scars on his back going down into the back of his pants. I helped him stand up and removed his pants. I treated this like I would taking care of a babe. I tried to see him as the defenseless babe that he had been.

After he was disrobed, I helped him to the kitchen and into the basin. The scars all down his back hurt my heart to see. He had been in a horrible situation from the look of it and the flashes I got while I touched him. He hissed as he sat down into the hot water.

Slowly, methodically, I helped him bath and scrub the blood off of him. While washing him, I was sickened to be able to feel his ribs. He had been mistreated in a big way at home. I wondered how his father let it happen. That wasn't the man I had known when Charlotte wed him. He must have turned a blind eye to the happenings going on in his own household.

After he was bathed, I put him in a nightshirt I had until I could come up with more clothes for him. I was going to have to leave the house to get them, but I wanted to make sure that he was fed and cared for before I left. I settled him into the other bedroom of my little house and went back to the kitchen to fix dinner. I decided to make a soup and cut a hunk of bread for him to eat. Starting in the morrow, I would feed him meals that would get an appropriate weight on him.

Once he was asleep, I left him alone in the room and went on a search for clothing for the child. The first order of business in helping him now he was clean was to tend to his physical and material needs. He was going to need food, sleep, clothes, and a safe environment. I was determined to help him with it.

Chapter 47

Charles stayed with me for two weeks before he began to open up to me. He told me about years of abuse that he endured by his stepmother's hand, and how she wanted his brother, William, to get the business, estate, and entire inheritance. He wouldn't talk about what happened that brought him to me. It was still too painful for him. When he slept at night, I would lie in bed and listen to him whimper and cry from the nightmares. I knew he would have to start talking about it soon or it would consume him.

We sat at the table for breakfast the morning after a night full of terrors, screams, and cries. It was time to talk about what happened. I watched him as he shoveled the eggs in his mouth like it was going to be the last time that he would be able to eat for a while. He always ate like it was his last meal.

"Charles." I waited for him to swallow and look up at me before I continued. "What happened the day you came here? If you are worried you will be in trouble, you won't. It won't leave this room, but you need to talk about it, my boy. If you don't, it will eat you alive."

Slowly, he set the fork on the table and pushed his plate away as if he instantly lost his appetite. "I killed her."

"Go on." I didn't need him to clarify who "her" was. I already knew.

"William died after eating some cake that was supposed to be for my birthday, and she blamed me. Said that I was supposed to be the one that died. I wasn't supposed to live past being a babe. She began hitting me with her fist then attacked me with a spoon. I didn't mean to hurt her. I grabbed the ax and began swinging it to get her away from me, but I didn't want to hurt her. She was the only mother I knew. I loved her."

Reaching out, I placed my hand over his and gave it a reassuring squeeze. "I know you didn't mean to, Charles. Sometimes we do things we don't mean to do in order to protect ourselves."

He had tears in his eyes. "After I hit her the first time, I couldn't stop. I wanted to, but couldn't. My arms kept swinging until she was dead. Even then, I hit her with it a few more times. I'm evil, and I am going to go to hell."

"No, Charles, you aren't evil. You are a young man that has been in an unbearable situation for his entire life. You deserve happiness." I didn't have the heart right then to tell him what his future held; how he was a lost soul.

***

"Focus, Charles. You have to channel your power. If you want to be able to get control, you have to focus." I encouraged as he worked on a spell.

"I've trapped a spirit before," he gloated.

"Having your mother's spirit tell you step-by-step how to do something isn't doing it. That's following directions and being instructed. How do you think your mother learned to control her gifts?"

He looked up at me then, all concentration broken. "Mama came to you?"

I nodded once. "Yes. How do you think I knew to find you? Now focus."

He turned his attention back to the crystal in front of him. I smiled proudly when it began to glow. He would figure out his power soon enough. Even though I was proud, it saddened me at the same time. I enjoyed having the boy here, but knew our time together was short.

He looked up at me, smiling hugely. When he looked at my face, the smile faded. "Isabella, what's wrong? I focused and did what you told me to. Are you angry with me?"

"No, Charles. I'm very proud of you. You are a quick study, and your magic is strong within you. I've never seen anyone catch on as quickly as you. However, we need to talk."

He sat on the couch beside me. "Are you ill?"

"No, dear boy. Just old. But we need to talk about you."

"What about me?"

"You are a lost soul."

"What does that mean?"

"It means you are cursed to walk this earth until you find what your soul is looking for." He frowned, tears building in his eyes. "Don't fret. It isn't as bad as it could be. You have to be extra vigilant to find what you are looking for. You can't stay in one place too long or you will catch unwanted attention."

"Can I make a spell to stop this curse?" Panic was lacing his voice.

"No, I'm sorry it doesn't work that way. You will find what you are looking for, I promise."

"How do you know?"

"I saw it. You will have several obstacles, Charles, but you will overcome them."

He nodded but from the way his brows were scrunched together, he was frowning, I knew he didn't believe it.

"All right. Now we need to focus on blocking. I'm going to teach you how to block others from being able to read you. It is important that you only let anyone know what you allow. Close your eyes and build a wall that will keep others out. This wall you are going to have to keep up at all times. When it is down, you become vulnerable. We don't want anyone to be able to know what's inside your head. Once you get the wall up and solid, we will work on making generic memories that will pass as genuine memories. We will build them so when others try to read you, that is what they will see and believe."

Wall building was harder for Charles than I thought it would be. He seemed to have a hard time clearing his head and only letting what he allowed bleed through. It was something that we were going to have to work hard on until he kept the wall up. I would randomly read him, just to see if he was doing it.

"Charles, you need to think of it as a castle wall if need be. I know you are having a hard time with this, but it has to be an impenetrable wall. No matter what someone does, you have to be able to hold the wall up and keep it strong. Some people will want to knock it down, but you can't let them."

He nodded. He closed his eyes, squeezing them tight. When he opened his eyes again, he was smiling.

I touched him, trying to read him. All I got was him sticking his tongue out. Laughing, I put an arm around him, pulling him into a hug. "Good job, kiddo."

***

After a month of rigorous training, I felt like Charles was as prepared as he was going to be. He could do any spell on demand and was good with runes and working with statues and crystals. His specialty was seeing ghosts, and he did that without a problem.

The downside was, he would interact with the ghosts as he saw them. If they spoke to him first, he would respond. That was something that no matter how hard I tried, I couldn't break him of that habit. It was something he did subconsciously.

"Charles, you need to stop talking to the spirits as you come across them. People will notice if you are talking to yourself. They frown on it. It will put you in a home or worse—label you a witch."

"They stopped burning witches and killing them though." He frowned like he couldn't figure out why it was a bad thing. "Father said my mother was special."

"Some people see it that way. Most see it as an affliction that you need to have beat out of you. The majority of the witch hunts have died down, but not here. This is why I'm teaching you control. Now you can hide it and save yourself from being murdered for being born special. Do you understand?"

"Yes, Aunt Isabella."

We had started having him call me aunt when suspicions rose about a boy living with me. We told those who asked that his mother had sent him to live with me and help me due to my age.

"Now I'm going to go to the market. You be a good lad while I'm gone and finish the potion. After you are done with that, please clean up."

"Yes, ma'am."

As I was walking out the door, I had a bad feeling but couldn't pinpoint what was wrong. I shook my head, thinking maybe I was paranoid. The hair on the back of my neck stood up as I headed away from the house.

Chapter 48

There was a commotion at the market, making me drop what I was doing and rush toward my house. I didn't know what happened or what was going on, but I knew it had to do with my house. Cutting through the neighbors' yards, I took the shortest path I could to my house.

I burst in the back door to find Charles curled up in a ball on the floor, crying hysterically. After a cursory glance around the room, I determined it was a potion or spell gone awry. Kneeling by the child, I stroked his hair and spoke softly to him. "Charles, what happened?"

"I thought I could lift the curse on my soul. I know you said it wasn't possible, but I was certain I could. I can do more than what even you believed. I wanted to do some good, to show you I was capable of anything."

I gathered him in a hug, assessing the situation while doing so. There were ingredients that could only be used for witchcraft lying about, and I wouldn't be able to get it cleaned up before the masses arrived. They would be here any moment. There were flames coming from the large cauldron I kept that I usually heated water over the fire with. Crows' feet, feathers, pig's blood, and an assortment of animal parts that were used for dark magic lay about.

"Charles, I need you to listen closely. We need to get you out of here, now. The witch hunters will be here any moment, and there is no hiding the potion ingredients."

I stood up and helped him to his feet. Taking the apron I was wearing, I wiped his eyes, drying them. I went to the desk and wrote down some names and addresses of people that would help him. I then jotted a note for him to carry and show the people when he went to him. After I finished that, I ran to the other room and packed a satchel full of clothes and grabbed another one. Going into the kitchen, I packed as much food as possible for his trip so he wouldn't starve while on his journey.

The whole time I prepared, he stood in the same spot watching me. When I came back to him, I helped him into a coat and handed him the satchels. He placed one on each shoulder. When I felt he had everything he needed, I led him out to the woods. "Go north to the road. Cross it and continue north. You will come to another road. Follow it east. When you get to the next town, look up the first address on the list. They will take you in."

"Aunt Isabella, I don't want to leave you. I'm scared."

I kissed his forehead gently. "It's time. You have to go. Now hurry, and whatever you do, don't look back. When you meet the man Bane, remember your roots. Remember your teachings. Don't let the darkness take over you. You are a good man, Charles Sebastian Wellington the third. Follow your path and your heart. God bless."

I watched as he disappeared into the shadows of the woods. I should have given him a lantern, but I didn't want the light to become a beacon to locate him. I was giving him his best chance at life and to succeed. I just hoped he remembered my words.

Reentering the house, I sat down in a rocking chair and slowly rocked back and forth while I waited for them to come and bust the door open. I knew I looked calm on the outside, but on the inside, my heart was broken. I now knew how it felt to lose a child. He wasn't mine, but it was close enough. Watching him cry as he left me was the hardest thing I have had to do, but I knew it was for the best. They were going to kill me. If he had been here when they arrived, they would have killed him as well.

The front door burst open. Firefighters, the sheriff, and several men pushed through the doorway. I didn't move, didn't speak. Just let them come in and do what they were going to do. One of the men was Andrew Agnew, Allison's father. They searched the room, then taking the rope they had brought with them, they tied me up.

"What happened here, witch?" One of the men leaned down and spoke in my face. His breath smelled of rotten meat and booze.

I didn't say a word. Just continued to stare at him. I wasn't going to give them the satisfaction of an answer.

"Are you deaf, witch?" he asked loudly, making my ears tighten. When I didn't answer, he struck me across the face. "You will answer me!"

"Enough, Jonathan." Andrew said. His voice was firm and calm. "No need for accusations until we know what happened. Striking an old woman is distasteful."

The man named Jonathan turned and faced Andrew. "Look around, Andrew. She is a witch. The explosion that happened was proof of that. The judge will take one look at this place and condemn her to death."

"That's for the judge to decide. We came only to see what the commotion was. Now we see it, there is no need to restrain her the way you are. Untie her, I will deal with the woman."

"Yes, Sheriff Agnew." The man was thoroughly reprimanded. He untied me and sulked away.

Mister Agnew knelt in front of me, placing his hands gently on my knees. "Isabella, what happened? This isn't a typical occurrence here."

His eyes were kind, but I couldn't tell him about Charles. I just sat there. I could taste blood in my mouth from the blow I received by Jonathan. If I had my way about it, he would be sorry that happened. I just needed the time alone.

Andrew lowered his voice and leaned a little closer so not to be overheard. "I know what you did for my family. Abigail told me everything. I am forever in your debt. I will try to protect you from this, but you know as well as I that it is out of my hands."

The only form of acknowledgement that I gave him was gently placed my hand on top of his. He sighed and stood up. Looking around the room, he finally spoke to the others. "Bag what you can. And for God's sake, put that fire out. Don't let her house burn down. I'll take her down to the jailhouse and she will stay in a cell until Judge Snyder determines her judgement."

I stood up and walked willingly beside Sheriff Agnew. He was a good man and did what was necessary, even when he didn't want to. He knew that without me, his daughter would be dead. He couldn't break the law for even me. He turned a blind eye to my helping, but this was too much to turn away from.

Once I was locked up, I sat on the edge of the bed and stared straight ahead. I knew my fate. I had read it when I touched Charles the first time. He was going to be the death of me, I just hadn't realized that it was so soon. I knew that I helped him as much as I could, but I wish I had prepared him for the kind of life he would be living from now on. He wouldn't live the high society life that he had grown accustom to, but he wasn't living that way anyway. I closed my eyes and sent a blessing of comfort to him.

***

"I sentence you, witch, to death. Prior to your death, you will be sentenced to time spent in the stocks, where all can see what a witch looks like and what happens to one," Judge Snyder announced.

It hadn't been much of a trial and the results didn't surprise me. I hadn't been given a chance to speak, but I wouldn't have said anything anyhow. I would have just kept my vow of silence. I hadn't spoken since I saw Charles leave. It wasn't hard not to when the voices that ran through my head were speaking enough for me. My power had been going haywire since I saw him off. It was as if all my training to keep myself sane had disappeared in a heartbeat.

The sheriff approached me and led me out of the courthouse to the church yard. I was placed in the stocks, and they were locked shut. It didn't take long for my back to begin to ache, but it was too high to kneel and too low to stand straight. That was part of the humiliation and punishment. They wanted physical pain as much as mental.

It didn't take long for the mob to make an appearance. They chanted things about death to all witches. Harsh whispers went around making up stories about things I had supposedly done. It went from helping people heal their children, which was the truth, to kidnapping children and cooking them for dinner.

The word around the stock was that I had killed the child that was staying with me and ate him for dinner. That was what caused the explosion in my house. I wasn't going to correct their stories, not that it would have done any good if I tried. I was a condemned witch. I no longer mattered. I was no longer a person.

Chapter 49

It had been a week that I spent in the stocks before they started throwing the rotting fruit and vegetables at me. It was supposedly my fault that the crops were beginning to fail. If I had been honest with myself, it was. I wanted them to know what they were doing and how I had helped, but I didn't want to try to prove it aloud. The sheriff put guards on me to keep the onlookers from harming me. It didn't help, but it was a nice gesture.

I hadn't eaten anything since being arrested and only had a few sips of water so I was losing my strength quickly. Sleep wasn't an option either. I knew that the sheriff had tried to convince the judge that I needed to be in at night, but he wouldn't see it. He wanted me to truly feel the evil that I was.

My head was spinning from lack of sleep and nutrition. I was beginning to hallucinate. I swore that I would randomly see Charles in the crowds, watching me with tears in his eyes. I knew that couldn't be right being that I sent him to Sullivan. I kept seeing Charlotte as well so I knew I was hallucinating.

It was late at night, and I could feel my life slipping away from me. All I had to do was give in and let go. It wouldn't be hard. I was starving, my throat was dry like cotton and dust. I looked up at the moon. It was full with blood on it.

"I shall not go without a gift to this town," I whispered. My voice cracked and scratched from lack of use. "I lay a curse on those who move to this place. Shall you feel the pain that those before you have caused. Shall your souls be stuck in purgatory and be treated as you treated others."

With that, my last breath escaped my lips and my soul was pulled from my body.

***

"It's about time you come back to visit," I told the young man standing before me.

I had spent years watching the town change and grow. We went from a few houses, courthouse, and church to a large town with colleges, schools, stores, and everything else needed. The times changed and so did the people. They became less involved with one another and more self-involved.

"I tried to come back sooner, Aunt Isabella." The young man sat on the grass next to where I had died. "Things have been more difficult than you prepared me for."

"I know. I wish I could have prepared you better."

He looked over at me. "You did the best you could. I owe you an apology. If I hadn't—"

"Stop. There is no need to live in the past." I chuckled at my joke. I was the past.

"Let me make it up to you."

I cocked an eyebrow at him. "How?"

"I met Bane just like you said I would. He is a great man. He has a vision that I can stand behind."

"I told you to be wary of him."

"Believe me, I have been. You don't think I would blindly follow someone after everything I've been through, do you?" He paused, watching me as I smiled. "Now, what I was saying is I have a place for you to live. You can be free of this wretched place. Come with me?"

He held out a hand to me. I studied his hand for a long moment before I placed mine on top of his. He stood up, and I was pulled into a crystal around his neck.

When I was released from the crystal, I was in a house. The room he released me in was a beautiful room decorated in blues. Blue had always been my favorite color. He stood at the doorway watching me.

"Is this suitable?" he asked.

I nodded. How could it not? I couldn't truly enjoy living in a house this beautiful as I wasn't alive, but I could pretend.

"Good. You may recognize parts of the house. It was built over the Wellington estate. More accurately, it was added onto it."

"Is she here?" I didn't need to mention who she was. He knew.

"Yes, but she won't be a bother."

I nodded. I had a feeling this house would become interesting. It was more than a feeling. Being around him, I had my power back. I knew how interesting it was going to get.

Black Zodiac Ghosts
8 and 9
Mother and Son

Chapter 50

Lexington, KY 1938

The Mother

"Come here you freak. You think you are better than everyone else because only thing wrong with you is your size. Let's see if you are a full-fledge woman." The world's largest man said as he forced me down in the hay, near the elephant pen.

He forced my legs apart, ripping my panties with one of his big, burly hands. I fought him with all my might, but he was ten times my size and fighting was futile. To me, it didn't matter how futile and useless it was to fight, I didn't want to be ruined. It was bad enough I was a freak, I hoped someday a man would come along and accept me for who I was, but I wanted to be pure and untouched for him.

My scream was cut off by his other hand covering my mouth and nose. I couldn't breathe. My heart began to pound as I struggled and prayed that I would get away from him unharmed. When he penetrated me and took my virginity, I cried into his hand. Tears poured down my face as I was overcome by pain.

His grunts drowned out any noise that my struggles may have made. He sounded like a rutting pig as he pounded into me. His grunts became faster as he moved harder and faster on top of me. I tried to distance myself from what was happening, but the pain was too much to bear. When he finally climbed off me, I curled up in a ball and cried. My body was wracked in tremors as I tried to breathe and make it through the pain.

He looked down at me and smiled. His teeth were yellowed and rotting. The smile was pure evil. "You fuck like a dead fish. Maybe next time you will ride me like a stallion."

After he walked away, I decided that wasn't going to happen. I would never find myself alone with him again.

The pain in my abdomen woke me with a start. The nightmares had been occurring since that night, but I was getting used to them. I rubbed my extended belly, trying to ease the pain that was settling there. I wasn't feeling the baby kick which was weird.

After I found out that I was pregnant, I planned on giving it up. After it was born, I was going to leave it at the fire station of whatever town we were working at the time. As time passed, however, I decided that I was going to keep it, being it would be the only family that I could call truly my own. After being manhandled by that monster, I vowed that I would never let another man touch me.

When the Ringmaster had found out what happened and that I was carrying a baby, the man suddenly "left" the carnival. I found that odd being he had been with it for years, and it was his home. I truly didn't care what happened to him or where he actually went because it meant I could stay with the show and have a way to support myself and the baby.

It didn't take long for the pain to return after it had eased. It stole my breath as my stomach tightened. It felt like I was being stabbed in the back. The pain was so intense I couldn't cry out. The only sound I could make was a breathy squeak. All I could do was lie on my side, curled around my stomach as I cried and wished the pain would go away.

There was a gush of wetness that began to run down my thigh. That was when the pain became worse and constant. It was back to back, no time to get a breath before another round hit. I finally was able to muster a scream, waking my bunk mate, the Bearded Lady. She rushed to my side.

"Rosie, are you alright?" Her voice was laced with worry.

"Help." The one word was all I was able to muster.

She looked down at my stomach and legs. "Oh my god, you are in labor. I'll get help."

Running from the bunk house, she was yelling at the top of her lungs. "Help! Rosie's having the baby. We need someone in here now!"

There was a frenzy of motion as people ran around trying to figure out what to do. Finally, the elephant trainer, Aaron, walked up. He was calm as a cucumber as he assessed the situation. Finally, he spoke. "I've helped Betsy deliver her last calf, Hugo."

"Aaron, she's a woman, not an elephant!" the Bearded Lady snapped.

"It's the same concept, Nancy. Now shut the hell up and let me help poor Rosie."

It seemed like an eternity of pushing, everyone yelling and trying to encourage me to deliver the baby. When it did finally arrive, Aaron placed the squirming, screaming infant in my arms.

"Congratulations, Rosie. It's a boy." He smiled and walked away.

There was a lot of cooing and awing over the baby. Nancy helped me sit up while I held the baby for the first time. He was larger than I had imagined he would be. It was difficult holding him due to my short arms, but I managed.

"What are you going to name him?" The Ringmaster asked. I hadn't realized that he was in attendance until he spoke.

Staring down at the life I had just created, I smiled. "Abraham."

It was a nice strong name. He would need the strength growing up here. The people in the show were the most loyal people around, until you had something they wanted or became no longer useful to them.

Chapter 51

Olathe, Kansas 1958

"*Open wide, Abe.*" I held the spoon to his mouth. He pressed his lips together and shook his head no. "Come on, Abraham. You have to eat it so you can be big and strong. You want to be a big boy, don't you?"

He crossed his arms over his chest and shook his head no. Typical child, never doing what I wanted him to do. I stepped up on the step-stool that I used to reach the top of his head when bathing him. It came in handy during mealtimes as well. I looked him straight in his dark blue eyes.

"Mommy says you need to eat. Now open your mouth. Don't make me put you over my knee and spank your behind."

His bottom lip stuck out in a pout. "Not hungry."

"Yes, you are. You haven't eaten since breakfast."

He finally opened his mouth, and I put the spoon heaping with grits in his mouth. He swallowed it and frowned at me. "Yucky."

"No, it isn't. Stop being such a baby." I kissed his forehead and climbed down. "If you finish your lunch, I'll let you have a snack."

I went to my lock box and opened it. Sticking my hand in it, I produced a candy bar. Abe loved candy bars and would do anything for it. Waving it in front of him, I ripped open the wrapper. His eyes widened. Shoving both hands into the bowl, he ate the grits by the handful until they were gone.

I gave him the candy bar and started to clean the bunk house.

We still shared the space with Nancy and any other temporary workers that we may have on the show with us at the time, but the majority of the time, it was just the three of us. The Ringmaster didn't like to bunk anyone else here.

Nancy was a lot of help when it came to taking care of Abraham. With my size, it had been difficult to do some things and she was always there to lend a hand. We had a pretty set routine in the bunk house and had separate chores to do. While I was doing laundry, she would babysit Abe. He would get into things he wasn't supposed to if we didn't keep a constant eye on him.

"Abe, Mommy is going to take the laundry down to the van. When I get back, I'll take you out of your seat. It will only take a minute. Mr. Aaron will be taking me to the laundry mat later today, and Aunty Nancy will keep an eye on you."

He nodded, but I was certain he didn't hear a word I said since he was so engrossed in demolishing the last of the candy bar.

***

"Ladies and gentlemen. Boys and girls. I present to you the World's Smallest Woman and Largest Baby," the Ringmaster announced. It was our cue that we were on display next.

The spotlights shone down on us. They were so bright, they were blinding. I stood on a small ladder next to the oversized high chair used for dramatic effect. The legs on it were three-feet high, so I looked much smaller than I was. The show was all about appearances.

Abe had to be bald. He wasn't allowed to have any hair anywhere. He didn't have any teeth either. That was a newer development from his love for sugar. His teeth had started to rot, so the Ringmaster thought it best to have all of his teeth pulled. He said that it would be better for the show and Abe's overall health. It didn't sound quite right, but I wanted what was best for my son.

We made a show of feeding Abe from a bottle and baby food in a large bowl with a giant spoon. I had to heft the spoon with two hands and put effort into feeding him. He made raspberries and covered me in green baby food. As the lights began to dim, Abe farted and it was more than a fart. The smell was instantaneous. The crowd gasped, groaned, then started laughing.

The lights went out and the Ringmaster spoke. "It appears that baby needs a change."

Helping Abe down, I led him through the dark out the back of the tent. I was going to have to hose him down before we went into the bunk house. He was too big for me to change his diaper with him on the bed anymore, so I would take him outside, take the diaper off, and use the hose, making sure the water was warm to clean him up.

We were in the middle of hosing him down, when the clown posse strolled up. They were laughing and joking, but stopped when they spotted us.

"When are you going to let that kid grow up?" Bongo asked.

"When are you going to stop getting in your mommy's makeup?" I retorted.

"Oh, the little woman has big words."

"Shut up, Bongo. Go make a kid cry."

"What are you going to do if I don't shut up? Have your monster of a kid sit on me? How old is that baby now? Twenty something?"

Turning, I sprayed him with the hose. I wished the water was ice cold, but unfortunately it wasn't since I was cleaning Abe.

"You fucking bitch!" Bongo yelled. "I go on in five, now I have to redo my makeup."

"Watch your mouth around my son." I snapped. "You better hurry if you don't want to be late. You know how the Ringmaster gets."

As they stormed away, I heard them talking about how they were going to get even with me.

I woke up to a rolled-up pair of socks being stuffed into my mouth. I tried to scream, but the cotton effectively silenced me and made me gag. Struggling to sit up, a burlap sack was placed over my head, and I was wrapped in something. I couldn't be sure, but I thought it was the sheet off my bed.

I was lifted and carried out of the bunk house. Being wrapped up with my face covered as it was, I was disoriented and not sure which direction I was headed. I felt like I was spinning. Fear ran through my body like a drug, making my heart race. I tried to keep my breathing under control, but it wasn't happening. Panic was keeping me from any rational thought.

Suddenly I was dropped and there was a loud thud above my head. I was completely still for what seemed an eternity. There was laughing going on outside of whatever I was in.

"Did you see her face?" A muffled voice asked. "It was hilarious. She looked like she saw a ghost."

"How long you gonna keep her here?" Another voice asked.

"As long as I want. It will be hilarious to see what her monster child does when he wakes up without mommy there. Maybe he'll cry like the baby he is."

"Do you think you are going too far?"

"Shut the fuck up."

The voices stopped after that. I tried to get free of what I was wrapped in. I tossed and turned every direction, causing a thumping on the sides of whatever I was in. There was a creak and then more weight was piled on top of me. Something was shoved down beside me, keeping me from moving. There was another thud.

I had to be in some kind of box. Probably a footlocker. They would have to free me soon. I just had to keep calm. Nancy would notice I was gone first thing in the morning and the gig would be up. Then I could get out of there and get back to Abe. He would be devastated if I wasn't there when he woke up.

My chest hurt from not being able to get a full breath in. The socks in my mouth were unbearable. I wanted to vomit and gagged every couple of minutes. The more I gagged, the worse it was. My stomach finally revolted and I retched, but with the socks stuffed in my mouth as far as they were, there was nowhere for the vomit to go, so it went the only place available: my nasal passage.

It completely clogged up my airway, and the little air I had been able to get was completely cut off. My heart began to race again. It felt like it was about to burst through my chest. My lungs burned and screamed for air. My mind raced, trying to come up with ways to be able to breath.

It wasn't long before I began to lose consciousness. I could feel my body shutting down, organ by organ. I was terrified and there was nothing I could do about it.

My last thoughts were on Abe, and how he was going to be an orphan. As my mind shut down, I realized something. It was his birthday. He turned twenty.

Chapter 52

The Son

Mommy was always there for me. I never needed to do anything on my own. It wasn't that I couldn't, she would rather do it for me. I loved Mommy taking care of me. She protected me from the nastiness of the world. We traveled with the show so we could stay together and be where we belonged.

Aunty Nancy helped Mommy a lot. She would watch me while Mommy was away doing things. I missed Mommy real bad when she wasn't around. I didn't have to spend much time without her. But while Aunty Nancy watched me, I got to do things I couldn't do with Mommy. She let me help with dishes or putting things away. She even let me sweep the floor.

Aunty Nancy thought that Mommy should let me do what other kids did. As I got bigger, she thought I would have been better off on my own in the real world. I didn't want to go to the real world as she called it. Mommy told me stories about how horrible people were and how scary it was.

The others in the show would talk about how dumb I was or what was wrong with me. They acted like I couldn't understand them when the spoke. I wasn't dumb. I didn't think there was anything wrong with me. I was just Baby Abe. They would snicker behind my mommy's back and talk about how I was a bastard child. I didn't know what they meant by that, but it didn't sound nice.

No one generally acknowledged me directly, but that was okay with me. I got nervous when people would talk to me. I never answered them. I don't think anyone knew that I could actually talk, I just chose not to. I wasn't sure if Mommy even knew.

I had to wear diapers even as I got bigger. It wasn't just part of the show. Mommy said that I had a sickness that kept me from learning how to use a big boy potty. Aunty Nancy said that Mommy just refused to let me grow up. Either way, I was still in diapers and had to have Mommy help change them.

When Mommy tucked me in, she sang me the lullaby that she had sang to me since I could remember. Then she kissed me on the forehead and made sure the blanket was tucked tightly around me, so I wouldn't fall out of bed.

"Goodnight, my handsome prince," she whispered as she snuck over to her bed. I took a deep breath, the scent of her laundry soap lingered in the air. Closing my eyes, I fell asleep.

***

Rays of sunlight shone into the bunkhouse, waking me. I sat up, looking around, confused. Normally, we were awake before the sun could fully shine in the window. Mommy would be up cleaning or prepping our costumes for the day. She wasn't anywhere to be seen and there wasn't anywhere to hide in the bunkhouse.

"Mommy?" I asked quietly. I didn't want anyone else to hear me speaking. It was best if they didn't hear how weird I sounded. Without teeth, I had a slur and lisp. I always had thought my voice sounded weird, but now it sounded even stranger.

Aunty Nancy yawned and sat up. First thing she did was pull a cigarette out of the pack she kept beside her and lit it up. After a couple of deep drags off it, she began to cough and hack like she was going to be sick. Once her coughing fit died down, she looked over at me.

"Where's Rosie?" she asked me.

I shrugged. Aunty Nancy didn't necessarily need an actual response from me. I never spoke to her. She did all the talking.

"I wonder why she didn't wake me before she left to keep an eye on you." Swinging her legs over the edge of the bed, she stood up and paced the room looking for my mommy. "Stay here. I'm going to go look outside. She will kill me if I let you wonder off."

She was gone for what seemed like an eternity before she came back into the bunkhouse. "Come on, Abe. We need to go looking for your mom. The van is still here so she didn't leave to do laundry, and I didn't see her anywhere else."

She waited while I climbed out of the bed and walked to her. She led me outside and we went on a search for Mommy. After coming up empty, she took me to the Ringmaster's trailer. Knocking on the door, she stepped back and waited for him to answer.

When he finally came to the door, he was wearing a robe. His hair was mussed and eyes were sleepy. "Why are you bothering me so early in the morning?"

"I'm so sorry, sir, but Rosie is missing." I could hear the panic in Aunty Nancy's voice as she spoke.

"What do you mean 'missing'?" His voice rumbled like he was angry. I took a step back and attempted to hide behind my aunt.

"We've searched everywhere, and she's nowhere to be found. She wasn't in bed this morning when we got up."

"Have you considered she may have just wanted to run an errand right quick?"

Aunty Nancy shook her head vigorously. "She didn't. She wouldn't go anywhere without waking me first to let me know. And she wouldn't leave Abe behind unattended. Plus, the van is here, and Frank hasn't seen her since after she cleaned up Abe after the show. I have a bad feeling."

She wasn't the only one. My stomach hurt and fear was beginning to grow in me. What happened to my mommy?

Chapter 53

The Ringmaster arranged a search party to find my mommy. He split everyone into groups, so we could search a wider area quicker. He has told us that it was imperative that we find her before the show tonight. He didn't want to call the police, just find her and bring her home.

He didn't think it was necessary to call them. The police were for regular people. We weren't regular people. We were freaks, carnies, the unwanted and invisible part of society. The police didn't care if one of us went missing. It was an act from God if we did in their eyes.

I stayed with Aunty Nancy during the searches. She was told that we had to stay home in case she came back. I had a feeling that she wasn't going to come back. I didn't know why I felt that way, just did. I was afraid I lost my mommy forever.

As the sun began to set, the search parties returned to the grounds. They are to get ready for their performances for the evening. The clowns were the first ones back. They whispered to one another as they walked to their trailer. The others followed suit as they made their way back. The tone of the grounds was quiet and dark.

Aunty Nancy worked on doing her make-up and brushing out her beard. She was going to be the first on stage—she usually was. I studied her while she freshened up. She had tear stains down her cheeks from crying off and on all day. Her beard, usually kept in a ponytail at her chin, was loose and fluffed up for the show. I never understood how she got it so long. I couldn't grow a beard, but if I had, then it would have been shaved as well.

"You stay here, Abe. I'll be back as soon as my performance is done." She patted my head as she walked out the door.

She hadn't been gone very long before I heard someone walking by the bunkhouse. I scurried to the door, ready to jump out, thinking mommy was back, when the voices I heard made me stop short.

"We shouldn't have done it." It was Charlene or Chancy, one of the clowns. "What are we going to do with her?"

"Shut up, Char. We agreed while in the woods that we weren't going to speak of it, and we would take care of it tonight after the show. We move on tonight and make a circus jump to our next stop in Toledo. No one will find her for days, if not longer. We will be long gone by then."

I knew the other voice to be Bongo. He was the one that had been being mean when Mommy put him in his place. I never liked Bongo. If I were honest, I never liked any of the clowns. They were mean and thought they were above everyone else, except the Ringmaster. He was the god of the show. His word was law.

"But Mike, we killed her. It was an accident. We should have gone to the Ringmaster. We should have done something." The woman's voice was frantic. "All Rosie did was embarrass you by telling you off in front of the others."

There was a slap and a cry. "I told you to shut the fuck up! And while we in make-up, my name isn't Mike. Know your place."

Red encroached my vision as anger boiled in my blood. If I understood what they said, and I was pretty sure I did, they killed my mother. I stormed out of the bunkhouse, grabbing Bongo by the throat. I squeezed and watched as his eyes began to bulge.

"You. Killed. Mommy," I growled. I was so angry I couldn't speak a full sentence or even think one.

I slammed him on the ground and grabbed a large stone that was next to his head. I slammed it into his head over and over. His skull collapsed under the impact and brains and blood splattered all over me.

Chancy screamed and began to run after I finished killing Bongo. I stood up and ran after her. Jumping, I soared through the air, landing on the ground close enough to grab her ankles. I yanked her toward me and began to strangle her. I didn't stop until she stopped moving and grabbing at the ground.

Standing up, I headed to the clowns' trailer. I was planning to kill every single one of them. I wouldn't stop until Mommy was avenged. As I walked past, I grabbed the whip used to train the elephant and a sword belonging to the Sword Swallower.

I was swinging both the whip and sword around as soon as I pushed into the trailer. There were screams as they whip slashed them and the sword bit into the skin of those closest to me. I dropped both, deciding I wanted to use my hands to kill them. I wanted to feel their lives slip away. I snapped a neck of a clown that was trying to escape with one swift jerk.

It only seemed like heartbeats before I had killed all except one of the clowns. He pulled a gun and was aiming it squarely at my chest. "Stop right there, freak. I'm-I'm not afraid to shoot you. You give all of us a bad name. You may have turned out decent if it wasn't for your crazy mother. That bitch got what she deserved."

The way he talked about my mommy threw me into a fresh rage. No one spoke about Mommy in such a way. I charged him, barely feeling the bullets as they found their home in my shoulders. I tackled him and yanked as hard as I could. I felt his arm come out of the socket. Grabbing the sword that had been forgotten on the ground, I began to chop away at him until he was pieces on the floor.

I stood up and looked down at my body to see I had blood dripping off me, pooling on the floor. I didn't know there was so much blood in a body. Turning, I headed to the door. I needed to get back to the bunkhouse before Aunty Nancy found out I was gone. I supposed she was going to keep an eye on me until mommy came back for me. She would come back.

When I opened the door to the trailer, there was a crowd of carnies standing there. They were all silent. The woman who walked on the tight rope looked past me and gasped. When she spoke, her voice was so soft she should have been difficult to hear, but her voice carried.

"He killed them all." Her hand came up to her throat and the men in the crowd descended upon me.

They dragged me to the tent. I didn't fight, though. I went with them willingly. Maybe they found Mommy and were taking me to her. I waited with the crowd while the tight rope walker went into the tent to speak with the Ringmaster.

When she returned, she nodded once and I was led inside. The tent was full of people, yet there was no noise. I was taken to the center of the ring. Looking around, I spotted Aunty Nancy who stood just outside the spotlight, tears streaming down her face. My arms and legs were bound with ropes and didn't know why. Where was Mommy? I thought they were bringing me to her. She wasn't there. Why was Aunty Nancy crying?

The Ringmaster's mouth was moving, but no words were coming out. He had the microphone to his face, so he had to be speaking. I cocked my head to the side, seeing if I could hear anything then. Nothing. The opposite ends of the ropes were tied to the four horses used for some of the acrobats' act. The horses were all facing different directions.

The Ringmaster turned and nodded. All the lights went out. A spotlight shone on me, darkness was everywhere else. I couldn't see anything beyond the circle of light. I couldn't even see Aunty Nancy anymore.

The horses started moving, forcing my arms and legs to go different directions. I fell back as they pulled. They didn't move fast. My shoulders popped first, causing me to cry out. It was then that I could hear again.

The crowd was chanting very softly. "Bad baby. Bad Baby. Bad baby."

The last thing I remember before the lights when out was a ripping feeling. It felt like I was pulled into pieces.

Everything went dark and quiet again. That's when I heard the voice that was music to my ears. Mommy. "Abe."

Chapter 54

Kirksville, MO Present Day

Bastian Bucco

I had to go to several shows trying to find them. The original carnival, circus, freak show, whatever had split up into several shows. They had to be in one of them. I knew they wouldn't be in separate shows, they would be together. The sightings and accidents had occurred in one, but then I found out that the company that owned it would shuffle their stuff around so it would be with a different show each time.

I was sitting in the crowd, watching the clowns drive a miniature car erratically. I couldn't help but roll my eyes at the ridiculousness of it. I was never found of the circus, even as a young lad. My parents took us once, and I hated it the whole time while my brother loved it. Of course, I felt like the freaks in the freak shows. I had never fit in anywhere.

The sound of a crash and screams pulled me from my musings. I looked up to see the car was flipped and now on fire. Clowns screamed and scrambled trying to get away from it. A small fire truck full of clowns pulled up. It stopped, and the clowns jumped down with a hose. The clown holding the nozzle pulled the handle, shooting some kind of white cream at the fire. It didn't extinguish the flames however. They did the exact opposite. Flames shot up in the air, causing a genuine reaction from the audience. The clowns retreated, leaving the flames to shoot higher into the air. Some of them had to be carried away from injuries do to the car being flipped.

What no one else saw were the ghosts that were standing in the ring, watching the chaos. One was a short woman that couldn't be taller than four foot. The other was twice the height of the first and was dressed up as a baby. It was definitely the duo that I had been searching for. They were the reason I had to leave behind Dana yet again. I was glad that she understood that I had a mission to complete.

Now I just had to get them to come with me. I doubted that they would come willingly. I didn't want to have to force them but probably didn't have a choice in the matter. I watched as the "baby" walked to the center of the tent where the poll was holding it up. He shoved against it as hard as he could, trying to break it. The pole looked sturdy and wasn't budging, so I wasn't worried that he would succeed. Then he picked up an ax that one of the clowns dropped in the all the commotion. He swung it into the pole. It bit into it, and the screams in the tent escalated. The crowd began to fight and try to escape before the entire tent went down on us. I sat calmly while others pushed and shoved, trying to get down the bleachers.

It didn't take long for me to be the only one left in the big top. I stood up, clapping. Both ghosts turned their attention to me.

"Bravo! That was a great performance. Did you see the crowd? Hear their screams? You scared the holy hell out of them. I have to say it was mighty impressive. And injuring those clowns—pure magic," I spoke as I slowly approached them. I didn't want to scare them away. I had spent way too much time looking for these two.

The Son looked at me, then back to his mother like he was uncertain of what to do. She stepped closer to me in a way that made me think she was trying to protect her young.

"I'm not going to hurt either of you. I have an offer for you."

"What offer?" She was glaring at me. If I wasn't used to working with malevolent spirits, I would have been nervous.

"I want to give you and your son a home."

"This is our home."

"Not anymore it isn't. It stopped being your home when you were murdered. You were both murdered by the people you considered family and friends. You were stuffed into a locker and suffocated. Your body was left in that footlocker until the stench caught someone's attention. Your son was quartered in a public arena, during one of the shows. That isn't a home. You don't belong here anymore."

"We won't come with you."

"You will have your chance to have a new family."

I watched as her expression changed. I knew that family was something that she had always wanted. It was something she had strived for. Her friend Nancy said as much when I talked to her, trying to locate the whereabouts of the ghosts. I had no problem using their desires to get what I wanted.

She shook her head no, and I knew I was starting to lose her. If they faded out before I had a chance to convince her, I would have to start the search all over. This could be my last opportunity. "Your son will be safe, and you will be together forever."

She looked back at Abe, and I knew I had her. She nodded, and he came closer. They held hands and turned back to me.

I said the enchantment to pull them into the crystal and smiled.

I was getting closer to having all twelve ghosts. Then I could finish this off once and for all.

Black Zodiac Ghost 10

BLACKSMITH

Chapter 55

Mass., 1900

Clang! Clang! Clang!

The sound of my hammer hitting the hot iron and anvil was music to my ears. It helped calm my nerves when they were agitated and soothed my soul. I was born to be a blacksmith and loved every minute of it.

My father had been a blacksmith before me. It was the only career that he was able to get as a freed slave. No one wanted to hire them, but a kindly old man took him under his wing and taught him the ways of blacksmithing. After the old man passed away, he left everything to my father who in turn kept the business successful and passed it down to me when he could no longer do it.

Sweat beaded on my forehead and I hit the metal with all my might. I was working on making a new hunting knife for Mr. Gunderson. He required a new one every few months. I only wished I had that kind of money to spend needlessly. My knifes were good quality and lasted more than a few months. The knife I had made myself when I first started learning to be a blacksmith was still sharp and I kept it on my hip.

The cowbell over the door clanged, alerting me of someone coming into the shop. I continued to hammer but made sure to acknowledge the potential customer. "Just a moment. I'll be right with you."

Satisfied with the progress of the knife, I put it in water to cool it and went to see who had arrived. I stopped short when I saw her. She had long brown hair pulled up in an intricate bun. Her eyes were the color of the sky. I was momentarily stunned by her beauty.

"Can I help you, ma'am?" I finally found my voice.

She turned and looked at me and smiled. "Yes, my husband ordered kitchen knives last month. I'm here to pick them up."

"What's the name?" I walked to the counter to look through my orders book.

"Williamson. Theodore Williamson." She stepped up to the counter, placing her fingertips along the edge of it. The ring on her finger glistened and sparkled under the light. I thought I remembered the order, but I couldn't see this beautiful woman with such a brute of a man. She was too delicate.

I found the name and walked to the back of the room to retrieve the blades. When I brought them back, I found Mrs. Williamson wandering around the shop looking at different blades that I had on display. She stopped to look at a dagger. It was small and meant to be easily concealed. I had made it as a sample for the madame of the local brothel. There were times when the women needed protection.

I set the knives on the counter then stepped up behind her. I watched as her finger gently glided across the blade and design etched into it. She traced the design before touching the hilt. She spoke softly, somehow knowing I was there. "This is beautiful work."

"Thank you, ma'am. I did the design myself." I wasn't sure why, but I felt compelled to let her know that the knife was solely my work.

She looked over her shoulder at me. "It is truly beautiful. You did a wonderful job."

"May I ask you a question?" I had a thought that had been nagging at me since she walked in the door.

"I suppose."

"Why are you picking up the knives? I have in my orders book that Mr. Williamson was going to be picking them up himself."

"He is out of town."

"Were you escorted?"

"How is that any of your business? Your job is to give me the knives, but if you have to know, yes. The carriage and driver are outside waiting."

I nodded, satisfied with her answer. "Come, let me show you the knives that your husband ordered." I led her back to the counter. I unwrapped the knives and gave her a few moments to look at them before I spoke again. "Do you believe your maid will enjoy them?"

She looked up at me and smiled. "We don't have a maid. My husband says that having a maid is a frivolous expense since he has a wife with no children."

The tone in her voice made me frown. I tried to smooth my expression quickly, but I knew she had seen it.

She confirmed she had seen it with a small humorless laugh. "Please, don't fret. God simply hasn't graced us with a child yet. It will eventually happen."

I nodded and changed the subject by explaining what each knife was and their use. When I finished explaining it to her, I asked, "Is there anything else I can do for you?"

"No thank you, Mister –"

"Smith, ma'am. I'm Byron Smith."

"I'm Mary. Mary Williamson."

She held out a hand for me to shake. It was a bold move for a lady of status, but there it was. I took her smooth, silky hand in my calloused one and shook it gently. Her hands were so small and delicate in mine, I was afraid I would break her.

She held my hand for a moment longer than proper, then pulled her hand away. Reaching into her handbag, she pulled out a couple of bills and handed them to me.

Turning away, I went to the register to get her change. While my back was to her, the bell above the door clanged. I looked back to see she was gone. I pulled the money and placed it under the register for when she returned for it. I was certain that she simply hadn't realized she overpaid me.

I hadn't returned to work when the door opened again. I turned half expecting Mrs. Williamson returning to collect her change, but it wasn't. A young man stood there, shifting his feet and looking nervous. My first reaction was that he was a thief, but when I studied him, I saw that he was simply nervous.

"Can I help you?" I asked, trying to put him at ease.

"I need a knife."

"Okay, let me show you what I have." I took him to the other side of the room to look at the different knives. While we looked, I asked. "What's your name?"

"Charles."

"Nice to meet you, Charles."

He picked out a knife, paid, and promptly left. I went back to my forge when the bell sounded again. I wasn't used to being this busy. I went back to the front, to see a woman standing there wringing her hands. She was wearing a maid's uniform.

"Can I help ya?"

"Yes, I need to order a sword."

I took her to the counter to take her order. After she finished explaining what she wanted, I wrote it down and went back to work. I had a lot of work ahead of me.

Chapter 56

I couldn't help myself. My mind kept drifting to Mrs. Mary Williamson. Her eyes, her smile. The gentleness of her touch. I could admit, at least to myself that I was completely smitten. I couldn't help myself. I wouldn't admit it to anyone else though. It was dangerous for a black man to even look at a white woman. If anyone found out that I liked her, I would be hanged. Or worse, tortured then hanged. It was a good thing that I would never see her again.

Knowing I wouldn't see her again, I questioned myself for the hundredth time as to why I was designing this dagger. I had her in mind when I started to work on it, and the next thing I knew I was making a blade specially for her. She would never get it and I would never sell it, but that didn't matter. It was for her.

The dagger was small, delicate like her. When I was satisfied with the shape of the blade, I sharpened it. It needed to be sharp for her. I wanted her to feel protected. I was going to make a sheath to go along with it. I wasn't as skilled at leather as I was iron, but I wasn't inept. I turned my thoughts back to the blade and how I was going to make it uniquely hers. I etched a design on the flat of the blade. It was a rose surrounded by swirls.

Once it was finished, I wrapped it in a cloth. Carrying it to the back of the room, I opened a trunk and gently placed it in there. I was going to keep it safe until I could get the sheath made and until she came back for it.

I laughed aloud at my ridiculousness. She wasn't coming back for it. She didn't even know it existed. She probably didn't know that I existed. It pained me to think that way, but it was true. I had only spoke with her that one time while she was retrieving the knives her husband purchased, yet I felt a connection. I thought she had felt it as well. The word husband echoed through my head. She was married and out of my reach. I should just put the dagger out on display to be sold or call the madame and see if she needed another.

The dagger stayed in the trunk where I put it for safe keeping. I locked it and pocketed the key. Turning, I headed back to work on the order of spikes that had come in. Using the tongs, I turned the spike so I could hammer it to a point.

When the metal cooled too much for it to malleable, I tossed it back in the forge to bring it back to smelting point. I crossed the room to get a drink of water. I didn't keep it too close to my workspace to keep it cool. As I sipped the water, my mind tried to wander back to Mary, but I forced it to stay blank. This was going to be harder than I thought.

The cowbell rang, I turned to see Mrs. Williamson standing there. She had the cloth that I had wrapped the knife set with in her hands. It was bulging, and I could see the top of a handle. I recognized the redwood that I used to for the handles of the knives they ordered.

I walked up and set the glass down. "Mar—Mrs. Williamson. Is there something I can do for you?"

"Yes. The butcher knife is nicked already. You were under strict instruction that they were supposed to be resistant to nicks." She set the knives on the counter in front of me.

I picked up the knife in question and studied it. The nick was odd looking. It appeared to be more of a gouge than a nick. I looked up at her. "What did you use this knife on? It looks like you used it on steel or something. Did you use it on bone?"

"It matters not what I used it on. It's my knife. Your work was guaranteed. Now fix it."

"Yes ma'am. I will get right on it. It shouldn't take too long to fix it." I headed back to my workspace. I heard footsteps behind me. I turned my head to see Mary following me. "Ma'am, I need you stay up front."

"Absolutely not. You messed up last time, so I am going to watch for myself to ensure you do it as you are supposed to. I want to see you work."

"I will have to take the handle off, so I don't burn it." I explained as I set the knife down on the anvil. With a couple swift movements, I had the knife disassembled and placed the blade in my forge. While the metal began to heat, I turned and crossed my arms over my chest, studying Mary. "I am heating up the metal so I can shape it back into its original shape. Then I will reattach the handle."

She came closer, just enough that she could feel the heat coming out of the forge but not close enough to feel the full impact of it. "I want to see how it's done."

The tone she used wasn't condescending, it seemed sincere. After the first meeting with her, the attitude she returned with had surprised me. I didn't think it was really her, but then I didn't truly know her, even though I felt like I did.

I explained step by step what I was doing as I fixed the blade for her. She stood off to the side, eyes glued to what I was doing. When I finished repairing the blade, I grabbed a rag and began to polish it. Once hit was back to its original luster, I reattached the handle and handed it to her.

"It won't nick again?" She asked, cocking an eyebrow.

"Only if you don't try using it on metal again, or whatever you used to cause that nick." I smiled as color rose on her cheeks. She looked down, almost like she was trying to hide a smile.

"I don't know what you are talking about." She turned and walked toward the front of the building.

"I'm sure you don't, ma'am."

"Call me Mary."

"Alright, Mary." I took the knife from her and set it back with the others, gently wrapping them in the cloth.

"How much do I owe you?" She pulled her coin purse out.

I placed my hand on hers. "Nothing this time as it was an err on my behalf, besides I owe you. You overpaid me."

"Don't worry about the money. It was a tip for how beautiful they are. Thank you for your generosity."

She gathered her knives and headed to the door. I opened it for her and held it as she walked out. When she disappeared down the busy sidewalk, I shut the door and groaned. I had hoped that I wouldn't have to deal with her again but wanted to at the same time.

I was sure that I would be seeing her again.

Chapter 57

I had been right about seeing Mrs. Mary Williamson again. She came to the shop as often as she could which was almost daily. She would just come in, roam around then leave on some days. Other days she would stick around and watch me work.

"Byron," She leaned against the wall not far from my forge.

"Hmm?" I asked as I turned the metal that I was currently heating.

"Will you teach me how to do that?"

Her question threw me off, so I just stared at her for a long moment. She looked so innocent and small against the wall. Her eyes were wide, making me think that she had possibly surprised herself by the question as well. Being a blacksmith wasn't woman's work. In fact, asking a woman to do anything like this would be inexcusable, however I didn't ask her, she asked me.

I nodded and stepped back a little so she could come closer and take over. "You will need to use the tongs to grab the metal out of the forge. Hold it tight, or you'll drop it. That's it. Now take it to the anvil. Easy. There you go."

I handed her the hammer. Standing behind her, I reached around, putting my hand over hers. I used her arm to demonstrate the force that had to go behind shaping the iron. After a few hits with my assistance, I let go and let her do it on her own. She was swinging the hammer like a professional within the first couple swings.

When the metal cooled too much to manipulate, she put it back in the forge and turned toward me. Jumping at me, she gave me a hug. "Thank you for letting me do that. It's so much fun. You are amazing, Byron."

The bell over the door clanged. I quietly excused myself from Mary to attend to the customer that just entered the shop. There was a woman standing there, wringing her hands. "Can I help you, ma'am?"

"Yes, I was wondering if you have any kitchen knives. I was at the Williamson's the other day and she has the most beautiful set of knives. She told me that she got them from here, that her husband ordered them from you."

"Yes, ma'am. Let me go in the back and get a set." I walked back through, past my workstation to see that Mary was standing statue still. Her eyes were large, but she had a smile on her face. She held her finger to her lips as I passed her.

I grabbed a set of knives, it was a set that I had originally made for the Williamson account, but Mr. Williamson didn't like the handles, so I redid them. I brought them back to the front, when I went past the anvil again, Mary was gone.

Arriving at the counter, I set the knives on the counter and unwrapped them for her to examine. "They are beautiful. Mary was right, you do a fantastic job."

She pulled out some bills out of her purse and handed it to me. I took them and rewrapped the knives tying them with a leather strap. I handed them to her. "If you need anything else, please come back. Thank you for your business."

She left without turning back. I watched as she climbed into the carriage that was out front and it quickly pulled away. Once it was gone, I turned and went back into the back to find Mary. I had to look everywhere for her.

I finally found her in my room. She was sitting in a chair, staring at the wall. I knelt in front of her. "You alright, Miss Mary?"

"Yes, Byron. Hearing Helen in there made me think. And I couldn't be seen by her, she would have told her husband who would have in turn told Theodore. I didn't care if she saw me, but I didn't want Theodore to become angry."

"What would happen if he got angry?"

She shook her head. "It doesn't matter. We won't have to worry about that." Standing up, she walked out of my bedroom, back into the main part of the store. She turned and looked back at me. "Thank you again for showing me how to forge. It was amazing."

"It was nothing, Miss Mary. You are a quick study."

Her lips touched my cheek, and I froze. I couldn't even blink. It was a shock. She smiled and stepped back. Gathering her stuff, she walked to the door. My eyes followed her, but I couldn't move.

"I'll see you tomorrow." She walked out without another glance back.

She was true to her word. Mary came back day after day, learning a little bit more each day. She took time to get to know me as a person as well. She didn't want to know only about forging. She asked me questions about my life outside of my job, which I didn't have one. I lived for work and that was it.

"So, you grew up coming here?" She sipped from the cup of water she had.

I nodded. "Yes ma'am. I have spent every day in this building since I was big enough to walk."

"And you live here?"

"I do. In the back room, I have everything I need to live comfortably. I don't need more than a bed and some food."

"That's sad." She looked down into her glass as if it held all the answers of the universe.

"Why is it sad, Miss Mary?"

She took her time answering. When she did answer she looked up and her eyes met mine. "You don't get to experience anything outside this building. The beauty of the world, the people. It can be magical out there, yet you stay here. You have never been travelling?"

I shook my head. "Miss Mary, staying here is safe. For people like me, it's best if I keep my head down and go unnoticed. I do just fine staying here and working. I'm safe and respected as much as I can for a black man."

"That's not fair." Her brows were burrowed together, causing little wrinkles to form on her forehead and between her eyes. I reached out and ran my thumb over the wrinkles on her forehead.

"Now, stop that frowning, Miss Mary. You will wrinkle that pretty skin. Life isn't fair, and I've come to accept that. It's the fate of my people. Maybe one day things will be different, but for now . . ." I trailed off because there wasn't more to be said. "You should be heading home now. It's starting to get late. Mr. Williamson will be worryin' about you if you aren't home soon."

"He won't notice. He won't be home until tomorrow. He's working out of town." She stepped up to me so we were practically touching.

My heart began to beat faster from the close proximity of our bodies. She smelled of sweet soap and lavender. It was a beautiful, just as she was. She pushed up to her tiptoes, lips brushing mine. I stood motionless, indecision flooding through me. Her lips were soft as rose petals. Her arms wrapped around my neck, bringing her closer.

Finally yielding, I responded to a kiss with one of my own. My arms came up and wrapped around her waist, pulling her closer. She moaned softly, her lips opening as if inviting me in. I deepened the kiss, then broke it as quickly as I started it.

"I'm sorry, Miss Mary." I paced away from her trying to get myself under control. My heart was pounding in my chest so hard that it was vibrating through my entire body. I ran my hands over my bald head, squeezing my neck. Turning, I looked at her. She was looking quite disheveled herself. "That can't happen again. It is improper. You're a married lady."

"I don't care." She took a step closer.

I held out a hand, trying to ward her off. "I do care. If anyone saw that kiss, I'd be a dead man. Miss Mary, I don't want to die."

"I want to live as well. I am only alive when I am with you." She came closer, causing me to back up. "Don't do this, Byron. Please. I need you. I have never felt like this in my entire life."

She wasn't the only one feeling things she had never felt. I felt things I had never before as well, but we were from two different worlds, so I couldn't pursue those feelings. If I were honest with myself, it wasn't safe for either of us. If we acted on the feelings, I would be killed, and she would be branded an adulterer or worse. I couldn't let that happen to her.

"You need to go now, Miss Mary. Please don't come back." It took all my will to send her away. I watched her face as tears pooled in her eyes and began to spill down her cheeks. Grabbing her coat, she pulled it on and took off out the door, letting it slam behind her.

I wanted to go after her, hold her, tell her everything would be alright, but it wouldn't. I could never see her again.

Chapter 58

She didn't come back the next day or day after. It hurt me every day she wasn't there, but it was what was best. I had to keep telling myself that over and over. I couldn't let myself fall into a trap where our lives were both imperil. Even if I were willing to risk my life, I couldn't and wouldn't risk hers.

I kept my mind busy during the day and late into the nights with work. I ended up being ahead of schedule on the jobs that I had. I was finishing up the railroad spikes that I had been paid to do almost a month ahead of schedule. It was ridiculous how busy I had to be to keep my mind off Mary. I missed her with my entire being and couldn't stand the thought of not being near her.

Dropping my hammer onto the anvil, I wiped the sweat off my brow and looked around. It was completely dark except for the glowing fire in the forge. I looked up at the clock it said it was half past twelve. I needed to get some sleep. If I could sleep.

As I curled up on the bed, I heard thunder rumble in the distance. Rain began to tap on the roof and windows. With a sigh, I climbed back out of bed, grabbing a couple buckets I kept in the room and strategically placing them throughout the building where there were leaks. Once that was done, I climbed back into bed.

The ticking of the clock and the tapping of the water dripping into the buckets echoed through the building. There was no way I was going to be able to sleep. I tossed and turned trying to get comfortable and drown out the sound. I could have sworn I heard Mary's laugh. Sitting up, I looked around, not seeing anything I cursed myself a fool and resituated on the mattress.

I finally started to doze when I heard a tapping on glass. I frowned and tried to ignore it figuring that it was just the rain pattering on the window from a shift in the wind. I heard it again, this time it sounded like a knock instead of a patter.

Resigned that the noise wasn't going to quit. I got up to go investigate what it was. As I passed through into the main part of the building, I saw an outline of a person outside the glass storefront. As I approached, I could see that it was a woman. I recognized the shape. It looked like Mary. I hurried to the door. Turning the lock, I unlocked and pulled the door open.

There she stood in front of me, in the pouring rain, just staring at me. I stepped to the side and helped her in the building. She was beginning to shiver and was soaked to the bone. I pulled her coat off her and walked away without a word. When I returned, I brought back a wool blanket and led her to the forge. I adeptly lit the forge and used the billows to heat it up. She needed to warm up and dry off quickly.

Once the fire was lit, I took went back to my room and returned with the comforter. I spread it out on the floor in front of the forge and helped her settle down on it. I sat beside her and watched her, waiting for her to speak. It was strange that she had come to me so late at night. The fact she was here at all was odd being I had made her cry when I kicked her out last time I saw her.

Her teeth chattered as she stared at the forge. She didn't speak at first, just stared at the flames. I could see the flames dancing in her eyes. She waited until her teeth were no longer chattering before she spoke. Her voice was soft, gentle, and full of hurt. Hurt that I knew I caused. "I couldn't stay away any longer. I'm sorry. I know you asked me to, but I can't stop thinking about you. My heart hurts to be away from you."

I didn't speak. Words weren't necessary. I pulled her into my arms and held her. Lowering my head, I rested my cheek on the top of her head. The smell of her shampoo filled my nostrils. I wanted to remember her smell for the rest of my days.

She pulled away and looked up at me. Tears threatening to spill over. "Are you going to send me away again?"

I shook my head no. I knew I should, but my heart couldn't take it again. I needed her with me as badly as she needed me. I was afraid of the consequences, but I couldn't worry about that now. The most important thing was in my arms.

She turned so she faced me and got to her knees. We were eye to eye when her mouth came down on mine. It only took the pressure of her lips on mine for me to decide that no matter what, this woman was the one that I wanted, needed, to be with for the rest of my days.

I pulled the blanket off her and began to unfasten her dress. I spread it apart with one hand, as I held her waist with the other. My hand touched her bare skin and she arched her back, bringing herself closer to me. I bared her shoulders pulling her dress down, effectively trapping her arms. My hands glided across her skin, which was as smooth as silk. Her fingers dug into my shoulders as my hands explored her body. I finished disrobing her, my mouth pulled from hers and I gently pushed her down to the floor.

Looming over her, I trailed kisses across her shoulders, making my way down toward her naval. I stopped at her nipples, my mouth covering one, hand covering the other. She moaned as I worked her with my lips, teeth and tongue. I then switched to give the other side some attention.

"Please," Mary begged.

I didn't think I would be able to control myself if I did as she asked, but I couldn't keep her asking. I spread her legs with one hand and unfastened my pants with the other. After freeing myself, I pushed my way into her. The sound she made as I entered her made my blood roar. I forced myself to move slowly at first. She urged me to speed up, I obliged. Before I realized what was happening, I was pushing into her as hard as I could. Her moans were of pleasure that urged me on. As I felt myself let go, she let out a scream and she went with me.

Holding onto her, I rolled so that I was lying on my back and she was lying on my chest. I hadn't wanted to squash her under my weight, so this arrangement worked better. It also got her off the cold hard floor. She was panting, her breathing as hard as my own. Gently brushing her hair back, I asked, "Are you okay?"

She nodded, her hair tickling my nose. "Better than fine. You, my love are magical."

I chuckled. "Are you sure you aren't the witch?"

Her head shot up. "Bite your tongue."

"I have better uses for my tongue than biting it."

I loved the flush that rose up on her cheeks at the implication of my statement.

A sobering thought occurred to me. "Mary, where does your husband think you are?"

She shrugged. "He isn't home. He wouldn't notice my absence anyway. We have separate bedrooms."

"How did you get here?"

"I walked."

"Alone?" I felt alarm rise in me. It was dangerous for a white woman to be walking alone at night. It was dangerous for any woman, no matter the breed or station.

"Aye, but no need to worry. I wasn't seen."

"That isn't what I worry about. You could have been hurt." My hands ran up and down her back. "The wife of someone as powerful as Mr. Williamson would bring in a pretty coin to anyone who dared take the initiative to apprehend her."

"That wouldn't happen."

"You don't know that, Mary. You can't go wandering around alone."

She sat up so she was straddling me. Leaning down, she kissed me softly on the lips. "Yes, sir. Now, let me help distract you."

She leaned forward, lips trailing down my chest. The woman definitely knew how to distract a man.

Chapter 59

We were lying in the floor in front of the forge still. It was as if moving from that spot wasn't an option. I didn't want to break the spell, and I wasn't sure what was going on in her mind. She was nestled up against my side, I was running my fingers lightly down her back. I looked at the hearth to see that the fire had died down to glowing embers, but we were keeping each other warm. She sighed and moved slightly so she was closer to me.

Looking down my chest, I saw her left hand. Her wedding band reflected the light of the dying fire. The sight of the ring brought me back to reality faster than dousing me with cold water.

"Mary?"

"Hmm?"

"We need to talk about something."

She lifted her head and looked at me. "What's wrong, Byron?"

"Why are you here?"

"What?"

"Why are you here? With me. You have a husband at home. Does he know you are gone? What's going to happen now?"

She sat up, pulling the wool blanket around her. "I don't want to have this conversation exposed."

I nodded and sat up as well. "I'm listening."

"You don't know Theodore. He isn't a good man. He isn't kind like you." She sat back on her haunches. "He is out of town on business again. He won't be back for two days. It's just me in the house by myself until he returns. He took the driver and the carriage with him."

"What do you mean he isn't a good man?"

"He is violent. I shouldn't speak ill of my husband but has done some devious things to get where he is. He has lied, cheated, and possibly killed. I'm not sure about the last, but I've heard the whispers in his office. I know that he married me just for my family inheritance."

"You didn't answer my first question. Why are you here?"

She leaned forward and kissed me on the cheek. "I can't get my mind off you. I have been drawn to you since I met you. I tried to stay away, but I couldn't. I wanted to see you right after I left. I knew I had to see you again. You are unlike any man I have ever met. You, unlike anyone else, took the time to show me how to do something that isn't considered ladylike. You are the most compassionate person I have met. You listen. I have never opened up like I have with you. You are special, Byron."

"You are special too, Mary. I'm not going to pretend I understand what is going on between you and Mr. Williamson. I just know what my feelings be. This can't be happening again." Even as I spoke the words, I knew that I wasn't strong enough to stay away from her. She was like a drug and I was addicted to her.

"I can't leave him, but I hate him." The venom in her words made me do a double take. "That's what is going on between me and Mr. Williamson. I have never truly loved him. I tried, but it was an arranged marriage. My parents made me marry him. I wish him dead, then I'd be free."

"Does he hurt you?" It was something that had been lingering on my mind. I hadn't seen any bruises, but that didn't mean anything. She had said he has been out of town so they could have healed while he was gone.

She didn't look at me, just looked away. Her reaction was answer enough. She wasn't being treated as she should be. It made my blood boil and I wanted to kill Theodore Williamson myself. I could rip him apart with my bare hands.

I held her close, gently stroking her hair. I wanted to take her pain away. I would do whatever I could to help her heal and get away from him.

Chapter 60

Our affair continued for months. She would sneak over to my shop when he was out of town. It was the best way to do things, so we weren't caught. It felt wrong, but at the same time it felt so right. She was the love of my life and I knew it. I would never love anyone else the way that I loved her. I had never been in love like this before either. I was helpless against it.

One morning there was a note sitting on the counter. I smiled knowing that Mary had left it behind for me to find. I picked it up, bringing it to my nose. It smelled of her sweet perfume. I carefully unfolded it and stared at the paper, slowly reading what she had written.

My love,

Come to me tonight. We can have dinner.

Love,

Mary

It was risky for me to go to her, but I would do anything she asked. I folded the note back up and went on with my day. The hours seemed to move so slowly. I was anxious and excited to see her, but there was a nagging in the back of my head that was warning me that it was a bad idea.

When the sun went down, I closed up the shop. I rarely had customers after dark. In the night was the prime time for me to do the majority of my forging since I was uninterrupted. Once the shop was dark, I slipped out the back door, locking it.

I made my way down dark alleys, keeping to the shadows on my way to Mary's house. I couldn't afford to be seen lurking around the white neighborhoods. I stopped at the back fence of her yard, staring at the house in awe. It was much bigger than I had imagined, especially since she said that she didn't have a cook or maid.

The house was a colonial size house with a wraparound porch. There was a light shining through the kitchen window, even though the rest of the house was dark. I climbed the fence and carefully walked through the yard to the back door. When I stepped on the porch, it groaned under my weight. Stopping for a moment, I waited to see if it would hold me. When I didn't fall through, I figured it was simply a loose board. I approached the door and stopped within arm's length of it.

Indecision washed over me. I desperately wanted to be with Mary, but that nagging feeling I had was back and louder than ever. It was telling me to turn around and go home. My momma had always told me to listen to my gut, but she also told me to follow my heart. My gut was saying go away, my heart said stay. I didn't know what to do.

Before I had to chance to make up my mind, there was a silhouette of a woman in the window of the door. When she came closer, I saw it was Mary. She opened the door a crack and slipped out. She motioned for me to follow, which I did without hesitation.

We went to the barn and she led me inside. She stood by the door, closing it after I crossed the threshold.

"What's going on?" I whispered. I didn't know why, but felt it necessary to keep my voice down.

She didn't answer right away. She crossed the room and lit a lantern. When she turned and looked back at me, she had a black eye. The right side of her face was swelled and she looked like she had been in a fight.

I rushed to her side. "What happened?"

A tear escaped her eye. Using my thumb, I gently wiped it away. She turned her head so I was cupping her face.

"Theo was home when I returned last night. When I refused intimacy with him, he became angry. He called me a whore and beat me when I refused him." She paused to sniffle. "Then he forced himself on me."

She began to cry. I held her close, trying my best to comfort her. What I wanted to do was bash his brains in with my hammer. All I could see was red and blood thundered in my ears.

The crying let up and Mary spoke again. "He knows I love another. He doesn't know who. He said he was going to kill me and my lover when he found out who it was. He used his belt to –" She cut off as a sob escaped her.

Seeing Mary hurt and in such despair made my mind up. I was going to have to do something about it. I held her until she calmed down. Kissing her forehead, I looked into her eyes. "Can you go visit your parents for a few days?"

"Why?" She dabbed at her eyes with her sleeve.

"Just do it. You need time away. I promise I will make everything better."

She nodded then kissed me gently on the lips. "Thank you."

"I love you, Mary."

"I need to get back." She stood and turned out the lamp, then slipped from the barn. I waited for a few minutes before I followed suit.

Once back in my shop, I paced, trying to calm myself. I was going to have to deal with Theodore Williamson. He hurt the woman I loved. It would never happen again.

Chapter 61

The following night, I made my way back to the Williamson's house. I held my hammer in my hand, carrying against my side so it would be less conspicuous. If anyone saw me, I didn't want them seeing my hammer. It was shit like that that would get a man like me arrested.

When I approached the house, walking straight to the back door without hesitating. I turned the knob, not surprised it was unlocked. Folks in these parts were very trusting. I didn't know the layout of the house, but I did know what Mary had hold me about it. I had a pretty decent idea in my head about how it was set up. From what Mary told me, the study, where Theodore spent the majority of his time was on the opposite side of the house from the kitchen, at the base of the stairs.

I turned the door knob and slowly pushed it open. It swung open silently, and I was grateful for the hinges being oiled. There he was sitting in his chair, facing the fireplace. The sight of him brought back the image of Mary covered in bruises. Anger washed through me again and I charged him without second thought.

Swinging my hammer, I caught him in the side of the head. He screamed and fell as the chair went sideways from the impact. I swung again, not giving him time to recover. There was a crunch as the hammer met his temple. Blood sprayed from his head. Turning the hammer, I used the claw end and continued to hit him in the head with it. I grunted with the effort it took to bust his skull open.

Brains and blood oozed from his head. His eyes were wide with the glassy stare that only death brought. I stood up slowly. Looking down at him, I spat in his face. As I stared at him, my head began to clear. Panic tried to rise to the surface from what I had done. I watched as blood spread around his body.

A blood-curdling scream broke me from the spell I was under. Spinning around, I saw Mary standing there, hands over her mouth, screaming into her hands. Her eyes met mine. I thought I saw them sparkle a split second before they widened and she went screaming into the night.

"Help! He killed him. That negro just murdered my husband!" She ran down the steps and down the sidewalk.

I ran out after her, confused. What was she doing? She wanted him dead and now he was. I helped her. I saved her from his abuse. When she turned left on the sidewalk and lights started coming on in houses around us, I turned and ran the opposite direction.

I couldn't understand what happened. She acted like she didn't know me when she saw me there, but the look in her eyes . . .

Arriving at the shop, I fumbled with the keys to unlock the door. I went inside, locking it behind me. Pacing the room like a caged animal, I stopped in front of the mirror when my reflection caught my attention. I was covered in blood. The dark red stained my skin. I stepped closer and looked into my own eyes. My mind raced as I watched myself. The events of the night and leading up to it ran through my head.

Realization struck me. Mary hadn't loved me. She played with my emotions to get what she wanted. Now that he was dead, I was going to be dead right along with him. It was just a matter of time. I had been played a fool, now was going to suffer the consequences.

There was a pounding on my glass door. I didn't answer and didn't come out of the back room. They were going to have to come in after me. I wasn't going to walk to my death willingly. There were voices yelling and pounding again. I tuned them out as I berated myself for being an idiot.

How could I fall for a woman that was so manipulative? I would have given her the world. I did everything I could to make her happy. I had been an idiot. What was worse, she had known I was one. I walked over to the trunk and opened it. There was the knife I had put away for her when I first met her. I placed it on the bed and wrote a quick note, placing it underneath the knife. I didn't know if she would get it, but I hoped she would.

There was a crash of glass shattering and the voices became louder. Heavy footsteps pounded on the floor as they raced through the shop to find me. A loud crash made me cringe. I didn't know what they knocked over, but it really wasn't my concern any longer.

The bedroom door busted open. Keeping my arms down at my sides, I stayed calm while I was rushed by the mob. A rope was tied around my arms and one around my neck. It took three men to pull me. I wasn't going to fight, but I refused to go easily. They were going to have to work for it.

I was taken to the center of town where there was a large oak tree. The tree was used for hangings and public executions. They tied me to the tree while I was 'tried' for my crime. It was a bunch of white men standing around me, shouting what I had done wrong and how I was going to die. Then they brought Mary out to the middle of the crowd.

She was wrapped in a blanket, tear stained cheeks. Other women were surrounding her, holding her and rubbing her back. They would take turns turning their heads toward me, daggers shooting from their glares.

"Would you try to tell us what happened, Mrs. Williamson?" One of the men asked.

I held my breath, waiting to see if she would defend me.

"This man, came into my home and killed my darling husband, Theodore. When I tried to stop him, he struck me." She turned her head so they could see her face and the bruises.

My heart sank. She was accusing me of the abuse that she received from the hands of her husband.

"We sentence, Byron Smith, to death." A man in a long black robe said. He turned and walked out of the crowd.

The women were ushered away and the men came closer. I closed my eyes trying to escape from my reality. As the name calling and throwing ideas out to what do to me began, I tried myself away from the nastiness. I thought back to the sweet embraces and kisses from Mary.

The first spike driving into my head caused me to cry out. I opened my eyes, but I couldn't see anything but blood. The second one was just as excruciating. As each spike dug its way home, I died just a little more. I could feel the hot blood running down my head. I tried to focus on that. As I began to die, my anger roared to life. I wanted to kill every single one of these men.

Then all went black.

Chapter 62

I roamed the shop, not sure what to do now. I knew I was dead. No one could survive what I had been through. I stopped at the forge, staring at the cold, unlit opening. It pissed me off all over again. I turned, determined that I was going to get even with everyone that was involved in my death.

My first victim was the judge. I found him in his bed asleep with his mistress. I took my hammer that appeared at a thought and beat him to death with it. After the first swing, the mistress woke up, but I killed her with one blow. Then I took my time beating him until his brains were nothing but a mushy mess on the bed.

The last person I went to see was Mary. I stood there, watching her. She sat in her chair, rocking slowly back and forth as she read a book. I stopped, considering simply walking away. Then I remembered the words that she said, the accusations of me beating her to death.

"Why?" My voice sounded eerie. It was a whisper on the wind.

She looked up from the book, searching the room. "Who's there?"

"I loved you."

Her eyes widened as she dropped the book on the floor and stood up. "Byron?"

She walked around the room, rubbing her arms. When she returned, she stroked the fire in the fireplace, bringing it roaring back to life. I stood behind her, watching her. My heart, if I still had one, ached for her. Yet the sting of betrayal was more than I could bear.

"You let them kill me!" I shoved her and she fell into the fireplace.

There was a whoosh and she caught aflame. She screamed and struggled trying to get out of the hearth. When she did get out, she tried running, but the flames ate up the clothing she was wearing burning her skin with it. I watched as she fell against the window. The drapes burst into flame and the entire house was eaten by the fire in minutes.

***

Present Day

I heard the clanging of metal on metal. It was like music to my ears. I hadn't heard that sound in a long time. Following it, I found my way to the noise. There was a man standing with a hammer at an anvil. I watched but didn't understand why he was simply hitting the hammer on the anvil without any heated metal.

The hammering stopped and the man turned to look at me. He smiled and set the hammer gently on the anvil. Holding his hands up in a harmless gesture, he spoke. "I'm not here to hurt you, Byron. I want to help you. I know you have been lost since you died. You got your revenge, yet can't or won't move on. Come with me."

"With you where? You can see me? No one has seen me in a long time." I crossed my arms. I wanted to kill him, but at the same time, I was willing to hear him out.

"To a house where you will be with others like you."

"Others like me? You mean murder victims? Or murderers?"

He shrugged. "A little of both. You will be welcomed. Plus, I'm sure there will be a little killing for you."

"I think I'll pass. I'll just stay here."

I turned away from him.

"I can't let you go." His voice sounded sorry.

"You can't stop me from leaving." The hammer was in my hand and I spun around on my heels swiftly, swinging the hammer as I went.

I missed him. He wasn't where he had originally been standing. I stopped, looking around. Next thing I knew there was a sucking sensation as I was being pulled somewhere.

***

Looking around, I was confused. How did I get in this bedroom? I walked toward the door, with every intention of leaving. When I tried to step over the threshold, a force threw me backwards into the room. I charged it again, determined to get out. No matter how I tried, I could get through the door. Then I decided that I was going to go through the wall. I was a ghost after all. That was as fruitless as trying the door.

Anger rushed through me. Taking my hammer, I started swinging, destroying everything in its path. Once the room was in shambles, I stood there, unsure of my next move. I felt like an animal, caged. If it was an animal the wanted, it was an animal they would get.

Chapter 63

St. Louis, MO 2000

The smell of cooked meats wafted through the air in the kitchen of my bed and breakfast. I took a deep breath, mouth salivating. I had to remind myself that it wasn't for me, it was special for my guests. My shredded barbeque pork was famous. It brought people in constantly. I lifted the lid of the crock pot and stirred it slowly. I added a bit of seasoning and put the lid back down.

A thought occurred to me. Going over to the deep freeze, I opened it to see how much pork I had left. It looked like I had enough for one more pork dinner. That meant I was going to have to get more. The idea made me smile. I enjoyed getting my meat. It always made me happy. Making my customers happy was a wonderful feeling.

There was a knock on my back door. I skipped over and opened it. There stood Derek. We had been dating for a while. I kissed him on the cheek and invited him in.

"You are in a good mood this morning, Ryan." He smiled as poured himself a cup of coffee. "You look absolutely beautiful."

I flipped my hair over my shoulder and blew him a kiss. "Thank you. I am in a good mood. It's an amazing morning. The B-n-B is full, so we are getting a lot of income. And everyone is anticipating the dinner for tonight. It's my shredded pork."

"Have enough for one more?" He pressed me against the refrigerator door and kissed me.

"For you? Always." I returned the kiss and wrapped my arms around his neck. "You know, we have some time before I have to have the breakfast out. We could . . ."

The implication was clear. I wanted sex. I stretched and nipped his ear. He laughed.

"Sorry, baby girl. I wish I could, but I gotta get going. I am helping dad with that new roof on the Henderson place."

I stuck my lip out in a pout. "I don't want you to."

"I'm sorry." He kissed me again. "I'll make it up to you. I promise."

He finished his coffee, placed the mug in the sink and walked back out. I turned and watched him leave. I hated to see him go. As soon as he was out of sight, I turned and went back to cleaning and singing, the turn down forgotten.

***

We were all seated in the dining room, eating dinner. I was at the head of a long table. It was something that I had grown up with. Everyone sitting at the same table, getting to know each other. It was part of the whole B-n-B experience. Derek sat at my right, where he belonged. The guests were all sitting randomly around the table. They had the choice to sit next to those who they came with or intermingle. I always encouraged intermingling.

"This meat is divine," one of the guests gushed. She was probably in her late 40s with dyed blonde hair. "I have never had pork this tender or delicious. What do you do to make it this good?"

I smiled. "It's a family secret recipe. If I told you, I'd have to kill you."

Giggles erupted around the table. I smiled and scooped a forkful of meat into my mouth. I preferred it without a bun. I felt a bun masked the flavors of the meat and seasoning.

I watched the guests quietly interacting with each other. There was one that I kept my eye on. He was a bigger guy, a lot of meat on his bones. He didn't say much, just sat at the other end of the table, shoveling food into his mouth. The way he ate reminded me of a pig. I could almost hear him snorting and oinking as he ate his chow.

Glancing at Derek, I couldn't help but smile. I reached over, touched his hand so he would look at me. I blew a kiss at him. He smiled and blew one back. I loved that he didn't get embarrassed to be affectionate in front of guests.

"Miss Jessop, may I ask how you got into the bed and breakfast trade?" a suit asked as he carefully set down his fork.

"It was a family business. My mother ran the bed and breakfast. When she fell ill and retired, I took over. I love meeting new people, so it worked." I flashed teeth at the suit. "I could just eat you all up."

After dinner, I cleaned up the plates and wiped down the table. My mind stayed on the man that sat by himself. I believed he said his name was Joshua. It didn't matter though. He wouldn't be around much longer. I was curious about him. If I pegged him correctly, he would be down in a bit for something to snack on, then I could find out about him.

Sure enough, I hadn't finished cleaning up the kitchen before I heard footsteps coming down the hall. I stopped and turned to see him standing there awkwardly at the door.

"Sorry, to bother you. I was just wondering if you had any milk. I have wretched heartburn." He looked nervous.

"Sure, come on in and help yourself." I waved him into the room. "Cups are in that cupboard over there and milk is in the fridge."

I watched as he moved around the room, getting his milk. He stood at the island, sipping on it. I approached and leaned against the island across from him. "Tell me about yourself, Joshua."

"It's Josh, and there isn't much to tell, Ms. Jessop." He shrugged as he took a drink of the white liquid.

"Call me Ryan." I reached over and touched his hand that was resting on the counter. "I would like to know more about you. Tell me about your family, your home, pets."

"I am kind of a nomad. I like to travel. This is just one stop on my way to the west coast. I'm hoping to make a living doing stand-up comedy or something along those lines. I don't have much family. Haven't spoken to them in years."

"That's too bad," I stuck a lip out. Yet perfect, I added silently. I stood up straight and walked around the counter. I cut a slice of the cake on the counter and brought it to him. "Here, it's one of my favorites. I think you'll like it."

I watched as he dug into the cake without a second thought. Sometimes it was too easy. People were too trusting.

Chapter 64

I hacked at the lump of meat, trying to cut it off the bone. This part was the worst. The rest of the process had been fun. My knife sliced through the tendons and ligaments detaching it from the bone. Pulling the hunk of meat free, I dropped it on the table with a plop.

I whistled while I trimmed as much of the fat off the meat as possible. If my dinners weren't so popular, I would consider not doing this part. Then again, I loved butchering my animals myself. The only part I had problems with was disposing of the leftover carcass. I needed a new way to do so. I had been doing what others before me had done—buried them in the crawlspace beyond the basement. I couldn't have too many questions about where I got my meats.

After I removed the cuts of meat I wanted, I dragged the carcass over to the hole, dropping it in. My breath heaved from the excursion of moving it. It was heavier than most of the animals that I had used. I took a moment to catch my breath before I covered up the remains.

Going back to my work station, I cleaned up the blood and put the meat in plastic lined paper like they had the butcher shop. When I carried the packs upstairs and put them on the counter. Going to the pantry, I opened the door and grabbed the key that was hanging on the wall. Unlocking the deep freeze, I placed the packs inside and relocked it when finished.

I rushed upstairs and took a shower in my private bathroom. I needed to get all the blood off. Somehow, I had gotten blood in my blonde hair and it took extra shampoo to get it out. Once done, I studied my reflection. My chocolate brown eyes were deep contrast to my pale skin. I was almost translucent. I cocked my head as I studied myself. Some people thought I was crazy, but I couldn't see it in my eyes.

I brushed the thought away and went back into my bedroom to get dressed. I decided while changing that I was going to make a roast with carrots and potatoes for dinner. That meant getting some of my meat and putting it in the crock pot.

***

I guess I became too greedy, cocky, whatever you wanted to call it. I had picked an especially large heifer for my next butchering. She was an obnoxious sort and held complete disregard for myself and my place. It made me mad, so she was an easy choice.

I watched as she shoveled the cake into her huge pie hole. It didn't take long for the sedative to overcome her. When she hit the ground, I grabbed her arms and dragged her to the basement door. I stopped long enough to unpadlock the door. With guest roaming about, one could never be too safe. I didn't want them roaming around in my work area.

Opening the door, I walked behind her and shoved. She rolled down the wooden stairs and landed on the cement floor with a thud. I hoped the fall didn't bruise the precious meat too badly. I shut the door, locking it from the inside and headed down the stairs.

Once I hit the landing, I grabbed her arms and pulled her to the table. There were meat hooks hanging from ceiling, I went over to the lever and turned it, lowering the hooks. There was no way I could lift her without them.

I walked over, grabbing a hook and shoving it into the hip. The pain woke the animal up and she screamed. It began to struggle and try to get away from me. Damn it, I thought. The tranquilizers that were in the cake weren't strong enough to keep this one down.

I cursed under my breath while I tried to regain control of the situation. I had never had to fight one like this. When she bit me, I saw red. Screaming, I slammed a fist into her mouth. Stupid cow. I would show her who was dominant. Reaching out, I grabbed the stick of the cattle prod I kept for emergencies. I shoved it into her side, the electric jolt strong enough to subdue her.

Finally subdued, I hurried up and hooked the other meat hook into her hip. This time she didn't move. Turning the lever, I raised the hooks back up, so she was hanging upside down. I tied her arms together so that she wouldn't be able to use them against me, if she happened to rouse. Grabbing a knife, I walked to her and slit her throat deeply. I knew that I sliced it deep enough that the tendons and veins were all slit.

Blood sprayed out of the wound like a sprinkler. I was soaked in it in a matter of moments. I couldn't help but laugh. It tickled when the blood hit me. Taking the knife, I slid it down the clothing, peeling them off like layers of an onion. Once the clothing was removed, I stepped back and waited for the majority of the blood to drain. I watched as it poured over the drain that was in the floor. I pursed my lips and glanced around. I was feeling impatient. I wanted to get to work.

An idea struck me. I looked down at my bloody clothes, then shrugged to myself. Stripping down, I tossed my clothes in the corner. I didn't want to mess them any further. Prancing over to the other side of the basement, I turned on the stereo I had set up there. *N Sync blared from the speakers, and I began to dance. I loved their music, it had such a beat. Dancing back to the heifer, I picked up the dropped knife and stood in front of her.

"You're all I ever wanted—" I sang along. Leaning forward, I pried the closed eyes open so they stared lifelessly at me. "If you hadn't been a bitch, well, okay, yeah that didn't matter."

I twirled. "What was that you say? You don't understand? Let me explain. No, stop and listen. You shouldn't have been so condescending. You would have been special and chosen nicely, but you couldn't be polite. Talking about my place with your nose turned up. You didn't have to stay here. You could have been to a different one or stayed at one of the hotels.

"Now I have to finish my work before the meat spoils. You will finally be a useful cow." Taking the knife, I sliced her from groin to breast, stepping back as the intestines and guts spilled out. They pooled onto the ground at my feet. Blood and guts spread across the floor, covering my toes and feet in blood.

I reached forward and pulled on the intestines trying to free them from the body. Once they had no more give, I sliced it, so it fell completely free to the floor. When I determined that she was cleaned out as good as I could get her from that angle, I lowered her to the table to keep working.

I talked to the animal, I like did with the others, and sang along to the radio. There was a thudding upstairs. I stopped and looked up at the ceiling. That was weird, I thought everyone was asleep. Shaking my head, I figured it was just a guest getting a snack. I turned up the radio, trying to drown out the noise of the guest moving about. It was distracting. Getting back to work, I didn't hear the basement door being kicked in.

Next thing I knew, I was surrounded my men in body armor and helmets. I looked around, confused. "What are you doing here?"

I didn't think about how it probably looked, me, elbow deep in the heifer's body.

"Don't move! Don't fucking move!" one of the men shouted at me. Guns were trained at me.

Slowly, I turned to face them. Smiling, I asked, "Are you here for a roast sandwich?"

"Get on the ground!" another shouted.

I cocked my head to the side, not fully comprehending. I was tackled, my face went into the blood. My arms were yanked behind my back, cuffs slapped on. I was jerked back to my feet now that I was cuffed and under their control.

"You're under arrest. You have the right to remain silent," the officer holding my arm Mirandized me.

"I have to finish butchering my meat. I have shredded pork to make and guests to tend. Can you guys come back tomorrow?" I looked back at the corpse on the table with longing. I needed to get things done.

They pulled me up the stairs, only stopping to wrap a wool blanket around me, covering my naked body. Led out, I was put into a police car. When the door was shut, I watched as the red and blue lights danced across my house. The only thought running through my head was the fact my meat was going to spoil.

Chapter 65

"*Miss Jessop, do you understand the charges against you?*" The judge asked as I stood next to my attorney.

"Charges?" I repeated. "I mean, yes."

"Your Honor, my client doesn't understand the consequences of her actions and does not understand the charges. She has lost her sense of reality." My attorney spoke up. My family paid her a hefty fee to help keep me out of prison. When my aunt had heard what happened, she had flown in from California and paid for the best legal team. "We wish to put in an insanity plea."

"Objection!" The prosecutor shouted as he rose from his seat. "Miss Jessop knowingly killed and butchered her guests at her business then cooked them up. If that weren't bad enough, she fed them to her other guests. We believe that Miss Jessop was fully aware of her actions."

"The hearing will be postponed while the determination of Miss Jessop's mental stability is tested." The judge banged his gavel, then stood up, dismissing the room.

I looked at my attorney. She had long brown hair, pulled back in a punishingly tight bun. Her face was plain but pretty. Hopefully, she was as good at her job as she was dressed. "What now?"

"You will go through psychiatric testing to see if you are able to withstand trial. After that, we will reconvene in court, and the based on the findings, the judge will make a decision on whether you should stand trial."

I nodded. Made sense I supposed. "Does that mean I can go home?"

She shook her head. "I'm afraid not. You will remain in custody while the testing is done."

***

I sat in my room, staring out the window. I hated being here. It was miserable. Since I was considered criminally insane, I was going to be locked in the asylum for the rest of my days. It wasn't a pleasant place. I listened to screams through the night, sometimes I was one of them.

The doctors didn't treat us as humans, but that was to expected. We were no longer human, we were crazy animals trapped in a cage together. Some of the patients tried to pretend to be human, others weren't that concerned.

I watched as a nurse pushed one of the inmates across the lush green grass of the backyard toward the garden. A couple others were playing chess, even though I was sure they were just going through the motions.

My door opened, making me turn to see who was coming into the room. It was Dr. Meissen. He was the doctor that was assigned to deal with me. He smiled as he shut the door behind him. "How are you today, Ryan?"

I raised an eyebrow. I didn't want to speak to him, but I knew I had to. It was part of the treatment. I was in maximum security of the psych ward, which meant I couldn't go anywhere unattended and the doctors and nurses kept stun guns on them. If we got out of control, we were stunned. After being stunned, we would be loaded with meds that were so strong, they had to put us in diapers because we were incapacitated for days afterwards.

With a sigh, I answered. "I'm fine. Dr. Meissen?"

"Yes?"

"Do you think I could have kitchen duty? I miss cooking and doing something," I pleaded, hoping he would relent.

"Not yet. Once I feel you have been rehabilitated to the point you are no longer a danger to the other patients, then we will revisit this discussion."

I nodded. There was no point in arguing with him. His word was law in that wretched place. I hated it. I missed my freedom. I missed being able to listen to my music and dance. I missed Derek. I sighed again.

"Are you still having the dreams?" Dr. Meissen studied my chart as he asked.

"No."

"Well, to be safe, I think we are going to up your dosage. There is a note here from the overnight charge nurse that you tend to be restless and have been sleepwalking."

"Yes, sir."

"If the pills don't work, I think we are going to need to do a more aggressive treatment."

A more aggressive treatment repeated over and over in my head. I knew what he meant by that as well. I had heard talk of the aggressive treatments. That was shock therapy or something horrible like that. One inmate claimed the doctor shot something into his brain making him be able to pick up radio stations. My roommate said that the treatment was shock therapy. She said they strapped her down and connected wires to her all over her body, including her vagina. They would flip a switch and electricity would go through all of her nerve endings, causing her body to convulse and tremor. It would scramble the brain. It was something I didn't want to try.

"Let's talk," the doctor sat down, crossing one leg over the other.

"I have nothing to say."

"Then answer me this. What made you make you special meals?"

"I wanted to treat them to something special. It was special. Everyone loved it."

"How did you choose your victims?"

I cocked my head. "Victims? Oh, you mean my animals? Easy, they chose me. I could tell they wanted to be something more than they already were."

"Did they know they were going to die?"

I shrugged. "I'm sure they knew. Deep inside they knew. If not, they wouldn't have come to me."

He sighed as he made notes to the chart. Snapping it shut, he stood up. "I'll have dinner brought to your room, and it will be an early bedtime for you. In the morning, you will join groups to see how you do in the group setting. Have a good evening."

When he left me alone, I looked back out the window. I was going to get to join the groups in the morning. It would be the first time I had been in the groups. All my sessions have been individual. I contemplated the thought of being with people again. It excited me. I couldn't wait until sessions.

Chapter 66

We sat in a circle like a group of friends that were just sitting for a visit, yet some of us were shackled. It was a comical sight, and I couldn't help but giggle. My roommate, Veronica, was in the group with me. She looked at me sharply like she was warning me to shut up.

"Hello, everyone," Dr. Meissen said as he looked around the group. "Let's welcome Ryan to the group. This is her very first group session."

There were murmurs of hellos and one emphatical "die bitch". I just sat there, staring at the doctor. He watched me with a smile on his face. Then he looked down at a notebook he held in his hands. He appeared to be reading something on it.

"Let's start with Veronica," he said looking back up. "Veronica, anything you want to share?"

"Um, let's see." She pursed her lips and tapped a fingertip on them. "I had a team meeting, and we don't think this is going to work. We need to reevaluate the staffing choices. We really like Ryan though and want her to become Senior VP."

I frowned. "Senior VP of what?"

"The company, duh."

I rolled my eyes and turned away. Veronica was certifiable. There was no company. We were all in the same crazy boat. Maybe I was just as certifiable. I shook that notion away. "You're nuts."

"Ryan," Dr. Meissen spoke up. "We respect everyone in this circle. We don't judge here. This is a nonjudgmental circle. We are all friends here."

"Are we?" I asked pulling up on my shackled arms. My arms were shackled to the chair so I could only raise them about chest high. "If we are, why am I, and a few others, chained like rabid dogs?"

"That is only a safety precaution, Ryan. Those of you shackled are done so for yours and our safety, until you are deemed safe."

"I never hurt anyone," I argued.

Eyebrows rose above his dark, thick framed glasses. "Never? If you never hurt anyone then why are you here?"

"People think I'm crazy."

"And are you?"

I pondered that for a moment. Was I? Slowly I shook my head no. "No, I'm not crazy."

"Is that why you were deemed mentally unstable and unable to stand trial for murders of more than ten people?" He leaned forward, putting his elbows on his knees. "They found the remains of multiple bodies buried in your basement, where you put them. Human meat was found in your freezer that you kept locked in the kitchen. Now, can you say you never hurt anyone?"

"I was helping people. I was feeding those in need. My guests and I donated to the local homeless shelters. I helped. I liked to help. I need to help. How can helping be harmful?"

"Homeless shelters," Dr. Meissen wrote something in the notebook before looking back at me. "Ryan, I am going to suggest that we carry this conversation on in private during our one on one session. Sound okay to you?"

I shrugged. He was trying to make me sound like a monster. I wasn't a monster. I was a good person that liked to help and cook. Feeding people was a passion of mine. I hoped one day he could see that. Maybe I could start helping and cooking again.

***

Time passed differently in the asylum than it did in the real world. I didn't know if it was because of the drugs or the crazies, but time seemed to stand still and fly at the same time. I wasn't sure how long I had been in there, but once I started following the doctor's rules and orders, I was allowed more freedoms.

They finally put me in the kitchen to cook as part of my therapy. It made me extremely happy to be able to cook again. One of the first things I did was bake a cake. Unfortunately, they didn't have anything that I would normally put in it, like buttermilk, but I would make do.

I was stirring the soup, wishing that I had some of my roast to go with it, but I didn't. I caught myself pouting, so I forced myself to stop. It wasn't doing me any good to pout. I added a dash of garlic and sang quietly to myself.

I felt the body heat from someone walking up behind me. "What are you cooking? Brains a la mode?"

I turned to look at the man standing behind me. He was bulky and wearing a yellow outfit, which meant that he wasn't a violent criminal. His crime was sexual in nature. I turned, crossing my arms, leaning my butt against the stove.

"You wish. I'm making vegetable soup."

He stepped closer. "I'll give you my meat."

He reached down, grabbing his cock and balls, giving them a squeeze and arching his hips closer to me. I raised my eyebrows and glanced down at his hand, full of himself.

Uncrossing my arms, I put one behind me as I arched my back toward him. His eyes drifted own to my chest like I planned. I grabbed the knife that was sitting on the cabinet, and in one swift movement, I had the knife pressed against the base of his penis.

"Okay, take a deep breath this is going to hurt." I shoved down, feeling the skin pop as he screamed a blood curdling scream. Before I could cut it completely off, we were yanked apart. I was shoved to the ground, nurses and aides piling atop of me. I felt the pinch of the needle biting into my skin and everything went fuzzy.

When things came back into focus, I was strapped to a bed in a hospital gown. I looked around the room, and I noticed I was in a basement. Frowning, I tried to sit up, but wasn't able to. I struggled against the restraints, but there was no give. I couldn't get out of it.

There were aides and doctors surrounding me. One was placing these stickers on me that had wires connected to them. I struggled more with no avail.

"Dr. Meissen, she's waking up, do we need to sedate her again?" one of the aides asked.

"No. She isn't going anywhere. I want to see her reaction to the treatment. Once she is ready, please clear the room. I would like to speak with the patient alone."

"Yes, Doctor."

They rushed around finishing up. I jumped and jerked one when of the aides put a sticker on my inner thigh. I felt like I was covered in those stickers and was terrified of what was going to happen next. I remembered what Veronica had said about the electroshock and the electrodes on the vagina.

When we were alone, the doctor sat down next to me. "Do you know why you are here?"

I licked my lips before speaking. "I don't even know where I am."

"You are in the basement of the building. We are doing a little electroshock therapy. You need a more aggressive treatment since you tried to castrate Donald in the kitchen."

"Donald told me to use it."

"I'm sure that's not what he meant. You know it's not okay to cook people. This should help clear your head."

He stood up and walked over to a control. He pushed a couple buttons and turned a knob. At first the buzzing was light, running across my skin in waves. I convulsed lightly, but it wasn't anything that I couldn't handle. Surprising myself, I giggled at the vibrating sensations. Dr. Meissen frowned at my giggles and turned the intensity up. It stopped tickling and started to hurt.

I screamed as pain rushed through me. It felt like my brain was vibrating on the verge of exploding and turning to mush. Thrashing, I involuntarily attempted to escape, but it was useless. There was no getting away from the torment. When it finally stopped, I continued to have little shivers of electricity rushing through me.

The doctor approached me, leaning over with a little penlight looking into my eyes. I followed the light, then crossed my eyes. I watched as he leaned closer. With a rush of adrenaline, I lifted my head, biting his nose with all my might. I felt it give and blood squirt as the tip of his nose came off in my mouth. I spat it out, spraying is face with blood and the chunk of nose.

He screamed, covering his face. He stumbled over to the control panel and hit a button. An alarm sounded then the electricity shot through me again, my screams mingling with his. Suddenly there was a frenzy of movement and everything went dark.

Chapter 67

Coming to, I found myself in a dark room with a straight jacket on. I struggled to sit up. It was a difficult task, but I succeeded. Standing up, I walked around the room taking everything in. Pressing myself up against the wall, I was surprised to find that it had some give. I was in a fucking padded cell.

Walking to the door, I stood on my tiptoes and peeked through the window in the door. All I could see was the door across the hall. I pressed my cheek against the window, looking down the hallway, first one way, then the other. Just more doors. There was no one in the hallway.

Disappointed, I turned and walked back to the bed, gently sitting down. My head pounded; eyes burned. I was miserable. If I thought about it, I could still feel slight tremors coursing through my body from the jolt. I needed some Tylenol or aspirin. Something to treat the pain. With nothing else to do, I lay back down on the bed and closed my eyes determined to sleep.

When I woke up, an aide was standing over me. He held a little cup that held my meds in it. I struggled to sit up, and he reached down, pulling me up using one of the arms of the jacket.

"Open." The one word held contempt. It was obvious he didn't want to be there.

I complied, letting him dump the pills in my mouth. I closed to swallow then opened back up, raising my tongue so he could make sure that I indeed swallowed the given pills. He nodded then walked out of the room, not closing the door. He was only gone for a moment. When he returned, he had a tray of food.

He fed me what was on the tray, barely giving me the time to taste it or even chew it. I was lucky that it was pureed or I would have probably choked on it. When it was empty, he stood and took the tray out.

Closing the door, he stood at the window and stared in at me in disgust. "Nurse Hanson will be in later to take you to shower and use the facilities. You will be forced to wear a muzzle, just like Hannibal Lector."

I could hear his laughter as he walked away. I was angry and disgusted. They were treating me like an animal. But I wouldn't let them bring me down. I would keep my mind and peace.

It didn't take long for Nurse Hanson to show up. She smiled apologetically as she placed the muzzle over my face. She helped me stand up and led me to the bathroom so I could relieve myself. She helped me clean up as much as possible, but the straight jacket wasn't allowed to be removed and a shower wasn't a possibility like the aide had said. The nurse did, however, wash my hair and clean my face around the muzzle.

"I'm sorry that we have to do it like this, Ryan. I know you wouldn't intentionally hurt anyone, but it's for your safety and mine. It's also protocol," she explained while she dried my hair. Setting the towel to the side, she began to gently brush it. She leaned down and whispered. "Dr. Meissen deserved what he got."

I smiled through the muzzle. At least someone sided with me.

***

I woke up hot. Sweating. Struggling to be vertical, I frowned. It wasn't just night sweats or boob sweat. It was a dry heat. I looked around, not sure why it was so hot. I stood and went to the door. The sound of an alarm going off startled me.

I could hear the other patients that were in isolation beginning to panic. I looked out the window, still not seeing anything. The alarm sounded like a smoke alarm. What in the hell was going on? As I watched out the little window, the temperature in the room increased exponentially.

Smoke began to pour into the room from the vents in the ceiling. Panic rushed through me as I pressed myself against the door. Why wasn't anyone coming to help? There should be firefighters, aides, someone coming to help us out of the cells.

There was a crackling as the ceiling caved, burning beams and embers falling on me. I screamed, trying to cover my face. I began to cough from the smoke and heat. My throat and eyes burned. I couldn't get a breath as the room heated up like an oven.

The flames began to bite at my skin as the cloth was burned away. The pain was so excruciating that I couldn't even scream. They licked their way up my legs and body, burning me alive.

Chapter 68

They rebuilt the asylum after the fire destroyed it initially. It took them some time, but when it was finished and opened for business, it looked better than ever. The new asylum looked less like a hospital and more like a home. The floors were still tiled, but there were rugs placed strategically to make it look less sterile.

I stayed at the asylum, tormenting the patients that resided there. Veronica had survived and returned after the rebuild. She had a private suite, as did the other patients that had survived the fire. It was the staff's way of apologizing for the mishap.

The fire had been electrical and started in the wall of the nurses' breakroom. The joke had been that the coffee pot had been overworked and needed coffee itself. That was what the nurses joked about, but the whispers that weren't spoken aloud was that it was the electroshock therapy equipment malfunctioning that caused the fire.

I made my way into Veronica's room. She was sitting at her desk coloring a picture. Her brows were drawn in a line of concentration. I stared down at the picture. I couldn't tell what it was, it looked like scribbles, but her brain had been pretty much mush since she had a lot of Dr. Meissen's treatments.

"Go away, you don't exist." Her voice was a murmur of a sound. Her words slurred from the medications that ran through her system.

"I do exist," I insisted.

"Nope. You died. Now shoo."

"Nuh uh. Not going anywhere."

"What do you want, Lector?"

"Don't call me that."

"Why? It's what the nurses called you. They still joke about you."

"I know, but that's not my name."

"You don't have a name anymore, you're dead and a figment of my imagination according to Dr. Meissen. He says that I'm having episodes from the trauma."

"Veronica, you may be batshit crazy, but you know you aren't hallucinating. It's me."

"Go eat someone." The tone was bland. I cocked my head not sure if she was serious.

I shrugged and left the room. Maybe killing someone would make me feel better. I was feeling anxious and annoyed. I needed to do something. I just roamed the halls constantly and bugged those who were able to see me, which weren't many.

I made my way to the kitchen. There was a man using hot oil making French fries. Using the anger and frustration I had pent up, I ran to him, shoving his face into the hot oil. When the tried to scream, the boiling oil entered his nose, mouth, and throat. When I let go, he fell backward. His face was blistered and blackening.

I grabbed a knife from the block and stabbed him in the heart. Watching the blood and life drain out of him made me feel giddy. I knew what I needed to do.

***

The young man entered the building, looking around. He looked surprised as he followed the social worker. I followed as he walked with her, listening to her discuss the perks of the asylum and updates done after the rebuild.

"We have the latest technology and updates in our building. Yes, there were issues with the electrical before, but it was an old building and hadn't been updated like it needed. Now everything is up to date and up to code. In fact, it exceeds the minimum requirements necessary for a facility such as this." She turned her head to look at the young man. "Mr. Bucco, can you tell me again why you are here?"

"My poor sister has lost touch with reality. I'm afraid she will hurt herself if left unsupervised. She needs more care than we are able to provide. I've heard some great things about this this facility." He smiled charmingly.

"Ah, yes. It is quite unfortunate when that happens." She led on, talking about the perks and upgrades of the building.

"Can I ask a question?" he asked while looking around.

"Anything."

"Did anyone pass away in the fire?"

"Um," she licked her lips. "I'm not entirely positive on that. There may have been a fatality or two."

I cocked an eyebrow to see the man, Mr. Bucco, doing the same. Even I could tell the social worker was lying. It was interesting how they didn't disclose the deaths.

"Oh, I thought I had heard something about it on the news." He rubbed the back of his neck. "If my sister hears of any deaths in the facility or the grounds, she will claim she sees the ghosts of the dead. She thinks she can talk to ghosts."

"I see."

The social worker was paged over the intercom and excused herself, leaving the young man in the sun room with some of the patients and aides. He roamed around the room, studying pictures that hung on the wall. He made his way to the far side of the room where there was no one around. I followed, captivated with this man.

His head turned slightly, eyes meeting mine. "I'm guessing you died in the fire."

His voice had been so soft I wasn't positive his lips even moved as he spoke.

I nodded. "You can see me?"

It was his turn to give me a slight nod. "You're Ryan Jessop, right?"

"How do you know?"

"I've been looking for you."

"Why?"

"I need you. I have a place for you in a home. A home where you will be free to roam and kill at your heart's content."

I scoffed at that. "No one allows murders."

"I'm not just anyone, if you haven't noticed. I mean, I'm talking to you, and you're dead."

"If anyone heard you, you would be put in here too. I mean, look at what you are doing to your sister," I whispered.

"I don't have a sister," he whispered back. "Like I said, I was looking for you, and I'm taking you with me."

He opened his hand, I hadn't seen him move, it had been in his pocket. He held a crystal that flashed with light before everything went dark.

The next thing I knew, I was in a pink bedroom. Everything was pink. The guy was standing there, leaning against the door. He smiled at me as I made eye contact with him.

"What in the actual fuck?"

He laughed. "Now, that isn't very lady like."

I raised an eyebrow. "Who says I'm a lady? I'm a psycho killer, remember?"

"Trust me, I haven't forgotten." He held a handout. "Welcome to your new home, Bane Manor. Cyrus Bane is the owner, yet is willing to give you free reign of the house as long as you don't try to kill him. Any guests are free game."

I narrowed my eyes at him. "Why did you bring me here?"

"You are a very special woman, Miss Jessop. You are needed for what Bane is planning. You are one of 12 key elements."

With that, he left me alone to my thoughts. I was special he said. I hadn't been called special in a long time. I didn't know why, but I had a feeling he was right. There was something different about this place. It pulled at me, and I couldn't figure out why.

Black Zodiac Ghost 12

Titan

Chapter 69

Des Moines, IA, 1990

The screams echoed off the walls of the empty warehouse. They were music to my ears. The sound of the screams was arousing. I could feel myself harden as the screams started and release as they died off. It was better than sex.

I stared down at the woman. Her dead eyes were wide, mouth hanging open. Her last thoughts had been of me and my ministrations. I used one finger and closed her mouth. I leaned forward and kissed her gently on the forehead.

"Sleep now." My voice rumbled into the silence. I raised my hand and closed her eyes.

I needed to get her put to bed. Crossing the room, I picked up the tarp. Spreading it out on the floor, I straightened it to its full size. I picked her up and carefully laid her down on it. I wrapped her up, tying the tarp in three places. I couldn't let any part of her show. She would get cold. I had to keep her warm as she was put to bed.

I loaded her in the back of my truck and climbed in. Turning the key, it roared to life. I pulled out and drove down the street a few blocks before I turned on my headlights. I drove for miles, through the lights of the city. Once I got outside the city limits, it was dark. So dark, that the bright setting on my headlights were necessary.

I drove for miles until I came across a dirt road. I turned onto the narrow path, carefully navigating into the woods. There was a gate that stopped any trespassers from going any further. Stopping, I climbed out and grabbed my sleeping beauty from the bed of the truck, slinging her over my shoulder. I knew that I wouldn't wake her by carrying her.

I opened the gate and walked through it into the darkness. I continued walking, occasionally shifting the woman over my shoulder. She was heavier than I remembered. I turned off the path into the woods. I had the perfect place for her rest. When I approached the spot, I gently placed her on the ground. I removed the tarp. She wouldn't need it now.

I turned to walk away then stopped and turned back. She had the view of the stars and could hear the trickle of a stream nearby. I was almost jealous of the serenity of her new home. Shaking my head, I turned away from her and began to walk. I had to get back to the warehouse. I had some cleaning to do before I went home.

***

I dropped my keys in the bowl by the front door that my wife had put there to specifically keep the keys in. I never understood why she had us put it in a bowl instead of buying one of those things that hung on the wall with hooks that said 'keys'. Whatever made her happy, I decided.

Pulling off my boots, I tossed them in the corner by the door and headed upstairs. I needed to shower before I went to bed. I never went to bed with the smell of my women on me. My wife, Christine, would have a fit. She was a mighty jealous woman anyway.

After showering, I put on a pair of sweat pants, then went to check on the kids. I opened the first door to see Brandon, sprawled across the bed, one leg hanging off. He reminded me of myself at that age. Well, mostly. Where he was social, I had been a loner. I pulled the door closed quietly and moved on.

The next door I opened was the girls' room. Emmy and Lydia were both asleep as well. Emmy was lying in her crib, sleeping similarly to the way Brandon had been. Lydia was curled in a ball in the middle of her bed. She was curled up so tightly and surrounded by stuff animals, she was difficult to see. Walking into the room, I covered Emmy up. She was little and I didn't want her getting cold. Her eyes were open a slit and it made me think of my woman asleep out in the woods. Leaning down, I kiss her on the forehead and walk out of the room.

I enter the master bedroom and silently cross the floor to the bed. Pulling back the blanket, I climb into the bed next to Christine. She shifted, eyes opening sleepily. She smiled at me and curled up next to me. My arm went over her, pulling her closer. I kissed her on the top of my head and drifted off to sleep.

The next morning, I went down to the kitchen, to see the kids were all up and eating breakfast. Christine was talking on the phone as she tried feeding the baby some kind of bright orange baby food. I walked to the coffee pot and poured myself a cup.

My head was pounding from lack of sleep. Sometimes my nights out went longer than they should and I suffered for it the next day. I hoped the black magic I was sipping would help get rid of the pounding behind my eyes. I sipped the hot liquid and felt the caffeine rushing through my body.

I joined the kids at the table and listened to them ramble about the events of the day before, school, and then they began to argue about who would get to play the Nintendo after they got home that evening. I listened quietly until Brandon threatened to hit Lydia.

"Brandon," I scolded. "you need to be nice to your sister. We don't hurt women. We treat them with respect and revere them. Now apologize."

"Sorry, Lydia." He mumbled under his breath as he stared down at his plate of bacon and eggs.

"Now finish up and get ready for the bus."

They finished eating and took off up the stairs. As soon as they disappeared, I turned my attention to my wife. She smiled at me while holding the phone on her shoulder and feeding the baby with her free hand.

"Yes, that'd be great. See you then." She pulled the phone from her ear and looked around like unsure what to do. Helping out, I took the phone from her, placing it on the base hanging on the wall. "Thanks, hun. You were out late last night."

I inwardly tensed, hoping she didn't notice. "Yeah, sorry. The game went longer than normal. I would have called, but I didn't want to wake you or the kids."

"It's fine. I'm not upset. Just an observation."

I turned away, rinsing out my mug. I was going to have to get ready to go to work. The factory job I had was what kept the bills paid and food on the table. I also needed to start planning my next outing.

"Kyle," Christine's voice interrupted my train of thought. "That was Mom. She will be here Thursday through the weekend. I know you are probably working and I have that seminar out of town, so she's keeping the kids."

"Sounds great." I repressed the sigh as I smiled at my wife. That was just great. All I needed was another person in the house. My mother-in-law had a habit of keeping a close eye on me. She had never liked me and tried to convince Christine to leave me. Now the bitch was going to be here.

I wished that I could kill her and be done with it. I couldn't, so I would just deal with her. I got my boots on and headed out the door for work.

Chapter 70

Work was hell in its own right. I stood at a machine and made sure that it ran smoothly for eight hours a day. The only time that I could leave was when I had someone to cover me. I hated the job, but I had to take care of my family.

When work ended, I went home, changed, and told Christine I was going to go have a few drinks with the guys from work. In reality, I was going to go watch my next woman. I had her lined up since right after I picked my last. Her name was Molly. She worked at the tavern that the guys spent their evenings drinking. It made it easier for me to keep an eye on her and stay close to the truth with Christine.

I walked in, spotting the guys huddled at the corner of the bar. I walked over to them and signaled for Molly to bring me a beer. She grabbed a bottle, popped the top and handed it over with a smile. I nodded my thanks, then turned my attention to the guys, well appeared to turn my attention to them. I knew where Molly was at all times though.

"Man, Johns is a dick." One of the guys complained after taking a pull of his beer.

"Right," I agreed. "He was up my ass most of the day."

"At least he didn't try to write you up for takin' a piss."

"He did give me a verbal warning for being a minute late from break." That still pissed me off. I wanted to punch the douchebag.

The bitch session continued, each guy trying to top the last with what Johns had done to them. I tuned them out while I drank my beer. My eyes drifted over to Molly who was leaning n the bar, talking to a patron. She smiled at him and jealousy twisted in my gut. She was mine, what was she doing talking to that buffoon?

I scrubbed a hand over my face and drained my beer. Those emotions weren't going to do anyone any good. Emotions made one sloppy and that's one thing I never was, sloppy. My actions had to stay practical and precise.

I ran my tongue across my teeth, then set the beer bottle down on the counter, signaling at Molly. She came back over with a new beer and handed it to me. The empty bottle disappeared in one smooth motion.

"Thanks," I murmured. She walked away after a smile.

At the end of the night, I stood there, while she figured up my tab. I slowly, methodically, tapped my fingers on the bar as she did the math. I had drank a little more than I normally did. I didn't mind waiting, it meant more time I got to spend with Molly.

"It comes up to eighteen." She smiled at me.

I pulled the cash out of my wallet and handed it to her, including a tip. I smiled and walked away, putting my wallet in my pocket as I strode out the door. Once in the parking lot, I climbed in my truck and pulled out of the lot and drove down the street, making a trip around the block. When I came back around, I parked, turning off my lights.

I watched through the window as Molly did through the usually clean up and closing routine. When she walked out the door, I felt the adrenaline rush me. I wanted to take her now, but I knew I had to wait. I wasn't ready for the next one.

She locked the door and walked to the sidewalk. I watched as she walked down the street. I hadn't realized that she didn't drive to work.

The temptation was almost too much to resist. She was helpless and alone in the night. She turned the corner and disappeared into the night.

Sitting there, I continued to stare at where she disappeared. I didn't have to follow her to know where she lived. I had lifted her wallet from her purse and got her address from her wallet a while back. I had also been able to replace it without her noticing. She would go another block before she reached her apartment building.

Finally, I started the truck and started to head home. Two blocks from the house, I changed my mind. Turning, I went to the warehouse district instead of the house. I needed to prepare things so I could add Molly to my collection. It was important for the process that everything was ready. I wanted everything perfect for Molly when she came to me. Once at the warehouse, I pull into my bay and climbed out of the truck. I went in and took inventory of what I had and needed. I planned on going to replenish my supplies after work.

Heading back to my truck, I knew I needed to get home before I was missed.

Chapter 71

It was time. I couldn't hold it inside anymore. I needed Molly. She needed to be in my collection. I went to the bar after work like I had been doing for weeks. The other guys weren't there, so I sat at the bar and Molly handed me a beer.

"Where are the guys?" She asked smiling.

I shrugged. "They should be along soon, I reckon."

"You guys do tip well." She smiled and walked away to a waiting patron.

I didn't care if the guys showed up or not. They never said anything about coming out, but I knew several of them did almost nightly. I would feel better if they didn't show up anyway. Maybe they wouldn't know I was here. The less people that knew I was at the bar, the better.

I stayed until closing time. After paying my tab, I smiled as thunder began to roll. I couldn't time it better if I tried. "Sounds like a storm is rolling in."

She sighed as she put the money in the register. "Yeah, hopefully, I can get clean up done and get home before the rain."

"Let me give you a ride."

She frowned at me. "Are you sure about that? I shouldn't. I should just walk home."

Rain began pouring down. "I insisted. What do you think is going to happen? That I'm going to kill you?"

She laughed and put her hand on my arm. "Don't be silly, Kyle. I wouldn't think that. I just don't want to impose."

"It's no imposition. I insist on taking you home. I can't let you catch your death."

"Okay, thank you. Just give me a few moments to get everything cleaned up and put away. I also need to make a deposit. Since you're offering to give me a ride, will you stop by the bank so I can do the night deposit? No, wait. Never mind. I can't ask that of you. I apologize. It's probably out of your way."

"Molly, calm down. We can do what you need to do. If you need to go by the bank, we will. It's okay." I gritted my teeth after speaking. Going by the bank would be stupid. It would put her with me on camera. But she didn't have to make it to the bank.

She nodded as she rushed around doing her cleaning up and closing things. She filled the deposit bag, placing it on the counter before she began sweeping. I waited patiently for her. I would wait all night if I had to. She was worth it.

As soon as she was finished with her closing, I led her out the door. She stopped to lock it, then ran toward my truck. I helped her in before going around to the driver's side. When I got in, she was laughing and wringing out her hair.

"Sorry, I feel like a wet dog."

"You're fine. Where to first?"

Her eyes widened for a second. "I forgot the deposit bag on the counter. Oh well, the morning manager can take it when he gets there. I'll just call him before I go to bed."

"How late do you stay up?"

"Umm. Late." She laughed a little. "Don't say it. I know, I shouldn't be up all night, but I can't help it."

Turning, I headed toward her apartment, but I had no intention of taking her home. The road before her stop, I turned suddenly. I could feel the look she gave me, but I didn't turn my eyes from her. I hoped she would keep quiet. I didn't want to fight with her while driving in the rain.

"Umm, Kyle. I live back there."

I didn't speak, just kept driving.

"Kyle?" There was a tremor of nerves in her voice. "You're starting to scare me."

She reached for the handle of the door. I couldn't suppress the smile. I had taken the handle out of the door, so it only opened from the outside. She started to panic and clawed at the window.

With a sigh, I knew that I couldn't let her attract attention to herself. With one swift move, I threw a fist at her, hitting her in the temple. Her head smacked the window and she went quiet. It was about time that she shut up. I couldn't stand when women got hysterical.

I pulled up to the warehouse. I looked over at the unconscious woman. She looked so peaceful. I hated to move her in fear that she would awaken. I should have used the chloroform, but there simply had been no time. I had to act quickly. I pulled the bottle out of the glove box. I opened it and poured a little into the rag I kept in there as well, placing it over her nose and mouth. It was better to be safe than sorry. I needed her to stay asleep until I got her inside and situated.

Feeling a little more confident, I climbed out of the truck and moved to her side. I opened the door, catching her as she lifelessly tumbled out of the truck. I shook my head at my own stupidity. I knew better than to not move the girl so she didn't fall. I didn't know what I was thinking. I had so many missteps that, that maybe I should just lock her up and come visit the next night.

That was a sound idea. I must have been tired. I needed to rest. Once I was rested, I could spend the entire day on Saturday with her. I would just tell Christine I had to work. It wasn't that far of a reach. They would probably schedule us for the weekend anyway so it wasn't a lie. I just planned on skipping out so I could spend time with my new woman.

Carrying her inside, I went over to the cage in the corner. I opened it with a foot and walked inside. It was tall enough for me to stand in, I wanted to give them plenty of room when they had to spend time alone. The cage was six feet long and wide. I had a cot in there and a bucket for water and an empty bucket that she could relieve herself in. If I could have installed a working toilet, I would have.

Gently, I place her on the cot, covering her up with the thin blanket provided. I kissed her on the forehead and backed out of the cage. I wanted to be there when she woke up, but it wasn't possible, I was afraid I would make another mistake if I stuck around. I hated making mistakes. I closed the cage and locked it with the padlock. Without looking back, I left and started the drive home.

Chapter 72

I wasn't able to go to Molly until Saturday. I had to spend time with the family or suspicions would be raised. I sat in my recliner, watching Emmy crawl around the floor, putting whatever she could get her grubby hands on in her mouth.

The news was on the television, but I hadn't been paying attention to it. I laughed as the little girl looked at me with a G.I. Joe hanging out of her mouth. It was quite a sight. My attention was pulled from her when an image on the screen caught my eye. Grabbing the remote, I turned up the sound so I could hear what was being said.

"A local woman has been reported missing," the news anchor started. Her face was solemn. Her face disappeared and was replaced by a photo of my woman. "Molly King was reported missing by her brother early this morning. The last she was seen was at Jack's Tavern where she works as a bartender. If you have any information on her whereabouts, please call the number flashing on your screen or your local police department."

"That poor woman," Christine spoke from behind me. "Jack's. Isn't that where you and the guys frequent?"

"Uh, yeah. It is. I've seen her there a lot. She's a nice lady." My heart picked up a bit. I worried that Christine was going to be suspicious, especially since I was out when the woman disappeared.

"That's too bad. People these days are monsters."

The words would have stung if it wasn't true. I was a monster and acknowledged it. I didn't have any other reason for doing what I did, except I enjoyed it. I had started it long before I met Christine. Part of me hoped when I met her, that my love and devotion to her would get me to stop killing. I mean, I couldn't kill her then. She had been too special. Now she was the mother of my children. Did I love them? As much as I could. Would I give up my passion for them? No. Maybe that was why I was a monster.

***

She was sitting in the corner of her cage when I walked through the doors, turning on the lights. She had her arms wrapped around her knees and eyes were swollen from crying. I approached the cage, showing her the bag I held behind my back. The greasy smell of fast food wafted through the air. She sniffed like an animal but didn't move.

Opening the door to the cage a little, I tossed the bag into it, closing the door quickly. I didn't want her to think she was going to have an opportunity to escape. There was no escape.

"Eat while I get everything ready for you," I told her and walked away.

I went to a chest, opening it. Ruffling through the clothes that were in there, I found the perfect little black dress for her. It was simple, yet elegant. She would look ravishing in it with her dark hair and eyes.

I laid it on the table while I went to the big metal cabinet and unlocked it. Inside the cabinet were weapons. Knifes, guns, hammers, pliers, just to name a few. I pulled out the blow torch, setting it on the cart next to me. I didn't plan on using it, but it looked scary enough. Scaring her was half the fun.

I pushed the cart next to my work table, then grabbed a stunner and the dress. I approached the cage, seeing the bag hadn't been touched. My temper flared, and I did what I could to tamp it down. It wouldn't do me or her any good for me to lose it. Things went too quickly when I lost my temper.

"You need to eat, Molly. I got your favorite, burger, and fries." I stood at the door of the cage. My fisted hand tightened on the dress as she continued to simply stare at me with tear-filled eyes.

"Kyle, please. Let me go." Her voice was harsh and scratchy. It was completely different from her melodious voice at the bar. "You don't have to do this. I won't tell anyone. I just want to go home."

"Hush now," I kept my tone soft and level. "Here, if it makes you happy, go ahead and change into your party dress, then we will bring your dinner out here and you can have some company. You're like me, not a fan of eating alone."

Slowly, I unlocked the cage and entered it, being sure to close the door behind me. If it were possible, she pulled into herself even further, making herself look smaller. I held the dress out to her, but she didn't move to take it.

Sighing, I pulled the gun and aimed it at her. "Molly, I don't want to hurt you. I really don't, but I will. Now you have to get dressed for me. If you don't, I'm going to have to shoot you."

Excitement filled me as I watched her remove herself from the corner. She was shaking like a leaf in the wind that was trying to hang on to the tree it was attached to. Her hands trembled so badly that she couldn't get her jeans unsnapped. I didn't help or even offer. I wanted her to do it herself. She had to do it herself.

Once she was changed into the dress, I smiled. "Now pick up the bag and let's go sit at the table."

I directed her to the table on the opposite side of the warehouse from my work area. I never mixed business with pleasure. I pulled the chair out for her, waiting for her to sit down. I was still a gentleman even if I was holding a gun to her head. Once she was seated, I pushed the chair in so she was sitting at the table properly.

I settled in across from her, setting the gun on the table near my hand. I just watched as she attempted to open the bag. She grabbed a napkin, opening it out and spreading it on her lap. It was such a prim and proper move, I smiled. I knew that she was the right choice. She was going to be a good one, while she lasted.

She slowly began to eat. I could tell from the look on her face, she was forcing herself to do so. It was erotic watching her tremble with fear as she did what I asked. As I watched her, I wondered what else I could make her do. How far I could go. It was tempting to try, but the glint from my wedding band caught my eye.

I hadn't fucked any of my women since I got married. It was important for me to remain faithful to my wife. She had changed me in some ways, that was one. Before, I would rape my women before killing them. It was a harsh reality, but true.

When she finished eating, I helped her out of the chair and moved across the room. I turned on the CD player, a waltz coming on. I held the gun to her head, while we danced. My arm that was on her waist could feel the tremors wracking through her body. When the song ended, I forced her up on my worktable.

I kept the gun aiming at her while I strapped her down. Her fear was so palpable, that I could taste it. It sent a surge of excitement running through me. I couldn't wait to hear her screams. Setting the gun to the side, I leaned forward, placing a gentle kiss on her lips. She cringed, trying to get away from me.

"Molly, Molly, Molly," I tsked. "You know better than that. I will have to teach you a lesson."

"Don't," her voice was a squeak of a sound, the fear choking her.

I picked up a scalpel and pressed it to her collar bone, pressing in, I made a small cut. Her whimper urged me on. I chose random places on her body to make small cuts. I worked my way down to her feet. I stopped and looked at her. I kept my eyes on hers as I made a small cut on the arch of her foot. She screamed out, causing excitement to surge through me.

I grabbed a salt block and scrubbed the bottoms of her feet. She cried, begged and pleaded for me to stop, attempting to kick away from me. Sighing, I set the block down. If she didn't want her feet scrubbed and exfoliated, then maybe she needed to be punished.

I pulled my belt off, folding it in half, hanging onto the buckle end of it. I flicked it, the belt shot out smacking the bottoms of her feet, causing more bleeding. When she was overcome with pain, she lost consciousness.

I cleaned the blood of my belt before putting it back on. I walked over to the side of the table grabbing the smelling salts to rouse her. I wasn't ready for Molly to sleep. When she began to stir, I placed a kiss on her lips. She jutted her chin and snapped, biting my lip, bringing blood to the surface.

I backhanded her out of reaction. Anger washed through me, erasing any kind of lustful emotion that I may have had for her. I grabbed the pliers and held her mouth open with one hand. Grabbing one of her front teeth with the pliers, I yanked as hard as I could. The tooth came out after a lot of resistance. She cried and screamed and I pulled another and another.

When she had no more front teeth on the top or bottom gums, I grabbed the scalpel and pressed it to her mouth. Holding her bottom lip out, I made an incision, then cut it off in one clean swipe. I threw the discarded skin on the floor.

"See what happens when you are bad?" I asked through gritted teeth. I was seething. She was no fun and I was going to have to end her now.

I grabbed a knife and slit her throat. The cut was so deep that I nearly decapitated her. Blood sprayed in an arc in the air. By the time the bleeding died down, Molly and I were both covered in blood. Turning, I walked away without looking back. I would dispose of her later.

I was going to have to figure out what to do with her. She didn't deserve to rest with the others. First, I had to get cleaned up. I needed to see Christine after the mishap, she always knew how to make me feel better.

Chapter 73

I crawled into bed, wrapping my arms around Christine. She sighed and scooted back so her ass was pressed against my stomach. I slid her hair out of the way and kissed her neck. She moaned a little and snuggled deeper into her pillow.

Rolling my eyes, I closed them, trying to get some sleep. She obviously wasn't in the mood to make love, but I ached for her. I needed to forget about the issues with Molly. I was going to have to deal with her in the morning. I would leave after a couple hours of sleep, telling Christine I was going to go hunting.

After tossing and turning, I finally fell into a light sleep. I couldn't have been asleep more than an hour or two before I woke back up. I knew that it would elude me until I took care of my mess. I could never sleep knowing my work area was a disaster. I sat up, sitting on the edge of the bed, and ran my fingers through my hair. Memories of losing my temper with Molly flooded me. I shouldn't have lost it. I knew better. I should have kept control.

Leaving her like that was a mistake as well. I knew I needed to clean up before I left. I always did. I couldn't afford to leave anything lying around. I rolled my neck and stood up. I had a lot to do and little time to do it.

As I was getting dressed, I heard Christine stir. She sat up and looked at me with heavy, sleepy eyes. "What are you doing? It's not even five yet."

"Go back to sleep, baby. I am going to go hunting for a bit. I'll try to be home before lunch." Crossing the room, I kissed her lightly on the lips.

She frowned when I pulled back. "What happened to your lip?"

Fuck! I had forgotten that Molly bit me. My mind raced as I thought about what I was going to tell her about the bite. I frowned and looked in the mirror. "I don't know. Must have done it in my sleep."

She didn't say anything, but I could tell that she didn't believe me. I finished getting ready under her watchful stare. I said my goodbyes as I walked out the door. I felt a sense of urgency to get to the warehouse, but I moved casually, methodically. I didn't want to raise any more suspicion.

When I pulled into the warehouse district, I slowed down. Something felt off. My truck crept down the street like I was trying to sneak in. The flashing blue and red lights made my heart pound. The police were here. Please don't let them be at my building. Please don't let them be at my building. I chanted in my head over and over. If I willed it hard enough, they wouldn't be.

I didn't. There were cops all over my building. There a van marked 'Medical Examiner' parked by the loading dock. I was truly fucked. I was sure I had my prints in there. It had never occurred to me that I should wear gloves. The warehouse was my safe haven. I drove past without trying to bottleneck too much.

Escape was my first instinct. I turned at the next road and made my way out of town. I needed to think, figure out my next step. I pulled off into the wooded area and grabbed the shotgun I had brought with me. I figured some hunting would clear my mind and bringing home a dead animal would be a good alibi that I was being truthful.

The more I thought about it, the calmer I became. There was no way they would be able to figure out it was me. The warehouse wasn't paid for in my name. Hell, I hadn't left anything that screamed me. Those cops were too stupid to check for prints. I was just overreacting. Everything will be fine.

I shot a deer, loaded it into the bed of the truck and went to a check-in station to give them my tag and have the deer checked. When that was done, I took it home and strung it up in the barn behind the house. Brandon would enjoy learning how to clean and gut the deer. It could be something we did together.

Upon entering the house, I noticed a tension that hadn't been there before. It made me uneasy. The house was also eerily quiet. The kids weren't yelling; television wasn't blasting. I checked my watch to see that it wasn't quite noon yet, so they should have been going crazy like usual. I walked through the house, to see where everyone was. It appeared to be empty. Christine had probably taken the kids out to lunch.

Walking into the bedroom, I stopped. Christine was sitting on the edge of the bed with a picture of us in her hand. She was holding it, letting it dangle toward the floor. She just stared at me, no real expression on her face.

"Where are the kids?" I asked, trying to act like her behavior didn't set me on edge. I crossed the room and began changing out of my coveralls.

"With my mother." Her tone was flat, but there was a sound of tears behind it.

I turned to face her. "What's wrong?"

She stood then, the picture hanging down by her side between two fingers. "You're cheating on me."

The phrase was so blunt, that I froze and frowned. "What?"

"You're having an affair, aren't you? That's what happened to your lip. Your lover bit you."

I slowly shook my head no. "I'm not having an affair. You don't know what you're talking about."

"I've spent the morning calling your friends. You don't spend as much time with them as you say you do, Kyle. How long have you been lying to me? Our entire marriage?"

Carefully approaching her, I placed my hands on her shoulders. "Christine. I am not having an affair. You're the only woman for me. I love you."

"Liar!" Her hand came up quick and struck me across the face.

My temper flared. I pushed her away from me, not wanting to hurt her. "Why the fuck would I lie to you? I chose you."

"You don't want me to leave, that's why. You've been staying out late more and more. You are distant. We haven't had sex in a month."

"We haven't had sex because you fall asleep as soon as your head hits the pillow." I countered.

"You used to wake me up."

"We have a baby. I thought you would appreciate the sleep."

"Why have you come home, clothes smelling of perfume?" Tears filled her eyes as she spoke. She blinked rapidly and angrily wiped at her eyes. "Your clothes have smelled like perfume too many times for it to be a coincidence. Who is she?"

The hurt in her eyes started to cause an uncomfortable feeling in me. I stood there, not knowing what to say. I couldn't tell her the truth and I wouldn't lie to her, so I said nothing. I watched as she shook her head and turned away from me.

She headed to the closet. Opening it, she pulled a suitcase out and placed it on the bed. She then walked around the room, packing stuff into the case. She filled the suitcase with clothing then closed it up.

"What are you doing?" I asked.

"Going to stay with my mother. The kids have plenty of clothing there for now. We will discuss what to do in a few days. I need time."

"No."

She swung around to stare at me. "What?"

"I said no," I spoke as I crossed my arms over my chest. "You are staying here. You will call your mother and have her bring my kids back immediately."

She shook her head and grabbed the suitcase off the bed. "It's too late for that, Kyle. I'm leaving."

As she shoved past me to leave the room, I grabbed her arm and yanked her backward. She yelped as she fell to the floor. She tried to scramble away from me as I stood over her. Her hand landed on the forgotten picture, breaking the glass. We both heard it crack, but neither of us acknowledged it.

"You aren't going anywhere. I've given up so much for you." I could feel my chest heaving as the anger burst through the flood gates and washed over me. "I shut off part of who I am for you."

"Wh-wh-what are you talking about?" she stammered.

"Me, you, everything! I didn't even want kids yet didn't say anything when you popped those little money eating brats out. I got a job I despise just so you could stay home and take care of those kids. You have inconvenienced my life, but I have dealt with it and happily because I love you." Grabbing her arms, I pulled her to her feet, so we were face to face. "I would have done anything you asked of me."

Tears streamed freely down her face as she watched me rage. She struggled to get out of my grip. That she would want to be free from me hurt and angered me more than I had realized. She was my world, but she didn't want to stay with me. I couldn't let her leave.

"I tried to stop killing for you." Once the words were out of my mouth, we both froze. I hadn't meant to say it and didn't know why it had come out. I had never even thought about uttering those words aloud to anyone now I practically shouted it for everyone to hear.

Her eyes widened in horror as my words sank into her heartbroken head. The color drained from her face and my gut reaction was to take pleasure from it. "Killing people? You're a murderer?"

Chapter 74

The look of terror and revulsion on her face did something to me that I couldn't fully understand. It was like a switch flipped and any emotions I had been feeling toward her were gone. Maybe not gone but buried. The thing was, I didn't feel anything.

I advanced and she retreated. It was like a game of cat and mouse. I enjoyed playing the cat. She scrambled to the other side of the bed. I continued to follow her until she backed herself into a corner. She pressed herself against the wall and began to sob.

She reminded me of my other women that I had taken to the warehouse. She was a trembling mess. It was exciting. I leaned over, grabbing her by the arms. I pulled her to her feet, smashing my mouth to hers in a hard kiss. She was limp and still. It was almost like kissing a doll.

When I broke the kiss, she just stared at me. I smiled, backing her onto the bed. I was finally going to get to relieve my sexual frustrations. Her hands came to my shoulders, digging her fingers into them. I nibbled on her neck. She slid her fingers up my face. I thought she was getting into the moment, but then she dug her nails into my face and racked them down my face.

The pain made me rear back and howl in pain. She kicked out, her leg connecting with my groin. I cupped myself and fell to the side. As I tried to regain my composure, I saw her scramble off the bed and out of the room. I had to move quickly to stop her, but it was hard to breath and pain was shooting from my balls to my stomach.

After several deep breaths, I was able to get up and go after Christine. I found her in the kitchen on the phone.

"This is Christine Coram; my husband is trying to —" I yanked the cord of the phone out of the wall. She screamed and whipped around to stare at me with the dead phone in her hand. "Kyle, please don't do this. You're scaring me."

"You started this, Christine. Now you've gone and called the police. They will be here soon. What the fuck were you thinking!" I could feel the spittle spraying from my mouth as I yelled. I lunged at Christine grabbing her by the throat. I held her down on the floor, reaching up, pulling a knife from the butcher block. I didn't have time to think, just act. As I began to stab her, my emotions broke free of the hold I had on them. "You were supposed to be my forever. I loved you. You turned on me. Look what you made me do."

My hands were slick with her blood. I continued to stab even when I felt her last breath escape between her lips. When I was finally worn out, I dropped the knife and stood. I walked almost drunkenly toward the stairs unsure of what my next move was going to be.

The door burst open as I placed my hand on the rail of the stairs. Turning, I stared down the barrel of a gun. The police had burst in and drawn down on me. I was guessing they had knocked on the door, but no one had answered, I had been busy.

"Get on the ground!" The officer in front shouted. "Hands on your head."

I wasn't going to go down easily. I began to kneel, raising my arms. Instead, I rolled to the side to make a run to the kitchen. I heard the guns firing, then the burning impact of them slamming into me. I hit the ground losing consciousness as I went.

Chapter 75

Present Day

"This is where Kyle killed Christine."

The voices roused me from the state of slumber I was in. It seemed like I had only faded for a moment. I wasn't sure how long I had been wherever it was that I had been. I followed them to the kitchen. A young woman that appeared to be around twenty stood by the kitchen counter, looking down at a spot on the white tile floor. There was a young man standing there with her.

"Are you okay?" He asked her, placing a hand on hers.

"Yeah, sorry. It's just. Well, this is hard for me. I haven't been here in a long time," she explained. I studied the woman. She looked familiar. In fact, she looked like Christine. Her voice was also similar to Christine's.

"I'm sorry. We can do this later if you would like." The young man smiled at her reassuringly.

"No. Let's do this now. If you follow me, I'll show you were Kyle died."

She walked from the kitchen quickly. I followed them to the base of the stairs. The carpet had been cleaned, but if you looked closely, you could still see a discoloration of where my body had lain.

"Here is where he was gunned down. He was making an attempt to escape the police when they fired. He had already stabbed Christine over fifty times." Her voice was distant as she spoke.

"Didn't you tell me that the house has been in the family ever since?"

"Yes."

"How are you related to the people that lived here?"

"I'm sorry. Christine and Kyle were my birth parents. After they died, my mom, grandma adopted us and changed our last name so that we wouldn't grow up with the stigma of being children of a murderer and one of his victims. I'm Emma."

"What do you remember about your birth parents?" He blushed a little. "Sorry if I'm prying."

"You're fine. I don't remember anything about them. I was a baby when everything happened. As I got older, I found out my father killed over fourteen women in his lifetime that authorities know of, including my mother. He was a monster."

"Why haven't you sold the house?"

She shrugged. "We decided as we got older that we didn't want anyone to have to live with the ghosts here. Bad things happened in this house."

So I was staring at my baby girl. I felt an urge to kill her. She looked just like her mother. The one who betrayed me. I made a couple steps closer with the thought of strangling her. I lunged, wrapping my fingers around her slender neck. I wanted to squeeze the life out of her. She was her mother reincarnated and didn't deserve to live.

The man grabbed her, pulling her out the front door of the house. I lost my grip as they went over the threshold. I cursed and began to rage. I strode to the window to see what was going on. The man held Emma in an embrace gently rubbing her back. I listened to their conversation.

"Are you okay, Emma?" he asked softly.

She nodded. When she spoke, her voice was rough. "I think so. What the fuck was that?"

I saw him hesitate, eyes drifting over to the window. It felt like he was staring straight into my eyes. He pulled Emma back to an arm's length and looked into her eyes.

"Maybe the dust was a little much for you. The place needs a good cleansing."

She frowned a little. "Maybe, but dust has never bothered me before. It felt like someone was trying to choke me."

"You were feeling highly emotional over what happened with your parents, so maybe that's what it was. You were choked on emotions, then the dust and everything was too much?"

She laughed a little. "You sound like you're reaching, Mr. Bucco."

"Call me Bastian. I've seen it before when people are in an old house that had a lot of emotion or something extremely violent happened in it. You were feeling what's called an empathetic impression."

"Okay Bastian, but it still feels like you're reaching."

"Let's get you out of here. I saw a diner on our way over. Let's get coffee and talk."

He led her down the stairs and away from the house. I watched as he helped her into the passenger side of a small car. When he walked around to the driver's side, he turned and stared at me. I had a feeling I'd be seeing him again soon.

***

My luck had turned for the better when I heard the front door open. I materialized there to see who had entered my domain. I smiled when I saw Emma, hands full of cleaning supplies. She walked to the kitchen and set the stuff on the counter. Grabbing a duster, she walked to the living room and picked up a picture frame that held a family photo in it. She ran her finger across the glass, before sighing and setting it back down.

She dusted the room, and I followed her. I wanted to kill her, but I needed to do it in the right place. I have had time to think about where and how I wanted to do it. I wanted to make it special. To take my time and savor the kill. What better place to do the deed than where I killed her mother?

When she worked her way back to the kitchen, I knew it was time to make my move. I lunged at her, knocking her to the ground. Sitting on her, so she couldn't move, I reached for a knife. I felt the handle slide into my hand. I wrapped my fingers around it, yanking it from the counter.

The first plunge missed because she moved her shoulder just enough. It grazed her shirt, blade bouncing off the tile. I wrapped one hand around her throat and squeezed to keep her still. Her eyes bulged and panic filled the. She bucked and struggled. An excitement raced through me I hadn't felt in a long time. The only thing that would make it better was if she could see my face as I killed her. I wanted to her see she was nothing but a means to an end.

I stabbed down at her again, this time the knife sliding home into her shoulder. She tried to scream, but nothing came out except a guttural sound from not having oxygen. I had to use so much force to pull the knife free from her shoulder that it came off the ground.

As I brought the knife down for a third time, there was a force stopping me from planting it into Emma's heart. I looked up to see the man that had been with her gripping the knife, trying to get it away. I put more force into it, determined to see her dead, but he wouldn't relent.

Releasing the knife, I smiled as he fell backward. I would just end her with my hands. I could already hear her gasping for air as my hand squeezed her neck. She tried to claw at my hand but was just scratching at her own neck.

"Hold on, Emma!" the man shouted. He chanted something.

I felt my grip loosening on her neck. I tried to keep it tight, but I couldn't. A pull was forcing me away from her. The last thing I heard before everything went dark and silent was him asking if she was okay.

Chapter 76

Bastian

I held the crystal in my hand, staring down at it. The ghost locked inside was sick and twisted. Even more so than the others I had captured for Bane. He had tried killing his own daughter and the look on his face when I had burst in the door had been lustful. It sickened me. He was the last one needed for the house, but I didn't want to let him out.

I would have to figure out something before I arrived back at the house. If I released him, everything would implode. The others had been halfway calm, even agreeable when I took them to the house, all but the Blacksmith.

What I worried about was if Kyle, or the Titan, figured out how to possess someone. His type of evil would taint everything it touched. I sighed and pocketed it. I would take him to the house for now, but I wouldn't release him. Not yet. He would have to be released only moments before the ceremony and the power was released. Only then would he be out of his crystal cage.

Black Zodiac Ghost 13
LOST SOUL

Chapter 77

I pulled into the driveway of the house and shut off the engine. This last capture had been the most difficult. I looked over at the crystal sitting in the passenger seat, seeing the aura of darkness surrounding it.

I'd dealt with murderous ghosts before, but nothing like this. They didn't all start as killers. They had been driven to the point of desperation where they felt it necessary to kill. Some only sought revenge, but others developed at taste for it.

This one was different. He had killed many people during his lifetime and would have killed more if he hadn't been stopped. The only reason he hadn't killed after death was because he had been tied to the house. Had it been up to me, I would have left him there or banished him.

Bane had other plans. He needed twelve spirits for the Black Zodiac. He wanted to open it and absorb the power within himself so he could wield it. It didn't matter what he was using them for, until Dana. She was the most beautiful, amazing being I had ever come across. I wanted to join her in the afterlife but didn't think that would be possible.

I held a secret. It was one I had to keep close to the chest since I discovered it when I was a young boy. If anyone found out my secret, well. . . I wasn't sure what would happen, but it won't be good. It was something that I kept so deep that only one other person had ever known about it, and she was the one that exposed me to it. Bane didn't even know it. If he did, he would probably use it against me or in his favor.

I shook my head as I walked into the house. It had once been a home, but it never felt like it. Now Bane had added onto it and made the house a monstrosity with something special in the basement. I went straight to his office. I needed to discuss this crystal with him.

When I opened the door, he was sitting at his large chestnut desk. He looked up at me, eyes glittering. I could see he was practically foaming at the mouth at the thought of the last ghost. His eyes dropped to my hand and the crystal.

"Why haven't you released him into his room yet?" Bane demanded, shutting the ledger in front of him. Electronics weren't feasible because we had so much ghostly energy in the house. The last computer we had exploded from the constant power surges. Cellphones and other simple electronics seemed to be fine, but the bigger ones couldn't handle the surges.

"We need to wait to release him." My grip tightened on the crystal.

Bane took his glasses off his face and cleaned them while studying me. "Why is that?"

"He's dangerous."

"I know he's dangerous. That's why I want him," Bane laughed.

"You hired me because you trust my judgment on this. I know these things." I felt anger rising.

"No, I hired you because you were willing to do what I want for a price. Don't forget I own your soul."

"No one owns me." I placed the crystal on his desk. "I'm not releasing him until it's time."

I turned to walk away. I hadn't made it three steps before I heard the distinctive click of a gun cocking. I turned back to stare at him incredulously.

"You will release him before you go." His voice was as dead as the expression in his eyes.

With a sigh, I nodded and left the room to prepare for releasing the Titan. As I made my way through the corridors, I knew I should have just chanced it and walked away. Would a bullet kill me? I didn't think so.

When I approached his room, I stopped. I couldn't shake the bad feeling washing over me. I would have to do something though. I decided that I would put spells on the room, completely encasing it so there was no chance he could get out, even by accident. It would be similar to what I did to the Blacksmith, just stronger. A lot stronger. Rolling up my sleeves, I got to work.

After releasing the Titan into his new cell, I went back down to Bane's office. He smiled at me when I walked through the door. He leaned back in his chair, folding his hands neatly on his desk. If I hadn't known any better, he would be the picture-perfect image of a grandfather. His graying black hair gave him the distinguished salt and pepper look. His smile was wide and charming. He appeared nice until you looked into his eyes. They were snakes' eyes. Sly and deadly.

"I assume that you are all finished up and Titan is comfortably situated in his room?" he asked, eyes glinting. It felt like he was looking for a reason to kill me.

"Yes, he's free. However, he can't leave the room until you summon him during the ceremony."

"Good. Good. I suppose that means that your job here is finished. I can get the thirteenth ghost myself." He reached into a drawer, pulling out his checkbook. He picked up his pen and filled out a check. Carefully, he pulled it out of the book and held it out for me. "Thank you for everything. Your help was greatly appreciated. Now, if you'll kindly see yourself out, I have work to do."

"How do you plan on getting the thirteenth ghost? You can't see ghosts, don't know how to trap them. You know nothing about them except they contain the key to what you want."

"That's none of your concern."

"Our contract was for thirteen ghosts."

"And I paid you for thirteen." He looked down at the ledger in front of him, clearly dismissing me.

I turned and strode from the room. On my way out the door, I stopped by an old China cabinet. Inside the cabinet was a statue. I studied it as resentment and anger bubbled to the surface. I had to turn from it, close my eyes, and take several deep breaths before I was calm again. When I opened my eyes again, the ghost of a young boy stood in front of me.

"Do you miss her?" he asked, studying me.

I shook my head no. "Never."

"But you think about her."

I knew he was prodding me, but I couldn't seem to help myself. He always had gotten the best of me. "Yes. I think of her. When I wake up from the nightmares of what she did to me, I think of her. Every time I see a child getting affection from their mother, I think of her. And I'm glad she's dead. I'm even more glad that she is trapped in there and can't hurt anyone else ever again."

"I miss her." His confession had me studying him. Besides being transparent, he just looked like a lost little boy.

"She killed you." I was blunt. I wanted him to see her how I did.

He shrugged. "She meant to kill you, not me. It was always meant to be you."

"I know." I turned and walked to the door. I had my hand on the doorknob when I stopped and looked back at him. "It should have been me."

With that, I left the house. I should have gone to talk to Dana. She would have made me feel better, but I didn't. I had to be realistic. There was no reason for me to be back at the house, so how could we have a relationship. Not only that, but she was a ghost. Made things more difficult.

I got in my car and pulled away, not glancing back in the rearview mirror. Now I could start my life over. Again.

Chapter 78

I had stepped at a nearby restaurant so I could have a late lunch while debating where to travel to next. Perhaps I would go out of the country. I had always wanted to visit England, but getting a passport could be difficult. Maybe not too difficult. I took a sip of my soda and listened to the small group of women seated at the table behind me.

"Are you really going to do it, Kate?" one woman asked.

"Yeah. I mean, what do I have to lose? I've already lost everything," Kate answered. There was a sadness in her voice that pulled at me. When she spoke again, her voice perked up. "Besides who can say no to living in a mansion?"

"What happened again?" another woman asked. I could hear the skepticism in her voice.

"I got a phone call from my uncle's attorney. Apparently, he died of a heart attack and left the house to me. I'm supposed to meet the lawyer tomorrow morning for a tour of the house and to get the keys."

"How are you going to pay for living in a house like that?" the first woman that spoke asked.

"Easy, Tammy. He also left me his entire estate which was worth millions from what the lawyer said. I'm the last living relative."

"I don't know. This all sounds funny to me," Tammy mumbled.

She was right. It sounded suspicious. I was mentally trying to figure out which mansion on I-44 they were talking about. The closest mansion I could think of was Bane's, and he wasn't dead.

The longer I listened to them talk, the certain I was that it was Bane's place. The Zodiac House. If I was correct, then Bane believed she was the thirteenth ghost, the key to opening the zodiac. I knew better. I knew who the thirteenth was and had no intention of letting Bane know. I wanted to use that to my advantage.

I may have originally agreed to help him get the ghosts to the house, but I heard whispers about what he planned to do once he absorbed the power. He wanted to bring hell to Earth. Even though I didn't care what happened to others, I didn't want to live in hell. My personal hell was bad enough. It was then that I determined that I would not tell him.

"Tammy, you worry too much. If it makes you feel better, you can come stay with me. At least for the first couple nights until you can see that it is completely legit," Kate offered.

I stopped listening after Tammy agreed. I had to find out if it was the house they were talking about. My gut told me it was, but the only way to be certain was to follow them.

***

I followed them from their hotel. We turned off the interstate at the UU junction. When they turned left, then right, my stomach dropped. I was correct about which house it was. I watched them pull in the driveway, but instead of following, I drove a little further down and pulled into a parking lot. I would have to get into that house without Bane knowing, but then Bane wouldn't be there if he were supposed to be her dead uncle.

I turned off my car, climbing out. I could think better while I moved around. Pacing was something my father always did when he was thinking, and I had always done it. I needed to get into the house undetected. I knew there were cameras all over the house. Plus, those women would be freaked out to find a strange man in the house with them.

An idea hit me. I would have to wait until dark, but I'd cut the power to the house then come in acting like the repairman. It would get me in the house without suspicion, and I could make sure everything was still secured. Especially Titan. He was an evil bastard. The others may cause issues, but he was the one I was worried about.

If I knew the Crone like I thought I did, she would do nothing to them. She just wanted to be left alone and have peace. Maybe she would keep the others away from them if need be. Dana was a wild card though. Kate was beautiful and had a beautiful white aura, so Dana would be insanely jealous. Her jealousy was always an issue.

I walked to my trunk, popping it to see if I had the appropriate gear with me to play the part of a power company employee. After digging around through different outfits, I finally found it. I opened a plastic bin and looked for the matching identification. It was important to look the part. Most people didn't question a person with the right ID with them.

The sun was setting when I decided that I should probably cut the power and get inside before dark. I had seen the lawyer leave hours ago, but the women were still inside. After getting dressed, I went to work.

Chapter 79

I approached the door and took a deep breath. It was now or never. I shifted my baseball cap down to cover my eyes a little more. Raising my fist, I rapped on the door. I rocked back on my heels while I was waiting.

The woman that Kate called Tammy opened the door a crack. "Who are you?"

"I'm Charles from the power company, ma'am. There is an issue with your electricity. I think I took care of the power from out here, but I need to get a look in your breaker box. It should only take a few minutes. I want to get the power back on and out of your hair as soon as possible."

"How do I know you are really from the power company and not some killer?" Tammy asked, glaring at me.

I handed her my ID tag so she could examine it. I watched her closely as she studied the ID then my face. After repeating the cycle several times, she opened the door wider and stepped out of the way to let me in.

"Make it quick." She handed my ID back as she spoke. "I'm not sure where the breaker box is, but together we can find it."

"Tammy, who's at the door?" Kate asked from the kitchen.

"An electrician. He's going to help us get the power back on."

"Good. How did he know that it wasn't on? I'm still on hold with the electric company." She came into the entryway with a cell phone in her hand. Hold music was coming from the speaker.

"We detected the surge that caused the power to go out. I was in the area and came to work on it," I explained. She looked skeptical as she stared at me. I wondered if she would believe the story I was telling. Finally, she ended the call and placed her cell phone back in her pocket. "Let's go find the breaker box."

She looked around, biting her lower lip. I could tell she had no idea where to look for it. It made sense because she was new to the house. Most people didn't go looking for the breaker box when they enter a house.

"I'm betting it's in the basement," I smiled helpfully.

She nodded and led the way to the basement. The stairs to the basement were dark and steep. I pulled out a flashlight and turned it on. I was going to offer it to Kate, but she had her cellphone out, using it as a light. I would never get used to that technology. Flashlights were an amazing thing if I were honest.

When we reached the landing of the basement, I saw William standing there. He had an evil smile on his face. It was the same smile I had seen a hundred times, right before something horrible happened.

"Welcome back, Charles," William said quietly.

I wasn't sure why he was talking so softly; I was the only one that could hear him. I simply glanced his direction and acted like I didn't hear anything. I heard him following me as we walked around the basement.

Finally finding the breaker box, I examined it. It wasn't like a normal box. I didn't know what the extra bells and whistles in it. I knew I was frowning at it, but I wasn't sure what to do. I just knew that with Bane, nothing was as it seemed so it wouldn't be smart to just flip switches.

Tammy stood so close I could smell the soap she used on her clothing. She was making me nervous. Then there was William. He was standing directly beside me, giggling. It made me even more uneasy.

"There. It says main breaker right there. Just flip it and the power should come on." Tammy reached past me to point at the switch.

"I don't think—" I started.

"It's an easy fix. Just flip it right there and your job will be done," she argued, cutting me off.

"Dealing with electricity can be a tricky thing. If we flip the wrong breaker, it could blow the grid." I spoke fast, trying to get her to back off and not do what she wanted.

"Maybe we should listen to him." Kate spoke up for the first time since coming down to the basement. "He is the electrician."

Tammy turned on her. "What kind of electrician doesn't know where the main breaker is?"

"He is just being cautious. This is a big breaker box," she reasoned, trying to calm her friend.

"Quit being a pussy. Let's flip the fucking switch, get some lights on, and get him out of here."

She shoved me to the side and grabbed the largest switch. She slammed it home. The lights flickered several times before they came on. A whirl of electricity powered up, making my stomach twist. Something wasn't right, and my plan had gone to hell.

I had hoped to have time to go through to house to make sure that all the strongholds were still in place and there was no way they could come in contact with the Blacksmith or the Titan. Now that lights were back on, I had no excuse to walk through the house. Unless I could get them to allow me to inspect.

"She shouldn't have done that," William said in a sing-song voice.

"What just happened?" I murmured hoping the ghost was the only one that heard me.

"You'll see." With that, he was gone.

"Looks like the power is back on. I'm going to need to do a walk through the house to make sure there isn't something causing the power to surge."

"Umm, okay." Kate shrugged.

"No. You need to leave." Tammy crossed her arms and glared at me. "You don't seem to know anything about electricity. You wouldn't even turn the lights back on. You acted like you were stalling. I bet if we call the electric company, they won't even know you who are."

"Go ahead. Call them. I'll wait," I bluffed. I crossed my arms over my chest and stared at her.

"This isn't necessary," Kate interjected. She placed a hand on Tammy's arm. "He was just being cautious. He is simply trying to do his job and ensure our safety. Let's just let him do that so he can leave, and we can get on with our lives."

"Fine, but I'll be watching every move he makes." Tammy frowned at Kate, then me.

I headed toward the stairs and climbed them back to the first floor. When I crossed the threshold into the kitchen, a bad feeling washed over me. I heard a cackling that chilled me to the bone. The ghosts were on the loose, and they were in the mood for fun.

Chapter 80

I led them into the study, where it was safest. Once we were there, I shut the door and searched the room. The failsafe was still in place and the room was fully protected from the ghosts. I was glad to see that Bane was smart enough to leave one room secure. I turned and smiled at the women, who were staring at me like I was crazy.

"It looks like everything is sound in here," I told them. "You stay in here while I go check out the rest of the house. It shouldn't take me too long."

"You really think I'm going to let you wander Kate's house alone?" Tammy snorted. "You are a real piece of work."

I was tiring of Tammy and her smart mouth already. I wanted to say fuck it and let them try to survive the ghosts alone. My conscience got the best of me, however. I knew I couldn't leave them defenseless with ghosts like Titan and Blacksmith. The others, maybe, but not them. They were the nastiest ghosts I'd ever come across.

"I have half the mind to just leave you to it and risk this house burning down. The original house, which is part of this one, is well over a hundred years old. The wiring may not be completely up to date. Are you willing to risk your friend's life because you are being a hard-headed bitch?"

They both just stared at me for a minute before Tammy turned and plopped down on a couch. Kate smiled weakly at me then sat beside her.

I walked out the door and turned back to them before I shut it. "Don't open this door."

Shutting the door, I walked down the hall toward the stairs. I could feel the ghosts moving around. There was a loud slamming noise. The impact was hard enough the walls quivered. I wanted to groan because I knew that woman would come out to inspect the noise. It almost sounded like a cannon had gone off.

At the landing, I looked down the hallway. The doors were all closed like they had been when I dropped off Titan. However, I knew that even though the door was shut, it didn't mean the ghosts were inside. They could walk through walls. The first door I went to was the Blacksmith's. Checking the door and protection runes, I felt confident that he was still tucked inside. The vibrations from him hitting the door on the door told me he was still there and pissed about it.

Running down the hall, I stopped in front of Titan's door. I inspected it carefully looking for any indication he had been freed. It didn't look like he had. I wasn't willing to open the door to find out. If I did, he would try to escape, kill me, or more likely both.

When I turned, William was standing behind me, grinning. I hated when he did that. It creeped me out. The look always made my stomach flip as memories tried to push themselves to the front of my mind.

"You know that won't hold them, right?" he asked.

"Yes, it will. It is the strongest magic I could find." I was confident that as long as none of the symbols or runes were damaged, the locks would hold up.

He giggled. "Charles, you are being stupid."

"I'm not Charles. The name is Bastian." I felt prickles at the back of my neck. I couldn't decide if it was from the name or the ghost standing directly behind me.

"Whatever you want to believe, Charles. The truth will come to pass. You will have to face your past some time."

I ignored William and turn to see who was behind me, but the closeness and the surge of hormones through me told me it was Dana.

"Dana." My voice came out hoarse. My throat was dry and scratchy from the saliva drying up from her just being near me. The woman did things to me that no one, dead or alive, had ever done. She made me feel.

Her bottom lip poked out. "Why didn't you come see me last time you were here, Bastian?"

"I was in a hurry. I planned on coming back to see you soon."

"No he didn't," William taunted me from behind. "He was told to leave by Bane and had no intentions of coming back for you. He's here for that woman downstairs."

Several emotions passed over Dana's face in a flash before settling on anger. "What? Is that true, Bastian?"

I hesitated only for a moment, unsure what to say. "I was told to leave, but you know I can't stay away from you. I love you. I'm not here for Kate."

"How did you know I was talking about Kate?" William asked with a lilt in his voice.

Dana crossed her arms and glared at me. "Good question. Is she prettier than me?"

I was on dangerous ground now. I wished I could punch William in the face. He was doing a good job instigating trouble. "Of course not, Dana. No one compares to you in beauty."

Out of the corner of my eye, I could see the knife she used to kill herself materialize in her hand. I had to get her out of the killing mood before she killed me, Kate, and Tammy. I reached a hand out to cup her face. I couldn't feel her face, but maybe she could feel the contact. She had an empty socket where her eye had been and cuts down her face and body where she had cut herself.

I ran my thumb across her bottom lip, then leaned forward to kiss her. I hoped it calmed her down because I wasn't in the mood for a knife in my back. Her hands came to my shoulders; thankfully nothing was in those hands.

I pulled from the kiss and smiled at her. "I'll come visit you in your room a little later. I have some stuff I need to take care of first."

"Okay. I'll be waiting." She turned to walk away. She walked a few feet before stopping and shooting a look at me over her shoulder. "Bastian. Don't make me wait too long."

I could hear the threat in her voice. Once she disappeared, I turned on William. "You need to keep your little fucking mouth shut. I would like to get out of here with everything intact. What do you think you are trying to do?"

"I want you to stay, Charles. I miss you." He tried to give me an innocent look, but I wasn't buying it. He had something else up his sleeve, but I wasn't sure what.

"Horse shit. And I'm not Charles."

"You used to be."

"That was a long time ago, William. Get used to it. I will never be Charles again."

He giggled as he faded away. "We'll see about that."

His voice echoed as he disappeared. I rolled my eyes at the theatrics but wasn't in the mood to provoke him back. I was just glad he was gone for the moment. The little bastard was never far though. He liked to follow me around when I was in the house. He started following me when he realized who I was.

I headed back toward the office to where Kate and Tammy waited. I needed to come up with a plan to get them out of the house even though Titan and Blacksmith were locked away. The others weren't friendly either, just a hair safer.

Chapter 81

I walked into the office to find one angry, pacing woman and one sitting calmly, looking at her cell phone. Tammy, the one pacing, stopped and glared at me.

"What did you find?" she demanded.

"There is a sparking wire in the attic. We need to turn the power back off, and in the morning, I'll have a crew come out and fix it, but you can't stay here tonight." I wanted to get them out of the house.

"I think you are full of shit. I called the electric company while you were gone, and they didn't know of any power outages." She stomped up to me so we were practically nose to nose. "Who the fuck are you?"

"I told you. My name is Charles. Charles Bartlett. I work with the electric company. I'm telling you we need to get out of the house now. If you insist on arguing, then fine stay, but I am cutting the power for everyone's safety." I really hated this woman.

"Maybe we should listen to him," Kate interjected. "I'm getting a bad feeling. He may not be from the power company like he said, but he seems genuinely worried."

She stood and walked to the seething woman. Resting her hand on Tammy's arm, she squeezed it lightly then smiled at her. I could see the calming effect that Kate had on the woman and it surprised me. I would have just decked the bitch and carried her out.

"Fine, but once we are outside, I'm beating this dude's ass." Tammy stormed to the door and flung it open.

She didn't see the ghost standing at the door, didn't hear him giggling, but I did. I walked past William, hoping to make it out the door without incident. Tammy grabbed the doorknob and turned it. It didn't turn. She yanked on it with no avail.

She turned on me. "What the fuck did you do?"

"I didn't do anything. Just fucking go." I felt a sense of urgency rush through me. We needed to get out of the house before something happened. I shoved her out of the way. "Let me do it."

I pulled, but the door didn't budge. The knob felt like it was stuck. Pulling a screwdriver out of my belt, I unscrewed the hinges of the door. There was no way I would remain stuck in the house. When I removed the hinges, I lifted the door pulling it from the frame. I froze when I saw the other side.

A metal wall stood in our way. I turned to look at the women standing behind me. They were both standing there like statues with the same dumbstruck expression on their faces. I let the door fall to the side and walked to the living room window. Pulling the heavy curtain to the side, I looked out. There was a sheet of metal there too. We were effectively and completely trapped in the house.

"Fuck, fuck, fuck!" I grabbed a chair and threw it across the room. It hit the wall and bounced off. I wasn't sure what to next.

"What's going on?" Kate asked, fear filling her voice. It sounded like she was about to cry.

Turning, I stared at her for a minute. I wasn't sure what to tell her. How could I tell her that her uncle had trapped her in a house, intending on having her die so he could become all-powerful? I wasn't sure why I cared about how she felt, but I did. I didn't want to hurt her, but I didn't know how to soften the blow. Plus telling her about the ghosts would make her think I was crazy, at least until one tried killing her.

"We're trapped." That was all that needed to be said for the moment.

"What do you mean trapped?" Tammy all but shouted the question at me. I was getting tired of her mouth.

"It means we have no way out of the house." I paced the room while I thought. There had to be another way out.

"Are you kidding me?" Tammy exploded. She turned on Kate. "We have no way out of this godforsaken place! I knew that it was a bad idea coming here. I told you this was a bad idea and it sounded fishy from the start. You were like, 'oh no it's legit.' I told you!"

"Hey now," Kate said in an offensive tone. She was frowning and stepped back a little. "You didn't have to come with me. You are the one that said you would come stay for a bit. Don't blame me for your choices. Yes, I chose to live here, but that was my choice. It's not that bad. I'm sure someone will be along soon to open the door."

As Tammy started in again, I stepped between the women. "Now is not the time to bicker. We have to be smart. I suggest we all go back to the office and discuss ways to get out. You have your phone still right, Kate?"

She nodded.

"Good. We will go in the office and you can call someone to come help get the door open." Even as I spoke the words, I knew no one would come. If they did, there was no way we were all getting out of here alive.

"I'm not going back into that stuffy office." Tammy crossed her arms and squared her shoulders. "I'll wait here."

"I wouldn't recommend that." I was trying to be diplomatic, but it was hard to do when the person you were talking to was as abrasive as sandpaper.

"Why not? Am I going to be electrocuted?" The tone was mocking. I would have left her to her own devices if I hadn't seen William creeping around the room to get a better view. Add that to the tingle on the back of my neck, and I knew we were in trouble.

"Just trust me on this. Let's go to the office, and I promise I will explain everything."

"No. I think it's time you tell us who you are and what you are really doing here now. I'm not going to trust you on anything."

The swish of air brushing past me caused me to jump back. The lightbulb in the lamp next to me exploded as the lamp flew across the room. Both women screamed as I cursed. I hadn't seen the bat until it came swinging at my head.

I ducked and felt the air of it move my hair. There stood Royce, the Mangled Captain. Anger coloring him with a reddish tint. He was pissed at me, and I knew it. I brought him here, but he seemed to remember his past also. I had hoped I would be long gone before he recognized me, but I wasn't that lucky.

I rolled to my left, springing to my feet. I grabbed Kate's arm and dragged her back to the office. I could hear Tammy close behind. Once inside, I slammed the door and leaned against it for a minute, trying to catch my breath. From the looks on their faces, I would have to tell them what just happened.

"What the ever-loving fuck was that?" Tammy asked breathlessly. Her eyes were wide, skin pale. She was terrified.

"Yeah," panted Kate. "I think it's time to tell us the truth."

I nodded and motioned for them to sit. For once, both did as I asked without argument or altercation. Once they were seated, I gathered my thoughts and spoke.

"My name is Bastian Bucco. I don't work for the power company; I work for a man named Cyrus Bane." I paused, watching their expressions. Kate immediately recognized the name as her uncle who died. "As far as I know, he is not dead. He wants to harness a power that he believes only you can help provide."

"How?" Her voice was small, almost childlike.

"With your spirit. This house is on a spiritual nexus. This nexus is a gateway to hell. Once it is opened, there is an incredible amount of power that can be wielded."

"How does he open this portal?" Tammy asked. She still sounded skeptical, but I didn't give a damn.

"With the power of the thirteen ghosts, they are the essence of the black zodiac. Each ghost represents part of the zodiac. The ghosts are the Golden Boy, Butcher, Cheerleader, Scorched Lover, Mangled Captain, Beauty Queen, Wretched Crone, Mother, Son, Psycho, Blacksmith, and Titan."

"That's only twelve," Kate whispered. "What's the thirteenth?"

"The Lost Soul. It is a soul that just continually roams the earth. Not immortal exactly, but doesn't die easily. It stops aging at a certain point in its life. The aging process won't start again until the soul has found its purpose."

"So how does Uncle Cyrus think I can help?" I could see the wheels turning in her head as she thought about what I was telling her. Her eyes widened. "So, are you saying that I'm this Lost Soul? How does he plan on using me?"

"Well, he needs your ghost, so he wants you to die. However, I know you aren't the lost soul, so we just need to get you out of here."

"How do you know that? How does anyone know this?" Panic rose in her voice.

I knelt in front of her. Taking both of her hands in mine, I squeezed them gently. "I know these things. He didn't discuss his plan with me, or I would have talked him out of it. I was told long ago about the lost soul. I know who it is, and as long as it stays with me, they are safe."

"So, let me get this straight." Tammy stood up so she could physically look down at me. "You want us to believe that ghosts are real?"

I nodded. "Yes."

We stared at each other until she looked away first. Yes, ghosts were real, and they were about to get a taste of what these certain ghosts could do.

Chapter 82

"*What do we do?*" Kate asked.

"Get your phone and try calling a friend to get us out of here," Tammy suggested.

For once I agreed with her. I nodded. "Yes, call someone for help."

She pulled out her phone. After staring at it for a minute she let it drop to the floor through her fingers. "Shit. No signal. Now what? Do we just stay in here? What happens if we leave the study?"

I stood and paced the room. "We stay in here as long as possible. If we leave the room, there will be ghosts after us. They don't care who you are, they like to kill. Well, most of them do."

"I have a question," Tammy asked, her sharp eyes on me. "How did these so-called ghosts get here? I mean it sounds like they are very specific types. The odds of them all culminating here seem odd."

"I brought them here." I shrugged.

"So, all this is your fault?" I heard the temper in Tammy's voice. She finally found someone to blame.

"In a way, yes. I brought them here so it's my fault they are here. But was it my plan? Nope. I had no say in it. Did I bring you here? No, so that wasn't my fault. If it makes you feel better, you can blame me though." I rubbed the back of my neck; I was already tired of this. "What I will do is try to help you get out of here alive. You need to stick with me and listen to me. No matter what, you do as I say. Got it?"

Both women nodded.

"We will stay in here as long as possible. This is the safest room in the house. Bane had me put spells up that will keep them out when the door is shut. They can enter when the door is open but can only go so far into the room. He didn't want them trying anything to him. He didn't make friends well."

"So, if we just stay in here forever, we will be fine?" Tammy laughed at the thought. The laugh was a sarcastic sound, on the verge of hopeless.

"For now, yes. I don't think the ghosts will let us stay in here forever though. They are going to start getting antsy and wanting to play. I wouldn't put it past some of them to find a way to get us out of here. I hope we won't be in here too long anyway." I hoped to buy time to come up with another plan. It was imperative we discover a way out.

Time seemed to creep as we sat around the office. There was no conversation, no noise. We just silently sat around the room. The women were both looking through books, but I couldn't sit still. I stood up and paced the room. I needed to keep moving. I never was good at sitting still. It had to be an effect from my childhood.

I pushed the thoughts away when they encroached my mind. I couldn't let the darkness. It was dangerous to let that stuff bog me down. I needed to focus on getting out of the house. I decided it was time to have a chat with William.

"I'll be right back. I'm going to step out for a minute." I started for the door.

"Wait." Panic laced Kate's voice. "You said we had to stay in here. It's not safe out there. You are going to leave us alone?"

"I'm going to just stand outside the door and have a talk with someone."

"Who?" Tammy asked. "You have a way to talk to someone from the outside? Why didn't you get ahold of them already?"

"They are from the outside." I sighed. I knew they would think I was crazy, but they asked. "I'm going to talk to one of the ghosts. William will talk to me."

"Who's William?" Kate asked.

"The first ghost, Golden Boy."

Tammy laughed. "You're going to talk to a ghost? You are certifiable."

"I may be, but he may know a way out." I turned and left the room before they could ridicule me any longer. Once the door was shut behind me, I looked around trying to find the little bastard. He wouldn't be too far from this door. He was like a shadow, always around. "William. Come here."

I crossed my arms as I waited. He needed to show up soon. I knew he was there, I could feel him, but I couldn't see him yet.

"Show yourself now."

"What do you want, Charles?" William's voice sounded like it surrounded me.

"Cute parlor trick, now show yourself. I need to speak with you, and I prefer to see you when we talk. You know this."

He materialized out of nowhere. I hated when he did that. It was ridiculous. His smile was sickening. That smile reminded me of the old days. The dark days as I thought of them, if I allowed myself to think of them, which I didn't.

"You rang?" he asked with a snarky tone in his voice.

"I need a way out of the house."

"Why would you think I know something like that? I'm just a ghost. The dead kid."

"You also know every nook and cranny of this house. You've been here forever. If there is a secret way out, you know it. I need to know. I need to get these women out before they are killed. If they die, their blood will be on your hands."

He laughed. "Oh no, brother. Their blood is on your hands, like the blood of others."

"They aren't dead, and what are you talking about?"

"I know what you are," he whispered softly. "We all do."

A chill ran down my spine. "Just tell me a way to get them out of this hellhole."

"Go to the basement. There is a large freezer. Move it and there is a door. Open the door and crawl through it. It opens out on the other side of the interstate. Well, that's what I have heard anyway." He shrugged. "It's hard to say since I haven't explored it myself."

The sound of the door opening made us both turn and look. Tammy and Kate both stood there.

"Sorry, I couldn't stand it anymore," Kate explained. "I'm feeling claustrophobic."

William giggled and both women shivered. They may not hear him, but it was obvious they felt his presence.

"Please, go back into the office," I pleaded. I hoped they would listen.

"Too late, Charles." With that, he disappeared.

Chapter 83

The impact caught me off guard. I hit the ground, all the air rushing out of me. I couldn't breathe. I stared at the ceiling waiting for my lungs to fill back up with oxygen. The Son hit like a train when he rushed people like that. I hadn't been on the receiving end of the hit until now, but damn.

The only way I could sit up was slowly. My ribs and side ached. I was certain they were bruised if not broken. Sighing, I looked around the room to take stock of what had happened. Mother and Son were standing in the living room, holding hands.

"What the hell, Abe?" I muttered.

They both just stared at me. Malice in their eyes. I hadn't expected the violence from them, but it shouldn't have surprised me. They were just the beginning of a night from hell. I struggled to my feet, not taking my eyes off them. If I did, they would probably attack again.

"What the fuck was that?" Tammy asked.

"That was the ghosts that you didn't think existed." I felt a wheeze while trying to breathe.

"Are you okay?" Kate placed a hand on my arm.

I nodded. "Yeah. I think I know a way out. Let's go."

We didn't make it into the kitchen before the next attack happened. Dana appeared out of nowhere, flinging her arm back and slapping Kate across the face.

"Bitch!" Dana growled.

Kate covered her face with her hand, tears filling her eyes. I knew she was scared, but it was different seeing it on her face. I wanted to make her feel better and didn't know why, but my first objective was to get Dana away from her.

"Dana, stop." I was as calm as I could be. I had to stay calm when dealing with her. "Dana, look at me."

She turned so she was facing me. Her eyes were livid. "What? How could you do this to me?"

I chanced a step closer. "I didn't do anything, Dana. Kate was brought here by Bane. This isn't her fault. She isn't responsible for anything."

"I know the look she is giving you. She is giving you the look that says she wants to fuck you. You are mine. Mine!" she screamed at me.

"I know, sweetie. I'm yours. I always will be, but you don't need to kill Kate to prove it. Please."

She glared at me. "You have never stopped me from killing before. You encouraged it. You even helped me kill, remember?"

"Yes, sweetheart. I remember. I also remember that we killed him because of what he was doing to you. He deserved it. Kate is innocent."

"Which makes her even more fun to kill," Dana purred. She stepped closer, running her hand from her neck to her breasts, then pinched her nipple. I felt myself harden, but I had to push those thoughts away.

"No, Dana," I rasped. It felt like I was strangling. "We can't kill her."

Her bottom lip stuck out. "You used to be fun."

"I know, and I'm sorry." I wanted to placate her enough for her to leave the woman alone. "I promise we will kill the next people that come in together. Okay?" I heard the gasp from Kate but didn't dare look at her. She would just have to understand and get over it. I wasn't trying to impress anyone here, just keep Dana from murdering her. ** move to down here since Kate can't hear Dana. Makes more sense here.

Finally, she nodded. She glared at Kate. "You touch my man, and I'll kill you. Do you understand?"

"Dana, she can't hear you, but I'll let her know what you said."

She looked at me and smiled. "I love you."

"And I, you."

She disappeared, and I let out a sigh. I turned to study Kate. She was pale, hand still covering her face. She had tears in her eyes, but her cheeks were dry. She looked like she wanted to cry but was too tough to actually do so.

"Are you all right?"

She nodded. "What was all that? You said you killed someone."

"I've done some bad things. That was – complicated. I'm not sure exactly how to explain Dana. She is the Beauty Queen. Killed herself because she didn't think she was perfect. She couldn't see the beauty within. She was very beautiful on the outside as well though. She just saw her flaws."

"You sound like you love her," Kate whispered as she removed her hand from her cheek. There was a red mark, with small scratches where Dana's nails connected.

"Like I said, it's complicated. Now we need to get out of here."

"Agreed. Where's Tammy?" Kate looked around.

I turned to help her look for the woman. We needed to find her and get out of here before anything else happened. I didn't see her anywhere in the hall. Grabbing Kate's hand, we made our way slowly through the main level, looking for the missing woman.

We entered the living room to find her standing in the middle of the room, wide-eyed. She was staring toward the wall. I inwardly cringed as I turned to see who she was staring at. To my shock and dismay, it was Titan. I didn't know how the hell he got out of the room, but there he was, standing there with a sick smile on his face.

"Tammy, back away slowly. No sudden movements," I instructed. I hoped that she would listen. I didn't want him to attack. It would be next to impossible to get him off her. I could barely get him off his daughter when he attacked her.

"H-How? How?" she mumbled.

"You need to back away from him." A sense of urgency washed over me. If I knew him, and I did, he would attack at any moment.

She made the mistake of looking away from him. Titan charged, but instead of going after Tammy, he knocked her out of the way and came toward Kate and me. She flew into the china hutch holding the statue. The glass shattered as the wood splintered.

I shoved Kate to the side so Titan would miss her and ended up tackled by the bastard myself. I rolled around with him, trying to gain the upper hand. It wasn't working very well though. I wished I had some iron on me or something.

"Bastian! What do I do?" Kate asked.

"Salt. . Or. . Iron," I gasped out. It was taking all my effort to keep him from killing me, making talking difficult.

I heard Kate run off while I fought him.

"You brought me here. You must die," he told me. His voice was soft, almost caressing. It made my stomach churn.

Suddenly, the weight and force of him disappeared as a fire poker flew above my head. Tammy stood there, staring down at me. Her expression bewildered.

"What the actual fuck was that?" she asked as she reached a hand out to help me stand.

"That," I gasped, trying to catch my breath. "Was a ghost."

"I could see it. Him."

"Some of them can pull enough energy to be corporeal, but it isn't often they can do that. Titan has a lot of anger built up, and that increases his energy." I hoped that explained it enough because I wasn't sure I could make it any clearer.

Kate took that moment to run back into the room with a box of salt in her hand. She looked around wildly for any signs of danger. When she saw us just standing there, the box of salt went down to her side, and she looked almost deflated.

"Charles Sebastian Wellington as I live and breathe," the voice that floated through the room, chilling me down to the bone. Fear gripped my stomach and bowels, making me nauseous.

It was the one voice I would never forget. The one that haunted me in my nightmares and when I was awake with my guard down. The voice was the evilest sound I had ever heard. I'd rather face the Titan, Blacksmith, and Psycho all at the same time repeatedly for all eternity than hear that voice again.

Slowly, I turned to see if maybe I was hallucinating. My breath caught in my lungs as my throat closed. What I saw horrified me more than anything else in the world.

Mother.

Chapter 84

My nightmares had come alive. When the china hutch broke, it freed my mother. I continued to stare at her, unblinking. I couldn't help it. I hadn't seen her since I was a child. Memories flashed through my head; I could not stop them. Growing up with that woman, her beating me for small infractions, sitting at the table, not allowed to speak. Being placed by myself after accidentally spilling a drink. My father's illness and death.

The scars on my back tingled at the sight of her. I closed my eyes for a moment, and when I opened them again, I hoped she would be gone. She wasn't. This was my nightmare come alive. She wasn't translucent either. She appeared to be solid.

I risked a glance toward Kate and Tammy to see if they saw her too. Kate's eyes were wide, and Tammy had a frown on her face. I was pretty sure that meant they could see her. Neither of them spoke nor moved. Just watched.

"Are you going to give your mother a hug?" Ingrid asked, forcing me to look back to her. Her arms were outstretched like she was waiting for me to embrace her. That wasn't going to fucking happen.

"No. You aren't my mother." The words sounded hollow, defeated, even to my ears.

"You have no idea how much I've missed you, Charles."

"I'm not Charles," I said automatically.

"Yes, you are. You are the spitting image of your father, my darling husband. Do you think I would not recognize my own son?"

"I'm not your son." I felt like a broken record. If I said it enough, it would make me believe it and make her go away. I just wanted her to go away. I needed her gone. I needed those memories she brought back gone. "You have no power over me."

"You're wrong, Charles. I am your mother. I have been with you since you were a babe. I was a wet nurse for you. You drained the life out of me. Then you turned into a little freak. One just like that witch you called a mother. She should have been burned at the stake. You should have been with her. Then we could have lived life like we were meant to. Without you."

Her words were like a slap on the face. I struggled to remain calm. I could feel the lump in my throat growing and my stomach continued to twist with the nerves. I took several deep breaths, trying to calm myself.

"William was supposed to grow up to be in charge of the family business and estate, but you wouldn't die! You wouldn't get out of the way and let him do what he needed to do. Your father insisted that it go to the oldest child, whether or not he was the most capable," she continued. Those were almost the exact things she told me before I killed her all those years ago.

"Leave me alone," I said weakly. The child inside me was coming to the surface, making me want to curl in a ball and cry. I struggled to keep him at bay. I needed to remember what the purpose of being in the house was.

"I will never leave you alone. I will spend the rest of eternity with you since you can't do what you are told. Do I need to remind you who's in charge here?"

"That's enough." Kate stepped forward, frown marring her features. "I don't know who you think you are but lady, you're dead. A ghost. You can't bother him anymore. Why don't you go back to hell where you came from?"

Mother laughed. "How precious. You have a slip of a girl standing up for you since you can't do it yourself. I knew you would grow up to be a weak, pathetic man."

She struck out with a speed faster than a blink of an eye. I reeled from the slap and was taken back a couple of steps. I didn't defend myself, just stood there and let the onslaught take place. When she hit me the fourth, maybe fifth time, Kate stepped in.

Kate threw a handful of salt into her face. Mother screamed and recoiled like it was acid. She then vanished like she hadn't been there. If I had to guess, she had gone into hiding. Kate turned and placed her hands on my cheeks.

"Are you okay?" she asked as I stared into her deep green eyes. "Do you want to talk about what that was?"

I shook my head no. I never wanted to bring that bitch up again. I just wanted to get out of the house and away from there forever. I never wanted to see the house or ghosts in it again. The thought stunned me for a moment.

I never wanted to see the ghosts again. The thought ran through my head again. I meant it. I was tired of dealing with ghosts. I wanted normal. I didn't know what made me feel that way, but I wanted to live the rest of my days as normally as I could. Without ghosts or murder.

"I'll be better once we get out of here. Let's go." I stepped back, and her hands fell away from my face. I ached a little at the loss of contact. I would think about that when I had time to think again.

I led the women to the kitchen where we were stopped in our tracks. There stood the Psycho, Ryan Jessop. Her hair was wild and eyes evil. She smiled at us and it looked like there was blood in her teeth. I didn't remember her looking like that when I trapped her, but I wasn't positive. I never looked that closely at the ghosts, except for Dana.

Psycho laughed. It was the same cackling sound I had heard coming from the basement. She held a butcher knife in her hand with blood dripping off it. I could see the blood leaving a puddle on the floor.

"Umm, is that blood?" Kate asked, stepping a little closer to me.

"Yep."

"Is that a crazy woman with a knife?"

"Yep."

"Is she going to try to kill us?"

I half shrugged. "Most likely."

"And we have to get past her to get out of the house?"

"Uh-huh."

"Fan-fucking-tastic."

I chuckled at her reaction. She didn't seem scared, more annoyed. I figured there was a point when you get so scared that it numbs you from the shock. Of course, the only one that tried to kill her directly was Dana.

She glanced at Tammy. "You ready for this?"

"Do I have a choice?"

"Nope."

"Then let's do it."

We walked into the kitchen and stopped. There was blood everywhere and an arm lying on the island in the middle of the kitchen. Blood slowly dripped from the fingertips. My mind raced as I tried to figure out who that had been. The three of us had been the only ones in the house. That I knew of anyway. We must have been wrong.

"Oh my god," Kate whispered.

It had to be a sight for someone not used to bloody situations. I was jaded due to the life I lived. I had seen a lot of blood and guts over my lifetime. It wasn't something you ever grew completely accustomed to, but it made you more desensitized to the sight than a normal person.

"Ryan, we don't want to bother you. We just need to get to the basement." I held my hands out in a defenseless gesture to show her we meant no harm. I lowered my voice and spoke softly to the women. "No sudden movements. Think of her like a rabid dog that you need to get around. You don't want her to set her sights you, or she will attack."

"Umm, out of curiosity. What did she do in her real life?"

"She owned a bed and breakfast where she killed her guests, cooked them, and fed them to other guests." I chanced a glance at Kate.

She rolled her eyes. "Delightful."

"Especially. Her roasts were famous."

"Wait. You're talking about Ryan Jessop," Tammy interjected.

I nodded once.

"I stayed at her bed and breakfast once. It was a cute place—" She trailed off as the implications of what I said hit her. "I think I'm going to be sick."

"Wait until we get out of here," Kate suggested.

We slowly crept through the kitchen. We didn't make it halfway before she came running toward us, laughing and screaming. I yanked Kate's arm, pulling her out of the way as the blade of the butcher knife came down. It embedded in the wall. Tammy grabbed the knife handle, yanking it out. She searched the room for the Psycho, but she was nowhere to be seen. Maybe we would get through there in one piece after all.

Chapter 85

Tammy kept the knife firmly in her grip as we walked to the basement. The door opened just as easily as before. We walked into the inky darkness as the door slammed shut behind us. There was a click of a lock engaging. I heard Kate gasp, then jiggle the handle.

"Yeah, you aren't getting that door open," I told her.

There was a sigh then Kate spoke. "I know, just had to try."

"The only way to go is down," Tammy groaned.

"Yep. Now let's go. William said there was a way out from down here." I knew that I was giving them a little hope. Maybe it would push them through until we could get out, hopefully alive.

"Who was all chopped to bits up there?" Tammy asked the question I had been wondering myself. "I thought we were the only ones in the house."

"That's what I thought too," I admitted. "So, if we weren't, then there is another way out. That person had to get in here somehow."

When we reached the landing at the bottom of the stairs, I stood there for a minute looking around. The basement had lights on when I left it earlier in the evening. I wasn't sure who turned off the lights, but the dark was eerie. I reached for my flashlight and switched it on.

The light landed on the freezer William had told me about. I signaled the women to follow me. Once over there, Tammy helped me push the deep freeze out of the way. When it was moved, I shined my light on the wall. To my dismay, a small gate door covered the way out with a padlock on it. I pulled on it, but there was no give.

"Fuck," I grumbled. We would have to come up with another way out or find something to cut the gate. I turned, shining my light across the room looking for a toolbox or something, anything that I could use such as wire or bolt cutters.

A loud click made all three of us jump. The lights came on. They were so bright I had to shield my eyes for a moment. When I removed my hand, I looked around, confused. The whole room had changed. A doorway that hadn't been there before was before us.

Tammy stepped toward the door before she stopped and turned back to us. "Where did that come from?"

I shrugged and Kate shook her head.

"Should we open it?" Tammy asked, glancing back at the door.

I opened my mouth to speak, then closed it on a sigh. I had no idea. I knew it was a bad idea, but we couldn't just stay where we were. Not being proactive made us sitting ducks. Finally, I spoke, "I really don't know. It's likely a trap, but I don't know who set it. It couldn't have been the ghosts, but then again, I don't put anything past them. That door isn't a good sign though. I figure it was put there by a human, most likely Bane, which means he's here somewhere too. None of this is a good idea."

"What do we do?" Kate asked. She wasn't looking at me though. She was staring at the door.

"I'll go through the door, you two keep looking for something to get that gate open. Once you do, you go through that tunnel and don't look back. It supposed to lead to the other side of the interstate. When you get out, call for help, leave, and never come back. I'll take care of everything here."

"We aren't leaving you," Kate insisted.

"Yes, you are. I'm the one he wants, not you."

Her brows furrowed together. "What are you saying?"

I leaned closer to her and whispered the words softly against her ear. "I'm the thirteenth ghost. The Lost Soul."

When I pulled back, her eyes and mouth were wide. "You are planning on sacrificing yourself for us, aren't you?"

"You don't deserve this. I am truly sorry that he put you through all this when it should have been me all along. Now please, do as I ask." I looked over at Tammy. "Make her do this. You both have to get out of here."

She nodded and put a hand on Kate's shoulder.

Taking a deep breath, I walked to the door and put my hand on the knob. Before I could turn it, there was a loud crash and a scream. I whirled around to see what was going on. Tammy was on the ground with the knife she had been holding plunged into her chest. Kate was on the ground beside her, crying unabashedly.

Tammy's breath was coming in struggles as her lungs filled with blood. She looked at Kate as she spoke. "Get . . . out . . . of . . . here . . . please. Find . . . a . . . out. Be happy. Find lo—"

The life escaped her with her final breath. Kate leaned over her, bawling. I looked around the room, trying to find who did it and to protect Kate as much as possible. Then I saw her. Mother. She stood off to the side, head held high, sadistic smile on her face.

"I should have killed the girl," she nodded toward Kate as she spoke to me. "You seem fond of the girl. That would have been a better punishment."

"You killed her because of me?" Even though I shouldn't have been surprised, I was. "She had nothing to do with me. It was just happenstance that I even met Tammy."

"Like it was happenstance that you let your brother eat your cake that killed him?" She cocked an eyebrow at me.

"You were the one that poisoned the cake, knowing that he never listened when you told him to stay out of stuff. His death is on you, not me." I stepped forward letting the rage carry me. "All this is your fault, Mother. If you would have cared, even a little bit, about me then all of this could have been avoided. If only you hadn't been such an evil bitch!"

"You finally acknowledge I'm your mother," Ingrid smiled at me. It made me nauseous to see it.

"You were never a mother to me. A mother is someone who gives a fuck about the child. Where were you when I cried myself to sleep after the night terrors I suffered from? When I was sick? The first time a ghost scared me? You weren't there. You were with your precious son, William. You were too worried about getting the family fortune." I lowered my voice. "That doesn't make you a mother. You only got the name because that was what I was told to call you. And you know what? I'm glad I killed you. I was relieved when I did it, and I would do it again. You are nothing to me."

I turned and helped a heartbroken Kate off the floor. She wrapped her arms around my waist, hugging me tightly. I hugged her back, surprising myself that I enjoyed the human connection. The warmth of a body. I pulled away back and looked down at her.

"Kate, I need you to listen to me. Find a toolbox. You have to get out of here. I can't see you die too. I'm going to take care of this. I told you I would get you out of here. I'm going to do my best to hold up that promise." I looked over her head to see the Wretched Crone standing there. "Do you know what we can use to get this gate open? I want her out of here, and it's time to face my future."

She nodded and disappeared. Reappearing in a corner, she looked down at a pair of bolt cutters on the floor. I rushed over and grabbed them. Time was of the essence.

I returned to the gate and cut the lock. It swung open soundlessly. Grabbing Kate's hand, I pulled her to the opening. I placed my flashlight in her palm, wrapping her fingers around the handle of it myself. I pushed her into the tunnel and blocked it so she couldn't come back out.

"Go. Get out of here."

Tears were still streaming down her face. "I'm scared. I don't want to leave you."

"You have to. If not, you will die too. I can't live with that. Go. Do as your friend wished. She wanted you happy. The only thing you can do is give her this dying wish." Then I did something out of character for me. I leaned forward and kissed her on the lips. "Kate, I wish I had the time to get to know you. Maybe take you on a date, but that isn't going to happen. Just know that you did something that no one else could do. You changed me. Helped me find myself again. There has been a part of me missing since I was a child. The compassion you showed me, a manipulative stranger, made me realize there is more to life than this. Thank you. Now go."

I watched as she disappeared into the tunnel. Straightening, I walked to the door of the mysterious room. The one thing I didn't tell her was that I had felt love for her. It was too soon to decide what kind, and I'd never be able to explore it, so it was best she didn't know.

I took a deep breath and let it out, trying to steady my nerves. Ready or not, it was time to face the music. And the monsters on the other side of the door.

Chapter 86

I opened the door and walked in without further hesitation. The only thing waiting would do for me is prolong the torture and this dull existence. The room was empty. On the floor was an engraved circle with different symbols representing the Black Zodiac. Standing in the center of the circle was Cyrus Bane.

He held a black leather-bound book in his hands, reading out of it. The cadence of his voice was almost mesmerizing, but I knew it was the words. He was speaking in a language that sounded like Latin, but it wasn't quite Latin. I couldn't pinpoint what was different about it, but I didn't recognize it.

He looked up from the book. His eyes widened for a moment then narrowed. He closed the book with a definitive snap and tucked it under his arm before he spoke. "What are you doing here, Bucco?"

"I came to stop you. I can't have you unleashing the demons from hell, and sorry, but your thirteenth ghost isn't available. She has escaped from this fresh hell." I smiled, rocking back onto my heels. "I guess you will have to cancel."

He laughed. The sound was as sinister as what he had been reading. "You are such a stupid fool. Did you think that I really wanted to kill that girl? I'm not as ignorant as you believe that I am. I researched the black zodiac and ghosts my entire adult existence. I know what I am looking for when it comes to ghosts. It just took finding the Lost Soul and everything would come together. That is you. You were the missing piece to get everything moving. And you did nicely."

I wasn't sure how he knew I was the Lost Soul. I had known for a long time, but no one had ever picked up on my trail before. As I stared at him, he continued.

"It took a lot of research, but I found you. You did a lot of traveling over the years, but you did leave clues. There were few pictures of you, and you kept your name similar to your given name until you came up with the last name Bucco. That was a nice touch, however, not good enough Charles."

"When did you figure it out?" I was genuinely curious.

"When you sold me the house. You said it was in your family for generations. The historical records of this house showed that there were no dependents born after the murders of Ingrid and William Wellington. The son of Charles Wellington the second disappeared and was suspected of the murders of William and Ingrid, but no one knew what happened to him. No records ever showed up about Charles the third again."

Damn it. Selling the house to him exposed my secret. If it was possible, I would kick my own ass for that. It hadn't occurred that someone would look that closely into the history of the house. Or the people that lived here. Yes, the murders had been big news back when it happened, but for it to still be known. Ugh.

"Now, you will have to die; however, there is a catch. It has to be by your own hand. I can't kill you. Why do you think the ghosts haven't touched you, except for Titan? That bastard can't follow instructions even when spelled to."

"I was attacked."

He laughed. "Of course, you were. They were trying to urge you to try to escape. They were supposed to drive you down here, which they did. Of course, I hadn't planned on the death of that other girl. Or that you would get Kate out. That was quite unfortunate. I was going to use them as leverage."

"Who was dead in the kitchen?" I wanted to keep him talking so I could come up with a plan. But then, I didn't need one. He couldn't kill me if he wanted this to work. The Lost Soul had to end his own life. That I hadn't seen coming.

"My lawyer, Mr. Bradford. He tried double charging me." He shrugged. "You know what they say, never trust a lawyer."

"I hate to burst your bubble, actually I don't, but I'm not going to kill myself, so I guess you will need to come up with a new plan." I shrugged then crossed my arms nonchalantly.

"I figured you'd say that. How about some one-on-one time with your mother? I've heard that she isn't one you get along with that well. I mean, you did kill her right?"

"Mother can't say anything or do anything to me that she hasn't done or said before. Mother doesn't affect me anymore."

"Really?" He scratched his chin.

"Yep."

"Let's find out." He slipped opened the book and read a few lines. There was a wind in the room, then suddenly I was back in the house how it used to be.

I looked around, confused. I was now standing in my room. It was arranged like it had been the last time I had been there as a kid.

William was sitting on my bed, toy soldiers in his hands.

"Charles, do you want to play war with me?" he asked innocently.

I looked at him with a frown on my face. "Do what?"

He held one of the soldiers out to me. "Play war. You can be the blue guys this time."

"No. You get mad every time we play if things don't go the way you want them to. I don't want to get into trouble again. Mother will be angry if you cry."

"I won't get mad and cry," William promised. "Please, Charles?"

I sighed. "Fine."

I took the solider out of his hand and sat on the floor. He hopped off the bed and joined me. As we played, I knew that he would get mad. He always got mad when he played soldier. Sure enough, we hadn't been playing ten minutes before he got angry.

"You can't take my troops from there," he growled.

"Yes, I can. I have you surrounded, and your general isn't able to escape to get help," I told him.

"No!" he screamed. "My troops are able to fight out of it."

"No, William they can't." I tried to reason with him. "How about one or two soldiers survive?"

"No! I want them all to survive. You cheat." He threw a soldier across the room and cried.

"William, calm down. You promised. Please, don't cry." I looked at the closed door. "I'm sorry. Calm down. Don't get me in trouble."

Panic choked me. I would get in trouble again. Mother didn't like it when William cried and wouldn't listen when I tried to tell her what happened. She never believed me when I told her what happened anyway. She would just accuse me of doing something to him.

"What is going on up there?" Mother demanded. William screamed, and I could hear her stomping up the stairs. She shoved my bedroom door up, glare settled on me. "Why is William crying?"

"He is mad that the game didn't go his way," I tried to explain quickly. I hoped she would believe me this time.

"William?" she asked, turning to him.

He hiccupped as he cried. "Charles is mean."

She grabbed me up by the hair and pulled me out of the room. "I don't know what is wrong with you. Why do you insist on being mean to your little brother? Do you resent him? Do you hate him?"

"No!" I cried as she yanked on my hair leading me down the stairs. I stumbled, but the only thing that kept me from falling was her grip on my head.

When we made it to the bottom of the stairs, she pulled me through the house into the kitchen. Hanging on the wall was a paddle in the shape of a hand. Holes were drilled into it. I couldn't decide if I was relieved that I was getting the paddle or upset. It didn't cause as much damage as the belt, but it still hurt.

She grabbed the paddle from the wall and turned toward me. "Drop your pants and bend over. You know the drill. If you can't be good, I will beat the evil out of you."

"Mother, I'm sorry. I won't make him cry again, I promise," I begged.

Her hand shot out and slapped me across the face. "I said, drop your pants and bend over. If you don't listen, so help me God . . ."

With trembling hands, I did as I was told. The first strike made me fall forward. She grabbed my shirt, yanking me back to my feet. As she swung the paddle, I could hear the air whistle through it. Each strike made my skin burn. I clenched my teeth and closed my eyes tightly trying to keep from crying out. The more I cried out, the angrier mother would get. When she finished paddling me, she hung the paddle up and walked from the room.

Slowly, I stood up. Pain radiated from my bum all the way up my back and down to my feet. There was a warm liquid feeling running down my leg. I reached back, gently touching my leg. When I brought my hand back, there was blood on my fingers. She broke open the skin. Sitting would be a chore.

I wiped the tears from my face and pulled my pants up, refastening my belt. I hated my life. I wished I didn't exist. I wanted to die. If I died, then maybe the afterlife would be much better than this one. Anything had to be better than this existence.

Chapter 87

The next thing I knew, I was back in that room in the basement. I had tears drying on my face. My bum still stung from the paddle. I remembered it, all of it. But I didn't remember wanting to die then. The thought had never crossed my mind during that incident. I remembered wanting to be somewhere else, living another life, but not dead. I shook my head, trying to rid myself of the memories.

"Oh, Charles. There are so many more memories that we can choose from if that one isn't good enough for you," she said softly. I didn't know when Mother showed up in the room. She must have been what triggered the memory.

"Go away. I'm not the kid you knew. I'm different. You can't turn me back into him."

"Why don't you go ahead and kill yourself. I know you wanted to as a child. You want to now. You don't fit in anywhere. You would have been found guilty of witchcraft if your father would have let me turn you in. You don't deserve to live. You aren't innocent."

"I know I'm not. I've made peace with that fact. You, however, will never change. When you do cross over, you are going to go straight to hell where you belong."

"You will be there right along with me, son," she sneered.

"Fuck you!" I spat at her. "You will never bring me down again."

"We'll see about that." She smiled at me.

The nightmares started again.

***

I was sitting in the corner of the room, knees drawn up to my chest, trying to fight the memories, but they kept bombarding me. I didn't hear the door open. Just the words going through my head.

Make it stop. I want to die. Don't make me do this anymore. I can't do it. I need to escape the pain. I want the pain to stop. Please make it stop. I want the pain to end. There is only one way to stop it. I have to do it. If I'm brave I will be safe.

I grabbed the knife that had been left in the room. I stared at the blade while I debated the best place to use it. Carefully, I lowered it to my wrist. If I cut down my arm, it should slice the entire vein open, and I would be free. Free of the pain and torment. Free to move on.

A hand landed on my arm. I jumped and looked up, trying to recognize the bright green eyes. Then it hit me. Kate was back. I shook my head and forced myself to stand. I felt a hand touch mine before taking the knife out of my hand.

"Bastian, are you okay?" The concern in her voice touched me in ways I haven't felt in a long time.

"I told you to leave, not to come back," I rasped. My voice was raw. I didn't know why, but it felt like I had been screaming.

"I couldn't leave you alone in here. You helped me; let me help you. We can do this together." She wrapped her arms around me in a hug.

"No," I pushed at her. "You have to leave. It's not safe."

As I stared at Kate, I could hear Dana's voice in my head. Kill her. She's trying to come between us. She doesn't want us to be together. She thinks that she is prettier than I am. She wants you for herself. We can't let her keep us apart. We have to be stronger than her. Kill her. It won't be hard for you to slit her pretty little throat.

"No." My voice startled Kate, but I still wasn't completely in the moment. "I won't hurt her. She's innocent. I told you that already."

"What?" Kate asked, frowning at me.

I shook my head. "Nothing. You have to get out of here. Come on."

"Not without you."

I growled. "Fine. Let's go."

We walked to the door, but it wouldn't open. It was locked. I punched the door and turned around.

"Fuck!"

"I didn't lock it," Kate promised.

"I know. It was a trap. Bane must have known that you would come back. He's smarter than I gave him credit for." We just had to wait for the other shoe to drop. We were once again trapped in the house, in a room. This time there was no way out.

"What do we do now?"

"We wait. If I'm right, we won't have to wait long."

She nodded. "Perfect."

I took her hand and squeezed it. "Thank you for coming back even though it was dumb."

"You're welcome. I don't think it was."

We would not agree on that, so I let it drop. There was no point in arguing with the last person I would ever talk to alive. I was flattered and touched that she came back for me. In my entire life, only one person had ever cared for me— Isabella. She had been there for me when no one else had.

Guilt washed over me. She had died because of me. I hadn't expected that wave of guilt. It was something I had accepted years ago and now it was eating at me. Mother's abuse must have gotten under my skin. I had always felt bad about what happened to Isabella. She had tried to warn me what would happen, but I wouldn't listen. I just had to practice magic. I had been young and stupid. I couldn't let it bog me down now. Not while Kate was in danger still. I needed to get her out of here.

When the door opened, I grabbed Kate and pulled her behind me, trying to hide her from view. Bane entered the room, eyebrows raised when he saw me. He looked around with a sly grin on his face.

"Where is the girl?" The tone in his voice was disturbing. It made the hair on the back of my neck stand up.

"I haven't seen her."

"Don't lie. I know she came in. You act like I'm stupid. I know she is here. It's not like hiding her is going to do any good. I'm going to get tired of these games."

"I'm not playing any games." An air of defiance washed through me. "And I'm going to get us out of here. Just wait and see."

"That may be amusing." Bane laughed.

"You will think amusing," I stepped closer to him, lowering my voice. "You will die before we get out of here, and I will burn this place to the ground. You will not rein in the power of the zodiac. I won't let it happen."

"You have no choice in the matter, Mister Bucco. You will die, and I will harness the power of the Zodiac."

Kate stepped around from behind me, standing at my side. She glared at the man who had been her father's brother. "You are a real piece of work. You set people up to die. How could you? You aren't my family. Dad would be ashamed of you if he were alive today. You aren't the man he said you were."

"I don't care if your dad would be ashamed of me or not. He's dead, and I was never fond of him. Just because he was my brother didn't mean I had to like him. You are a silly girl to think that his opinions of me would matter." He grinned. "Not that you will be alive much longer to tell me more."

He launched himself forward, straight toward Kate.

Chapter 88

Everything seemed to move in slow motion as Bane grappled with Kate on the floor. The struggle didn't last long before he slammed her head back. It connected with floor with a loud crack. Kate went limp instantly.

Bane got to his feet and turned to me. "Now you will do as I say. Take the knife and slit her throat."

"Fuck you!" I spat in his face.

He pulled a gun from behind his back and aimed it at Kate's head. "I was hoping you would say that. Then listen up. If you want her to live, you know what you have to do."

I shook my head no. "I'm not killing myself."

Suddenly, I knew that I wasn't alone. William was standing beside me looking up at me. "This isn't going to end well, Charles."

"I know. I'm sorry."

"For what?"

"For what I have to do. And everything else."

"It's fine. Just do it, Charles. Isabella wants you to know that you are strong and smart. She would tell you herself, but she's busy."

"Doing what?"

"Holding Mother back."

"Who are you talking to?" Bane demanded.

I shrugged. There was no point in lying anymore. "My brother."

He cocked the gun and glared at me. "Do it, or I will kill her."

"How do you expect me to do it? I don't have anything to do it with."

He pulled a vial out of his pocket and held it out for me. "With this."

I took it from his hand and stared at it. I didn't need him to tell me what it was, I already knew. It was poison. It would be a nasty way to die, but I couldn't let him kill Kate.

"If I do this, you have to let Kate go."

"I'll consider it."

"No. There is nothing to consider. You let her go, or I don't do this. Then you have to find another way to open the nexus."

"Fine. She goes free. Now drink up."

I opened the vial and sniffed the contents. I couldn't smell anything I hoped it tasted the same way as it smelled. I didn't take my eyes off Bane. He lowered the gun down to his side while I examined the contents.

"How fast does this work?" I asked, stalling. I hoped I came up with another plan.

"You'll be dead within minutes."

I nodded. Out of the corner of my eye, I saw Kate shifting. Her hand was reaching for the knife she dropped during the struggle with Bane. Her fingers gripped it as I put the bottle to my lips. Without warning, I flung the contents of the vial in Bane's direction, watching as it splattered in his face.

He screamed, covering his face with his free hand, gun momentarily forgotten. That was when Kate sprung to her feet. She didn't hesitate. Taking the knife, she plunged it into his heart. She twisted the knife clockwise then yanked it out. Blood spurted from the wound. Bane mouth opened and closed before he dropped to his knees. Kate kneed him in the face and watched as he fell to the ground.

"Now we need to get the hell out of here before the ghosts go crazy." I pulled the knife from her bloody hand.

Kate just stood there staring at the man bleeding out on the floor. She blinked a couple times as if waking up from a dream. Her eyes widened as she turned to face me.

"Oh my god. Did I—" she trailed off.

I turned her so she was facing me. I didn't want her to see the man dead on the floor. She didn't need to see what she had done.

"You did what you had to do to protect us. Kate, you saved my life." I studied her green, troubled eyes.

She nodded.

Looking over her shoulder, I watched as the blood filled the crevices of the design on the floor. When the blood touched the first symbol, it lit up. My eyes widened. Apparently, I didn't have to kill myself after all to open the nexus. It just had to be freshly spilled blood.

"Kate, we need to get out of here now." I pulled her to the door and turned the knob. To my surprise, it opened effortlessly.

Leading her through the door, I shut it firmly behind us. I pushed her toward the tunnel and urged her to go into it.

She turned, her green eyes blazing. "No. I'm not going without you. We are in this together."

"It's dangerous for you. I'm going to deal with the house. I can't let anyone else come in here to the madness," I explained.

"What are you planning on doing?"

"I'm going to burn this hell hole to the ground. That should take care of the nexus as well." At least I hoped.

"Let's do it."

We turned and came face to face with Dana. Of course it couldn't be easy. She was going to be a difficult one to deal with. I didn't know how she would react to me holding Kate's hand.

"You should have killed her when you had the chance," Dana pouted. "Now I'm going to have to do it for you. Maybe kill you, too. If I do, then we can finally be together forever. That's what you want, isn't it?"

"Dana, I can't deal with us right now. I have to get her out of here safely. You aren't going to kill her. I won't let you. We already discussed this." I paused. I knew what I was about to say would royally piss her off. "We can't be together. I have to right my wrongs."

"What!" she screamed. The sound was so intense that even Kate shivered. She couldn't see or hear Dana, but she felt the power. "You promised."

"I know I did. But Dana, things change. I've changed."

"No, you haven't. You are still you. You enjoy killing, I can feel it deep inside me." She ran her hand from her collar bone to her chest. This time I didn't react to it like I had in the past.

"It's over Dana. I'm sorry."

I pulled Kate with me but held her close to protect her from Dana's wrath. I hoped she wouldn't attack us, but I couldn't guarantee she would behave. Then she did. I felt the knife bite into my shoulder.

"Fuck," I hissed. It hurt more than I thought it would. I spun around to face her. "Dana. Knock it off. You are better than this."

"I'm going to kill both of you," she growled.

She was interrupted by a tremor that shook the foundation of the house. We all froze. I glanced back to the closed door. There was a glow coming from underneath it. I had to hurry if I planned on Kate and I getting out alive.

I yanked her arm as we ran up the stairs. I could feel the blood running down my arm, but I ignored it and the pain. Reaching the top of the stairs, I remembered the door had locked behind us. I reared back and kicked it with all my might. The door cracked and buckled under the force. It fell forward onto the floor.

Running to the stove, I blew out the pilot light. After the light went out, I turned the knobs on all four burners turning on them on, so gas was released into the room. I did the same for the oven, leaving the door open.

Nodding in satisfaction, I took off to the living room fireplace. I had to move quickly, or we would be poisoned by the carbon monoxide. Skidding to a stop in front of it, I grabbed the long matches used to light a fire and attempted to light the fireplace.

"What are you doing?" Kate spoke for the first time since before Dana attacked.

"I'm making a bomb, so to speak. Once the gas reaches the fireplace, it will ignite and explode. House will be gone." I said fumbling with the matches. I couldn't get the fucker to light.

"Here." She pulled a Zippo from her pocket and flicked it open. She lit the lighter and handed it to me. "It was a keepsake from something of my past. I don't need it anymore. If you put it in the fireplace, it should catch the logs on fire."

"Good idea." I set the Zippo in the fireplace and turned to Kate again. "Let's get out of here. Together."

She nodded and we ran back toward the basement to our freedom.

Chapter 89

We stood in front of the tunnel leading to freedom. There was a rumble and the door to the room with the nexus in it exploded. I saw the ghosts slowly appearing in their places of the zodiac symbol. That wasn't supposed to happen. They shouldn't have been summoned to their places without my death.

"What the fuck is going on?" I asked myself. If the nexus opened, we would all be in trouble. "That shouldn't be happening. I didn't die to start the process. It was supposed to take my death."

"That's not exactly right," Isabella spoke from behind us. I whirled around to stare at her. "What do you mean?"

"What?" Kate asked, looking around.

"Hold on, Kate." I held a hand up to her. "What are you talking about, Aunt Isabella?"

"Bane wasn't correct on how the nexus opened. There may have been some. . . alterations to his book before he got it." She inwardly smiled, but it was a sad smile. "Any fresh death would open the nexus as long as the words had been spoken and the twelve ghosts were there."

"Then why was there talk about the thirteenth ghost?" I had a sick feeling in my stomach.

"The thirteenth ghost isn't for opening the nexus. It's meant to close it. The Lost Soul is to find himself and close the nexus to keep it from ever being opened again."

"How?"

"I think you know how already." She stepped closer and kissed me on the forehead. "I am proud to call you mine. You have grown so much through the years. That darkness that was inside you has shrunk. You are a good man, Charles."

I nodded. I knew what I had to do. I had always known. Isabella faded away, and I knew that she had been taken to her spot on the Zodiac. I turned back to Kate. "I need you to listen carefully. I mean it. You have to do exactly as I say."

"Okay." Her voice was soft. I could tell she was scared.

"Everything will be okay, but it's time for you to go. The house will blow at any minute, and you can't be here for it. I don't want you to die. Everything I've done today is to keep you alive."

She stepped closer putting her hands in mine. "I'm scared."

"There is no need to be afraid. All you have to do is go through that tunnel and not look back. This time whatever you do, don't come back. You won't live if you do."

"You need to come with me," she insisted. "Please."

"I have to stay here. It's my destiny."

"I don't believe in destiny. I need you."

"No, you don't. You are a strong woman. Look at you. You've done more in the last twenty-four hours than most do in a lifetime. You've faced evil and are still innocent."

"I'm not innocent. I killed a man."

"You didn't kill a man. You saved my life. Kate, you saved my soul. If you hadn't come back for me, I would have eventually given in and ended my life to stop the torment. Now I have to stop the nexus from releasing hell on Earth."

I did something I didn't plan on doing. I leaned forward and kissed her. It felt real, right. I knew it would be the only time I would ever feel that.

"I don't want to leave you," she whispered.

"I'll always be with you," I whispered back. I heard the whoosh of the gas igniting. "Now go. Hurry."

"I—" she paused.

I could smell the smoke as it worked its way through the venting. "Go now!"

She walked into the tunnel then turned back to me. "I love you."

I smiled. It was the first time anyone said that to me where I felt they were being honest. It may not be a romantic love and we could never explore it, but it was love all the same. "I love you too. Now go."

She sniffled as she walked disappeared into the darkness. When I could no longer hear her, I turned and made my way back into the room with the ghosts.

Once inside the room, I walked to the middle of the symbol and stood, waiting. I would not have to do anything but stand there. The fire would get me as soon as the flames reached the kitchen.

"I'll see you all in hell," I whispered as I heard the explosion from upstairs and everything when dark.

***

Kate

I was standing on the side of the interstate when the house exploded. I dropped to the ground to keep from being hit with debris. Sirens wailed in the distance, coming too late to put out the fire .

My heart ached as I lifted my head to look up at the remains of the house. Flames were shooting up in the sky, black smoke billowing from it. I had lost everything in that house, but also gained something. I gained the knowledge I wasn't alone. Bastian, Charles, whatever his name truly was, was still with me. I could feel the warmth of his presence.

I wished I had a chance to know him better. Maybe I wouldn't have felt the same for him as I did, but now I would never be able to find out. He had saved me in more ways than one. If it hadn't been for him, I would have died in that house along with Tammy.

My heart wrenched thinking about Tammy. She had been my only true friend in a long time. Now she was gone. I wasn't sure how I would explain what happened to the police when they questioned me, but I would have to come up with something. There were multiple dead bodies in that house, if they didn't all burn to ash.

The next few hours were a whirlwind of activity. I was wrapped in a blanket by a fire fighter and placed in an ambulance while I was looked over. After the police came and questioned me, I was released to go, however my keys were in the house, and I had no way to go anywhere.

Go to the parking lot of the store a little way down. A voice in my head told me. I didn't question it, just walked. When I reached the parking lot, there was a car sitting there. It looked like it was abandoned.

When I got closer to it, I saw the keys were sitting in the cupholder. I opened the car door and climbed in. After inspecting the car, I realized that it was Bastian's. I smiled to myself. He was still with me. I put the key in the ignition and turned it over. The car roared to life. I pulled out of the parking lot and turned left, away from the house, fire, and excitement.

I didn't know where I was going, but I was determined to live a life that was worth living. This was my second chance, and I would make the most of it.

Zizi Cole, a born and bred native of Missouri, resides in a small town with her two boys and cat. When she isn't writing, she likes to spend time with her children and do some reading.

She is a writer of horror, and more recently, has branched out into the realm of fantasy. She's been an active member in the Indie community-making the best-seller list in her categories, she has also been nominated for several awards including "Best Horror Author". Zizi's co-authored fantasy, Afflicted, won second place for "Best Retelling" with Enchanted Anthologies in 2017. Her DAMNED series also took third place for "Best Horror" with Wild Dreams Publishing. She looks forward to meeting her fans at events and connecting with them on social media.

CONNECT WITH THE AUTHOR

Facebook

www.facebook.com/zizicole85

Twitter

www.twitter.com/zizicole

Goodreads

www.goodreads.com/zizicole

Instagram

www.instagram.com/authorzizicole

Website

www.zizicole.com

www.ingramcontent.com/pod-product-compliance
Lightning Source LLC
Chambersburg PA
CBHW020629020726
47494CB00001B/111